Alfred Monnin

Life of the curé d'Ars

Alfred Monnin

Life of the curé d'Ars

ISBN/EAN: 9783337333799

Printed in Europe, USA, Canada, Australia, Japan

Cover: Foto ©Raphael Reischuk / pixelio.de

More available books at **www.hansebooks.com**

Life of the Curé d'Ars.

Life of the Curé d'Ars.

OF

THE CURÉ D'ARS.

from the French of

THE ABBÉ ALFRED MONNIN.

——— ———

BALTIMORE:

KELLY & PIET.

1865.

CONTENTS.

1*

     CONTENTS.

PREFACE TO THE AMERICAN EDITION.

The holy life of M. Vianney, better known as the Curé of Ars, can scarcely fail to be of the deepest interest to all. The work is written with the utmost simplicity, by one who was well acquainted with the saintly priest whose life is described. It is also touching to observe, that God has chosen here, as elsewhere, "the foolish things of this world to confound the wise;" for the worldly learning of the Curé of Ars was nothing compared with the supernatural powers granted him by Almighty God for the benefit of souls.

The book places briefly before the reader's mind the *family, pastoral, heroic, hidden* and *apostolic* life of the good priest of Ars. It is well to study these various parts which make up a life simple at once and saintly. Each portion is read with ever increasing interest, and the charm of freshness is added by the childlike manner in which the truth is related.

We see here how divine grace perfects nature; how that heavenly gift causes a resemblance among the saints. Each saint has special gifts of nature, and these, far from being annihilated, are perfected, so that they are rendered hand-

maids of the great work,—the salvation of souls.   In the
present case, we perceive naturally good dispositions im-
proved and elevated to the supernatural order.

There is that breathing of piety in the work which makes
one desire to be better; the mere reading of the Life of the
holy curé will enkindle love for God and the things of God.
How much more, then, its thorough study?

We commend the Life to the reading of all those who
desire to advance in the path towards Heaven.

PREFACE.

In presenting to the Catholics of England the following Life of the Curé of Ars, few words are needed. The reputation of sanctity which surrounds the name of M. Vianney makes all commendation superfluous. A common consent seems to have numbered him, even while living, among the servants of God; and an expectation prevails that the day is not far off when the Church will raise him to veneration upon her altars.

It would seem as if God were dealing with us now as He dealt with the world in the beginning of the Gospel. To the corrupt intellectual refinement of Greece and Rome, He opposed the illiterate sanctity of the Apostles; to the spiritual miseries of this age He opposes the simplicity of a man. who in learning hardly complied with the conditions required for Holy Orders, but, like the B. John Colombini and St. Francis of Assisi, drew the souls of men to him by the irresistible power of a supernatural life. It is a wholesome rebuke to the intellectual pride of this age, inflated by science, that God has chosen from the midst of the learned, as His instrument of surpassing works of grace upon the hearts of men, one of the least cultivated of the pastors of His Church.

It would be needless to anticipate the outline of the following narrative, which is brief in itself; and for this Preface one or two general observations will suffice. No one can read the Life of the Curé of Ars without being reminded of that of St. Francis and his companions. There is a homely and rural beauty about it which vividly recalls the plains of Umbria and their simple inhabitants; Dardilly, Ecully, and the "Chante-merle," remind us of Foligno, Perugia, and Gli Angeli; and the lowly and lonely pastor wandering among the corn-fields and the orchards of Ars is such a picture of evangelical poverty as we read in the *Fioretti di San Francesco.*

Another supernatural beauty in this life is the peculiar nature of the miracles by which God manifested His love and care of His servant; such as, the multiplication of the corn in the *grenier,* the wine in the barrel, and the flour under the hand that was kneading it for the oven. No one can read them without remembering the lives of the Prophets Elias and Eliseus, with the wonderful and homely beauty of their miracles, the visible revelations of the loving Providence which invisibly is interwoven with all our lives, and ministers to all our needs.

And lastly, it is impossible to read of the days of unresting toil, till his wasted frame was carried from the confessional to his chamber, and the nights of unceasing prayer, in which he gazed with eyes radiant with supernatural light upon God Incarnate on the altar, without remembering One who "had not so much as time to eat," and who, when the toil of the day was done, "went up into a mountain alone," and "continued all night in the prayer of God."

One of his spiritual children said of him, "He would gaze at the Tabernacle with a smile which gladdened the heart. I have seen it many a time myself; it seemed as if he *saw* our Lord. I was always struck with my own spiritual misery before God, when I saw, by the light of the sanctuary-lamp, that wasted and withered form, and that brilliant glance fixed upon the door of the Tabernacle, with an expression of happiness which it is impossible to describe."

The special features of this most supernatural life appear to be, evangelical poverty of spirit, and the two fruits which spring from it,—the sweetness which, as St. Francis of Sales tells us, is the perfection of charity, and the radiant peace which beamed from his countenance, his words, his tones, and every action of his life.

In a word, the one great truth taught us by the whole history of the Curé of Ars is the all-sufficiency of supernatural sanctity. A soul inhabited by the Holy Ghost becomes His instrument and His organ in the salvation of men. To such a sanctity the smallness of natural gifts is no hindrance, and the greatest intellectual power without it does little in the order of grace; for souls are to be won to God, as God created and redeemed them,—by love and by compassion; and it was this which shone forth with a surpassing splendor in all the life of this great servant of Jesus, and concealed even the wonderful gifts of discernment and supernatural power with which he was endowed.

It remains only to add, that the following narrative has been derived from the Life of the saintly Curé written at the command of his Diocesan, the Bishop of Belley, by his friend and fellow-laborer, the Abbé Monnin.* By the kind permission of the Abbé Camélet, Superior of the Congregation of which M. Monnin is a member, this very interesting work is now presented, in substance, to such English readers as may not have access to the original, in the earnest hope that some hearts among us may thus be stirred to the veneration, and, in their measure and degree, to the imitation, of this devoted servant of God.

H. E. M.

St. Mary of the Angels, Bayswater,
    Feast of the Assumption, 1862.

-----

* Le Curé d'Ars, par l'Abbé Alfred Monnin.   2 v. Paris, 1861

LIFE

OF

THE CURÉ OF ARS.

CHAPTER I.

Birth and Childhood of Jean Baptiste Vianney.

Who has not felt the question rise to his lips, as he closed the Life of St. Vincent of Paul, or the holy founder of St. Sulpice, Are there such men now, or have they ceased altogether out of the land? Is heroic sanctity a thing of the past, or, if it still exist, is it so wholly hidden as to be no longer a note of the Church?

To these distrustful and half-querulous thoughts our Lord vouchsafes at times to give an answer, by casting a sudden light upon some obscure corner of His vineyard, where such a life as that before us has been consumed for Him; thus showing us that a man of the nineteenth century may bear as deep an impression of His own Divine image as any form which has come down to us from the past.

The life of the Curé of Ars, as described by one who witnessed and shared his labors, is in itself a more signal miracle than any of those by which it was glorified; and that life was lived in our own time by "a man like unto us," not two days' journey from the homes where we have been sitting at ease.

Jean Baptiste Marie Vianney was born at Dardilly, a village not far from Lyons, where his humble forefathers had dwelt for many generations. Their simple farmhouse, with its little courtyard before it, stands near the entrance of the village, amid scenery of singular beauty,—a succession of vineyards, meadows, and orchards, intersected by clear streams, broken by deep valleys, and shadowed by hanging woods. All the scenes surrounding his infancy were lovely to look upon, and the moral and spiritual aspect of his home was no less fair. "It was the dwelling-place," says the Abbé Monnin, "of one of those honest families of farmers, in which have been perpetuated, from age to age, the traditions of labor and of prayer, and whence have sprung during the last fifty years the greater number of our priests, our soldiers, and our religious." The house of the Vianneys had been known from time immemorial as the home of the poor, the well-known resort of all the wandering beggars, who were accustomed to seek and find a nightly shelter beneath its hospitable roof. An Apostle tells us that they who thus welcome the poor of Christ have entertained angels unawares; and such a one crossed the threshold of the Vianneys, when, on a sultry July day of the year 1770, Benedict Joseph Labré came to ask a night's lodging among the mendicants who daily crowded the courtyard. There was nothing in the outward aspect of the wanderer to point out to the good farmer that he was harboring one whose place was to be hereafter on the altars of the Church; but who shall say what influence the prayer which repaid his simple hospitality may have had upon the future sanctity of the child, who was to make his own humble name illustrious? It was a saying of the Curé of Ars, that "wherever the saints pass, God passes with them." May not his own birth and predestination have been the fruit of this *passing of God* over the hospitable threshold of his father? One thing is certain, that his birth took place in the course of the very same year in which the miraculous power of Benedict Labré was most signally displayed in the cures wrought at his tomb.

The parents of Jean Marie, Matthieu Vianney and Marie Beluse, possessed, in a high degree, the traditional virtues of their race. Matthieu was a pious Christian, and a thoroughly honest man; to the virtues which distinguished her husband, Marie added a sweetness and tenderness of character, a gentleness of manner, and an elevation of mind which sprang from a deeply interior spirit, and fitted her to be the mother of a saint. Before the birth of the second of her six children, Marie had often offered him to God and the Blessed Virgin, and had even made a secret vow, should God accept her desire, to consecrate him to the service of the altar; with this view he received in baptism, on the the very day of his birth, the names of Jean Baptiste and of Marie. It is said, perhaps without sufficient authority, that the woman who attended his mother at his birth, went out suddenly, as to consult the stars, and exclaimed on her return, without much consideration for the state of her patient, "This child will be either a great saint or a great villain." Matthieu Vianney, who entered the room as she finished her sentence, rebuked her sharply and laughed at her prediction; but the shaft rankled in the anxious mother's heart, and was not drawn forth till, reassured by the early marks of her child's precocious piety, she could say to herself: "He will be a saint, then, my little Jean Marie." Like the mother of St. Bernard, Marie Beluse watched for the first dawn of reason to turn her child's earliest thoughts

to God.   At eighteen months old he had already learned to
to join his little hands in prayer, and to lisp the names of
Jesus and Mary.   M. Vianney used often to tell how his
mother would always come herself every morning to awaken
her children, that she might see that they offered their
hearts to God, and secure the first thought and the first
action of the day for Him.

"You are very happy," said some of his friends to him,
"to have had so early a love of prayer."

"After God," said he, "it was the work of my dear
mother; she was so good. 'Do you see, my little Jean
Marie,' she would say, ' if I were to see you offend the good
God, it would give me more pain than if it were one of my
other children.'   Virtue," added he, "passes from the
heart of a mother to the hearts of her children, who do
willingly what they see her do."

At three years old Jean Marie already began to retire
into solitary places to pray.   When he could yet hardly
speak, he loved to join in all the devotions of the family.
He was the first to kneel down at midday or sunset to recite the Angelus with infantine gravity.   The first present
which he received from his mother was a little statue of
the Blessed Virgin.   He prized it, not as a child's toy, but
as an object of pious veneration.   It was the surest remedy
for all his childish troubles.

"Oh, how I have loved that image !" said he, more than
sixty years afterwards; "I could not bear to part with it
day or night; and I could not have slept quietly, if I had
not had it beside me in my little bed."

On the rare occasions when some of the troubles which
to childhood seem irremediable, drew tears from his eyes,
it was quite enough to give him an image or a rosary, and
he was consoled at once.

In the long winter evenings he would sit for hours by his mother's side, talking with her of God and holy things, till her heart swelled with joy that her long-cherished hopes were thus being realized in the early sanctity of her child. Devotion to the Blessed Virgin was the sentiment earliest developed in his soul.

"You have long loved the Blessed Virgin," said his assistant priest to him one day.

"I loved her even before I knew her," replied he; "it was my first affection. When I was quite little I had a pretty little rosary, to which my sister took a fancy; she wanted to have it. This was one of my first troubles. I went to consult my mother about it. She advised me to give it up for the love of God. I obeyed; but it cost me many tears."

All these holy affections grew with his growth; prayer was his delight before he understood it to be his duty. It was the spontaneous language of his lips, which were never profaned by any of the coarse and unbefitting words so commonly learned by village children. He was shielded from the knowledge of evil by the pure atmosphere of his father's house, and he seldom left his mother's side but to retire to some quiet corner to pour out his heart to his heavenly Mother.

When he was about four years old, he one day disappeared and could nowhere be found. His mother, having long sought him with increasing anxiety, found him at last on his knees, in a corner of the stable, praying most fervently. Suppressing her feeling of joy and admiration, she reproved him severely for the trouble and anxiety he had occasioned. "Why, my child, have you caused me all this uneasiness, and why have you taken it into your head to hide yourself from me to say your prayers?"

"Mother, forgive me," said the child, throwing himself into her arms; "I did not mean to grieve you. I will never go there any more."

Another time, a neighbor, who was not particularly devout, said to his father, "I think your little fellow takes me for the Devil; he does nothing but make the sign of the cross when I am present."

His mother, fearing that, young as he was, he might be already beginning to affect singularity and to wish to attract notice, remonstrated with him upon the subject. He listened with great docility, and replied: "I did not know our neighbor was looking at me; but ought not we to make the sign of the cross at the beginning and end of our prayers?"

When the neighbors saw the extraordinary devotion and recollection with which the child assisted at Mass, they would say to his parents, "You must make your little son a priest." But the time was at hand when that most intense desire of the mother's heart seemed destined to bitter disappointment. The revolution, which swept away throne and altar, barred the way to the sanctuary. A day came when the little church of Dardilly opened its doors no more for holy Mass; the bell no longer called the faithful to prayer; every indication of Christian feeling was forbidden under the name of liberty. Jean Marie was then only in his eighth year; but the seed had been sown too deeply in his heart to be scattered by the cold blast of infidelity which swept over his unhappy country; the more deeply hidden, the more strongly was it rooted. As he beheld all the things which he loved and revered fall around him, he gathered them up and stored them in his heart. He was no longer to kneel beside his mother at the altar of God, and, like St. Mary Magdalene of

Pazzi, inhale the fragrance of her Communion ere yet admitted to receive his Lord. Few and far between were now the blessed seasons when, in fear and haste, the faithful were summoned to some carefully-guarded hiding-place to hear the Mass said by some proscribed and persecuted priest, at peril of his life and their own. What was to replace the daily Mass, and the frequent visit to the Blessed Sacrament? Even the indwelling of that Divine Spirit, the Lord and the lifegiver, that best Consoler, by Whose ministry Jesus is made present to us in His Sacraments, and in Whose Person He is present even without them. What was to stand in the place of the deserted and desecrated sanctuaries of apostate France, where her few faithful children might no longer find their God? Even her silent valleys and lonely woods, and her free, pure mountain tops, where the step of the spoiler and the infidel came not near to disturb them. With God in his heart and the holiness of nature around him, Jean Marie passed peacefully through that terrible time. He was now come to the age when country boys of his class have to begin to labor for their daily bread. Matthieu Vianney had four or five cows in his stable, an ass, and three sheep. It had been hitherto the office of the elder brother to keep them; now it was Jean Marie's turn to lead them out to browse in the little close near the house, and in the long days to take them to the more distant pastures belonging to the farm. It would seem that our Divine Lord, Who has been pleased to reveal Himself to us under the touching name of the *Good Shepherd*, has a special love for the shepherd's life. Shepherds were the first to approach Him on earth; and He has often made the life of a shepherd the preparation for that of a pastor of souls. Such was the first seminary of St. Vincent of

Paul; such was the school in which Jean Marie Vianney was trained for the interior life; the solitary communing with God, in which he was enabled hereafter to persevere under the overwhelming pressure of his life-long labor for souls. To him, in those evil days, that life was a special blessing. The daily Sacrifice was taken away; the church-bells were silent, except when forced

"to send around
The bloody tocsin's madd'ning sound."

But under the free sky, by the light of the silent stars, the lonely boy conversed with God, and learned of Him that heavenly wisdom by which he was hereafter to make many wise unto salvation. And already, even at that early age, he was beginning to exercise his ministry for the souls of others. There is at a little distance from the village of Dardilly a lovely little valley, which, from the number of those birds which congregate there, is called *Chante-merle* (the thrush's song); this was the young shepherd's most frequent haunt; thither he loved to lead his ass and three sheep. His young companions, who all loved him well, used to hail his approach, as he appeared among them with a staff in one hand and his inseparable image of the Blessed Virgin pressed to his bosom with the other. On a little hillock, by the side of an old willow, which is still to be seen there, he placed his dear Madonna upon an altar of turf, and having knelt to pay his homage to her, he invited the other shepherd-boys to do the same. Never was he so happy as when he saw them all kneeling around his beloved image; then, having recited a Hail Mary with fervent devotion, he would rise and gravely address his young companions, who listened with devout attention, upon the devotion to the Blessed Virgin. Sometimes, indeed, they would get tired of listening, and desert the sermon for some more stirring exercise. Jean Marie, being thus left like his patron to make his voice heard in the wilderness, would console himself by retiring into some silent corner, where he installed his beloved image in the hollow of a tree, and kneeling at its feet he passed long hours in prayer.

"We have visited," says M. Monnin, "with pious curiosity and religious reverence these scenes of our saint's infancy. We have taken delight in wandering along the paths which the foot of the little shepherd had so often traced. Long did our eyes rest on the peaceful landscape before us, as we mused upon the influence of nature over the heart of man. It was here, then, O God of the poor, God of the little, the humble, and the weak,—it was in this unknown spot of earth that this child lived alone with Thee, with Thine angels, and with the works of Thy hand; it was from among these coppices, whence his childish prayer arose to Thee, that Thou wast pleased to call that priest, that apostle, that man of God! Here didst thou train him for Thyself, amidst the horrors of those days of blood, far from the two-fold torrent of anarchy and impiety which was then deluging France, and covering her with ruins. Here wast Thou slowly preparing him to become one of the glories of Thy Church. When he rose from his knees to return to his little flock, he went forth from Thy presence, carrying in his heart Thy spirit of poverty, of humility, of sweetness, of obedience, of sacrifice, and all those precious germs which we have seen in later years developed into sanctity."

One day, the little shepherd, who was then but seven years old, in company with a neighbor's child of the same age, named Marion Vincent, was leading his ass laden with corn to the mill at St. Didier. It was very hot, and the

two children stopped in a narrow lane to rest in the shade.
Their childish talk now became more intimate.

"I think," said Jean Marie, "that we two should get on
very well together."

"Yes," said Marion, "and if our parents like, we can
marry!"

"Oh, no, no!" vehemently exclaimed Jean Marie; "for
me never! Do not let us talk of it; never let us talk of it
again."*

Had that child already heard the voice of the Holy
Ghost, revealing to him the joy of sacrifice, the glory of
virginity, and the emptiness and nothingness of all earthly
things as compared with invisible blessings? Certain it is
that, even from that early age, all his thoughts and emotions
seem to have been concentrated in the desire to serve God
and to unite himself to Him alone.

Next to God, Jean Marie loved the poor. The unbounded charity, which was one day to be identified with
his very life, already inflamed his young heart. With him,
the heart seems to have outgrown and absorbed the other
faculties; for he was in no way remarkable at this time for
graces of mind or gifts of intellect.

We have a touching picture of the hospitality of that
poor farmhouse to the homeless beggars, of whom the
country was full. At nightfall they would present themselves, sometimes twenty at a time, and were all sure of a
resting-place in the *grange.* In the winter, Matthieu Vianney took care to have a large sparkling fire of fagots kindled in the kitchen to warm them. Then a huge pot of
potatoes was placed upon the hearth, which the children

* Marion Vincent, who is still living in a house close to that of the
Vianneys, told this childish incident herself to M. Monnin.

afterwards consumed together with the poor, and seated at the same table with them. After supper, all said night prayers together, and then the master of the house went to marshal his guests to their resting-places,—some in the barn, some in the cellar. The great delight of Jean Marie was to assist his parents in the exercise of their noble and holy hospitality. He brought in all the beggars whom he could meet with, and once succeeded in collecting four-and-twenty. His greatest joy was to find little boys or girls of his own age, or younger still. He brought them to the fire, one after the other, beginning with the youngest; he would beg fruit from his parents' table for them, and add to it all that he could save from his own food. Then he inspected the state of their clothing, and begged from his mother, whose tender compassion he well knew, a shirt for one, a vest for another, a pair of trousers for a third, and shoes for a fourth.

When he met with children of his own age, he set to work to teach them the Our Father, the Hail Mary, the Acts of Faith, Hope, and Charity, and the chief truths of religion. He taught them that they must be very good; that they must love the good God very much; never complain of their lot, but bear its hardships patiently in the prospect of eternal life. Though he discreetly addressed his exhortation to the children, their elders would listen to him with grateful and admiring wonder. Such was the early childhood of Jean Marie Vianney; such the freshness of the morning dew sent to prepare his soul to bear the burden and heat of the day which was before him.

The grace which, like an aureola, had surrounded him from his cradle, increased from year to year. As he passed out of early childhood, it was but to advance from the ignorance of evil to its detestation. Such was the innocence of his childhood, that he has been heard to say: "I knew nothing of evil till I learned to know it in the confessional."

His own first confession, from the impossibility at that time of approaching the Sacraments, was not made till he was eleven years old. The fury of the revolutionary storm had by that time in some measure abated; some of the proscribed priests had reappeared, and together with them some pious Sisters of the Order of St. Charles, who labored under their direction in the neighboring parish of Ecully to prepare the children of the few faithful families who pressed around them for confession. Jean Marie was sent to the house of his grandfather at Ecully, that he might be at hand to receive their instructions. From their hands the aspirants for first Communion passed into those of the missionary priests, who assembled them, now in one house, now in another, and always at night, to elude the vigilance of the republican police. We have no precise information as to the circumstances attending the first Communion of the saintly boy. It took place, in all probability, in the year 1799, in the house of the Comte de Pingeon. Though the first heat of persecution had then passed away, so unquiet still was the state of the times, that the Curé of Ars used to tell of the loaded wagons of hay, which were drawn up against the door of the barn which served as a chapel, to screen the worshippers from malicious observation. The peculiar circumstances which make it difficult now to find authentic records of the acts of religion solemnized in those dark days, must have impressed them the more deeply upon the hearts of the worshippers. No outward circumstances, indeed, were needed to enhance the thrill of awful delight with which, for the first time, Jean Marie Vianney must have received his God; but, for that life of sacrifice, what could have been a fitter preparation than such a first Communion as the children of France were then wont to make?

"The altar," says M. Monnin, "encircled only by the parents and some few friends upon whose fidelity entire dependence could be placed, was usually prepared in a granary, or some upper chamber, to be out of the reach of observation. There, before daybreak, in the strictest secrecy, the holy Sacrifice was offered. There was something in the precautions necessary to keep suspicion and hostile observation at bay, and in the mystery which accompanied all the preparations for the great day, which told of a time of persecution, and breathed of the air of the Catacombs. The soul of the young communicant could not but be deeply and permanently impressed by all the circumstances attending his first participation of the *Bread of the strong* in those days of trial and apostasy. If the flowers of first Communion are ordinarily the presage of the fruits of riper years, truly must the heart of our saint have been on that blessed day a sanctuary fragrant with the presence of the Divine Spouse."

His sister Margaret gives her testimony to the perfection of his conduct in their daily home-life.

"Our mother," says she, "was so sure of Jean Marie's obedience, that when she met with any repugnance or delay on the part of any of us to do her bidding, her plan was to call my brother, who always obeyed at once, to do what she wanted. She would then hold him up as an example to us, saying, 'You see he never complains, or hesitates, or murmurs. You see he is far on his way already.' It was very seldom that his example failed to lead us to follow him. He generally went to work in the fields with the other members of the family. He did his part of the work conscientiously, and so long as all worked together, everything went on happily; but one day when he was sent to the vineyard alone with François, he tired himself out with trying to keep up with his brother, who, in his capacity of elder, felt bound in honor to surpass him. In the evening poor Jean Marie complained to his mother that François went on so fast, that he could not keep up with him. ‘François,’ said she, ‘go on a little more slowly, or else give a helping hand now and then to your brother; you see that he is much younger and weaker than you; you must have a little compassion for him.’ ‘But,’ replied François, ‘Jean Marie is not obliged to do as much as I. What would be.said if the elder did not keep ahead of the younger?’

“The next day a religious, who had been driven out of her convent by the revolution, and was living with her family at Dardilly, gave my brother, whom she loved very much on account of his piety, a little figure of our Blessed Lady, contained in a hollow cylindrical case, which could be opened or shut at pleasure. This present,” continues Margaret, “came just in good time, and my brother thought he had now found a sufficient auxiliary against the overactivity of François. The next time, therefore, that they were sent to the vineyard together, he took care before he began his work, to place his little statue at a short distance before him, and as he advanced towards it, he begged the Blessed Virgin to enable him to keep up with his elder brother. As soon as he came up to it, he again nimbly picked it up, put it once more before him, and seizing his pickaxe made head against Francois, who chafed in vain at not being able to pass him, and told his mother in the evening (not without a slight tone of pique) that the Blessed Virgin had helped his little brother well, and that he had done as much work as he. Our mother, like a wise and prudent woman, only smiled and kept silence, for fear of exciting any emotion of self-love."

In the midst of these toilsome labors, the pious child never lost the habit of interior prayer, nor the sacred Presence of God. "When I was alone in the fields," the Curé of Ars would often say, "with my spade or my pick-axe in my hand, I used to pray aloud; when I had companions with me, I used to pray in my heart." And he added, "Oh, how happy should I be, if now, when I am cultivating souls, I had as much time to think of my own, to meditate and to pray, as I had when I was cultivating my father's fields! There was some relaxation at least in those days; we rested after dinner before we set to work again. I stretched myself on the ground like the others and pretended to be asleep, but I was praying to God with all my heart. Oh, those were happy days!"

"Oh, how happy I was," repeated he less than a month before his death, "when I had nobody to guide but my three sheep and my ass! Poor little gray ass! he was full thirty years old when we lost him. In those days I could pray to God quite at my ease; my head was not broken as it is now. It was like the water of the streamlet, which has only to follow its bent."

"A premature wisdom," says M. Monnin, "had revealed to this child that the kingdom of God is within us, that God weighs the heart and not the work, that He looks not at what we do, but at why we do it. It is in the secret laboratory of the intention that the gross metal of our commonest actions is transformed into purest gold. What is a glass of water in the universe? Give it to a poor man, and it is the purchase-money of eternity. The whole of human life consists in little actions which accomplish great duties. Jean Marie understood this. He did much (in the words of the *Imitation*) because he loved much; he did much, because what he did, he did well." As he went and returned to his work, he always recited his rosary or some other prayers. If he met with children of his own age, he would persuade them to go with him, and teach them the Catechism as they went along.

One evening as he was returning from the vineyard with his elder brother and a band of laborers, he had taken his rosary in his hand, and was telling his beads as he walked a little behind the others. One of the vintagers said to François in a tone of mockery, intending to be heard by Jean Marie, "And you, François, why don't you mutter Pater-nosters with your brother?" François, colored a little; but the generous child continued his prayers without being in the last degree disconcerted, or making any reply.

After the hard labor of the day, he would spend the evening in studying the Catechism, the Gospel, or prayers, which he learned by heart, and then set himself seriously to meditate on them till, overcome by sleep, he was obliged to retire to his bed. He had no taste for any of the usual amusements of children; his one recreation in his leisure moments was to make little clay figures of priests and nuns, or altars and candlesticks. He set a certain value upon these handiworks, but would give them readily to any one who would undertake to enable him to go to Mass, by doing some of his work for him. He would then leave them all and run off to Mass, where he would be seen on his knees in a corner, with his eyes cast down, his body immovable, absorbed in profound contemplation, and often shedding abundant tears. After Mass he never failed, having first made his thanksgiving before the Blessed Sacrament, to pay a visit to the image of the Blessed Virgin. He then returned to his work with a light heart and bright countenance. Sometimes his brother or companions would amuse themselves with hiding his tools during his absence. Nothing ever put him out of humor; he would seem quite to enjoy the joke, and when he found out the culprit, would thank him for taking care of his tools, and promise to do the same turn for him another time.

The Curé of Ars dearly loved the remembrance of these days of rustic labor, and would often speak of them to his intimate friends. "When I was young," he used to say, "I tilled the ground. I am not ashamed of it; I am nothing but an ignorant husbandman. I often used to say to myself, as I struck my pickaxe into the ground, So shouldst thou cultivate thy soul; so pluck up the evil weeds to prepare it for the good seed of the good God."

CHAPTER II.

His first studies—He is drawn for the conscription—His escape and
concealment.

At length the revolution had worn itself out; and France, weary of herself, had taken shelter under the strong hand of Napoleon. One of his first acts was to restore a measure of liberty to the Church. But the deep wounds which had been inflicted on her were beyond the power of soldier or statesman to heal. Her temples were reopened, and her altars raised again; but her faithful priests had perished on the guillotine, or pined away in exile, and who was to minister in their stead? The town of Ecully was especially happy in receiving for its pastor the Abbé Balley, one of the confessors for the faith, who during the Reign of

Terror had often ministered, at the peril of his life, to the spiritual wants of its pious inhabitants. His first care, on taking possession of his cure in February, 1803, was to collect around him the boys and youths of his flock; and it was not long before an intimate relation was established between the new Curé and the saintly boy of Dardilly. The sight of the holy priest at the altar made a great impression upon Jean Marie. He longed to see and speak with him; and the first effect of their conversations together was to rekindle a desire which had long lain dormant in his heart,—to devote himself, soul and body, to the service of the suffering Church of Jesus Christ. As a child this had been an instinct, at eighteen it was a vocation. "If I were ever a priest," he would say, "I would win many souls to God." He had opened his heart to his parents on the subject just after his first Communion; but under the dark cloud which then hung over the Church in France, they shrank from giving their consent. Jean Marie took the course which he afterwards recommended to so many others. He committed his vocation to God in obedience and prayer, until it should please Him to remove the obstacles which then stood in the way of its accomplishment. The Concordat which followed the battle of Marengo, in 1801, made so great a change in the aspect of ecclesiastical affairs, that he felt the time was come to lay his long-cherished hope before the good Curé of Ecully, and ask his counsel and aid for its fulfilment. M. Balley gave him the most decided encouragement, and sent him away with a promise to do everything in his power to assist him. His parents no longer made any opposition to the wishes of their son, who now took up his abode with his mother's relations at Ecully, to be near his friend and patron. So much was he beloved at Dardilly, that all the neighbors

wished to share in the expense of his education. A pious
widow begged and obtained the favor of washing his clothes,
and thought herself well repaid by the opportunity thus
afforded of paying him an occasional visit.

The little farm of Point-du-jour, which was Jean Marie's
home for two years, was, no less than his father's house,
sheltered from all worldly and evil influences, and here also
his piety continued to increase in proportion to his faithful
correspondence with Divine grace.

But here a new and severe trial came upon him. He
was free to devote himself to the life which had long been
the choice of his heart; every outward obstacle was removed, but now his path was crossed by one which seemed
insurmountable. His education had been utterly neglected.
He knew nothing but the science of the saints. At an
age when other youths have finished their classical studies,
he was but beginning Latin; and what was more depressing still, he had no natural talents to enable him to cope
with these disadvantages. His conception, we are told,
was slow, and his memory unretentive. He made little or
no progress. His kind instructor did his best to encourage
him, and to give him a little confidence in himself; but at
times the poor boy was fairly disheartened. On one of
these occasions he asked leave to go home and see his
parents. M. Balley gently refused. "What good would
that do you?" said he kindly. "Your parents would only
think that your labors and their sacrifices had been all
in vain; and be too glad of the opportunity to keep you
at home; and then farewell to all our projects, farewell
to the priesthood and the salvation of souls." Such words
never failed to restore the courage of Jean Marie, and he
would plod again at his weary task with unflinching assiduity. It was not to be always in vain. A sudden

inspiration one day entered his mind, which, after consulting his director, he carried into effect. He made a vow to go on foot, asking alms as he went, to the tomb of St. John Francis Regis; to ask, through his intercession, the gift of sufficient learning to enable him to become a good and faithful laborer in the vineyard of the Lord. His prayer was heard. St. John Francis Regis, to whom he ever afterwards bore a special devotion, obtained for him the grace he had asked in a measure which astonished his master and those who had felt most hopeless of his success. No sooner was he domesticated with his relations at Ecully than the young student arranged with his cousin Marguerite, who was housekeeper, the way in which he wished to be treated. She was specially charged, for instance, never to put any seasoning into his soup. "Be sure," he would say, "to serve my soup before you put in any of your milk or butter. I want neither the one nor the other." When she was faithful to these instructions, Marguerite was rewarded by seeing him bright and cheerful, and sometimes by the gift of a medal or a picture; if she swerved from them, as she sometimes did, from accident or design, Jean Marie would reproach her seriously, and go about looking melancholy and out of heart. "He ate his soup on these occasions," said she, "as if each mouthful was choking him."

Here he carried on his old practice of collecting all the houseless poor he could find, and bringing them for a night's lodging to the farm. On his way one day from Ecully to Dardilly, he met a poor man without shoes; he immediately took off a new pair which he had on, gave them to him, and arrived at home without any, to the great dissatisfaction of his father, who, charitable as he was, was not inclined to carry things quite so far as his son.

Though instances like this betokened no great share of what the world calls common sense, Jean Marie had already a large measure of that gift of counsel, which is its supernatural counterpart, and by which he was in after life so eminently fitted for the office of director of souls. An example of this occurred during his residence at Point-du-jour. One of his cousins received a letter from a friend who had lately entered a monastery, painting in most attractive colors the delights and advantages of a religious life. The young man was exceedingly affected and disturbed, and for many days endured a most painful struggle between the desire to share the happiness thus set before him, and the claims of duty to an aged father and mother, who had no other earthly stay but himself. No sooner did these Christian parents come to the knowledge of the conflict that was going on in his heart than they said to him, "You belonged to God before you belonged to us; it is His will that is to be ascertained; go to your cousin and ask his advice. He is so wise and reasonable that we may safely follow his judgment." The letter was accordingly delivered to Jean Marie, who, having read it, said, without a moment's hesitation, "Stay where you are, my friend; your aged parents want you to help them, to comfort them, and to close their eyes: this is your vocation."

The years thus went peacefully by at Point-du-jour till a new blow fell, which seemed destined to be the death-stroke of all his hopes. In the autumn of 1809 the young student was drawn for the conscription. As soon as he had reached the age which rendered him liable to be called upon, M. Balley had taken the precaution to have his name inscribed on the list of students for the priesthood, this inscription constituting an exemption from military service; but by some oversight the entry was never made. An order to join the troops at Bayonne came upon him and his whole family like a thunder-clap. Parents, brothers, sisters, and friends were all overwhelmed with grief and consternation. He alone, on whom the blow fell with most stunning weight, kept up his courage, and sought to rekindle theirs. Matthieu Vianney made an ineffectual attempt, at an enormous cost, to procure a substitute for his son; but two days after the affair had been arranged, the young man who had undertaken to fill his place changed his mind, and left the money which had been paid him on the door-step of the house.

The self-control which Jean Marie had exercised brought on a severe attack of illness, and instead of sending him at once to Bayonne, the military authorities were obliged to place him in the hospital at Lyons. During the fortnight he remained there, he received visits from several members of his family, among others from the good cousin Marguerite, who had been his kind hostess at Point-du-jour. "As soon as I heard," says she, "that he was in the hospital, I hastened next day to see him. It was on a Sunday. I found him in bed with fever. When he saw me crying, he could scarcely forbear to do the same. I sat down by his bedside, and he began to speak to me of the holy will of God, and submission to His decrees, in such beautiful and touching words, that I wish I could repeat them. As I listened to him, it seemed as if my heart was changed, and I had less difficulty in accepting, as good and adorable, whatever it may please God to send us, however bitter it may seem to nature. I cannot remember the expressions he used; but the effect of his words was to infuse such consolation into my heart, that I felt quite calm and resigned. As the day declined he ceased to speak, and urged me to share the portion of food which was brought to him.

'Your example,' said he, 'will give me courage.' I did as he wished, but he ate very little; and as it was growing late, he said, 'Go now, or you will be benighted. Tell my parents that I am better, and that I expect soon to be able to join my regiment.'"

At the end of a fortnight he was considered fit to travel, but was seized with a fresh attack of fever on the road, and laid up again at the hospital at Roanne, from whence, as soon as he felt well enough, he wrote to his parents. During the six weeks which he spent at Roanne, he was visited by his parents, and almost all his kindred and friends, and received moreover the most tender and assiduous care from the good Sisters of St. Augustine, to whom the charge of the hospital was intrusted. Under their good nursing he rapidly regained his strength, and was appointed to make one of a detachment then forming at Roanne to join the army in Spain. The devoted soldier of Christ was on the point of being forced to enlist in the most murderous and manifestly unjust of all the wars in which the headlong ambition of Napoleon engaged him. But He who was soon, by the feeble breath of His Vicar, to cause the weapons to fall from the frozen hands of his *invincible* legions, was at no loss to deliver from the eagle's talons the shepherd-boy, who was to be His own chosen champion against the army of Lucifer.

The whole chain of providential events by which this deliverance was brought to pass is a remarkable comment upon that motto of the saints: "In silence and in hope shall be your strength." Jean Marie offered neither resistance nor remonstrance; but on the day fixed for the departure of his column, he went to pray in a church. He forgot the time, and let the hour pass by at which he was to present himself at the office. When he appeared, he was loaded with invectives and reproaches by the recruiting officer, who threatened to send him in chains from brigade to brigade till he should reach Bayonne.

Some more kindly spirits interposed on his behalf. "What is the use," said they, "of using force? The poor boy has no idea of deserting, or he would not have come to present himself."

This reasoning prevailed; and he set out upon his journey, having no thought of deserting, but with a sort of conviction on his mind that he should not join his corps. He went on his way with a heavy heart and a sad countenance; his longing desire for the priesthood and his intense repugnance to every other career, especially that of arms, strengthening with every step he took. He remembered how, in his peaceful home, he used to pity the poor young men whom he had seen forced from their firesides by the pitiless conscription; he thought with shuddering horror of the deserters he had seen dragged along in chains by the soldiers, answering by frightful curses the cruelty of their guards. Was his life to be spent among such as these?

To drive away these dark thoughts, he took out his rosary, and turned to the blessed Mother of God,—his never-failing refuge in distress. At that very moment a stranger accosted him in a tone of great kindness, asking whither he was going, and why he seemed so sad. Jean Marie told his story. The young man bade him follow him, assuring him that he had nothing to fear, and at the same time took up his knapsack to carry, which was very heavy, and which, being still weak from his late illness, he could scarcely drag along. Jean Marie followed his guide without raising any objection, perfectly ignorant as to his destination, but resigned to anything that might befall him, except, as

he afterwards said, falling into the hands of the *gens
d'armes.*

They travelled thus all day long through woods and by
mountain tracks, avoiding as much as possible highroads
or frequented paths. Jean Marie was sinking with fatigue;
but the kind words and looks of his companion seemed to
give him strength and courage. At ten o'clock at night
they halted for the first time at the door of a lonely house.
The stranger knocked; a voice answered from within, and
a man and woman appeared at the door, having risen from
their beds to ascertain who was asking their hospitality at
that hour of the night. The stranger exchanged a few
rapid words with them in a low voice; and from that day
forward M. Vianney never either saw or heard of him, nor
did he ever, according to the testimony of those most intimate with him, discover who he was.

Can we help here calling to mind the angelic companion
of the young Tobias? Whether, however, this remarkable deliverance of the servant of God was effected by human or angelic agency, we cannot fail to recognize in it
the loving providence of Him who "guides the just by
right paths, and keeps him in all his ways."

The good people to whose care he had been commended
received him most hospitably. While he ate his supper
in company with the husband, the wife put snow-white
sheets on the only bed in the house, which they compelled
him to occupy. The next morning his host, who was a
young shoemaker newly married, told Jean Marie that he
had not means to maintain him, nor work for another pair
of hands, but that he would show him a place in which he
would be perfectly safe. Jean Marie made no difficulty
in trusting himself to his protector, who guided him to a

village called Nöes, at the entrance of the great forest of the Madeleine, on the borders of the departments of the Loire and the Allier. Strange to say, the person to whom his friend the shoemaker took him was the Maire of the Commune; a singular protector for a refractory recruit. The good man received him with the greatest kindness, told him he had nothing to fear, and found a safe lodging for him with a good widow, the mother of four children, who was loved and respected by the whole village.

"I have known many holy men and holy women," the Curé of Ars used to say, when speaking of his protectress; "but the two most beautiful souls I ever met with were M. Balley and the Mère Fayot."

She received the fugitive as a mother would welcome a long-looked-for child.

The more effectually to conceal him from the search of the military, it was thought desirable that he should assume the name of Jerome, under which, being anxious to do something to requite the kindness of his benefactors, he opened a little school, where he labored from morning until night to instruct the children of the village. Jean Marie Fayot, the widow's eldest son, from whom M. Monnin learned most of the details here given of M. Vianney's residence at Nöes, shared his room on his first arrival there, and relates that whenever he woke in the night he always found him murmuring prayers. He communicated several times in the week, though he went to confession only once a fortnight, and the Curé of Nöes was noted for the strictness of his principles. He was so modest, recollected, and exemplary in all his conduct, that pious persons would come from the neighboring villages to make his acquaintance, and to pray or sing *cantiques* with him. When the return of summer and the press of field-work emptied his

school, he turned his hand to other labors; and during the
haymaking worked so hard in the service of his neighbors,
that he brought on an attack of inflammation of the chest,
which confined him for several weeks to his bed.

The villagers of Nöes understood the value of their guest,
and were so much afraid of losing him that they used to
station scouts on the surrounding heights to give notice of
the approach of the soldiers. One day he was driven to
seek shelter in a hay-loft over a stable, where he was
nearly suffocated by the quantity of hay heaped upon him, and
by the effluvia from the stable. He was obliged to remain
there for some considerable time, and used afterwards to
say that he had never suffered so much as on that occasion,
when he made a solemn promise to Almighty God, if He
would vouchsafe to deliver him from that fearful extremity,
never to complain of anything again, whatever might happen to him. "And I think," he used to add with touching simplicity, "I have pretty nearly kept my word." He
was very fond of talking of his stay at Nöes. That place,
with its simple, kindly people, had wound itself closely round
his heart. He would have liked to have been nominated
to its cure, and to have ended his days there; and in 1841
he said to Jean Marie Fayot, who came to Ars to make his
confession to him, "If I ever obtain permission to retire
from the sacred ministry, I mean to come and die in the
midst of you, or else at the Great Chartreuse." He never
forgot his debt of gratitude to the good widow Fayot, and
when he first became a priest used to write to her once a
year. Nor was her affection for him less warm and sincere. She was overcome with joy at the news of his elevation to the priesthood; and when, some weeks afterwards,
she heard that he was appointed Vicaire of Ecully, nothing
could restrain her from setting forth to pay him a visit.

M. Vianney used often to tell the tale of the good woman's
arrival at the presbytery, which happened in the midst of
a meeting of all the neighboring clergy, the Vicar-General
and other dignitaries being present. Not in the smallest
degree disconcerted at the appearance of these august per-
sonages, she no sooner caught sight of her Jean Marie, her
"dear boy," in his soutane, than she made her way straight
through them all, and throwing her arms round his neck,
gave him a hearty and motherly embrace.

CHAPTER III.

He returns home—Resumes his studies—The Seminary of Verrières—
Of Lyons—He is ordained Subdeacon—Priest.

PEACEFULLY and even happily as the days of his exile
went by, the thoughts of Jean Marie could not but often
turn wistfully to that sacred vocation which seemed again
to have eluded his grasp, and to the beloved home in which
all his earthly affections were centred. The strength and
tenderness of these human affections formed a remarkable
feature in a character so entirely detached from self, so
wholly consecrated to God.

It is a quality not always discernible in Saints, but seldom absent from such among them as have been enabled
deeply to stir and win the hearts of men. It was consecrated by the Divine tears which fell upon the grave of
Lazarus; it burned in the fervid words poured forth from
St. Bernard's bursting heart over his brother's bier; it

makes the name of the "dear St. Elizabeth" to be still a household word in Protestant Germany; it draws us to love St. Teresa even more than we reverence her; and attracts the alien and the heretic of our days, no less than of his own, to the sweet spirit of St. Francis of Sales. It is the cord of Adam, by which the human heart is drawn and bound to the Son of man, through those who have borne most visibly the image of His Divine humanity.

The long absence of Jean Marie, and their painful suspense as to his fate, had weighed heavily on his parents. His poor mother fell sick with sorrow and anxiety; she sought for consolation from the good Curé of Ecully; but strong in his own assurance of the purposes of God for that elect soul, he grew half angry with what he considered her want of confidence, and sent her away with a reproof, which bore, notwithstanding, encouragement with it. "Go away, go away; one day your son will be a priest." The trouble of Matthieu Vianney was aggravated by the vexatious inquiries and threats of the recruiting-officer, who could not be persuaded that he was ignorant of the place of his son's concealment.

Meanwhile the widow Fayot, who had been ordered to drink the waters at Charbonnière, a village not far from Ecully, paid a visit to the parents of her *protégé*, and assured them of his safety and well-being. The poor mother's heart revived again, and overflowed with gratitude to God, and to those who had been His instruments of good to her beloved child. He was alive and well, happy, and esteemed and beloved as he deserved, and she asked nothing more. Matthieu Vianney was not so entirely satisfied. When his anxiety for his son had been set at rest, he remarked somewhat drily, "Since Jean Marie is now quite well, he ought to join his regiment. I am threatened every day with the loss of all my property unless I make known the place of his concealment, of which I am wholly ignorant. I do not choose to suffer any longer for a rebellion which brings us all into distress by the expense which it entails upon us." "Your son," said the widow, "shall not leave us; take my word for it. He is worth more than all your property; and if you should succeed in discovering his hiding-place, I would find another for him, and every member of our commune would do the same."

This state of concealment was not, however, to last much longer. In the conscription of 1810, his younger brother volunteered to fill his place; and, strange to say, by the intervention of the same officer who had hitherto so fiercely resented his departure, the exchange was accepted, and the fugitive was free to return. There was a great excitement of mingled joy and sorrow among the good people of Nöes at the news of the good fortune of M. Jerome. They vied with each other who should contribute most largely to the outfit which was to enable him to make a creditable appearance at home. A tailor from Noanne was sent for to make a new soutane, which, for the satisfaction of his friends, he was obliged to put on before his departure. His hostess presented him with her wedding napkins; and another charitable woman forced upon him all the money she had by her, replying to his vehement remonstrances, "Be quiet; I am still rich; I have my fortune in my stable." The poor woman was fattening a pig for the market. And so they let him depart, first exacting a solemn promise that, if possible, he would some day return to Nöes to be their curé.

Free from all danger of the law, and at liberty to pursue the vocation of his choice in peace and hope, the young student returned to his home after fourteen months' absence. His mother's joy cannot be described. The son who was to her an object not less of reverence than of love, was to leave her no more; for her blameless life drew to its close, and she died the death of the just while he was still pursuing his studies under the Curé of Écully.

At the end of about two years after his return, his good friend judged that it would be better for him to finish his training at a seminary, where he might be helped onward by the collision of other minds. Jean Marie was therefore sent to the Petit Séminaire of Verrières to pursue his course of philosophy. Here he had many opportunities of exercising and making progress in humility. His companions, seeing no deeper than the surface, and discovering that he was inferior to most of them in intellectual acquirements, set him down as something not far removed from a simpleton, and treated him accordingly. His backwardness arose, however, far more from want of culture, and the frequent interruptions by which his course of study had been broken, than from any deficiency in his natural powers, which, though not brilliant, were by no means wanting in solidity; but the conviction of his own intellectual inferiority, which was deepened by the slight estimation in which he was at this time held by youths of his own age, was no doubt a part of the providential training which was to make him so perfect in humility. It was not long before a very different estimate began to be formed of him. Prejudice gave place to cordial admiration when longer intercourse revealed the deep wisdom of this ignorant youth; the reaction began with the masters, learned and discerning priests, who, although at first they had failed to appreciate the high qualities of their slow and timid student, were soon filled with admiration of his uniform and consistent piety. His fellow-students were not slow to make the same discovery, and, as is common with young and generous natures, conscious of having been guilty of injustice, they now manifested a love and admiration for their companion as enthusiastic as their former contempt had been galling. To shield his humility, however, from the dangers attending over-popularity, this general approbation roused the jealousy of one of his fellow-students, who pursued him with the most bitter and unrelenting hostility. The insults heaped upon him by this envious and evil-minded young man were met with a sweetness and patience, which for a long time seemed to serve no other purpose but to exasperate the malice of his enemy. At length, however, the hour came when meekness was to obtain the victory over wrong. From taunts and insults the furious youth one day proceeded to blows: instead of manifesting the slightest resentment, Vianney knelt at his feet and asked his pardon. The demon was cast out, and the unhappy youth, who had so long been his slave, knelt in his turn to ask and obtain the forgiveness of him whom he had so cruelly persecuted.

Having finished his course of philosophy, Jean Marie returned, in the July of 1813, to begin that of theology, under the direction of the Abbé Balley. "In this study," says M. Monnin, "he felt no longer the dryness, the disgust, and the difficulty which had more than once nearly discouraged him in his previous course." His teacher, indeed, thought it advisable to simplify his mode of instruction. A secret presentiment told him that the Holy Spirit would put the finishing stroke to the work which he was preparing; that He would do for the intellect of his pious pupil what He had already done for his heart, and in His own good time teach him all truth. After a year or two of assiduous care on the part of the master, and persevering efforts on that of the disciple, M. Balley thought he might venture to present him for examination at the Great Seminary of Lyons. Alas, this presentation was to lead to the. greatest of all those humiliations by which it pleased God to achieve in his soul that interior work of universal abnegation which was to render him hereafter an instrument of such admirable pliancy in His hands.

"When God," says M. Monnin, "has made choice of a soul, and predestinated it to something great, He marks it with His own seal, and that seal is the cross."

Jean Marie no sooner appeared in the awful presence of the examiners than his self-possession entirely deserted him, his memory became a blank, and to the questions addressed to him he returned incoherent and inconsequent replies, which gave all present the impression that he knew nothing whatever of the subjects of his examination. He was somewhat summarily dismissed. M. Balley, who of course, had his full share of his pupil's discredit, went at once to the superior of the seminary, and requested him to come the next day with one of the Vicars-General and ex- amine the disappointed candidate in private. The result of this second trial was, as he had hoped, satisfactory. Jean Marie was admitted into the Great Seminary of St. Irenæus to prepare for holy orders.

The impression left of him upon the minds of his fellow-seminarists is thus given by M. Monnin: " He grew visibly in humility, sweetness, and piety; these virtues could hardly be concealed from the observation of his fellow-students, but the acts of self-denial and penance, by which the new man is formed upon the ruins of the old, were known to God alone. He had already acquired so great a command over himself as to make it his one aim to do always that which is most perfect. He was never seen to infringe a rule, even in the minutest point. Never was he heard to speak in time of silence, to talk apart during recreation, or to show coldness or discourtesy to any of his companions. He conversed with all indifferently, without choice or partiality, making himself all things to all, that he might win them to Christ. Though his taste and disposition led him by preference to converse on religious subjects, he never sought to introduce them with a view to set forth his own familiarity with them, or in any way to gain credit to himself. He accommodated himself to every subject, every mind, and every character, without constraint and without affectation, and always kept himself as much as possible out of sight."

We find, also, from the testimony of his contemporaries in the seminary of Lyons, that the inferiority of M. Vianney's attainments has been much exaggerated. One of them tells us, indeed, that "whenever M. Vianney was questioned, either upon doctrines or morals, it was always in French, because he could not speak Latin; but his answers, though short, were always correct and exact."

Another writes thus: " He knew little of Latin, having begun his studies late, and gone through them very rapidly; but he knew quite enough to understand the approved authors in philosophy and theology. As far as I could judge (for we were not in the same class) he was not strong in philosophy; there were many others, however, no farther advanced in it than himself. To describe him as an ignorant person is a great mistake." It was a mistake, however, shared and fostered by his own singular humility. When, in after years, some of his intimate friends were speaking of the time when he studied under M. Balley, he objected to the word. " I never *studied*," said he. " M. Balley was so kind as to spend five or six years in trying

to teach me something, but he only threw away his Latin
by trying to cram it into my bad head."

This excessive self-distrust was the occasion of many precious acts of interior humility; it was his delight to unite
himself to the humiliations of his Divine Master, as he
poured forth his soul before Him in the Blessed Sacrament,
and thanked Him with holy David that He had made him
" the laughing-stock of those that were round about him."

Meanwhile the time for his ordination drew near, and
the directors of the seminary were still in a most painful
state of indecision. Were they to reject a subject whose
piety and regularity had won him the esteem of all, or
were they to present him for holy orders deficient, as they
knew him to be, in the learning usually required of candi-
dates for the sacred office? But for the intercession of his
friend and master, M. Balley, Jean Marie would in all probability have been sent back to tend his three sheep, and
the many thousand souls he was destined to feed with the
bread of life would have never known his pastoral care.
M. Balley, on hearing of the difficulties in the way of his
pupil's ordination, sought an interview with the Vicar-General, M. Courbon, who administered the diocese of Lyons
in the absence of the Archbishop, Cardinal Fesch. M.
Courbon was remarkable for his gift of discerning merit,
and his skill in employing those who possessed it. M. Balley's words produced their full effect; and when he was
consulted on the ordination of the unapt scholar, he seemed
to reflect for a moment, and then said,

" Is this young Vianney pious? Does he say his rosary
well? Is he devout to the Blessed Virgin?"

" He is a model of piety," replied all the directors with
one voice.

"Very well," answered the Vicar-General, "I will receive him. Divine grace will do the rest."

The Curé of Ars used often to say, "There is one thing for which M. Balley will find it hard to answer before God, and that is, for having made himself responsible for an ignorant creature like me."

The Abbé Vianney was ordained sub-deacon at Lyons by the Bishop of Grenoble, in the absence of the Cardinal-Archbishop. One who was at his side during the ordination observed that, when he arose after the prostration, his countenance shone with holy joy; and as the procession returned from the cathedral to the seminary, chanting the *Benedictus*, he pronounced the words, *Et tu, puer, Propheta Altissimi vocaberis; præibis enim ante faciem Domini, parare vias ejus,** in a tone which rang long years afterwards in the ears of his old friend and companion. It seemed prophetic of his future course.

M. Vianney received deacon's orders in the July of the following year, and six months afterwards was ordained priest in the cathedral-church of Grenoble.

God alone, to whom he then offered the holocaust of his whole being, knows what passed in that devoted heart when the long-desired and often-delayed moment came for the completion of the sacrifice. We can guess it only by the burning words which would escape him when he spoke of the surpassing dignity, the unspeakable blessedness, and withal the tremendous responsibility, of the office then laid upon him.

---

* "And thou, child, shalt be called the Prophet of the Most High; for thou shalt go before the face of the Lord to prepare His ways." (*St. Luke* i, 76.)

CHAPTER IV.

He is appointed Vicaire of Ecully—Death of M. Balley—M. Vianney
is nominated Curé of Ars—His labors for the reformation and sanc-
tification of his parish.

M. VIANNEY was ordained priest on the 9th of August,
1815, at the age of twenty-nine. It is not known where
he said his first Mass. It was probably, however, at Ecully;
and he was certainly assisted by M. Balley, who had asked
and obtained his favorite pupil as his vicaire. Great was
the mutual joy of master and scholar in being thus asso-
ciated together, and great was the rejoicing among the good
people of Ecully. "We loved him," said they, "when
he was a student among us; he edified us then by the holiness of his life. What will it be now that he is a priest?"
Nor were they disappointed. He was soon in possession of
the confidence of all around him, and his confessional was
continually surrounded. The first confession he ever received was that of his beloved master M. Balley, who chose
him at once for his confessor. On the eve of great feasts
he passed the day and part of the night in his confessional,
leaving himself scarcely time to say Mass, recite his Office,
and snatch his single and scanty meal.

"He had not," says M. Monnin, "two weights or two
measures; he made the perfection which he preached to
others the inflexible rule of his own actions." He was severe to himself, gentle and indulgent towards others, especially to the poor and lowly. His heart and his purse were

open to all. One instance among many has been preserved of his tender charity. He had persisted for a long time in wearing a cassock so old and ragged as to call forth the frequent remonstrances of his friends, who told him that the dignity of his office called for a more suitable exterior. He would answer, " I will see about it ;" but still his slender salary melted away in alms, and the ragged cassock continued to be worn. At last, having been beset more urgently than usual, he determined to put the sum necessary for the purchase of a cassock into the hands of the tailor's wife. Some days afterwards he received a visit from a lady, whom her own abundant alms, and the troubles of the times, had reduced to the extremity of distress. At the end of a conversation which wrung his heart by the picture of noble suffering thus exhibited, the vicaire hurried to the tailor's wife, and asked her for his money. The good woman, who by no means wished to lose a job for her husband, brought forward a hundred good reasons against restoring the money, each more luminous and eloquent than the last. " Yes, yes, all very well," was the only reply of the determined vicaire ; " but give me my money, and we will see about it afterwards." And the price of the cassock found its way to the noble lady through an unsuspected channel. The life which the holy curé and his young vicaire led in common was that of the strictest religious order. They said the canonical office together at a fixed and invariable hour ; they slept in their clothes ; they made a day's retreat every month, and the spiritual exercises every year.

M. Vianney was never weary of expatiating on the holiness, the talents, and the virtues of his venerated master. " I should have been good for something in time," he used to say, "if I had always had the blessing of living with M. Balley. It was enough to make one love God only to hear

him say, 'My God, I love Thee with my whole heart.' He
repeated it continually all day long when he was alone, and
ceased not to do the same in his chamber at night till he
fell asleep." So severe were the austerities practised by
these two holy priests, that the Vicar-General was constrained to use his authority to moderate them. The aged
servant of God was soon, however, to find rest. At the end
of two years from the time of M. Vianney's ordination, his
beloved master was taken away, leaving a double portion of
his spirit upon him. M. Balley committed to his care all
his instruments of penance. "Take these, my poor Vianney," said he, "and be sure that nobody sees them after
my death, or they will fancy I have done something for
the expiation of my sins, and will leave me in purgatory
till the end of the world;" then laying his trembling
hands upon the head of the young priest, who was sobbing
at his feet, he blessed him, saying, "Farewell, my dear
child; courage; persevere in the love and service of our
good Master. Remember me at the holy altar. Farewell;
we shall meet above."

"He died," said M. Vianney, "like a Saint as he was,
and his pure soul departed to add new joy to Paradise."

The people of Ecully tried hard to obtain the pupil of
M. Balley for his successor; but M. Vianney steadily refused a post which he accounted himself inadequate to fill.

Three months afterwards he was appointed Curé of Ars.
"Go, my friend," said the Vicar-General; "there is but
little of the love of God in that parish; you will enkindle it."

Ars is a little village of the ancient principality of Les
Dombes, now the department of Trévoux. In the year
1818 none of the roads existed which now break the monotony of its features. The houses were scarcely visible

amid the thick foliage of its fruit-trees. They were scattered here and there without any regard to symmetrical order, only clustering a little more thickly round the ancient steeple of the same date with the fine old feudal castle which commands the village from the north. A silent peace, bordering upon melancholy, is the characteristic feature of the villages which lie sequestered among the wooded valleys of the Dombes; the streams flow lazily along, to pay their tribute to the Saône; the air is heavy and relaxing, a circumstance not to be forgotten when we attempt to appreciate the superhuman life of unflinching and unremitting labor which was led in so depressing an atmosphere.

The population of Ars is wholly agricultural. The loving veneration which they have at all times borne to their pastors shows that these poor villagers are susceptible of deep impressions, and faithful in preserving them. At the re-establishment of religion in France, the Abbé Berger had been appointed Curé of Ars; and he remained there nearly to the time of M. Vianney's arrival, in the beginning of Lent, the 9th of February, 1818. The new curé came in most apostolic poverty. The furniture which he had inherited from his holy master consisted of a wooden bedstead and some coverlets, of which his charity soon dispossessed him, inventing such arrangements for his night's lodging as would have amazed M. Balley himself.

It is said that, when he first caught sight of the roofs of his parish, he knelt down to implore a blessing upon them. When asked if this were true, he made his usual reply on such occasions, "It is not a bad idea." The people of Ars were not slow to discover what a treasure they possessed in their new curé. Those who heard his first Mass were struck with his extraordinary fervor, and with the saintliness of his whole bearing. The general impression was strengthened

by the report of frequent visitors from Ecully, where his
loss was still bitterly deplored. The simple peasants, rude
and uncultivated as they were, failed not to discover that
their pastor was a man of prayer, a priest in very deed after
the heart of his Divine Master. In the beautiful words of
his friend and biographer, "his heart was a most pure vessel of mortification and prayer; and, like the thurible
which his hand waved at the feet of his Lord, it was ever
open towards heaven, and closed towards earth; exhaling
continually that precious incense which burns to purify the
air, and consumes itself in neutralizing the invisible yet
fatal miasma around it."

With him the priest was all in all, the man nothing.
M. Vianney was destitute of all natural means of attracting
interest or commanding admiration. He had none of the
ordinary graces of youth, nor had he yet attained that
spiritual beauty which glorified his old age. His face was
pale and angular, his stature low, his gait awkward, his
manner shy and timid, his whole air common and unat-
tractive. There was nothing in his appearance, except its
asceticism, and the singular brightness of his eyes, to impress the mind of an ordinary observer.

No sooner was the new curé installed in his parish than
he chose the church as his dwelling-place. He would be
seen for hours together kneeling perfectly motionless in
the midst of the sanctuary, "bathing" (to use his own expression) "in the flames of love which issued from the
Divine Presence on the Altar." He entered the church at
daybreak, and remained there till the evening Angelus.
There he was sure to be found whenever he was wanted.
"How we loved," say the notes of Catherine Lassagne, a
pious woman of whom we shall hear more hereafter, "to see

our good curé in the church at his prayers, especially at daybreak! While reciting his office, he would gaze at the tabernacle with a smile which gladdened the heart. I have seen it many a time myself; it seemed as if he *saw* our Lord. I was always struck with my own spiritual misery before God, when I saw, by the light of the sanctuary lamp, that wasted and withered form, and that brilliant glance fixed upon the door of the tabernacle with an expression of happiness which it is impossible to describe."

The curé, whose home was in the church, had little need of a presbytery; hence the forlorn and dismantled aspect which that abode began even now to wear, and which in after years so forcibly struck those who were admitted within its lonely walls. It seemed the dwelling-place of a spirit, so utterly destitute was it of all things needful for the body. We have few details of the early years of our holy curé's pastoral life; enough, however, remains to show us that they were full of severe and long unrequited toil. The notes of Catherine Lassagne give us the following picture of the state of the parish when he first undertook its pastoral care. "Ars," says she, "at the time of M. le Curé's arrival, was in the utmost spiritual poverty: virtue was little known, and less practised; nearly all its inhabitants had forsaken the right way, and neglected the care of their salvation. The young people had nothing in their heads but pleasure and amusement. Nearly every Sunday they assembled together on the green, a few steps from the church, or, according to the season, in the village taverns, to indulge in dancing and amusements of every kind." They were, in fact, remarkable among the villagers of the neighborhood for a headlong and reckless devotion to pleasure. How is their pastor to stem the tide? He has but two weapons: one, as we have seen, pursuing prayer, and the daily offering of the all-prevailing sacrifice; the other, the faithful and fervent preaching of the Word of God. To this last he attached very great importance, and he spared no pains in preparing his sermons. He would shut himself up for days together in his sacristy, devoting to this employment every moment which he had to spare from his spiritual exercises. When he had finished writing his discourse, he would recite it aloud by himself, as if from the pulpit. In this laborious preparation he faithfully persevered, until he attained in time that marvellous facility which characterized his preaching in the later years of his life. But he had another way of preaching, not less effectual.

"The world," it has been well said, "belongs to him who loves it best, and does most to prove his love;"* and it was by the might of love that M. Vianney mastered the hearts of his people. They felt that he loved them, not only as a whole and in a general way, but with the discriminating and individual love of the Sacred Heart itself for each severally and alone. No child could pass him in the street without receiving a smile or a caress; no trouble was beneath his notice, no sorrow too trifling for his sympathy. Without ever for a moment forgetting, or suffering others to forget, the dignity of his sacred office, he would enter uncalled the dwellings of his poor people, and converse familiarly with them on their family matters, till he found an opportunity, without any abrupt or harsh transition, to speak to them of divine things. Many a soul was brought back to God by these simple pastoral visits.

Notwithstanding the laxity which generally prevailed at this period among his parishioners, M. Vianney was not

* L'Abbé Mullois, *Manuel de la Charite.*

without the aid of a few faithful souls, already prepared to yield a hundredfold for the seed he cast among them. Of these, the most influential, both from her position and her piety, was the lady of the Castle, Mdlle. d'Ars. Her youth (she was at this time sixty years of age) had been spent under the eye of a most pious mother, who had early trained her in the purest precepts of the Gospel; while her manners had all the refinement and high cultivation of the society in which her early days had been spent, and possessed the peculiar grace and fascination of a highbred Frenchwoman of "la vieille cour." Mdlle. d'Ars, as the mistress of a household, exactly answered to the picture of "the valiant woman" presented to us in Holy Scripture. The daily routine of her home was regular and quiet as the order of a convent. Every one, from the mistress to the lowest servant, was at his post. Her own time was divided between prayer, the care of her household, and visiting and working for her poor. Her own personal habits were those of the strictest self-denial. When M. Vianney saw her one day come to Mass ankle-deep in snow, he could not help saying to her, "Mdlle., you really ought to have a carriage."

"My good curé," replied she, "I have calculated what it would cost me, and find it would be a good round sum, and I should have so much the less for my poor."

Besides her other devotions, Mdlle. d'Ars said the Canonical Hours daily. The château was not only a house of prayer, it was the refuge, the hospital, the bank, and the pattern of the whole country round. Mdlle. d'Ars was the first to appreciate the eminent sanctity of her new pastor, and her esteem and veneration of his virtues grew with every remaining year of her life. She was in the habit of presenting him with a bouquet of white lilies for his feast-day. One year, having been prevented from making her offering as usual on the vigil of St. John the Baptist, she brought it to him in the sacristy on the morning of the feast. M. Vianney, having admired the beauty and freshness of the lilies, laid them down on the sill of a south window, where the burning sun must naturally have withered them in a few hours. At the end of a week they retained their sweetness and brilliancy, to the great astonishment of all who heard of the fact. "Mdlle. d'Ars," suggested the curé, in his ingenious humility, "must certainly be a saint, for her flowers to live in this way."

M. Vianney chose the same means for the renewal of his parish which had proved so successful in the hands of M. Olier for the reformation of St. Sulpice. His first desire was to establish in his church the perpetual adoration of the Blessed Sacrament; but where was he to find adorers? Among a poor agricultural population, depending upon daily labor for daily bread, whom could he find to watch before the tabernacle? First, there was the noble châtelaine, the pious lady of Ars, who would have desired nothing better than to abide, like the aged Anna, day and night in the temple; next, a simple peasant, a good father of a family, an unlettered husbandman, whose fervent piety was the joy of his pastor's heart. Whether going to his work or returning from it, never did that good man pass the church-door without entering it to adore his Lord. He would leave his tools, his spade, hoe, and pickaxe, at the door, and remain for hours together sitting or kneeling before the tabernacle. M. Vianney, who watched him with great delight, could never perceive the slightest movement of the lips. Being surprised at this circumstance, he said to him one day, "My good father, what do you say to our Lord in those long visits you pay Him every day and many times a day?" "I say nothing to Him," was the reply; "I look at Him, and He looks at me."* "A beautiful and sublime answer," says M. Monnin. "He said nothing, he opened no book, he could not read; but he had eyes,—eyes of the body and eyes of the soul,—and he opened them, those of the soul especially, and fixed them on our Lord. 'I look at Him.' He fastened upon Him his whole mind, his whole heart; all his senses, and all his faculties. There was an interchange of ineffable thought in those glances which came and went between the heart of the servant and the heart of the Master. This is the secret, the great secret, of attaining sanctity. To be saints, is to form the image of Jesus Christ within us; and to form Jesus Christ within us, what must we do? We must look at Him often, and look at Him long; for the more we look at Him, the more we shall love Him; and the more we love Him, the more shall we be led to imitate Him."

A poor widow, la mère Bibot, who came with him from Ecully, lived near the church, and kept house (if so it may be called) for the curé, made a third in this little group of worshippers, which was completed by the arrival of Mdlle. Pignaut, a person already highly esteemed at Lyons for her piety, and who now left that city to live under the pastoral care of M. Vianney. She took up her abode under the widow's humble roof, to pass the remainder of her days in almsgiving and prayer.

Now was the heart of the holy curé glad within him. His Lord would no longer be left alone: he had formed a little court around Him. At whatever hour you entered the church, you would find at least two adorers, one in the

---

* "Je l'avise, et il m'avise."

sanctuary, the other in the chapel of the Blessed Virgin. The day which had been begun by the offering of the holy Mass, was ended by the recitation of the Rosary and of night prayers in common. This evening exercise was not long confined to the five who first joined in it. It was announced by the sound of the bell, and it was the joy of the curé's heart to see, one by one, members of almost all the village households come in after their daily toil for a half-hour of prayer before they went to rest. He never failed to preside at this evening devotion from its commencement till his death, except when absent on missions to the neighboring villages. On no other occasion did he ever pass a single night out of his parish.

Another aim which was continually before him was to bring his parishioners to a more frequent use of the Sacraments. At Ecully the practice of frequent Communion had been established by the pastoral vigilance of M. Balley; it was unknown at Ars. Mothers of families and some of their daughters, when the mania for dancing happened not to be upon them, would communicate at the great feasts; but nothing more was thought of. "I have nothing to do here," said the holy curé, with many a sigh; "I am afraid I shall lose my soul. Oh, if I could but once see our divine Saviour known and loved! If I might distribute His most Sacred Body daily to a number of fervent communicants, how happy should I be!"

It was not long before this desire of his heart was also granted. The same little band of devout souls who had led the way in the establishment of evening prayers, and the perpetual adoration of the Blessed Sacrament, now formed the nucleus around which he was enabled to form a goodly company of frequent and fervent communicants. To aid and expand the growing spirit of devotion among his people, M. Vianney lost no time in establishing two devout confraternities : that of the Blessed Sacrament for the men, and that of the Rosary for the women, and especially the young girls of his flock. His mode of proceeding in the establishment of this latter society was characteristic. One Sunday evening after Vespers he noticed some of the giddiest of the village girls, whom he had vainly tried to draw to the evening Rosary, waiting in the church for confession. " Here," said he to himself, as he quietly watched them from his place in the choir, " is my confraternity of the Rosary ready made." When he saw them ranged round the confessional, " My children," said he, " we will, if you please, say a chaplet together to ask the Queen of Virgins to obtain grace for you to do well what you are about to do." He then began the prayers, and the girls duly responded. It was all that was wanted. From that hour many of them dated their conversion. One of them, at that time the lightest and most pleasure-loving of the party, told Catherine Lassagne that she felt so much confused and disconcerted when M. Vianney proposed to them to say the Rosary, that she could hardly make the responses. " I believe," added she, " that it was at that moment he obtained my conversion." She became afterwards a model of piety and regularity. These were some of the holy curé's first victories ; the tide was beginning to turn ; but many a long year's hard struggle was before him ere yet the field was won.

He had begun, as we have seen, by drawing together around him, and to the feet of our Lord, a little company of chosen souls, to go forth with him to the help of the Lord against the mighty. He was no longer alone. Their prayers, alms, and communions stayed up his hands when over-wearied with the struggle, and one by one the strongholds of evil fell before him. The noisy revelry of the tavern and the dance, and the inveterate practice of Sunday labor, gave way, by slow yet sure degrees, before the meek yet unflinching perseverance of his assault. "Do not distrust the providence of God," he would say, when his poor people were tempted on a fine Sunday to place their crops in safety; "He who made your corn to grow will assuredly enable you to gather it in." Those who trusted to his word were never known to repent of their confidence.

"I was at Ars one summer," writes M. l'Abbé Renard, "during the hay-season. The week-had been rainy, with the exception of a few intervals of sunshine, during which the peasants had mowed their fields. On Saturday night the hay lay on the meadows, too wet to be carried. A glorious Sunday morning succeeded it; but though all their crops lay in danger of perishing, not a haymaker was to be seen in the fields. Happening to meet one of the peasants, I said, by way of trying him, 'My friend, will not your crop be spoiled?' 'I am not afraid,' said he; 'God, who gave it to me, can preserve it for me. Our good curé will not have us work on Sunday; we ought to obey him.' God blessed this obedience, as He always does; those who were faithful to it lived at their ease on the produce of their land; those only were ruined who worked secretly on Sunday; for, as one of these good people said, 'With us human respect is turned the other way.'" But the holy curé was not content with forbidding labor and repressing noisy amusements on Sunday; he taught his people to find a blessed substitute for both in the ever-open house of God, which scarce sufficed to contain the number of worshippers who flocked to Mass, and returned to the mid-day catechizing, and again to Vespers, Compline, and Rosary. At nightfall, the bell a third time called the whole parish, as one family, together, to listen to one of their pastor's simple and touching homilies.

"At this distance of time," says M. Monnin, "when, in consequence of the number of strangers who have been induced by the pilgrimage to settle at Ars, a second formation has covered this primitive vegetation, it has become difficult to trace the deep labors of our great husbandman; but five-and-twenty or thirty years ago Ars was a veritable Christian oasis. 'I have often walked in the fields in harvest-time,' said a frequent visitor of Ars, 'without hearing a single oath or a single unseemly expression.' I once remarked this to one of the peasants, who replied with great simplicity, 'We are no better than other people; but we should be ashamed to do such things so near to a saint.' At the sound of the mid-day Angelus the men would stop in the midst of their labor and recite the Ave Maria with uncovered head. No scenes of drunkenness, none of the quarrels which are its unfailing consequence, are to be seen. Such is the attendance at the Sacraments that an ordinary Saturday evening at Ars is like the eve of a great festival elsewhere, so great is the throng around the confessional. In what other of our parishes do we see women, and even men, at their prayers in the church at two or three o'clock in the morning, and again at night after a hard day's toil?

"I know there are still some hardened sinners who resist all the efforts of their pastor. Evil will glide in everywhere, and seems to be rendered more intense in its perversity by the neighborhood of any great good; but any one who knows Les Dombes, or who will be pleased to remember what was the state of Ars before the arrival of M. Vianney, and what is still the state of the surrounding parishes, will account the change which he has wrought among his own people the greatest among the miracles of this holy priest of Jesus Christ."

CHÀPTER V.

He restores and ornaments his church, and builds several chapels— His devotion to St. Philomena—His labors for souls within and without his parish.

NEXT only to his zeal for the salvation of souls and the purification of those living temples of God, was the care of M. Vianney for the order and beauty of His material sanctuary. The austere lover of poverty was even lavish and prodigal where the glory of God's house was to be maintained. When he came to Ars, he found his little church cold and empty as the hearts of the worshippers. His first care was to replace the high altar, which was actually falling to pieces from age and neglect, by one more worthy of its sacred purpose. It was a joyful day to him when the fine new altar was erected at his own sole charge ; for he would have counted it shame to ask the aid of others till he had exhausted his own resources. Next, the old carving of the choir was renovated, under his direction, by the hand of the village carpenter, to the great delight of the people of Ars, who looked upon the bright coloring which was laid on with no sparing hand as a masterpiece of art. They learned of their curé to care for the house of the Lord, and to aid him to the best of their power in celebrating the festivals of the

Church with due solemnity. The feast of Corpus Christi was the dearest of all to his heart. He took great delight in arranging a procession of children, arrayed at his own cost, in white, who were to strew flowers before the Blessed Sacrament, when borne in glad procession round the church.

"Come, my children," he would say, with that smile which went to every heart, "you will be very good, very modest, very recollected. You will remember that you are before the good God, and stand in the place of the angels. You will say to Him from the bottom of your hearts, 'My God, I love Thee!' In order to please our Lord, your souls must be as white as the dress you wear."

M. Vianney found a ready and zealous helper in his pious labors, in the Vicomte d'Ars, who had formed a close friendship with him when on a visit to his sister. This pious nobleman, who was the very model of a devout layman, on his return to Paris, sent him a splendid tabernacle, candlesticks, and reliquaries for his new altar, together with some rich vestments and banners, a remonstrance, and a splendid canopy.

The joy of the holy curé at the sight of all these magnificent presents was almost infantine. He went about the parish calling upon his people to rejoice with him.

"Come, good mother," he said to one of his good old women, "come and see something beautiful before you die."

He was not happy till he had thought of a way of expressing his gratitude to God. On the following Sunday he said to his parishioners:

"My brethren, you have seen what M. d'Ars has just done for us. Well, I intend to lead you all in procession to Fourvières,* to give thanks to the Blessed Virgin, and

* A celebrated shrine of our Blessed Lady, and place of pilgrimage, near Lyons.

make an offering to her of these riches. She will bless
them. We will consecrate ourselves to her at the same
time in that sanctuary where she shows herself so mighty
and so gracious. She must convert us."

The proposal was heartily responded to; and on the feast
of St. Sixtus, the patron of the parish, the procession set
forth, scarcely a soul being left behind.

"It would have been a good day," says Catherine, "to
attack the village; for there was no one left at home to
defend it."

The rural procession is still remembered, the gorgeous
banners contrasting with the humble dress of the villagers
and the emaciated and mortified appearance of their saintly
pastor.

"That day," says M. Monnin, "has remained as a me-
morable epoch in the remembrance of the people of Ars.
It drew down graces upon their little corner of the world,
which, in after years, was to attract pilgrims from all the
ends of the earth to this new suburb of Fourvières. It
marked out to them the precise period of a great religious
transformation. At the same time it shed a sudden light
upon the soul of the holy priest. His heart swelled with a
sense of joy unknown before, which seemed like a revelation of the future glory of his humble village."

"I was a prophet once in my life," said he, not long
before his death; then interrupting himself, as if he was
afraid of his words being taken seriously, he added play-
fully, "O evil prophet! prophet of Baal! I predicted that
a time would come when Ars would not be able to contain
its inhabitants."

The next work of M. Vianney, after the restoration of
the choir and altar, was to erect several small chapels, not

only for the purpose of enlarging the church, but to assist the devotion of the faithful. The first was in honor of his patron, St. John the Baptist, who, according to a tradition formerly believed at Ars, appeared to him in the early days of his ministry there, and revealed to him that he desired to be especially honored in that church, and that by his intercession many sinners should there be brought back to God. Some days after this chapel had been opened and blessed, M. Vianney said to his parishioners:

"Were you but to know what has passed in this chapel, you would not dare to set foot there. If it shall so please God, He will make it known to you; as for me, I will not utter another word about it."

Nothing more was ever known. "It was," says M. Monnin, "one of those half-revelations which seemed to escape him unawares, and the imprudence of which (as he accounted it) he hastened in his humility to repair by endeavoring to efface the remembrance of them. Certain, however, it is, that the chapel of St. John was always especially dear and venerable in his eyes; it was the scene of his life-long labor for souls, and from thence, by the slow martyrdom of his confessional, he passed to his reward."

A remarkable circumstance occurred just after the completion of the chapel of St. John. The holy curé had exhausted all his funds, and was in great perplexity how he was to pay his workmen. He had recourse to his unfailing aid, the Blessed Virgin, and went to take a turn in the fields with his rosary in his hand. He had scarcely passed the bounds of the village, when he was respectfully saluted by a stranger on horseback, who inquired after his health.

"I am not ill," replied he; "but I am in a good deal of trouble."

"Do your parishioners cause you uneasiness?"

"On the contrary, they are far better to me than I deserve; but the fact is, that I have just built a chapel, and have not the means to pay my workmen."

The stranger, after seeming to reflect for a moment, drew out of his pocket twenty-five gold pieces, which he placed in the hand of M. Vianney, saying,

"M. le Curé, this will pay your workmen. I recommend myself to your prayers."

He then rode off at full speed, without giving M. Vianney time to thank him. This was the first, but by no means the last, time that he received unexpected and mysterious assistance of the like kind.

The second chapel erected by the holy curé was dedicated to his chosen patroness, St. Philomena. The relics of this virgin saint had been discovered at Rome, in the cemetery of St. Priscilla, on the 25th of May, 1802. On the entrance of the tomb which contained them were carved the symbols of virginity and martyrdom,—an anchor, three arrows, a palm, and a lily,—with the legend,

[Fi]lumena, pax tecum. Fi[at].
(Philomena, peace be with thee. Amen.)

Within appeared the relics of the saint, with an urn still bearing the traces of the blood shed for Jesus Christ. These precious remains were afterwards translated to Mugnano, in the Neapolitan territory, where many signal miracles were wrought at the shrine of the young martyr. The devotion spread from Italy into France, where new wonders attested her power with God, Who chose, as the agent for promoting the glory of His saint, the humble curé of an obscure village.

Mysterious and wonderful is the sympathy which thrills through the communion of saints, unbroken by distance, undimmed by time, unchilled by death! The child went forth from her mother's arms to die for Christ; the lictor's axe cropped the budding lily, and pious hands gathered it up, and laid it in the tomb; and so fifteen centuries went by, and none on earth thought upon the virgin martyr, who was following the Lamb whithersoever He went, till the time came when the Lord would have her glory to appear; and then He chose a champion for her in the lonely toil-worn priest, to whom He had given a heart as childlike and a love as heroic as her own; and He gave her to be the helpmate of his labors, and bade her stand by him to shelter his humility behind the brightness of her glory, lest he should be affrighted at the knowledge of his own power with God.

"The love of the Curé of Ars," says M. Monnin, "for his *dear little saint*, as he called her, was almost chivalrous. There was the most touching sympathy between them. She granted everything to his prayers; he refused nothing to her love. He set down to her account all the graces and wonders which contributed to the celebrity of the pilgrimage of Ars. It was all her work; he had nothing whatever to do with it."

At the close of the fifth year of M. Vianney's labors at Ars, his superiors determined to place him where his burning zeal for the salvation of souls might have a wider sphere of action. He was appointed to the cure of Salles, an important place in the canton of the Beaujolais. There was everything attractive to nature in the proposed change to a pure air, a bright sky, and lovely scenery, from the dull and heavy atmosphere of the Dombes. He refused not to go at the voice of obedience; but he was equally ready to remain in his obscure village, when the will of Divine Providence was manifested that there was to be his abode for life. His poor furniture was actually twice packed up, and twice brought back from the banks of the Saône, the swelling of the waters rendering it impossible to cross the river. His poor people had been inconsolable from the first intimation of his approaching removal. Mdlle. d'Ars, in the energy of her grief and displeasure, wrote, in one of her familiar letters, of nothing less than *strangling the Vicar-General*. The impending evil was happily averted by milder means. The parishioners, having ascertained that their pastor had no desire to leave them, and no wish but for the accomplishment of the will of God, took advantage of the providential delay occasioned by the swelling of the river, to address so effectual a remonstrance to the Vicar-General as induced him to cancel his appointment, and leave their beloved curé at their head.

"From that time forth," says M. Monnin, "M. Vianney identified himself more and more with his parishioners. All his thoughts were concentrated upon them ; their peace was his peace ; their joys his joys ; their troubles his sorrows ; their virtues his crown. He bound himself to their souls, as the serf to the land he tills. His horizon in this world was henceforth bounded by the limits of that little spot of Christian earth, where all the providential preparations of his life were to find their accomplishment. His activity was to have but one end,—the glory of God by the salvation of the souls there committed to his care."

Ever distrustful of himself, M. Vianney would frequently call some of the neighboring priests to his aid, and on these occasions the Divine blessing rested no less on their labors than on his humility.

"I believe," says Catherine, in her notes of this period,

"that it is impossible to calculate the number of the conversions which M. le Curé obtained at the time of the jubilee by the prayers, and above all by the Masses, which he offered for his parishioners. There was such a renewal of fervor that almost all set to work with their whole might to free themselves from their sins. Human respect was *turned the other way*. Though M. le Curé had engaged another priest to help him, almost all chose to go to confession to their own pastor. In the sermon which he preached at the close of the exercises, M. le Curé was able to say, in the joy of his heart, 'My brethren, Ars is no longer Ars. Not for many years past has so great a change taken place in this parish. I have assisted at many missions and jubilees, but never at one like this.' It is true," adds Catherine, "that this fervor has in some degree cooled, but our good God still keeps the upper hand. Religion is generally reverenced among us, and those who practise it respected."

Before the time when the influx of pilgrims made it impossible for him to leave his post for a single night, M. Vianney frequently repaid the assistance afforded him by the neighboring priests on these occasions by undertaking the care of their flocks in case of absence or sickness.

In the beginning of the year 1823 he was called upon to take part in a mission given at Trévoux by the priests of the Society of the Chartreux at Lyons. M. Vianney would set off on foot, with his surplice over his arm, in the severe cold of a winter's night, when his Sunday labors were over, and return to his post on Saturday evening in time to hear the confessions of his parishioners. He took up his quarters with M. Morel, an old friend, who had been his fellow-student at Verrières. "I can be more at my ease with you," said he; "and I shall not be pressed to eat, as I should be elsewhere."

This mission lasted for six weeks, and he was nearly weighed down by the labor which fell to his share. So great was the press which surrounded him, that on one occasion the confessional, which was not very firmly fixed, gave way.

He was always the first in the church in the morning and the last at night, and on one occasion was so completely exhausted by his labors, that M. Morel was obliged to take him on his shoulders and carry him half dead to his room. He could hardly be persuaded even then to take a restorative, till Madame Morel bethought herself to say to him:

"M. le Curé, you give other people penances, and expect them to perform them. Well, now, let me give you one to-day, and drink what I bring you."

"Ah, well," said he, with a smile, "what woman wills, God wills;" and he accepted his penance.

On the eve of the general Communion, at the close of the mission, M. Morel went at nine, at twelve, and at two o'clock, in the vain hope of extricating his guest from the dense crowd which surrounded him. He at last made his way to the confessional, to drag him away by force, when he was assailed by the unanimous exclamation:

"If you take M. le Curé away, we shall not return, and you will have to answer for it before God!"

"What!" cried he indignantly; "yesterday M. Vianney did not leave the church till midnight, and was at his post again at four o'clock in the morning. How much time has he had for sleep? His bed has not even been touched. To-day, as yesterday, he has his office to say, and at four o'clock as usual he will be here again. Tell me, you who grumble, would you do as much?"

And having thus put the murmurers to silence, M. Morel took the good curé by the hand, who was too much worn out to offer any resistance, and led him away to his house.

The fame of the conversions wrought at Trévoux spread throughout the neighboring parishes, and M. Vianney was thenceforth beset with petitions from others of his brethren in the priesthood, to confer the like benefit upon their flocks. M. Monnin gives the names of six parishes in which he labored with the same marvellous success as at Trévoux; "yet in this incessant toil for the souls of others," adds he, " he neglected not his own. His heart ascended continually to God in fervent ejaculations; he gave a considerable time to meditation, to the reading of the lives of the saints, and to visits to the Blessed Sacrament,—no short and passing visits, but long hours prostrate before the tabernacle. Labor was with him but the prolongation of prayer; he was always speaking to God, or of God; loving Him, or moving others to love Him. Neither does it appear that his own parish ever suffered from these frequent evangelical journeys. He accepted the office of missionary only when he could do so without neglecting his duty as a parish-priest."

We may judge of the impression left by him upon those who remember these missionary labors, by the following lines, addressed by a good priest, after his death, to the Bishop of Belley :

" I must go back forty years to retrace my first recollection of this venerable man. It was in the year 1820, when I was about ten years old. We were practising, in the court of the college where I was studying, to strew the flowers for the procession of Corpus Christi, when I saw a priest come in of a very simple, poor, and humble exterior. One of my companions whispered to me : ' That is the Curé of Ars; *he is a saint;* he lives upon nothing but boiled potatoes.' I looked at him with amazement. As some of us addressed him in a few courteous words, he stopped for a moment, and said with a kind smile, ' My friends, when you are strewing flowers before the Blessed Sacrament, hide your hearts in your baskets, and send them amid your roses to Jesus Christ.' Then, without paying any other visit, he went straight across the court to the chapel, to pay his homage to the Master of the house in His tabernacle. I have forgotten nearly all the names of my fellow-students, and almost all other circumstances of that time; but the words of that priest, his visit to the Blessed Sacrament, and the speech of my companion, have never been effaced from my memory. I was especially struck (for I was a greedy boy) with the idea of a man who *lived on potatoes*. I felt, without exactly knowing why, that this implied something great and wonderful, and it was probably this which kept the other circumstances in my mind.

"Ten years afterwards, by a combination of circumstances which belong to the history of the loving providence of God towards me, I found myself in an ecclesiastical seminary. Then the thought of the mortified priest, who was so devout to the Blessed Sacrament, recurred to my mind. During that interval, he had grown much in reputation among men, and although his renown had not reached the height which we have seen it attain in the last fifteen years of his life, there was already a great sensation about him. Men came to him from all parts : the good for edification, sinners to pour their sins and remorse into the bosom of the man of God. The miracle of his life, so inconceivable in its austerity, excited the wonder and admiration of all. It was, indeed, incomprehensible how he could live on so small an amount of nourishment. Many other marvels were related of him; and these rumors, strange and unwonted in our days, have been since fully confirmed."

Surely, as he passed across that college courtyard, *God* (in the saintly priest's own words) *passed with him*, and impressed that ideal of mingled austerity and sweetness, the very type of sacerdotal sanctity, upon those children's hearts.

CHAPTER VI.

Foundation of the *Providence*—Miraculous interpositions attending it.

It was in the year 1825, the seventh of his ministry at Ars, that M. Vianney founded the asylum for orphan and destitute girls, which, under the name of *Providence*, became afterwards the model of so many institutions of the same kind throughout the length and breadth of France. The miracles which illustrated the commencement of this humble and unostentatious work of charity laid the foundation of the wide-spread fame which attracted multitudes to Ars, who would never otherwise have heard of the sanctity of its holy curé.

Like all the works of God, the *Providence* had a small and noiseless beginning. M. Vianney had long silently brooded over his desire to find some shelter for the poor girls whom he saw exposed to continual temptation from the twofold danger of want and ignorance. A large house, well suited for his purpose, was about this time erected behind the choir of the church; upon this he cast a longing eye. "If that house were mine," said he, "I would turn it into a *Providence* for poor destitute girls. I should have but a few steps to go from the church to visit my little family, to catechize them, and take my meal there. The *Providence* would give me my bread; I should give it in return the Word of truth, which is the bread of the soul. I should receive from it the nourishment of the body in exchange for the food of the soul. I should like this well."

The idea grew and strengthened in his mind, but he would first lay the matter before God; and with this view he proposed a Novena to the Blessed Virgin. "She so dearly loves the poor," said he, "who are the friends of her Son, that she will assuredly come to my assistance." And that he might not seem to tempt God by expecting miracles, he set himself to do what he could on his own part.

No religious vowed to holy poverty ever carried that distinctive virtue of the Gospel to a higher degree of perfection than the Curé of Ars. He took our Lord literally at His word, and taking no thought for the morrow, constantly anticipated both the small stipend of his cure, and the slender patrimonial portion which he received from his brother François.

In 1822 he writes to him thus:

"MY DEAR BROTHER: Together with an account of my health, which continues much the same, I must tell you that if you can contrive to send me my pension for the whole year, it will be a great convenience to me, as I have just made an important purchase for my church. If you could even advance me that of the coming year, it would be still better. My brother-in-law Melin has kindly pro-

mised to give me a hundred crowns.for a work of charity,
but that will not be enough. I venture to hope, my dearest brother, that you will do me this favor."

On this occasion, as his small income would not suffice
for the purpose in hand, he sold all that he possessed, and
purchased the house for the sum of 20,000 francs, which
was about the value of his share of the property at Dardilly.
When he had bought the house, he had not money to pay
the legal expenses of the purchase. The next difficulty
was to find suitable persons to take charge of the establishment. His first idea had been to place it in the hands of
religious, and his thoughts had turned to the Sisters of St.
Charles, in grateful remembrance of the care with which,
under the Reign of Terror, they had prepared him for his
first Communion. He saw reason, however, to alter his
plan, and resolved to place at the head of his infant undertaking two young persons of his own training, whom, without suffering them to aspire to the religious character, he
had long exercised in all the virtues which belong to it,—
obedience, humility, simplicity, and absolute dependence
upon Divine Providence.

Benoîte Lardet and Catherine Lassagne were both distinguished for their sound practical sense and solid piety.
The one was to be, in his own words, the *head*, the other
the *heart*, of the new foundation. To Catherine Lassagne
we owe not only the facts here related by M. Monnin concerning the *Providence*, but, as we have already seen, many
of the details of the holy curé's ministry before the period
of M. Monnin's personal knowledge of him. She thus
describes the opening of the *Providence:*

"All the provisions which the two foundresses found on

their entrance into the house were a pot of butter and some
dry cheeses, sent by a charitable young lady. They brought
with them from home their beds, their linen, and a few
other articles of absolute necessity. On the day of their
entrance *there was no bread.* After they had cleaned the
house, they thought of returning home *till they should have
something to eat.* But they said one to the other, ' Let us
stay; perhaps Providence will send us something for dinner.' Providence did not fail them. The mother of one
of them thought of her daughter, and sent her her dinner,
which she shared with her companion, who a little while
afterwards received her own. They had all they wanted,
and the next day made some bread." A few days afterwards they were joined by a good widow from a neighboring village, and then by a young woman named Jeanne
Marie Chaney, who was strong enough to act as an *arm* to
heart and *head.* She did the hard work, made the bread,
washed the clothes, and worked in the garden. "M. le
Curé," continues Catherine, "began by opening a free
school for the little girls of the parish; he soon afterwards admitted some children from the neighboring parishes, who were also taught gratuitously, but who paid for
their own board. He received as many as we had room
for; but our space was then very narrow. M. le Curé provided for everything, and supplied all our daily needs.
Not long afterwards a person from Lyons came to reside at
Ars, who, without wishing to fix herself at the *Providence,*
took pleasure in the society of the directresses. She had
property, and took upon herself the expense of the house-
keeping, which was a great relief to M. Vianney. She
also helped him to purchase land for the support of the
house."

The good curé was now able to receive a few poor children. He began with two or three orphans, and in a very short time that little handful swelled to sixty, lodged, fed, and clothed at the expense of the *Providence*, preserved from vagrancy and its consequences, and sheltered from the dangers and scandals of their former way of life, in an atmosphere impregnated with the sweet odor of Jesus Christ. In order to receive this number, it was necessary to build; and now "M. le Curé became architect, mason, and carpenter. He spared himself no labor, but made the mortar, cut and carried the stones with his own hands; interrupting his beloved work only to go to his confessional." Thus was founded the *Providence* of Ars, in faith and prayer and poverty, as have been all houses which the Lord hath built. When shall we learn thus to cast ourselves and our works upon him? So only can we inherit the promises which belong to the poor in spirit, and enter upon the enjoyment of that *kingdom*, that free and royal spirit of joy and confidence in God, which it is our Father's good pleasure even in this life to give unto the poor. All our miserable anxiety about the means for carrying on His work comes of our having still some lurking dependence upon our natural powers and gifts and possessions,—the boats and nets which we have left to follow Christ. It comes of our still creeping timidly along the shore, instead of casting ourselves boldly upon the wide ocean of His providence, whose almighty hand is ever stretched out for our support, and whose unchanging voice still breathes in our ear, " Why are you fearful, O ye of little faith ?"

"Now it was," says M. Monnin, "that M. Vianney began to enjoy that ample credit on the secret funds of Divine Providence which eventually enabled him to realize whatever he desired. He found bankers wherever Providence has agents; and the agents of Providence are everywhere."

"When he had a little money," says Catherine, "he went at once and bought corn, wine, and wood; all the rest came of itself."

Sometimes, however, our Lord permitted these His faithful servants to fall into straits and difficulties, from which they could be delivered only by His own gracious and immediate intervention. The following facts are attested by eye-witnesses who are still living.

One day the stock of flour at the *Providence* was exhausted; there was no baker in the village, and eighty mouths to feed. What was to be done? The superioress, Benoîte Lardet, was' at her wit's end. One of the mistresses proposed to Jeanne Marie Chaney, who made the bread, to bake the handful of flour which was left, while they waited for more.

"I have been thinking of it," said she; "but we must wait to hear what M. le Curé says."

Accordingly she went to tell him their trouble.

"M. le Curé, the miller has not sent us back our flour, and we have not enough left to make two loaves."

"Put your leaven," said he, "into the little flour you have, and to-morrow go on with your baking as usual."

Jeanne Marie did exactly as she was told to do. We learn the result from her own words.

"The next day, I know not how it happened, but as I kneaded, the dough seemed to rise and rise under my fingers; I could not put in the water quick enough; the more I put in, the more it swelled and thickened, so that I was able to make, with a handful of flour, ten large loaves of from twenty to twenty-two pounds each; as much, in fact, as could have been made with a whole sack of flour."

This fact, with all its details, was related to M. Monnin by Jeanne Marie Chaney, who made the bread, by Catherine Lassagne and Jeanne and Marie Filliat, who witnessed the miracle.

"Oh, how pleased we were," added they, "to eat this bread!"

Another day the orphans wanted bread; there was neither corn, flour, nor money in the house. For once the good curé's heart failed him. He thought God had forsaken him on account of his sins. He sent for the superioress, and said to her with a very full heart:

"We shall have to send away our poor children, then, since we can no longer find bread for them."

He went first, however, with a vague feeling between hope and fear, to look once more into the granary. He slowly ascended the stairs, followed by Jeanne Marie Chaney, and opened the door with a trembling hand. The granary was full, as if corn had been thrown into it by sacksful. M. Vianney hastened down to tell this great wonder to his children.

"I distrusted Providence, my poor little ones," said he. "Our good God has well punished me."

This was the interpretation which his humility always put upon any especial mark of Divine protection; he regarded it as a loving chastisement for his want of trust in God. The mayor of Ars, Antoine Mandy, who has often told the tale to his children, and a number of the principal inhabitants, hastened, at the rumor of the miracle, to see the wonderful corn; and the miller, as he filled his sacks with it, declared that he had never handled such fine wheat.

The Curé of Ars always attributed this miracle to St. John Francis Regis, whom he had constituted guardian of his *Providence*, and whose relics he had placed in the midst of his provision of corn.

Some years afterwards, Mgr. Devie, then Bishop of Belley, wished to extract for himself a direct testimony as to this extraordinary fact. On the pretext of inspecting the orphanage, he asked to see the granary; and suddenly turning to M. Vianney, who was not on his guard, he said, in a simple, indifferent tone, raising his hand to a certain height, "The corn came up so high, did it not?"

"No, Monseigneur," replied M. Vianney, raising his hand higher; "it was as high as this."

M. Monnin has often heard him say: "One day, when I had nothing left to feed my poor orphans, it came into my head to hide the relics of St. John Francis Regis in the little corn we had left. The next morning we were very rich."

The following circumstance was related to M. Monnin by Jeanne and Marie Filliat, the witnesses and instruments of the fact related. Marie, having gone down into the cellar, discovered that the wine was running out of the cask. She ran to the *Providence*, and said to M. Vianney, "I think the wine is all running out."

"There is nothing to make yourself uneasy about," replied he very quietly; "He who has permitted the wine to run out can easily bring it back again."

Marie Filliat returned to the cellar with her sister, and found that the wine had indeed been running at such a rate that there was none left in the cask. She took up, as quickly as possible, the little she could recover; and, as soon as she had ascertained that there was no farther escape, poured what she had saved back into the cask. By the side of this large barrel there stood another, capable of containing 100 bottles, which was only half full. The two sisters thought they would pour its contents into the large cask. When they had done this, one of them put her finger to the hole at the top, from which they had removed the peg. The other began to laugh, saying, "Do you want to find out whether it is full?"

Well might she laugh, since they had poured about sixty bottles of wine into a cask made to hold two hundred.

"Yes," replied she, "it *is* full; and so full that I can touch the wine with my finger. Try yourself."

She did so, and remained speechless with astonishment.

"This wine," added they, "like that of the marriage-feast at Cana, was most excellent, and far superior to what we were accustomed to drink at the *Providence*."

On another occasion Catherine relates that M. Vianney wished to divide a dish of vegetables among the children.

"He gave such large portions to each," said he, "that I felt sure it would not go round the table, and I ventured to say to him : 'M. le Curé, if you go on like that, you will not have enough for all; it is impossible.' He paid no heed to my warning, but went round the table, helping everybody plentifully, and yet left some in the dish. I could not believe my own eyes."

On another occasion M. Vianney was in sore perplexity for money to pay for a large quantity of corn which he had purchased for the orphanage from one of his parishioners, who had already granted him a considerable delay. He took his staff and his rosary as usual, and walked out into the fields, recommending his beloved children to our Lord and His blessed Mother. Just as he reached the boundary of his parish, a woman suddenly crossed his path.

"Are you M. le Curé of Ars?"

"Yes, my good woman."

"Here is some money which I have been desired to give you."

"Is it for Masses?"

"No, M. le Curé; only remember the giver in your prayers."

Notwithstanding his humility, M. Vianney was often constrained to say, with a grateful smile, on occasions of which this is only one among many: "We are certainly rather the spoilt children of our good God." Many a time did he find considerable sums of money in his drawer, which he was certain he had never placed there.

"When I think," said he, "of the care which my good Lord has taken of me, and recall to mind his goodness and mercy, my heart swells with joy and gratitude. I know not what to do. I see nothing around me but an abyss of love, into which I would desire to plunge and to lose myself. I have felt this especially on two occasions. When I was studying, I was overwhelmed in sadness" (probably from the difficulties he met with in his studies, and the fear of being compelled to give up his longing desire for the priesthood). "I knew not what to do. I can see the place now. I was passing by the house of la mère Bibot, when I heard these words, *as if some one whispered them in my ear:* 'Be at peace; thou shalt one day be a priest.'

"At another time, when I was suffering under great depression and anxiety of mind, the same voice said to me distinctly, 'What has ever yet been wanting to thee?' And, indeed, I have always had all I needed."

"I have observed," said he one day to the directresses of the *Providence,* "that those who have large incomes are continually complaining: they are always wanting something. But those who have nothing, want for nothing.

It is good to abandon oneself solely, unreservedly, and forever, to the guidance of Divine Providence. Our reserves dry up the current of His mercies, and our distrust stops the course of His blessings. I have often thought that if we were to depart from our state of poverty, we should not have wherewithal to live. Let us, then, abide peacefully in the arms of that good Providence which is so careful of all our wants. God loves us more than the best of fathers, better than the tenderest of mothers. We have but to submit and resign ourselves to His will with childlike hearts. These poor orphans are not really your children; you are not really their mothers; and see whether they distrust your care and tenderness. It is confidence which God looks for from us before all things. When we have intrusted our interests to Him alone, His justness and goodness are pledged to aid and succor us."

The plan of the *Providence* of Ars was in some respects peculiar. Persons were received of all ages, and of every variety of previous condition. The most destitute and abandoned were the most freely welcomed. Girls of fifteen, eighteen, or even twenty, who had been suffered to grow up in habits of vagrancy, and in total ignorance of their duties, were there received and reclaimed; and it was this class, says Catherine, which afforded some of the most blessed examples of conversion and perseverance. Others were received at six or seven years of age. None were ever sent away till they had made their first Communion. Generally speaking, no one finally left the *Providence* before the age of nineteen, though many of the younger girls went to service in the summer, and returned to spend the winter under its sheltering roof. No inmate of that happy home was suffered to leave it till a safe abode had been provided for her by her pastor's care. For such as had a vocation to religion, he chose the congregation in which he judged they might best serve the Lord, and provided them from his never-failing providential supplies with all that was necessary for their reception. For others he procured a marriage-portion, to enable them to enter some Christian household; while he placed others in decent servitude, under a careful mistress, who would be a mother to them.

It might have been expected that the mixing of girls and children of all ages, indiscriminately gathered together, would have been attended by many evil consequences; nor can we account for the success of the work of the *Providence* except by the sanctity of its founder. The same hand which had formed the mistresses gently moulded the pupils. There were, of course, subjects who either proved incorrigible or failed to persevere; but these instances were the few among many. "All the good which this house has effected will never be known," said M. Vianney, "till the Day of Judgment."

The type upon which he had founded the *Providence* was rather that of a very poor and very pious family than of an ordinary school or charitable institution, in the order of which, however excellent, there is always more or less that is artificial and out of harmony with the previous habits and probable future lot of its inmates. The Sœur Rosalie would have seen nothing there contrary to the strict principles of common sense, which made her regard the overnicety and comfort of the generality of orphanages as a worse preparation for a life of extreme poverty than even the most miserable and ill-regulated home. St. Francis of Assisi himself would not have thought his chosen bride too richly clad or softly lodged if he had been bidden to share the black bread of the *Providence.*

"The favorite virtue of the holy curé," says M. Monnin, "was visibly impressed on his work. It would have been impossible to surpass the mistresses and the pupils in detachment from worldly possessions, indifference as to human aid, liberty of spirit, and absolute dependence on Divine Providence. They looked for no protector, they desired no friend, but God. We know how powerfully we constrain His mercy to come to the aid of works undertaken simply for His love. Their confidence in Him was blind, boundless, infantine; it was the motive of all their works, and the supply of all their needs. One of the directresses was once asked, by a person who took great interest in the house, how many orphans they had under their care. She answered, with the utmost simplicity, *that they did not know.*

"You do not know?"

"No, indeed; God knows, and that is enough for us."

"But suppose one of your pensioners were to run away?"

"Oh, we know them too well, and our hearts are too full of them, not to find out the loss at once."

The instruction given to the children embraced none of the modern systems of learning; but it was solid as far as it went. They learned, according to the measure of the capacity of each, and her probable future need, to read, write, sew, and knit.

For their spiritual benefit, M. Vianney began that course of daily catechetical instruction which in after years was listened to with breathless attention by pilgrims of all classes and degrees from France, Germany, Belgium, and England. "He came every day at the midday Angelus, after the dinner of the community, when the single room had been swept which served for refectory, schoolroom, and workroom, and, leaning against the end of one of the tables, spoke to the poor orphans for an hour together of the chief truths of the faith, and the fear and love of Almighty God." The principal subjects of these instructions were the happiness of serving God, the beauty of holiness, the frightful deformity of even the slightest faults, the duty of shunning the occasions of sin, of resisting temptation, of frequenting the Sacraments, prayer, the nothingness of this world, the dignity of the soul, reverence and love for all men, and compassion for the poor.

He denounced with especial energy sins against holy purity.

"In order to understand the full horror of these sins, which the devils tempt us to commit, but which they do not commit themselves, we must know what it is to be a Christian,—a Christian, created to the image of God! a Christian, the child of God, the brother of God, the heir of God! a Christian, the object of the complacency of the Three Divine Persons! a Christian, whose body is the temple of the Holy Ghost: this is what is dishonored by sin. We were created to reign one day in Heaven; and if we are so miserable as to fall into this sin, we become the abode of devils. Our Lord has said that nothing impure shall enter into His kingdom. And how, indeed, shall a soul which has wallowed in this filth appear before the pure and holy God?

"There are some souls so utterly dead and corrupt, that they grovel in their pollution without perceiving it, and without having any power to free themselves from it. Everything leads them to evil; everything, even the most holy things, reminds them of evil: they have these abominations continually before their eyes, like an unclean animal which delights and wallows in filth. Such souls are abhorrent to the eyes of God and His holy angels.

"See, my children, our Lord was covered with thorns to

expiate our sins of pride; but for this accursed sin He was scourged and torn to pieces, for He tells us Himself that after His scourging they might have numbered all His bones. O my children, were there not a few pure souls here and there to make amends to the good God, and disarm His justice, you would see how we should be punished! For now this crime is so common in the world, it is enough to make one tremble.

"We may say, my children, that hell is vomiting its abominations upon earth, as a steam-vessel pours forth its smoke. The devil does all he can to pollute our soul, and yet our soul is our all; our body is but a mass of corruption: go to the churchyard, and see what it is we love when we love our body.

"As I have often told you, there is nothing so vile as an impure soul. Those who have lost their purity are like a piece of cloth steeped in oil; you may wash it and dry it, but the stain will always come out again upon it: and so it needs a miracle to cleanse the impure soul.

"There is nothing so beautiful as a pure soul. Did we but understand this, we should never lose our purity. The pure soul is disengaged from matter, from earthly things, and from itself. Therefore it is that the saints have always ill-treated their bodies; therefore did they refuse them all but what was strictly necessary; such for example as to rise five minutes later, to warm themselves, to eat anything they liked. See, what the body loses, the soul gains; and what the body gains, the soul loses.

"Purity comes from heaven; we must ask it of God. If we ask it, we shall obtain it. We must take great care lest we lose it. We must shut our heart against pride, sensuality, and all other passions, as we close our doors and windows against the entrance of robbers.

" What joy is it to a guardian angel to have the care of a pure soul! My children, when a soul is pure, all the court of heaven looks down upon it with joy.

" Pure souls shall form a circle round our Lord. The purer we have been on earth, the nearer shall we be to Him in heaven. When the heart is pure, it cannot help loving, because it has found the source of love, which is God Himself. ' *Blessed*,' says our Lord, ' *are the pure in heart; for they shall see God.*'

" My children, we do not understand the power which a pure soul has over the heart of God. It does not do the Will of God, but God does its will. Look at Moses, that most pure soul! When God would have punished the Jewish people, He said: ' *Pray not for them; for Mine anger must burst forth against this people.*' Yet Moses did pray, and God spared His people. He suffered Himself to be appeased. He could not resist the prayer of that pure soul. O my children! a soul which has never been stained by that accursed sin obtains all it will from God.

" To preserve purity, three things are necessary: the practice of the presence of God, prayer, and the Sacraments; and again, the reading of holy books—this nourishes the soul."

Of pride he would speak as one who well knew the human heart:

" Pride is that accursed sin which drew the angels out of Paradise, and cast them down into hell. This sin began with the world itself.

" See, my children, we sin by pride in many different ways. One person will show pride in his dress, in his language, in his manner, even in his way of walking. Some people walk in the street with an air which seems to say to all who look at them, 'See how tall I am; how stately I am; how gracefully I walk!' Others, when they have done anything well, are never tired of talking of it; and if they fail are miserable, and think that people will have a bad opinion of them. Others are ashamed to be seen with the poor, and always seek the society of the rich. If by chance they are admitted into some great house, they boast of it, and take pride in it. Others take pride in talking. If they are going to visit some rich person, they examine what they are going to say, they study fine language; and if they are at a loss for a word, they are mortified, and fear to be laughed at. But, my children, this is not the way with a humble person. Whether he is laughed at, or esteemed, or praised, or blamed, or honored, or despised, or attended to, or neglected, it is all one to him.

"My children, there are some again who give large alms, to gain credit by it. You must not do so. These people will gain no fruit by their good works. On the contrary, their alms will turn into sin.

"My children, a proud person always thinks that what he does is done well. He wishes to domineer over all who come in his way; he is always in the right; always thinks his own opinion worth more than other people's. This is not the way to go on. A humble, well-informed person, if his opinion is asked, gives it in all simplicity, and then leaves others to give theirs. Whether they are right or wrong, he says no more.

"St. Aloysius Gonzaga, when he was a student, if found fault with on any occasion, never tried to excuse himself. He said what he thought, and never troubled himself about what others might think; if he was wrong, he was wrong; if he was right, he would say to himself, 'I have often been wrong before.'

"My children, the saints were so dead to themselves, that they cared very little whether others were of their opinion or not. People in the world say, 'Oh, the saints were simple!' Yes, they were simple in the things of the world; but as to the things of God, they understood them well. They knew nothing about the things of the world,—true enough; because they thought them of so little importance that they paid no attention to them."

On Sin.

"See, my children, how sin degrades man. Of an angel, created to love God, it makes a demon who will curse Him throughout all eternity. Oh, if Adam, our first father, had never sinned, and if we did not sin daily, how happy should we be! We should be as happy as the saints in heaven. There would not be an unhappy person upon earth. Oh, how blessed would this be!

"It is sin, my children, which brings all calamities upon us, and every kind of scourge,—war, pestilence, famine, earthquakes, fire, hail, storms, tempests,—everything which brings suffering and distress upon us. See, my children, a person in a state of sin is always unhappy. He may do what he will, but he is weary and disgusted with everything; while he who is at peace with God is always content, always joyful. O blessed life! and blessed death!

"My children, we are afraid of death,—and no wonder. It is sin which makes us fear death; it is sin which makes death fearful and terrible; it is sin which affrights the sinner at the moment of that last dreadful passage. And, O my God, there is cause enough for fear. To think that he is accursed—accursed of God! The thought makes

one tremble.　Accursed of God! and why?　Why do men
run the risk of being accursed of God?　For a blasphemy,
an evil thought, a bottle of wine, a moment of pleasure.
For a moment's pleasure, to lose God, the soul, and heaven
forever!　We shall see our father, our mother, our sister,
our neighbor, who dwelt so near to us, ascend to heaven,
body and soul; while we shall descend. body and soul into
hell, there to burn forever and ever.　The devils will seize
hold of us.　All the devils whose counsels we have followed will come to torment us.

"My children, if you were to see a man preparing a
large pile, heaping fagots one upon another, and he were
to tell you, 'I am making ready a fire to burn myself, what
would you think of him?　And if you were to see this same
man approach the pile when lighted, and throw himself
into the flames, what would you think of him?　We do
the same when we commit sin.　It is not God who casts
us into hell; we throw ourselves into it by our sins.　The
lost will say, 'I have lost God, my soul, and heaven, by
my fault, by my fault, by my grievous fault.'　He will
spring upward from the furnace, only to fall back into it
again.　He will feel an eternal craving to rise, because he
was created for God, the greatest and most exalted of beings, the *Most High*,—as a bird in a room flies up to the ceil-
ing and falls back again.　The justice of God is the ceil-
ing which imprisons the damned.

"There is no need to prove the existence of hell.　Our
Lord speaks of it Himself in the history of the wicked
rich man, who cried, 'Lazarus, Lazarus!'　We know very
well that there is a hell; but we live as if there were none;
we sell our souls for a few pieces of money.　We put off
our conversion till the hour of death; but who can assure
us that we shall have time and strength at that fearful mo-

ment, which all the saints have dreaded, and at which the powers of hell, knowing that it is the decisive point on which eternity depends, gather themselves together for their last assault?

"There are many who have lost faith, and never see hell till they enter it. They receive the last Sacraments; but ask them whether they have committed such or such a sin. Oh, get an answer if you can!

"The elect are like the ears of corn which escape from the reaper's hand, and like the bunches of grapes left after the vintage; the damned are like the sheaves piled up in the granary, or the grapes pressed down in the wine-vats. They fall into hell fast as the snowflakes on a winter's day. A saint was asked, at the moment of death, at what he was looking so fixedly.

"Oh," replied he, 'how terrible are the judgments of God!'

"St. Hilarion said, 'Wherefore dost thou fear, O my soul? For eighty years hast thou served the Lord.'

"And we,—perhaps we have never served the good God as we ought for two days! There are some who offend God every moment of their lives; their heart swarms with sins, as an ant-hill with ants.

"No, truly, if sinners would but think of eternity,—of that terrible *forever*,—they would be converted at once. Cain has been in hell these six thousand years, and he is but at the entrance. Those who do some good, who have some virtue, spoil it all by self-love: these are good works lost. My children, we sprinkle pride, like salt, over all that we do. We like our good works to be known. If your virtues are seen, you rejoice; if your defects are perceived, you are sad. I observe this in a great many people: a single word of blame disturbs and disquiets them.

This was not the way with the saints; they were pained if
their virtues were known, and pleased that their imperfections should be seen. The devil writes down our sins, our
angel guardians all our merits. It is certain that all the
thoughts and actions of our life are written down; let us
labor that the angel guardian's book may be full, and the
devil's empty."

On our Last End.

"There are many Christians who actually do not know
why they came into the world.

"Wherefore, O my God, didst Thou place me in this
world?'

" 'That thou mightest be saved.'

" 'And wherefore wouldst Thou have me to be saved?'

" 'Because I love thee.'

"The good God created us and placed us in the world
because He loves us; He wishes to save us because He
loves us.. To be saved, we must know, love, and serve
God. This is now our business. Oh, what a blessed life!
How blessed it is, how great it is, to know, to love, to serve
God! We have nothing else to do in this world. Every-
thing else we do besides this is so much time lost. We
must act for God alone, and put our works into His hands.
When we wake, we must say, 'I desire to-day to act for
Thee alone, O my God; I will submit to whatsoever Thou
shalt send me, as coming from Thee; I offer myself to
Thee in sacrifice. But, my God, I can do nothing without
Thee. Do Thou help me!'

"Oh, when we come to die, how bitterly shall we regret
the time we have given to pleasure, to useless conversation,

to rest, instead of employing it in mortification, in prayer, in good works, in thinking of our misery, in weeping over our *poor sins!* It is then we find out that we have done nothing for heaven.

"O my children, how sad it is! Three-fourths of the Christian world labor only for the gratification of this miserable carcass, which will soon rot in the earth; while they think not of their poor soul, which is to be happy or miserable forever. They want common sense. It is enough to make one tremble.

"Men of the world say that salvation is too difficult a work. Yet there is nothing easier: to keep the commandments of God and of the Church, and to avoid the seven deadly sins,—this is all; or, if you like it better, to do good and avoid evil.

"Good Christians, who labor to save their souls and to work out their salvation, are always happy and contented; they have a foretaste of the happiness of heaven; they will be happy for all eternity; while bad Christians, who are losing their souls, are always miserable; they murmur, they are sad, they are *dull as stones*, and they will be so to all eternity. What a contrast is here!

"Here is a good rule for our conduct: to do nothing but what we can offer to God. Now, we cannot offer Him detraction, calumny, injustice, hatred, revenge, impurity, dances, plays, &c.; and yet the world is full of nothing else. St. Francis of Sales said of dances, that they were like mushrooms,—the best of them were good for nothing. Mothers say, 'Oh, I watch over my daughters;'—they watch over their toilette, but they cannot watch over their hearts. Those who have dancing in their houses incur a terrible responsibility before God; they are responsible for all the evil which is done, for the bad thoughts, the evil speaking, the jealousy, the hatred, the revenge, which are its consequence. Ah, if they did but understand this responsibility, they would have no dancing. Like the authors of bad books, bad pictures, and bad statues, they are responsible for all the evil which these things shall produce as long as they exist. Oh, it is enough to make one tremble!

"See, my children, we must consider that we have a soul to save, and an eternity awaiting us. The world and its riches and pleasures shall pass away, but heaven and hell shall never pass away. Let us take care, then. The saints did not all begin well, but they all ended well. We have begun ill, let us end well; and we shall one day go to dwell with them in heaven."

The Sacraments.

"My children, why are there no Sacraments in other religions? Because there is no salvation there. We have Sacraments at our disposal, because we belong to the religion of salvation.

"We are bound to give hearty thanks to God for it, for the Sacraments are the sources of salvation. It is not so in other religions. The Jansenists* have Sacraments, it is true; but they are of no use to them, because they imagine that the perfect only can receive them.

"The Church has no desire but for our salvation; therefore she lays it upon us as a precept to receive the Sacraments, because she desires that we should always be in a state to appear before God.

"My children, how sad a thing it is for a soul to be in a

---

* A remnant of these heretics exists at Fareins, a parish near Ars, under the name of Farinists.

state of sin! It may die in that state; and all that it has
done is then without merit in the sight of God. Therefore
it is that the devil rejoices when a soul is in a state of sin,
and perseveres in it, because he thinks that it is laboring
for him, and that he shall have it at the hour of death.
When we are in sin, our soul is all corrupt and vile; it is a
spectacle of horror and disgust. The thought that the
good God beholds it ought to bring it back to itself. And
then, what pleasure is there in sin? There can be none.
We have fearful dreams that the devil is seizing us, that
we are falling down a precipice. Reconcile yourself with
the good God, have recourse to the Sacrament of Penance;
you will sleep as tranquilly as an angel. You will be glad
to wake in the night to pray to God; your mouth will be
full of thanksgivings; you will rise with great facility to
heaven, as an eagle cleaves the air. After this, your soul
aspires to something higher still, which is the Blessed Eucharist. My children, there is nothing so great as the Holy
Eucharist. Weigh all the good works in the world against
one good Communion, they would be but like a grain of
sand in comparison with a mountain. Say a prayer when
you have the good God in your heart; God can refuse you
nothing when you offer Him His Son and the merits of His
holy Death and Passion.

"My children, you remember the story which I have
told you before of a holy priest who was praying for his
friend. It would seem that he had a revelation that his
soul was in purgatory; and it came into his mind that he
could do nothing better than offer the Holy Sacrifice for its
repose. At the moment of consecration he took the Sacred
Host in his hand, and said: ' Holy and Eternal Father, let
us make an exchange. Thou holdest the soul of my friend

which is in purgatory, and I hold the Body of Thy Son which is here in my hand: well! do Thou deliver my friend, and I will give Thee Thy Son with all the merits of His Death and Passion.' At the moment of the Elevation, he beheld the soul of his friend, all radiant with glory, ascend to heaven. Well, my children, when we want to obtain anything of the good God, let us do the same after Holy Communion; let us offer Him His well-beloved Son, with all the merits of His Death and Passion; He will be able to refuse us nothing.

" My children, if we did but understand the value of Holy Communion, we should avoid the slightest fault in order to be permitted to receive it more frequently. We should keep our souls pure in the sight of God. Listen, my children; I suppose that you have been to confession to-day; you will watch over yourselves; you will be happy in the thought that to-morrow you will have the joy of receiving the good God into your heart. To-morrow, again, you will still be unable to offend Him; for your soul will be all embalmed with the precious.Blood of our Lord. O blessed life! blessed life!

" O my children, how glorious throughout all eternity shall be the soul which has frequently and worthily received the good God. The Body of our Lord will shine through our body, His adorable Blood through our blood; our soul will be united to the Soul of our divine Lord throughout all eternity. There will it enjoy peace and perfect happiness. My children, when the soul of a Christian which has received our Lord enters into paradise, *it increases the joy of heaven.* The angels and the Queen of angels come to meet it, because they recognize the presence of the Son of God in that soul. Then is that soul overpaid for all the pains and sacrifices it has endured on earth. My children, we may know when a soul has received the Sacrament of the Eucharist worthily. It is so drowned in love, so penetrated and transformed, that it is no longer to be recognized as the same in word or deed. It is humble, gentle, mortified, charitable, and modest. It is at peace with all the world. It is capable of the most sublime sacrifices. In short, it is no longer the same.

"All our good works put together can never equal the Sacrifice of the Mass, because they are the works of men, and the holy Sacrifice of the Mass is the work of God. Martyrdom is nothing in comparison with it; for martyrdom is the sacrifice which man makes to God of his life, while the Mass is the sacrifice which God offers for man of His Body and Blood. Oh, how sublime is the office of the priest! If he did but understand its greatness, he would die. God obeys him; he says two words, and our Lord descends from heaven at his voice, and encloses Himself in a little Host. God looks upon the altar, and says, 'This is My beloved Son, in whom I am well pleased.' He can refuse nothing to the merits of that oblation. If we had faith, we should discern God hidden in the person of the priest, like a light behind a glass, like wine mingled with water. A priest, after the Consecration, felt a moment's doubt whether his words could have power to bring our Lord down upon the altar; at the same instant, the Host appeared all red, and the corporal tinged with blood. If we were told that at a certain time a man would be raised from the dead, we should run with all speed to see it. But is not the Consecration, which changes the bread and wine into the Body and Blood of God, a far greater miracle than the raising the dead to life? We should always devote a quarter of an hour at least to preparation for hearing Mass; we should annihilate ourselves before the good God, after the example of His profound annihilation in the Sacrament of the Eucharist, and make our examination of conscience; for to hear Mass worthily we must be in a state of grace.

"If we knew the value of the holy Sacrifice of the Mass, or rather, if we had faith, we should have more zeal to hear it. All the prayers of the Mass are a preparation for Communion; and the whole life of a Christian ought to be a preparation for this great action.

"We ought to labor to be in a state to receive our Lord daily. How deeply humbled ought we to feel to see others approach the holy table, while we remain motionless in our place! How happy is the guardian angel who guides a faithful soul to the holy table! In the primitive Church they communicated daily. When Christians grew lukewarm, *blessed bread* was substituted for the Body of the Lord: it is both a consolation and a humiliation; it is blessed bread indeed; but it is not the Body and Blood of our Lord.

"There are some who make spiritual communion daily with blessed bread. If we are deprived of Sacramental Communion, let us replace it as far as we may by the spiritual communion which we may make every moment of the day; for we may always have a burning desire to receive our good God. After the reception of the Sacraments, when we feel the love of God growing cold, let us instantly make a spiritual communion. When we cannot go to the church, let us turn towards the tabernacle; no wall can shut us out from the good God; let us say five *Paters* and five *Aves* to make a spiritual communion. We can only receive our good God once a day; a soul enkindled with Divine love makes up for this by the desire of receiving Him every moment of the day.

"O man, how great thou art, nourished by the Body and

Blood of God! Oh, what a sweet life is this life of union with God! It is heaven upon earth. No more troubles, no more crosses. When you have had the happiness to receive the good God, you feel for a few moments afterwards a certain joy and delicious consolation. It is thus always with pure souls; for this union is their strength and their bliss."

The Sweetness of the Real Presence.

"Our Lord is there, waiting for us to visit Him and ask Him for what we want. How good He is! He accommodates Himself to our weakness. In heaven, where we shall be triumphant and glorious, we shall see Him in all His glory: if He had manifested Himself to us in this glory now, we should not dare to approach Him; but He hides Himself, as in a prison; as if He said to us, 'You do not see Me; but that matters not: ask of Me what you will, and I will grant it.' It is there in the Sacrament of His love that He intercedes continually with His Father for sinners. To what insults does He expose Himself by thus remaining in the midst of us! He is there for our consolation; there we ought to visit Him frequently. How acceptable to Him is a quarter of an hour snatched from our occupations or our idle time, to be spent in praying to Him, in visiting Him, in making reparation to Him for all the indignities which He receives! When He sees pure souls come eagerly to Him, He smiles upon them. They come with that simplicity which is so pleasing to Him, to ask pardon for the insults heaped upon Him by sinful and ungrateful souls. What happiness do we feel in the presence of God, when we are alone at His feet before the sacred tabernacle! Come, my soul, redouble thy fervor; thou art alone to adore thy God; His eyes rest upon thee alone. That good Saviour is so full of love for us, that He seeks us everywhere.

"He is there as a Victim: see, it is a prayer most pleasing to God to ask the Blessed Virgin to offer the eternal Father His divine Son, all bleeding and mangled, for the salvation of sinners; it is the best prayer we can offer, since all prayers are made in the name and by the merits of Jesus Christ. Again, we should thank God for all the indulgences which purify us from sin. But we pay no heed to them. We trample upon indulgences as we trample upon the ears of wheat after the harvest.

"See, there are seven years and seven quarantines for hearing the Catechism; three hundred days for reciting the Litanies of the Blessed Virgin, the *Salve Regina*, and the *Angelus*. So does the good God shower down His graces upon us; we shall be sorry at the end of our life that we have not profited by them. When we are before the Blessed Sacrament, instead of looking around us, let us close our eyes and our mouth; let us open our heart, the good God will open His; we will go to Him, He will come to us— the one to ask, and the other to receive; it is as a breath passing from one to the other. What sweetness shall we find in forgetting ourselves to seek God! The saints lost sight of themselves to see God alone, to work for Him alone; they forgot all created objects, to find Him alone: it is thus that they attained heaven."

The Sacrament of Penance.

"My children, it makes one tremble to think how few receive the Sacraments with due dispositions. There are some who fan themselves while the priest is giving them absolution ; others are trying to remember whether they have left out any sin, and then ask : 'Have you given me absolution ?'' My children, remember this, that when the priest gives you absolution, you have but one thing to think of,—that the Blood of the good God is flowing over your soul, to purify it, and make it as bright as it was made by its baptism. A soul which has received absolution is like an infant newly baptized : heaven is open to it, as to that little angel.

" My children, when we find a little spot on our soul, we must do what a person does who has the care of a beautiful globe of crystal. As soon as a little dust settles upon it, she takes a sponge and makes it all clear and bright again. So, when you perceive the least spot upon your soul, reverently take holy water, do some good work to which the remission of venial sin is attached—an alms, a genuflection to the Blessed Sacrament, hearing Mass, and the like.

" My children, it is as with a person who has a slight illness—there is no need to send for the doctor; he will get well of himself. He has a headache—he has only to lie down and rest it. He is hungry—he has only to eat. But if it be a serious illness, or a dangerous wound, then we must call in the physician, and take the remedies he prescribes. So, when we have fallen into some great sin, we must have recourse to the physician, who is the priest, and the remedies, which are the Sacraments.

" My children, the goodness of God in instituting this

great Sacrament is past our comprehension. If we had had a favor to ask of our Lord, we should never have thought of asking this. But He foresaw our weakness and our inconstancy in good, and His love led Him to do for us what we should never have dared to ask.

"My children, many people make bad confessions almost unconsciously. They say, 'I don't know what ails me.' They are tormented in mind, and know not why. They are wanting in the agility which takes us straight to the good God; there is something heavy and burdensome upon them which wearies them. My children, these are the remaining sins—often only venial sins—for which they retain an affection. There are some even who tell all their sins, but do not repent of them, and thereupon they go to Holy Communion. Here is the Blood of our Lord profaned. They go to the holy table with a certain repugnance. They say, 'Yes; I have confessed all my sins. I know not what ails me.' And they communicate in this doubt.' Here is an unworthy Communion, made almost unconsciously.

"My children, there are some who profane the Sacraments in another way. They have concealed mortal sins for ten or twenty years. They are continually tormented; their sin is always present to their mind; they always intend to confess it, and always defer the confession. This is a very hell on earth. Then perhaps they ask to make a general confession, and tell their sins as if they had only just committed them; they will not confess that they have concealed them for ten or twenty years. Here is a bad confession. They ought to add also, that during all that time they had neglected their religious exercises, and no longer felt the same pleasure as formerly in the service of God.

"My children, we run the risk also of profaning the Sacraments when we seize the moment of a noise being made round the confessional to confess the sins of which we feel most ashamed. People quiet their consciences by saying, 'Well, I accused myself of them, so much the worse if the confessor did not hear me.' So much the worse for you who have acted so deceitfully. Others speak very quickly, or take advantage of a moment when the priest is not paying particular attention, to get over their worst sins. My children, we must pray hard for repentance. After confession, we must plant a thorn in our heart, and never lose sight of our sins. We must do as the archangel did to St. Francis; he pierced him with fierce darts, which never left him."

Of the Order to be observed in the Practice of Virtues.

" Prudence teaches us what is most pleasing to God, and most profitable for the salvation of our souls. We must always choose what is most perfect. If two good works present themselves, one in favor of a person whom we love, the other in favor of one from whom we have received an injury, we must give the preference to the latter. There is no merit in doing good when we are led to it by a merely natural impulse. A lady asked St. Athanasius to find a poor widow to live with her towards whom she might exercise charity. When she next saw the Bishop, she reproached him with having sent her a person so good and gentle that she was no help to her on the way to heaven. The saint next chose the most illtempered, discontented, and troublesome old woman he could find, who pleased her well. It is thus we should act; for there is no great merit in doing good to one who is loving and grateful to us in return.

" There are some persons who never think themselves

sufficiently well treated; they take everything that is done for them as their due. They make an ungracious return to their benefactors, and repay every kindness with ingratitude. Well, these are the objects we should choose for our kindness. We must use prudence in all our actions, seeking not to follow our own taste, but to do what is most pleasing to God. I suppose that you have some money which you intend to give for a Mass : you see a poor family in great misery, and in want of bread; you will do better to give your money to these poor people, because the holy Sacrifice will be offered all the same : the priest will not fail to say the holy Mass; while the poor creatures might perish with hunger. You wish to pray to the good God, to spend your day in the church; but you consider that it would be more useful to labor for some poor person whom you know to be in great want. This would be far more pleasing to God than to spend your day at the foot of the tabernacle."

On Temperance.

" The third cardinal virtue is temperance. It is to temper our imagination, not to let it gallop as fast as it will; to temper our eyes; to temper our mouth—there are some who must always have something sweet and nice in their mouth; to temper our ears—not to let them hear vain songs or unprofitable conversation; to temper the smell—there are some who perfume themselves so as to make all who come near them sick; to temper our hands—there are some who always want to wash themselves when the weather is hot, and who are always seeking things which are soft to the touch; lastly, to temper our whole body, that poor machine of ours—not to let it go loose, like a runaway horse

without bit or bridle, but to restrain and tame it. There
are some who are lost in their bed; they are content to lie
awake, that they may feel how comfortable they are. This
is not like the saints. I don't know how we are to get beside them. But mark this : if we are saved, we shall have
to stay an immense time in purgatory, while they flew
straight to heaven to see the good God. That great saint,
Charles Borromeo, had a grand cardinal's bed in his room
for every one to see; but by the side of it he had one made
of fagots, which nobody saw; and this was the one he used.
He never warmed himself; and it was remarked, by those
who came to see him, that he kept himself in a position in
which he could not feel the fire. Such were the saints.
They lived for heaven, and not for earth; they were altogether heavenly, and we are altogether earthly. Oh, how
I love those little mortifications which are seen by no one,
such as to rise a quarter of an hour earlier, or to rise a few
moments in the night for prayer! But some people think
of nothing but sleep.

"There was a hermit once who made a royal palace for
himself in a hollow tree; he lined it with thorns, and
hung three heavy stones over his head, so that whichever
way he moved he was sure to hurt himself, either against
the thorns or the stones : and we think of nothing but to
find good beds, in which we may sleep well at our ease.

"We may abstain from warming ourselves; if seated
uncomfortably, we may refrain from changing our position;
if walking in the garden, we may deny ourselves the
pleasure of eating some fruit which we like; or at table we
may abstain from some dish more savory than the rest;
we may refuse to look at something attractive or curious,
especially in the streets of a great city. There is a gentleman who sometimes comes here, who wears two pairs of

spectacles, to prevent him from seeing anything. But there are some heads which are always in motion, some eyes which are always in the air. When we are walking in the streets, let us fix our eyes on our Lord bearing His cross before us; on the Blessed Virgin, who is looking at us; on our guardian angel, who is at our side. How beautiful is this interior life! it unites us with the good God. And so, when the devil sees that a soul is striving to attain to it, he endeavors to turn it aside by suggesting a thousand chimeras to the imagination. A good Christian pays no heed to him, but advances farther and farther in perfection, like a fish which plunges deeper and deeper in the water.

"We want to get to heaven, but quite at our ease, without putting any kind of constraint upon ourselves. This was not the way with the saints. They sought to mortify themselves in every possible way; and in the midst of all these austerities they enjoyed infinite sweetness. How happy are those who love the good God! they do not lose a single opportunity of doing good. Misers employ every means to increase their treasure;—they do the same with regard to the riches of heaven—they are always amassing more and more. We shall be surprised, at the day of judgment, to see souls so rich."

On Hope.

"My children, we are going to speak of hope. This is what constitutes the happiness of man upon earth. There are some in this world who have too much hope, and others who have too little. Some say, 'I will commit this sin again; it will not cost me more to confess four sins than three.' This is as if a child were to say to his father, 'I am going to give you four blows; it will cost me no more than to give you one. I shall ask pardon for them all together.' This is the way we treat the good God. We say, 'I shall amuse myself this year; I shall go to dances and taverns; and next year I will be converted. When I want to return to the good God, He will receive me; He is not so hard as the priests make out.' No; the good God is not hard, but he is just. Do you think that He will accommodate Himself to all your fancies? Do you suppose that when you have despised Him all your life He will come and throw Himself on your neck? Oh, no, no! There is a measure of grace and a measure of sin, after which God withdraws Himself. What should you say of a father who should treat a good child and a naughty one exactly alike? You would say, 'That father is not just.' Well, neither would God be just if He were to make no difference between those who serve Him and those who offend Him.

"My children, there is so little faith now in the world, that men either hope too much or else despair. Some say, 'I have sinned too deeply; the good God cannot pardon me.' My children, this is a grievous blasphemy; it is to set bounds to the infinite mercy of God. You may have committed sin enough for the perdition of a whole parish; but if you confess and repent of it, and would not commit it again, the good God has forgiven it.

"There was once a priest who was preaching upon hope and the mercy of God. He encouraged others, but was himself in despair. After the sermon a young man pre-sented himself for confession. Having made the avowal of his faults, he said, 'Father, I have committed a great many sins; I am lost.' 'What do you say, my friend? We must never despair.' The young man rose: 'Father, you

tell me not to despair, and you yourself——.' It was a
flash of light. The priest, in amazement, drove from him
that thought of despair, became a religious, and, in the
end, a great saint. The good God had sent His angel, in
the form of this young man, to teach him that we must
never despair.

"My children, the good God is as prompt to forgive us,
when we ask Him, as a mother to snatch her child out of
the fire."

The Word of God.

"My children, the Word of God is no light thing. The
first words of our Lord to His Apostles were these: 'Go
and teach;' to show us that instruction is the first thing
necessary for us.

"My children, how have we learnt our religion? By
the instructions which we have heard. What gave us a
horror of sin? what has shown us the beauty of virtue?
what has inspired us with a desire of heaven? These instructions. What has taught fathers and mothers the duties they have to fulfil towards their children, and children
their duties to their parents? Once more, these instructions.

"My children, why are men so blind and so ignorant?
Because they pay no heed to the Word of God. There are
some who never say so much as one *Pater* and *Ave* to ask
for grace to hear it aright and to profit by it.

"I believe, my children, that a person who does not
attend as he ought to the Word of God, will not be saved;
he will not know what is necessary for salvation. But
there is always hope of a person who is well instructed.
He may stray into all kind of evil ways, but there is always

hope of his returning to God, though it were only at the hour of death; whereas an uninstructed person is like one in his agony who has lost consciousness. He knows neither the heinousness of sin, nor the beauty of virtue, nor the worth of his own soul; but grovels from sin to sin, like a reptile which crawls along in the mire.

"See, my children, in what estimation our Lord held the Word of God. To the woman who cried, 'Blessed is the womb that bare Thee, and the breasts which fed Thee,' He replied, 'Rather, blessed are they who hear the Word of God, and keep it.'

"You see, my children, that our Lord, who is Truth itself, makes no less account of His Word than of His Body. I don't know whether it is worse to have distractions during Mass than during instruction. I see no difference. By distractions during Mass we lose the merit of the Death and Passion of our Lord; and by distraction during the instruction we lose His Word, which is Himself. St. Augustine says it is as bad as to take the chalice after the Consecration, and spill it on the ground under our feet.

"My children, people would feel a scruple in missing Mass, because they know that they would thereby commit a grievous sin; but they feel no scruple in missing the Catechism. They think that there is no fear of offending God grievously on this point. At the day of judgment, when you are all around me, and the good God says to you, 'Give Me an account of all the instructions which you have heard, and of those which you might have heard,' you will think very differently. My children, people go out in the middle of the Catechism; they amuse themselves by laughing, they pay no attention, they think themselves too learned to come to Catechism. Do you think, my children, that all this will be passed over? Oh, no; believe me, the good God will settle it very differently.

"See, how sad it is! Fathers and mothers stay outside during the instruction: yet they are bound to instruct their children; and what are they to teach them? They are not instructed themselves. All this leads, by a short road, to hell. It is a grievous thing indeed.

"My children, I have observed that there is no time at which people are more inclined to go to sleep than during the instruction. You will say, 'I am sleepy.' If I were to take up a violin, everybody would be in motion, everybody would be on the alert. My children, we listen to a priest if we happen to like him; if not, we turn him into ridicule. We must not act thus *humanly*. It is not the *shell* we should look at. Whatever the priest may be, he is always the instrument which God makes use of for the distribution of His sacred Word. You pour your wine into a vessel, and whether it be of gold or copper matters not; if the wine be good, it is good all the same. My children, I often think that the greater number of Christians who perish, perish for lack of instruction; they do not understand their religion. Suppose, for example, a man who has to earn his bread by his daily labor. It comes into that man's head to do great penances, to pass the half of his night in prayer. If he is well instructed, he will say, 'No, I must not do that, because I shall not be able to do my duty to-morrow if I do. I shall be sleepy, and the least thing will make me impatient; I shall be tired all day long, and able to do nothing. I shall not do half as much work as if I had a night's rest: I must not do this.' Again, my children, a servant will have a wish to fast; but he has to spend his whole day in hewing wood or tilling the ground. What would you have him do? Well, if that servant is well instructed, he will think to himself, 'But if I do this, I shall not be able to give satisfaction to my master.' What is he to do then? He will eat his breakfast, and mortify himself in some other way. This is what we ought to do; we ought always to act in the way which will give the greatest glory to God.

"A person knows that another is in great distress, and takes from her parents wherewith to relieve him. Assuredly she would do far better to ask than to take. If her parents should refuse her, she will pray to God to inspire some rich person to give alms in her stead. A well-instructed person has always two guides who walk before her,—*Counsel and Obedience.*"

Decay of Faith.

"It is with faith as with grace. When a person has an inspiration to turn to God, and disregards it, the good God takes His grace, and bestows it upon another who will make better use of it. *This is the whole secret.* It is as with a father who wishes to give something to one of his children. If that child refuses it, and despises his father's gift, his father will say to him: 'Oh, you don't want it? Very well. I will give it to your brother.' And so with us. The good God bids us forsake sin, and give ourselves to Him. We will not do it, and the good God bestows His grace elsewhere.

"My children, when the faith existed in countries which are now idolatrous, we in these lands were pagans. Those countries gradually lost the faith; it then came to us. Now we despise it, and it will return whence it came. I was speaking some time ago to a missionary, who assured me

that in the islands where he was stationed almost all the
inhabitants were Catholics. He told me that they had
built thirty churches in a year. My children, there is so
little faith among us now, that a priest told me, a little
while ago, that when he went to visit a sick parishioner to
speak to him about confession, the sick man said to him,
' M. le Curé, let us speak of war.' Then he called a servant, and said to him, ' Go and draw a bottle of wine; I
want to drink with M. le Curé.' As he was going to drink,
he said, ' You have got two glasses; you have taken mine.'
Alas, poor man, his sight began to fail him; but he would
never consent to make his confession. Before he died, he
insisted upon being carried to his granary; and he said, as
if speaking to Death, ' Oh, no, not yet; not this year. I
have too much to do. Next year, if you will.' Then he
was carried into his cellar, saw all his provision of wine, and
said again, ' Not this year.' But he was obliged to depart
all the same.

"I have heard of another who could never be persuaded
to take holy water; of another who would never make the
sign of the cross. O my children, this shows what a state
we are come to, and that it is a sad thing when the faith
has left our hearts. My children, another priest, who was
administering the last Sacraments to a sick person, said to
him, ' My friend, make an act of contrition.' ' Father, I
don't know what it is.' ' It is asking pardon of the good
God for all our sins.' ' Oh, I know nothing about it;' and
so he died. O my children, how sad this is! Let us pray
to the good God not to suffer us to lose faith.

"There are some who are always repeating, ' The priests
say what they choose.' No, my children, the priests do
not say what they choose; they say what is in the Gospel.
The priests who came before us said what we say; those

who come after us will say the same. If we were to say
what is not true, the Bishops would soon forbid us to
preach; we say nothing but what our Lord taught before us.

"My children, I am going to give you an example of
what comes of not attending to what the priests say. Two
soldiers were passing through a place in which a mission
was being given. One of them proposed to his comrade
to go to the sermon. They went; the missionary was
preaching on hell. 'Do you believe all that this curé
says?' asked the best of the two. 'Oh, no,' replied the
other; 'I believe these are only fooleries told to frighten
people.' 'Well, for my part,' said the other, 'I do believe it; and, as a proof of my belief, I intend to leave the
army and enter some religious house.' 'Go where you
will; I shall continue my journey.' He fell ill on the way,
and died. The other heard of his death in the monastery,
and prayed to God to reveal to him the state of his companion's soul. One day as he was praying, his comrade
appeared to him. He recognized him, and asked, 'Where
are you?' 'In hell; I am damned.' 'Unhappy soul! do
you now believe what the missionary said?' 'Yes, I
believe it. The missionaries are wrong only in one thing;
they do not tell of a hundredth part of the torments which
are suffered there.'"

On the Eve of Ash Wednesday.

"My children, the Church tells us a thing to-morrow
which is well fitted to humble us. Lay carefully to heart
these words: 'Remember, man, that thou art dust.' I
shall say this to myself, and I shall say it to you also.

"Look at that man who struggles, who makes a commotion, who wishes to domineer over every one; who thinks himself to be some great one; who seems to say to the sun, 'Depart hence; let me enlighten the world in thy place.' Some day that proud man will be reduced, at the most, to a handful of dust, which will be carried on from river to river until it is lost in the sea.

"See, my children, I often think that we are like those little clouds of dust which the wind collects upon the road, which turn round and round for a moment, and then disappear.

"See, we have brothers and sisters who are dead. Well, they are now reduced to that little handful of ashes of which I have been speaking to you."

The labors of the holy curé for these poor wandering lambs, now folded by his care, were fully repaid by the fervent and tender piety which prevailed among them. Their eyes would sparkle with joy when their good father came, in some rare moment of leisure, *to talk to them about the good God.* Sundays and Thursdays were days consecrated to adoration of the Blessed Sacrament, in reparation for the injuries and insults offered to our Lord in that mystery of His love.

When the elder girls, who were the most fervent, heard of any scandal or profanation of the holy name of God, they would ask permission to spend the night in prayer, and relieve each other, hour by hour, that the nocturnal adoration might not be interrupted. Besides this, they practised mortification of the senses, like good religious in the best-regulated convent.

"We were happy in that house," adds Catherine, "because all was done to edification."

The deathbeds of some of these poor girls were very

blessed. One, who when in health had greatly dreaded death, said to her mistress on the evening before she died : "I suffer indeed in my body, but I am so joyful in heart. I did not think it would be so sweet to die." She asked her companions to sing a hymn, and sang it with them till her last breath.

Benoîte Lardet had lived like a saint, and like a saint she died. A few days before she breathed her last, she saw her sister weeping at her bedside. "Why do you weep?" said she; "would you keep me in this world? *I cannot yet used to it.*" When told that her illness was mortal, she exclaimed: "Oh, what joy! I am going to see my God!" Not many days afterwards, He whom she had served so faithfully in His poor and ignorant members called her to Himself.

CHAPTER VII.

How the Curé of Ars became a saint—The sufferings he inflicted on himself.

It is from the period of the foundation of the *Providence* that M. Monnin dates the commencement of the *heroic life* of the Curé of Ars. "Those," says he, "who did not approach him till the later years of his life, when the habit of sanctity had become a second nature to him; when the practice of the most heroic virtues had become so familiar as no longer to cost him an effort; when, united with, and transformed into, Him, who is the Way, the Truth, and the Life, he had become one with Him, loving what He loves, hating what He hates, never changing tone or look, whatever might befall him; following every movement of that Divine Master, with Whose Heart and will his own were inseparably united; those who knew him in those days admired a work finished and perfected. But they would have much mistaken had they imagined that the Curé of Ars had become a saint without the toil and effort by which alone saints are made.

"'Who are these,' says one of the ancients in the Apocalypse, 'who are around the Throne before the face of the Lamb, clothed in white robes, and having palms in their hands? Who are they, and whence come they?' And he is answered, 'These are they who are come out of great tribulation.' This is the law of sanctity; and it was not given to our saint to escape it, or to unite himself by any other means to Him who is the Saint of saints.

"Through how many tribulations, conflicts, and trials did he pass before he reached the lofty summit on which we have seen him so tranquilly reposing! So true are the words of St. Catherine, that never from the beginning to the end of the world has our Lord willed, or shall He will, that anything great should be accomplished but through much suffering.

"Sanctity is the fruit of sacrifice. It is a death, and a new birth; the death of the old man, the birth of the new. There is no death without its suffering, no childbirth without its pangs."

Of the sufferings of our holy curé, some were inflicted by himself, some by the devil, some by good and some by evil men; some, and those the most intense of all, by the hand of God Himself. And first of those which were self-imposed. There are few, even among the saints, whose lives bear the marks of a more systematic and unflinching

crucifixion of the whole man, a more uniform practice both
of exterior and interior mortification, than we find in the
portrait traced of him by those familiar with the details of
his daily life.

Claudine Renard, the pious widow who had the charge
of washing his linen, and rendering him such other little
services as he could not refuse to receive at her hands,
could rarely obtain admittance into the presbytery. On
the few occasions when she contrived to effect an entrance,
after doing her best to put the poor furniture in order, she
sometimes proceeded to make the good curé's bed. She
thus discovered that, one by one, he had cast aside all the
bedding he had brought with him from Ecully, till nothing
remained but the straw palliasse; and that finding even
this too luxurious, he had put a board on the top of it.

"And besides," said Catherine, when relating these
particulars, "there is hardly any straw left now in that
poor bed. He takes it out by degrees, till at last there
will be nothing left but the wood. Then he will be satisfied. We have tried sometimes secretly to put in a few
handfuls, but it only made him take out more; for if he
felt his bed a little less hard, he would pull out the straw,
and throw it into the fire. We discovered this by finding
the ashes in the fireplace."

It was accidentally found out afterwards, that, to satisfy
his increasing thirst for suffering, M. Vianney was in the
habit of discarding his bed altogether, and sleeping on the
bare floor of the granary with a stone for his pillow.

His favorite food consisted of some pieces of the coarsest
black bread bought out of the basket of some poor man.
The Abbé Renard, in a memoir drawn up by him of the
early days of the holy curé's ministry, tell us that he had
often witnessed the joy with which he ate this most dis-

tasteful food. If he perceived the disgust which his companion felt at the sight of it, he would laugh and invite him to share his dinner, saying, " It is a blessing, dear friend, to be permitted to eat the bread of the poor; they are the friends of Jesus Christ. I feel as if I were sitting at His table."

When these delicacies were not to be procured, his ordinary meal consisted of potatoes, which he boiled himself once a week. Sometimes, when his own stock of potatoes had come to an end, he has been seen, with his basket in his hand, begging his week's provision from door to door. He took our Lord at His word, and left the whole care of his life, and all that belonged to it, to the pledged care of His Providence. He never withheld an alms because it would leave him without provision for the morrow, or even for the day.

A neighbor one day brought him a loaf of fine flour, which she had made on purpose for him. She went back to fetch some milk; and believing that he had been long fasting, she wished him to eat the bread and milk in her presence. No persuasions could induce him to consent. At last an idea struck her, which would account for his pertinacious refusal.

" I see, M. le Curé," said she, " you have no bread left." True, indeed; a beggar had passed while she was gone, and the whole loaf of bread had been deposited in his wallet. M. Vianney seemed determined, in those days, to try how long human nature could be supported without food. He sometimes reduced himself to such a state of weakness, as to be obliged to lean against the forms or walls of the church for support. When, after long days of fasting, he could hold out no longer, he would take a handful of flour, and, moistening it with a little water, make a few *matefaims*,* which served him for his single meal.

Catherine tells us that she had often heard him say: "Oh! how happy I was in those days! I had not the whole world on my hands; I was all alone. When I wanted my dinner, I did not lose much time over it. Three *matefaims* did the business. I ate the first while I was baking the second; and while I was eating the second, I baked the third. As I finished my dinner, I arranged my fire and my stove, drank a little water, and that was enough for two or three days."

It has, in fact, been ascertained that the Curé of Ars often passed several days together without taking any nourishment whatever, when he desired to obtain some special grace for himself or his parishioners, to make reparation for some scandal which had wrung his heart, or to do penance for some grievous sinner, whom he judged too weak in courage, or in contrition, to perform it for himself. When asked how a confessor was to act in order to exact due reparation for sin, and at the same time show necessary consideration for the weakness of sinners, he said, " I will tell you my recipe. I give them a light penance, and do the rest in their place."

He had great confidence in the efficacy of fasting as a means of appeasing Divine justice, and a weapon against the evil one.

" The devil," said he, " laughs at disciplines and other instruments of penance; or, at least, if he does not laugh at them, he cares little for them; but what puts him effectually to flight is the privation of food and sleep. There is nothing which the devil dreads so much, and nothing

<hr>

* A thin cake so called in the Dombes.

which is more pleasing to God. I experienced this during the five or six years when I was alone, and could follow my *attrait* without being remarked. Oh, what graces did the Lord vouchsafe to me at that time! I obtained everything. I wanted from Him."

His assistant priest once said to him : "M. le Curé, it is said that at one time you could easily pass a whole week without eating."

"Oh, no, my friend," replied he; "that is an exaggeration. The utmost I ever did was to go through a week upon three meals."

He has acknowledged on other occasions having abstained from all nourishment for whole days together, and sometimes for forty-eight hours. The habitual rigid abstinence which he practised appears from a remark which escaped him one day, when a batch of baking at the *Providence* had been very successful: "Well, for once I must be greedy, and eat as much as I want." It is positively affirmed by Catherine that he has passed a whole Lent without consuming two pounds of bread. He even tried to live without bread altogether. Claudine Renard caught him one day eating a handful of grass.

"What, M. le Curé," said she in amazement, "are you eating grass?"

"Yes, my good mother Renard," answered he with a smile; "it is an experiment which I am trying; but it does not answer."

"It is very plain," said he, long afterwards, in a moment of affectionate familiarity, to his assistant priest, "that we are differently formed from the beasts. I once tried to live like them, upon grass; but I lost all my strength. It seems that bread is necessary to man."

Bishop Devie once asked him : "Did you ever try to live

upon roots and grass, like your predecessors, the fathers of the desert?"

"Monseigneur," replied he, "I did try it once for a week; but I could not go on. I am not a saint like them."

"One day," says Catherine, "I tried to persuade M. le Curé to take a little more nourishment. I said, 'You will never hold out, if you go on living in this way.' 'Oh, yes,' replied he gaily. 'What says our Lord? *I have another food to eat; which is, to do the will of My Father, who hath sent Me.*' Then he added, 'I have a good *carcass*. I am tough. As soon as I have eaten something, no matter what, or slept a couple of hours, I can begin again. When you have given something to a good horse, he sets off upon the trot again, as if nothing ailed him; and a horse hardly ever lies down.'"

The best horse, however, may be overridden, and M. Vianney was sometimes forced to acknowledge that he could do no more.

"There are days when I can really hardly speak; especially about seven in the morning, and seven in the evening; but I always find strength to speak of the good God."

At evening prayers his voice was sometimes scarcely audible. · He was asked once, why he spoke so loud when he preached, and so low when he prayed.

"Because, when I am preaching," said he, "I have to deal with those who are deaf or sleeping; but when I pray, I have to deal with the good God, and He is not deaf."

In fact, he always went to the very limit of his powers.

"My good curé," said Mdlle. d'Ars, "do take a little more care of yourself, if you would not give me continual distractions. When I hear you recite the Rosary in that feeble, worn-out tone, I find myself saying, instead of 'Holy

Mary, Mother of God, pray for us,' 'My God, have pity on him, and give him grace to go on to the end.'"

Sometimes the good lady got fairly angry with him, and threatened to complain of him to the Archbishop; and, indeed, M. Courbon, the Vicar-General, who looked upon him as in some sort a child of his own, remonstrated with him, though without effect.

The only occasions on which M. Vianney relaxed, in any degree, the habitual austerity of his life, were when he was called upon to exercise hospitality to a brother priest. On these rare occasions, he would send to Mdlle. d'Ars; or, if there was not time to reach the castle, Mdlle. Pignaut, or Claudine Renard, would provide a dinner, simple indeed, but very different from his ordinary fare, which he would make a show of sharing with his guests, while, in the words of one who enjoyed his hospitality on one of these occasions, "he ceased not to discourse of heavenly things, like a man absorbed in God." It is an instance of what has been before observed, of the strength and tenderness of his home affections, that he showed the same consideration for any of his relatives who came to see him. When his nephew and niece from Dardilly paid him a visit, some little addition was always made. He sat down to dinner with them, whereas he always took his solitary meals standing; carved for them, and courteously did all the honors of the table, encouraging them to eat, and eating with them of whatever was before them. But as these good people said, "When we were at Ars, we felt neither hunger nor thirst; *it was always like the day of our first Communion.*"

Then M. Vianney would ask kindly after all his old friends at Dardilly, and dwell upon his childish reminiscences, asking particularly after the old apple-tree, under the shadows of which the reapers had been accustomed to dine and sleep.

We are told of a very characteristic banquet, to which the good curé invited Mdlle. Pignaut and the widow Renard, who, to satisfy a little womanly curiosity, often teased him to give them an entertainment in return for the many repasts they had provided for his guests. He could do no less, they said, than invite them in return.

"One evening, then," says Catherine, "when M. le Curé had laid in a fresh stock of his favorite black bread, he went to visit his neighbor.

"'Claudine,' said he, in a livelier tone than usual, 'you are to come to my house at once, with your daughter and Mdlle. Pignaut. I want you all three.'

"Exceedingly pleased, and above all exceedingly curious to know what M. le Curé wanted with them, the three women arrived at the presbytery.

"'What do I want with you?' said he, as soon as they came in; 'I want you to sup with me. Are you not pleased? Take chairs, and sit down. What a feast we are going to have! We will eat the bread of the·poor—the friends of Jesus Christ—and we will drink the good water of the good God. So much for the body. And then we will·read out of the lives of those holy Saints who were so penitent and so mortified. So much for the soul. And so now let us set to work.'"

The good curé had arranged his table, and spread his feast: in the middle was a basket filled with the bread of the poor; on the right, a large folio volume of the Lives of the Saints; on the left, a pitcher of water, with a wooden cup.

At the sight of this grand preparation, Claudine Renard,

who was in the secret, exchanged a look with M. le Curé, and smiled; the other two were a little disconcerted. Without seeming to notice their confusion, M. Vianney blessed the table, and offered a piece of bread to each.

"I dared not refuse," said Anne Renard, when she related the story. "I got to the end of my piece of bread, and so did my mother; but poor Mdlle. Pignaut, do what she would, could not manage to swallow hers. She was on thorns the whole time the visit lasted, having never been invited to such a feast before. She never tried to get another invitation."

M. Vianney would certainly have wanted the necessaries of life but for the watchful care of Divine Providence in commissioning one pious hand after another to supply his wants.

On the death of the good widow Renard, her place was filled by a pious woman, who went by the name of Sœur Lacon. She carried on a perpetual warfare with the holy curé to induce him to mitigate in some degree the inflexible austerity of his life. She would slip unawares into the presbytery, and leave withinside the provisions which M. Vianney had refused to receive from her. Great was her self-gratulation on such occasions, until, on the following morning, she would recognize her gift in the wallet of the first beggar who came to ask alms at her door.

Catherine's journal contains an amusing account of one of these skirmishes between Sœur Lacon and her incorrigible pastor:

"She had made a beautiful pie for M. le Curé, which, when baked to perfection, she took out of the oven, and hid in an old cupboard in the presbytery kitchen, thinking it would be sure to be safe in that deserted corner of the house. She impatiently awaited M. Vianney's return in

the evening; and as soon as she heard him come in, she
said to him, in the most insinuating tone in the world, 'M.
le Curé, will you have a little piece of pie?'

"'Certainly,' replied he, immediately; 'I should like it
very much.'

" Delighted with so unusual an acquiescence, she flew to
her hiding-place, when, alas, no pie was to be found! What
could have become of it? Had M. le Curé found it out,
and given it to some poor man? This was really too much.
She went up stairs in great indignation.

"'M. le Curé, this is too bad. My pie was my own; I
did not give it to you.'

"'Why did you put it in the presbytery, then?' replied
he, very quietly. 'I conclude that what I find in my house
is my own, and that I have a right to dispose of it.'"

Poor Mdlle. Lacon, as Catherine tells us, had taken a
great deal of trouble to give M. Vianney this surprise; and
was the more to be pitied, as she was upwards of seventy,
had one leg shorter than the other, and had great difficulty
in moving about, on account of her rheumatism.

" M. le Curé, however," adds she, "only did it to try
her; for he knew that she was a good soul, and that the
more sacrifices he led her to make, the more would she advance in the ways of God."

That she *was* a good soul, free from malice and guile,
appears from her proposing, a few days afterwards, to M.
Vianney to make him some *matefaims.* He consented with
a readiness which might have led her to suspect mischief.
But in the innocence of her heart she set to work to mix
her flour; and, being doubtful of her own skill, called
in Mdlle. Pignaut to counsel. M. Vianney watched all
these preparations with a malicious eye. When they were
finished, the dish was solemnly placed before him. He

joined his hands, and raised his eyes to heaven, as if about to say the *Benedicite;* and then, while all around were devoutly making the sign of the Cross, he took up the dish, ran down stairs with it, and distributed the contents to the poor.

M. Vianney was often to be met hurrying along with something concealed under his cassock. He would go about, knocking at one door after another, till he found some one to receive his alms, which it was his great object to bestow with the greatest possible secrecy, and unknown, if possible, even to the objects of his bounty. An old blind woman, who lived near the church, was on this account a special favorite. He would enter her cottage softly, and deposit his gift in her apron without speaking a word. She would feel with her hand what he had given her, and, supposing she owed it to the kindness of some of her poor neighbors, would answer, " Many thanks, good woman ; many thanks;" to the great delight of M. le Curé, who would go away laughing heartily.

M. Vianney, after some of his long fasts, often came home from the church so utterly exhausted, that he was unable to stand. On these occasions he would laugh merrily, and seem as much delighted with himself as a schoolboy who has succeeded in some mischievous frolic.

One day, as Catherine tells us, he felt so faint in the confessional, that he said to himself, " You had better come out while you can, or they will be obliged to carry you." So he dragged himself, as best he could, to the *Providence,* when he arrived panting for breath, and as pale as a corpse. He asked for a little eau de Cologne.

" Well, Monsieur," said Catherine, as she brought it to him, " you must be quite happy this time ; you have carried things far enough to-day." And indeed, said she, "under his pale and sunken features we could perceive the radiance of an exceeding interior joy." It was the joy of victory over a vanquished enemy; and that enemy whom he thus triumphed over and laughed to scorn was himself. He would take nothing but a little eau de Cologne; and as soon as he could stand, hastened into the next room to catechize the children.

"When the catechizing is over," says Catherine, "he finds his little earthen pipkin by the fire containing some milk just colored with chocolate. He generally takes his meal, if meal it can be called, standing by the chimney corner, and often drinks his milk without putting any bread into it at all; the whole is concluded in the course of five minutes. When he is in a hurry, he returns to the presbytery with his pipkin in his hand; so that any one who met him going through the streets would take him for a beggar who had just received an alms. He is never better pleased, nor in a merrier mood, than on these occasions."

It was thus that he contrived to add humiliation to mortification. An ecclesiastic, who had come to Ars on purpose to see him, met him thus eating his dinner as he went along. "Are you the Curé of Ars, of whom every one speaks?" said he, in great astonishment and disgust.

"Yes, my good friend; I am indeed the poor Curé of Ars."

"This is a little too much," said the priest; "I had expected to see something dignified and striking. This little curé has no presence or dignity, and eats in the street like a beggar. It is a mystery altogether."

The words were repeated to M. Vianney, who delighted to tell the story. "The poor good gentleman," said he, "was fairly caught; he came to Ars to see something, and found nothing."

A second interview, however, brought this contemptuous visitor under the power of the singular fascination which the *little curé* exercised over all who came within its sphere. He made a good retreat under his direction, and no longer wondered what men came out into the wilderness to see.

The dress of M. Vianney corresponded with his fare. Though a great lover of order and cleanliness, he never allowed himself more than one cassock at a time. It was washed and mended till it would no longer hold together, and not till then would he consent to replace it by a new one. It was the same with his hat, which was worn till it was perfectly shapeless; and with his shoes, which were never approached by brush or blacking. Thus arrayed, he would present himself at the ecclesiastical conferences or other meetings of the clergy, which he made a point of attending, meeting all the raillery of his brethren by the invariable reply, "It is quite good enough for the Curé of Ars. Who do you think would take scandal at it? When you have said, It is the Curé of Ars, you have said all there is to say."

"Thus was it," says M. Monnin, "that he became a Saint,—by sparing himself in nothing, little or great; by applying fire and steel to the most sensitive parts of his being. Such, at the period of his history at which we have arrived, was the Curé of Ars. Having overcome the slavery of self, he was free to follow every impulse of the Holy Ghost. He had removed all the hindrances, and broken all the bonds, which could attach his heart to anything below the Supreme Good. His will soared above this world, in union with the will of God. His views, his desires, his affections, were, so to speak, deified; his expanded heart included all creatures in its wide and fraternal embrace. He had but one wish,—that God's name should be hallowed : His kingdom come ; His will be done on earth, as it is in heaven." With him, as with St. Paul, to live was Christ; and it was manifest to all who saw him, that Christ lived in him.

CHAPTER VIII.

The sufferings inflicted on him by the devil.

To the ceaseless warfare which, as we have seen, this holy priest waged with his own body, was added a sensible persecution from the powers of evil, as rare in these days as the heroic sanctity which called it forth. M. Vianney thus described the first of these fearful visitations, which took place just after the foundation of the *Providence:*

"The first time the devil came to torment me was at about nine o'clock at night, just as I was going to bed. Three great blows sounded on the outer door, as if some one were trying to break it open with an enormous club. I immediately opened my window, and said, 'Who is there ?' but I saw nothing. So I went quietly to bed, recommending myself to God, the holy Virgin, and my good Angel. I had not fallen asleep, when I was startled by three more strokes louder than the first, not on the outer door, but on that which opens upon the staircase leading to . my room. I arose and called out a second time, 'Who is there ?' No one answered. When the noise began, I

thought it might proceed from robbers, who had been
attracted by the valuable gifts of M. d'Ars, and therefore
began to take precautions. I got two courageous men to
sleep in the house, in order to assist me in case of necessity.
They came for several successive nights, heard the noise,
but could discover nothing, and remained fully convinced
that it had another source than the malice of men. I was
soon convinced of this myself; for one winter's night, when
a quantity of snow had fallen, I heard three tremendous
blows in the middle of the night. I sprang hastily from
my bed, and ran down stairs into the court, thinking that
this time I should catch the evil-doers, and intending to call
for help. But to my great astonishment I saw nothing, I
heard nothing, and what is more, I saw not a trace of foot-
prints upon the snow. I had no longer a doubt that it was
the devil who wanted to terrify me. I resigned myself to
the will of God, beseeching Him to be my guardian and
defender, and to draw near to me with His holy angels
whenever my enemy should return to torment me." M.
Vianney acknowledged that at the beginning of these
nightly visitations, while their cause was still uncertain, he
felt as if he should die of terror in his bed, his teeth
chattered, his blood froze in his veins, and his whole body
became rigid as a corpse. He could not close his eyes, and
his health became visibly affected. Charitable neighbors
used to take it by turns to watch armed in the belfry, or in
some adjoining house commanding the entrance to the
presbytery, and to sleep in the room next to that of M.
Vianney. Sometimes they were terribly frightened. The
village blacksmith had established himself one night with
his gun in the room adjoining that of the curé, when, in
the middle of the night, he heard a noise as if in the same
room with him, as if all the furniture were flying in pieces

under a storm of blows. He cried for help, and M. le Curé instantly came to him. They searched in every corner, but nothing could be seen.

As soon as M. Vianney felt convinced that the noises were preternatural, he dismissed his useless guard, and in time grew accustomed to them.

This persecution went on with more or less of violence for a period of thirty years. It had been preceded by one so much more terrible as to make the exterior conflict light in comparison. The holy curé was for a long time haunted by a continual and piercing terror of hell. He seemed to see it always beneath his feet, and to hear a voice telling him that his place there was marked out for him.

The fear of being lost pursued him day and night, and in comparison with it all succeeding terrors seemed endurable. Yet what must have been the fortitude which, for thirty years together, could hold out under this nightly torture of the nerves, this continual sensible presence of the powers of evil, and return to the daily labor for souls with a brow as unruffled, and a voice as calm and soothing, as if none but ministering angels had been suffered to come near his bed!

M. Vianney was usually awakened at midnight by the three loud knocks which betokened the presence of his enemy. After making a horrible noise on the staircase, the demon would enter the room, seize the curtains, and seem to be tearing them to pieces, so that the curé was astonished in the morning to see them uninjured. Sometimes he pulled the chairs about, and disarranged all the furniture, as if he were hunting for something, calling at the same time in a tone of mockery, " Vianney, Vianney,

thou *eater of potatoes!** we shall have thee yet! we shall
have thee yet! We have thee! we have thee!" At other
times he would howl in the court below, or imitate a charge
of cavalry, or the tramp of an army on the march; or he
would seem to be hammering nails into the floor, cleaving
wood, planing boards, or sawing, like a carpenter busy at
work in the inside of the house; or he would drum upon
the table, the chimney-piece, the water-jug, or on whatever
would make the greatest noise. Sometimes it would seem
to M. Vianney as if a whole flock of sheep were driven over
his head. Once, when he felt more than usually worn out
by the continual din, M. Vianney said, "My God, I willingly make Thee the sacrifice of a few hours of sleep for
the conversion of sinners." The infernal flock instantly
departed; there was silence; and he slept in peace. At
one time, for several successive nights, he heard a clamor
of voices speaking in unknown tongues; "as if," said he,
"troops of demons had been holding their parliament in
the courtyard."

These occurrences were of course much talked of.
"They excited," says M. Monnin, "many rumors and
much contradiction. They had the disadvantage of taking
place in the night, which is the accomplice of error, and
lends a vague uncertainty to the things it covers, which
criticism and incredulity know how to turn to account;
while the profound solitude in which the Curé of Ars enveloped his life made examination difficult. Yet it was
not to be supposed that M. Vianney was either deceived or a
deceiver. Those who knew him, knew that he would have
preferred death to the least deviation from truth. Neither
had he the temperament of a visionary; he was not in the

---

* Mangeur de truffes.

smallest degree credulous; he had all the qualifications for a trustworthy witness—good eyes, good ears, good judgment. And these things took place, not once, but a hundred and a hundred times in a year, and that for a period of thirty years together. They were attested by himself a thousand times. There was no subject on which he was more willing to speak." In Catherine's notes, written at the very time of the beginning of this persecution, many of these occurrences are noted down, day by day, from the mouth of M. Vianney himself. For instance :

" M. le Curé has several times said to us, in the last few days, ' I don't know whether they are rats, or whether it is the *grappin;** but they come in great troops over my granary, and tramp up to my bed. You would take them for a flock of sheep. I can scarcely sleep at all. Sometimes I take a stick and knock upon the floor, to make them quiet; but they go on just the same.' "

" 2d July, 1823. M. le Curé said to us, ' I don't know whether rats sing, but there is one always singing in my room. He climbs singing upon my bed at night.' "

" Oct. M. le Curé begged us to enlarge his palliasse, because the devil throws him out of his bed. ' I did not see the devil,' added he ; ' but he has several times seized hold of me, and thrown me out of my bed.' "

" Oct. 18th. M. le Curé told us yesterday that the devil had tried to kill him."

The brethren of the Curé of Ars were by no means inclined to give credit to any supernatural agency in these occurrences, for which they were industrious and ingenious in discovering natural causes. " It is a mistake," says M.

---

* A nickname by which M. Vianney was accustomed to call his infernal enemy.

Monnin, "to represent the clergy as a credulous body of men. Credulity is in an inverse ratio to faith. Those who know not God are credulous from the sheer necessity of believing something, which is an instinct so strong, so imperious, in the heart of man, that he would rather believe too much, believe everything, than believe nothing. He would rather renounce all reason than give up all faith. But he who has submitted his reason to the Divine teaching of faith, feels no need of believing anything but what God has revealed, and the Church teaches.

"The brethren of M. Vianney sought, then, in the immoderate fasts and vigils of the holy man for natural and physiological causes of these diabolical manifestations; an explanation more summary and convenient than satisfactory. 'If the Curé of Ars,' said they, 'would live like other people, if he would take his proper amount of sleep and nourishment like them, this effervescence of the imagination would be quieted, his brain would no longer be peopled with spectres, and all this infernal phantasmagoria would vanish.'"

At the time when these prejudices were at their height, an occurrence took place which was related to M. Monnin by one of the eye-witnesses, who offers to attest the following relation by his signature: In the winter of 1826, M. Granger, the venerable Curé of St. Trivier-sur-Moignans, requested M. Vianney, for whom he had a very great esteem and veneration, to join the missionaries who were about to give the exercises of the great jubilee in his parish. M. Vianney consented to his neighbor's wish, and remained at St. Trivier for three weeks, preaching occasionally, and hearing many confessions.

The vexations which he endured from the demon formed the subject of frequent conversation among the clergy present, who amused themselves much at his expense. "Come, come, dear curé; do like other people, feed better; it is the only way to put an end to all this diablerie."

One evening his critics took a higher tone; the discussion waxed warm on their side, and the raillery grew more bitter and less restrained. It was agreed that all this infernal mysticism was nothing in the world but reverie, delusion, and hallucination; and the poor curé was openly treated as a visionary and a maniac. "Your presbytery," said they, "is nothing better than an old barn, without either order or arrangement. The rats are quite at home there; they play their pranks night and day, and you take them for devils!" The good curé said not a word in reply to these sage admonitions, but retired to his room, rejoicing in the humiliation.

A few moments afterwards, those who had been so witty at his expense wished each other good night, and retired also to their respective apartments, with the happy indifference of philosophers, who, if they believed in the devil at all, had very little faith in his intermeddling with the affairs of the Curé of Ars. But, behold! at midnight they are awakened by a most terrible commotion. The presbytery is turned upside down, the doors slam, the windows rattle, the walls shake, and fearful cracks seem to betoken that they are about to fall prostrate. Every one was out of bed in a moment. They remembered that the Curé of Ars had said, "You will not be astonished if you should happen to hear a noise to-night." They rushed to his room; he was resting quietly.

"Get up!" they cry; "the presbytery is falling!"

"Oh, I know very well what it is," replied he, smiling. "Go you to your beds; there is nothing to fear."

They were reassured, and the noise ceased. An hour afterwards, when all was quiet, a gentle ring was heard at the door. The Abbé Vianney rose, and found a man at the door, who had walked many miles in order to make his confession to him. He went at once to the church, and remained there hearing the confessions of a great number of penitents, until it was time for Mass. One of the missionaries, M. l'Abbé Chevalon, of pious memory, an old soldier of the Empire, was so struck by this strange adventure, that he said, when relating it, " I made a promise to our Lord never again to jest about these stories of apparitions and nightly disturbances; and as to the Curé of Ars, I take him to be a saint."

The coincidence of the occurrence of these noises with the arrival of the penitent for confession, is one instance out of many in which a more than usual manifestation of diabolical fury proved the presage of some more than common manifestation of the Divine mercy to sinners. M. Vianney would often rise, after a harassed and sleepless night, to find strangers waiting at the door, who had travelled all night to make their confession.

He learned at last to rejoice in the visits of the *grappin*, as tokens of an approaching harvest of souls. During a mission which he gave at Montmerle, and which proved remarkably successful, the devil dragged him in his bed round the room, as he himself told the Abbé Toccanier, at that time Vicaire of Montmerle, and afterwards his friend and coadjutor at Ars.

One of the demon's customary modes of annoying him was to cover a favorite picture of the Blessed Virgin, and an image of St. Philomena, with mud and filth. M. Renard has himself seen the former so disfigured that the features were no longer distinguishable.

Towards the end of his life, M. Vianney was left comparatively at rest from these disturbances, and for the last six months before his death they ceased altogether, as if the enemy had withdrawn his forces in despair. We will give only one more instance of his baffled malice, in the words of M. Monnin, who was an eye-witness of the scene he describes, which took place about three years before the death of the holy curé, and when he was acting as his coadjutor in the absence of M. Toccanier:

"It was one morning during the first celebration of the Quarant' Ore at Ars. The crowd was immense; the work of God in the souls of the worshippers was deeper and more striking than ever. As I was setting out early to go to the church, I was struck on the threshold by a smell of burning, so stifling and penetrating that I could hardly stand. I hastily crossed the market-place. Holy Mass, catechizing, and some few confessions kept me engaged till seven o'clock. When I had finished, I found the whole village gathered round the presbytery. I should have imagined that some misfortune had happened, had I not observed the general expression on the faces around me to be that of mirth. They were laughing, joking, and calling to each other from one end of the square to the other; and the words *lit* and *grappin* were all that I could distinguish amid the clamor. 'What's the matter?' said I, approaching one of the groups. 'What! don't you know that the devil set fire last night to M. le Curé's bed? Come and see, come and see!' And I saw in fact some men carrying the half-burnt remains across the court. I entered the house, and went straight to M. Vianney's room, where I found everything in disorder, and all the traces of a fire hardly yet extinguished. The bed, the curtains, and all around it,—a few pictures which owed their only value to the devotion of M. Vianney, and of which he had said a few days before that *his good saints* were the only things in the world to which he felt a little attachment, and that he would not consent to sell them, because he wished to leave them to the missionaries,—all had been consumed. The fire had stopped only at the casket which contained the relic of St. Philomena; and its progress was arrested there as if by a line drawn with geometrical precision, burning all which was on one side of the holy relic, and sparing all on the other. It went out as it had been kindled, without any apparent cause; and what is most remarkable, and even it may be said miraculous, it was not communicated by the heavy serge curtains to the flooring, which, being black with age and smoke, would naturally have taken fire like so much dry straw. Another remarkable circumstance was, that M. le Curé, who came in in the midst of all this disturbance and confusion, did not seem so much as to perceive it. He met several persons carrying the remains of his furniture, without asking them a single question. I found him in the sacristy; but when I addressed a few words to him on the event which had set the whole country in commotion, he shrugged his shoulders, and answered only by a gesture of indifference. It was not till after holy Mass, when he was writing on the pictures for distribution, that he suddenly interrupted his employment. I can see him now with his pen raised, his eyes, with their deep and sweet expression, fixed full on me. 'For a long time past,' said he, 'have I been asking this grace of the good God, and He has heard me at last. To-day I think I am really the poorest man in the parish. They all have their beds,—and now, thank God, I have none.' And without another word, he went on signing the pictures presented to him. 'Poor M. le Curé!' said I, in a tone which he took for pity, but which expressed only admiration. 'Oh,' replied he, 'there is less evil in this than in the slightest venial sin.'

"At midday, when he came to see me, we discussed the matter a little more at length. I told him that it was generally considered to have been a malicious trick of the devil, and asked him if such was his own opinion. He answered me very decidedly, and with the greatest possible composure. 'Certainly, my dear friend; it is very manifest. As he could not burn the man, he wished to console himself by burning his bed. He is very angry,' added he; 'which is a good sign; we shall soon have a great deal of money, and a great many sinners. The devil is never more provoked than when he sees us use the same money which corrupts and ruins souls, to promote their salvation.' And, in fact, during the course of that week there was a most extraordinary movement at Ars, and M. Vianney received several important sums for the support of the missions.

"He spoke to me also of the Quarant' Ore; of the benefits of that holy institution, and the joy which the visible presence of the Blessed Sacrament added to the ordinary blessings of the pilgrimage. His eyes were filled with tears, and his soul seemed to flow forth in each word he uttered. 'This is another kind of flame,' said he, 'another kind of fire,—it is a fire of love.'"

It may naturally occur to us to inquire whether the supernatural noises heard by M. Vianney were audible to others. Besides the instances already given, M. Monnin relates two others, one related by M. Renard, who heard it from the Abbé Bibot himself, the son of the good widow of Ecully. M. Bibot came to Ars in 1829, to make a retreat under the holy curé, who received him with fatherly kindness, and insisted upon his taking up his quarters in his house.

"I was particularly intimate with this young priest," says M. Renard; "and the first time I met him after his arrival at Ars, our conversation turned upon the marvels with which the whole country at that time rang. 'You sleep at the presbytery,' said I; 'you can give me some news of the devil, then. Is it true that he makes a noise there? have you ever heard him?' 'Yes,' replied he; 'I hear him every night. He has a wild sharp voice, like the cry of a wild beast. He takes hold of M. Vianney's curtains and shakes them violently. He calls him by his name. I have caught these words distinctly: "Vianney, Vianney, what are you doing there? Get along! get along!"' 'Do not these cries and noises terrify you?' 'Not exactly; I am not easily frightened; and, besides, the presence of M. Vianney reassures me. I recommend myself to my guardian angel, and manage to get asleep. But I sincerely pity this poor curé; I should not at all like to live with him always.' 'Have you ever asked M. le Curé any questions on this subject?' 'No; I have several times thought of doing so, but have been withheld by the fear of giving him pain. Poor curé, poor holy man, how can he live in the midst of such an uproar!"'

"In 1842," says M. Monnin, "a soldier came to Ars, who was at that time attached to the gendarmerie of our department, and was waiting among the rest of the crowd till M. Vianney should come to his confessional. To pass away the time, he took a few steps towards the presbytery. This man's heart was heavy with recent sorrow, which had left a vague religious terror upon his mind, impelling him, he scarcely knew why, to the confessional. Still he hesitated; truth at once attracted and repelled him.

"As he was slowly moving towards the presbytery, he was startled by a strange sound, which seemed to come from the window. He listened, and heard a strong, shrill, piercing voice, such as might be that of a lost spirit, repeat several times, 'Vianney, Vianney! come, come!' The poor man's blood froze within him with horror at the infernal cry. Just at that moment the church-clock struck one, and M. le Curé appeared with a light in his hand. He found the poor man overcome by terror, reassured him, and before asking him a single question, or having heard one word of his history, he astounded him by saying, 'My friend, you are in great trouble; you have just lost your wife in her confinement. But take courage, the good God will come to your assistance. You must set your conscience in order first, and then you will more easily arrange your affairs.' 'I no longer attempted to resist,' said the soldier; 'I fell on my knees, like a child, and began my confession. In my trouble I could hardly put two ideas together; but the good curé helped me, and revealed to me things, to my inexpressible amazement, of which he could have had no natural knowledge. I did not believe that any one could thus read the heart.'"

Mysterious noises and footsteps used also to be heard at the *Providence*, and at one time they continually found pieces of meat in the soup on abstinence days. They would empty the saucepan, and fill it again with water fresh drawn from the well; but all to no purpose, the meat would reappear at the bottom. At last they went to ask the curé what was to be done. "Serve the soup, and eat it all the same," said he; "it is the *grappin* who does it,—laugh at him." The plan succeeded, the meat appeared no more. "We became so accustomed," says Catherine, "to these tricks of the devil, that they ceased to surprise us." It was a penalty which they paid for the fatherly care and kindness of their holy pastor.

CHAPTER IX.

The sufferings inflicted on him by men.

" You shall be hated of all men for My name's sake;" "of the world, for it hated Me before it hated you;" and not of the world only, for they who hate you " shall think that they do God service." The Curé of Ars would have wanted one essential mark of sanctity, if the persecution of demons had not been accompanied by the persecution of men, and if the persecution of sinners had not been aided and countenanced by the persecution of good men, that never-failing companion of heroic sanctity. He had his full share of this bitter chalice, and it was filled for him by his brethren in the priesthood.

" While," says M. Monnin, " the reputation of our holy curé swelled rapidly, passed from mouth to mouth, and brought to his feet an ever-increasing number of penitents, his brethren began to murmur. Some felt a natural distrust, and perhaps unconscious jealousy, at seeing the guidance of souls transferred from their own hands to those of a simple and unlearned priest, whose talents they had been accustomed to hold in slender estimation. They found an excuse, in a pious anxiety for the salvation and direction of their flocks, for bitter criticisms and ill-disguised tokens of jealous displeasure. We shall not be astonished at this susceptibility and these suspicions, if we call to mind how much of human infirmity still outlives the most generous efforts to subdue it, even in the least imperfect soul. Others, and they, it must be confessed, the most numerous, were naturally and blamelessly alarmed at an excitement so novel and strange. Unaccustomed to the prodigies which sanctity was wont to work in other days on the mass of a people, they were astonished; they could not comprehend it; they shook their heads incredulously, and dreaded the effect which might be produced on a skeptical and scoffing generation, by the sudden reappearance of a power now forgotten and almost disbelieved.

"Another thing which helped greatly to strengthen the prejudices against M. Vianney was the fact of his confessional being continually besieged by a crowd of penitents, especially of the female sex, who seemed as if they came for no other purpose but to try and show forth his patience by their wearisome importunity.

"Poor souls, and worthy of all compassion, who, untrained by the hand of obedience, persist in seeking themselves instead of seeking God, and drag their incurable miseries from confessor to confessor, in order to find, not guidance and peace, but permission to follow their own will, and to make themselves wretched in their own way!

"Ars soon became the rendezvous of these unquiet spirits; and it may easily be conceived how much the reputation of M. Vianney (ere yet it was established beyond question by signal marks of sanctity) must have suffered by the reports which they carried home. They made him say all manner of inconceivable things; twisting his words to suit their own views, and strengthening themselves by his supposed authority in contradiction to the direction of their ordinary confessor.

"Thus were many excellent men, who were far from doubting the rectitude of his intentions, led to doubt his prudence, and the wisdom of his mode of direction."

Some parish-priests threatened to refuse absolution to any of their people who should go to confession to the Curé of Ars. Others publicly preached against him.

"In those days," as he once said himself, "they let the Gospel rest in the pulpits, and preached everywhere on the poor Curé of Ars."

"Those who did so, were not," says M. Monnin, "bad priests; they thought they were giving glory to God by combating superstition, and defending the faith against dangerous novelties and wild enthusiasm. They verily thought they were doing God service."

M. Monnin once asked the holy curé whether this distressing opposition had ever deprived him of peace. "The cross deprive one of peace!" said he, while a heavenly expression passed over his countenance. "It is the cross which gives peace to the world; it is the cross which ought to bring peace to our hearts. All our miseries come of our not loving the cross. It is the fear of crosses which gives weight to the cross. A cross borne simply, and without those movements of self-love which exaggerate its suffering, is no longer a cross. A suffering borne in peace is no longer a suffering. We complain when we suffer. We have much more reason to complain when we do not suffer, since nothing so likens us to our Lord as the bearing of His cross. Oh, blessed union of the soul with our Lord Jesus Christ by the love and power of His cross! I do not understand how a Christian can dread and fly from the cross. Is it not also to fly from Him who vouchsafed to be nailed to it, and to die on it for the love of us?" Another time he said, "Contradictions bring us to the foot of the cross, and the cross to the gate of heaven. To get there, we must be trampled on, vilified, despised, crushed. None are happy in this world but those whose hearts are at peace in the

midst of earthly sorrows.   They taste the joy of the children of God. All troubles are sweet when we suffer in union
with our Lord.   To suffer, what does it matter?   It is but
for a moment.   If we could but go and pass a week in
heaven, we should know what this moment of suffering is
worth.   We should think no cross heavy enough, no trial
bitter enough.   The cross is the gift of God to His friends.
Oh, how blessed a thing it is to offer ourselves every morning as a sacrifice to our good God, and to accept whatever
may befall us in expiation of our sins!   We must ask for
the love of crosses, and then they will become sweet.   I
had some experience of this during the course of four or
five years.   I was well calumniated, well contradicted, well
despised.   I had plenty of crosses,—almost more than I
could carry.   I set to work to ask for the love of crosses;
then I was happy.   I said to myself, Truly there is no happiness but in this.   We must never look from whence crosses
come.   They all come from God.   He gives them to us as
means whereby we may prove our love to Him.

He welcomed these humiliations for another reason.
They delivered him from the continual dread of hypocrisy,
with which he was filled, by the homage so generally paid
him.   "At least," he said to himself, "I am not deceiving
everybody.   There are some who estimate me at my true
value; how thankful ought I to be to them!   They will
help me to know myself."

Here we recognize the attitude in which saints meet
calumny and reproach; even as the King of saints stood
before Pilate, with His eyes cast down as a convicted cri-
minal.   Men of the world suffer wrong as heroes; ordinary
Christians as martyrs; saints as penitents.   Nor is there
either affectation or delusion in their estimate of themselves.
Humility is but another name for truth.   They who dwell

in the light of God's presence see their own stains to be
darker than the blackest slander can paint them, and accept contempt and ignominy as simply their due. "We
indeed justly," said the first who entered heaven by the
way of the cross; and the words have been echoed by all
the saints of God through the eighteen centuries which
have rolled on since his beatification. They have moved
along their *Via Crucis*, not with the proud step of conscious virtue, and the upward glance of injured innocence;
but on their knees, with their heads veiled, and their eyes
cast down, answering "mea culpa" to their accusers, and
"we indeed justly" to their crucifiers. M. Monnin gives
us an instance of this saintly temper which occurred at this
period of his friend's life, and which reminds us of a like
circumstance in the life of Boudon:

"A letter was brought to him one day containing the
following words: 'M. le Curé,—when a man knows as little of theology as you do, he ought never to enter a confessional.' The rest of the epistle was in the same strain.
This man, who could never find time to answer any of the
letters which daily poured in on him in increasing abundance, appealing to his wisdom, experience, and sanctity,
could not refrain from expressing the joy and gratitude he
felt at being at last *treated as he deserved.* He immediately
took a pen, and wrote as follows: 'What cause have I to
love you, my very dear and very reverend brother!' (The
letter was from a brother priest, who has since repaired his
fault by asking the holy man's pardon on his knees.) '*You
are the only person who really knows me.* Since you are
so good and charitable as to take an interest in my poor
soul, help me to obtain the favor which I have so long
asked, that, being removed from a post for which my ignorance renders me unfit, I may retire into some corner to

bewail my miserable life.   How much penance have I to do! what expiation to make ! what tears to shed !' "

At about the same time, a meeting was held of some of the most influential clergy of the neighborhood, which came to the resolution of making a formal complaint to the new Bishop of Belley of the imprudent zeal and mischievous enthusiasm of this ignorant and foolish curé. This their intention was made known to M. Vianney, in a letter written by one of the party in the bitterest and most cutting terms. This was not the first time that he had been threatened with the displeasure of his Bishop; and, believing himself fully to deserve it, he looked for nothing less than an ignominious dismissal from his cure. " I was daily expecting," said he, " to be driven with blows out of my parish; to be silenced; and condemned to end my days in prison, as a just punishment for having dared to stay so long in a place where I could only be a hindrance to any good."

One of these letters of accusation happening to fall into his hands, he indorsed it with his own name, and sent it to his superiors. " This time," said he, " they are sure to succeed, for they have my own signature."

Ars was now included in the see of Belley, once filled by the chosen friend of St. Francis of Sales, which had been recently restored, and conferred on one well worthy to succeed him. " Mgr. Devie," says M. Monnin, " was the friend, the benefactor, the counsellor of many of his priests; the master and the model of them all. Chosen by God to restore the glory of his little church after long years of widowhood and humiliation, none ever laid a firmer or a gentler hand upon the ruins of the sanctuary, or the souls committed to him. Such was Mgr. Devie, the last man in the world to be carried away by false reports, or evil surmises. He no sooner beheld M. Vianney than he loved him; he loved his simplicity, his mortification, and his poverty. He warmly took his part on all occasions. "I wish you, gentlemen," said he once, at a numerous meeting of the clergy, in a tone which shut the mouths of the scoffers,—"I wish you a little of that folly at which you laugh; it would do no injury to your wisdom."

To satisfy himself as to the prudence and discretion of the holy curé, the Bishop sent his vicars-general to Ars, to see him at work, and question him as to his mode of proceeding in the guidance of souls. Without a thought of justifying his conduct, he explained everything with the greatest candor and simplicity; concluding with an earnest petition to be relieved from a burden far too heavy for his feeble powers. "I want to go into a corner," said he, "to weep over my poor sins."

Some time afterwards, Mgr. Devie recommended him to submit to the counsel of the diocese any difficult cases which might occur in the course of his ministry. "Out of more than 200 cases which he sent us," said this learned prelate, "there were only two on which I should have formed a different judgment. His decisions were invariably correct, and his practice irreproachable."

The hearty approbation and admiration expressed by the holy Bishop for M. Vianney bears the greater weight from the fact that, as M. Monnin tells us, "by a particular dispensation of Divine Providence, he never did anything to encourage the works of his zeal; but, on the contrary, in several instances was unintentionally the means of thwarting them."

We have hitherto only spoken of the persecution of the good, the cross laid upon him by mistaken, and for the most part well-intentioned men; but the Curé of Ars bore too many tokens of resemblance to his Master not to be honored by the enmity of the world. That enmity was exhibited in a tissue of vile and slanderous attacks upon that which, of all earthly blessings, is dearest to a holy soul,—the spotless purity of his fame. Strong hearts have been crushed, and lives of vigorous usefulness have been blighted, by the blast which now fell upon him. A few evil, prying eyes, a few venomous tongues, and the prince of this world needs no more to blacken the fairest fame, and set the brand of hypocrisy upon the saintliest life. The Curé of Ars, that man of austerest penance, so simple and candid in his speech, so grave and modest in his bearing, was represented as a vile hypocrite, a man of evil and scandalous life. He received anonymous letters, filled with scurrilous insults, and infamous placards were fixed upon the walls of his presbytery.

"These calumnies," said M. Monnin to him one day, "must have been the work of very wicked men."

"Oh, no," replied he, "they were not wicked, only they understood me better than other people. Oh, how glad I was," continued he, "to see myself thus trampled under foot by all men, like the mud in the streets! I said to myself, 'Well, now your Bishop must treat you as you deserve. He must now drive you out with blows.' And that thought consoled me and sustained my courage."

"But, M. le Curé, how could they accuse you of leading an evil life?"

"Alas, I have always led an evil life. I led the same life then that I do now. I have never been good for any-thing."

"In saying this," adds M. Monnin, "he was uncon-scious of the testimony he was bearing to himself, for the life he was then leading was before our eyes. That marvellous, supernatural life he had, then, always led."

"I should be sorry," added he, "that God should be offended; but, on the other hand, I rejoice in the Lord at all that can be said against me, because the condemnations of the world are the benedictions of God. I was afraid of being a hypocrite when people were making some account of me, and I am very glad to see that unfounded estimation changed into contempt."

To a priest who came to him one day, to complain of a wearisome and vexatious opposition which he was enduring, "My friend," said he, "do as I do; let them say all they have to say. When they have said all, there will be no more to say, and they will be silent."

M. Monnin anticipates a suspicion which may arise on hearing of the atrocious calumnies heaped on this holy priest, that perhaps the very innocence and simplicity of his character might have made him less circumspect in his demeanor than prudence requires. "Nothing," he tells us, " could be farther from the truth. He regarded every indication of that over-sensibility, in which some persons indulge towards their director, as a dangerous snare, an injury to humility, and a hindrance to that sweet and uniform simplicity which goes straight to God, without a thought of self, or of those who lead us to Him. With him, nothing human, however innocent and lawful, was suffered to intermingle with direction. Thus, while he endured with incomparable sweetness and patience the whims and scruples of his penitents, he never indulged them in long conversations, frequent and useless interviews, or any other aliment of vanity or self-love. It was therefore against every appearance of probability that these injurious reports and detestable suspicions arose to poison the air around him; and yet there was a period when priests and laymen, men of piety and men of the world, seemed leagued in one confederacy against him; the outrages and violence of the one serving as a corollary to the prejudices of the others."

Meanwhile nothing interrupted the uniformity of his habits, or disturbed the placidity of his soul. He hid within that heart, so tranquil yet so desolate, the points of the weapons which pierced it to the quick, and appeared outwardly as calm, as sweet, as gracious, as little solicitous about his own reputation, as easy of access, as ready to enter into the most trifling concerns of others, as if unconscious of the burden of a blighted reputation and a wounded spirit. Never was there a shade of sadness on his brow, or a note of querulousness or sharpness in his voice. He practised to the letter the maxim so often on his lips, "*The Saints never complain.*" Like his Divine Master, *he held his peace.* Nor did he, as so often happens in times of oppressive sorrow and suspense, lose the presence of mind and freedom of action necessary for the due fulfilment of his daily duties. Never did he carry a more loving exactness into the discharge of his pastoral office in the pulpit and the confessional, than at the time when these very labors were made the fuel of the fiery furnace in which he was to glorify God. When asked how he could possibly, under the continual threatening of dismissal, and amid the wearing vexation of this strife of tongues, have preserved the energy of mind, and the self-command necessary to labor on with unabated ardor and perseverance, "We do much more for God," said he, "when we do the same things without pleasure and without satisfaction. It is true that 1 daily expected to be driven out; but meanwhile I worked on as if I were to remain here forever."

It does not appear that during this time of fiery trial

from his fellow-men, M. Vianney had to endure the far
more excruciating interior sufferings which were his portion at another period of his life. "I was never so happy,"
said he, "as in those days; the good God used to grant me
everything I desired." It was also at this time that the
concourse of pilgrims to Ars began to increase in so wonderful a manner. "Men came," says M. Monnin, "from all
countries, far and near, to this reprobate, this ignorant, insane man, this hypocrite, to lay open the most secret recesses of their conscience, to consult him on the most intricate questions, to recommend themselves to his prayers.
His great miracles and his great works supported by large
alms date also from this period."

This persecution lasted for about eight years. The holy
priest lived it down. Never, during that long trial, did
word or look betray a ruffle upon that supernatural serenity,
which reflected the image of God upon his soul. It often
happened that they who came to Ars to revile and blas-
pheme, were softened and subdued by the very aspect of
one who could be hated and suspected only at a distance.
"It was impossible," says M. Monnin, "to insult him to
his face." The sight of that serene countenance, with its
expression of transparent simplicity, was enough to change
slanderers into friends.

The prejudices of the clergy were sooner dispelled, as
they had arisen rather from misconception than from malice;
and during the later years of his life M. Vianney was regarded by his brethren in general with the most cordial and
unvarying respect and admiration.

CHAPTER X.

The sufferings inflicted on him by God.

" A CHRISTIAN," says St. Augustine, " must suffer more than another man, and a saint more than an ordinary Christian."   It was God's purpose to make M. Vianney a saint; and therefore, in addition to the sufferings inflicted upon him by himself, by the devil, and by men, his Divine Master gave him to drink of that bitterest draught of His own chalice, which wrung from Him the exceeding bitter cry, " My God, My God, why hast Thou forsaken· Me?" The light which had gilded the clouds that rose around him from earth and hell was withdrawn, and he entered into that thick darkness, which Divine love never suffers to overshadow any soul, but such as it has gifted with special strength to endure it.   The Abbé Baux, who was for many years the confessor of the Curé of Ars, affirms that his soul was habitually subject to the bitterest desolation.   Our Lord hid from him the immense good which He was working by his means.   He believed himself to be an utterly useless being, devoid of piety, understanding, knowledge, discernment, or virtue.   He was good for nothing but to injure and ruin everything—to disedify everybody—to be a hindrance in the way of all good. ' In the humility of his heart, he shed tears over his sins, indevotion, and ignorance, while at the same time the generosity of his courage led him to throw himself in all his helplessness and weakness into the arms of his Lord.

"God," said he, almost in the words of St. Francis, "has showed me this great mercy, that He has given me nothing on which I could rely, neither talents, nor wisdom, nor knowledge, nor strength, nor virtue. When I look at myself, I can discover nothing but my poor sins. Yet He suffers me not to see them all, nor to know myself fully, lest I should despair. I have no resource against this temptation to despair, but to throw myself before the Tabernacle, *like a little dog at his master's feet.*" "He was continually haunted," says M. Monnin, "by confusion for faults past, and by fear of faults to come; by the constant dread of doing ill on every occasion."

It would be difficult to overrate the intensity of such a trial to a man overwhelmed, as he was, with labor for souls, and compelled to give instant decision upon cases involving the eternal salvation of those who hung upon his words as the oracles of God. His intense appreciation of the sanctity required of the ministers of the sanctuary was another source of suffering. He was speaking one day with deep sadness of the difficulty of corresponding with the sanctity of a priest's vocation, when the young ecclesiastic with whom he was conversing said to him, "But still, M. le Curé, there are many good men among the clergy."

"What do you say, my friend?" replied M. Vianney. "Assuredly there are many good men among us! Where should they be found, if not among us? But," continued he, with increasing animation, "*to say Mass, one ought to be a seraph;*" and he began to weep bitterly. Then, after a pause, "See, my friend, I place Him on the right, He remains on the right; I place Him on the left, He remains on the left! *If we really knew what the Mass is, we should die!* We shall never understand how blessed a thing it is to say Mass till we are in heaven. My friend, the cause of

all the misery and relaxation of the priesthood is the want
of due attention to the Mass. My God, how pitiable is the
state of that priest who does this as an ordinary thing!
There are some who have begun well, who have said Mass
so devoutly for some months; and afterwards"—again his
voice was choked with tears. "Oh, when we consider what
it is that our great God has intrusted to us, miserable creatures that we are! What does the mischief is, all this
worldly news, this worldly conversation, these politics, these
newspapers. We fill our heads with them; then we go and
say our Mass, or our Office. My one great desire would be
to retire to Fourvières, having no charge of any soul but
my own; and after I had said my prayers well, to spend the
rest of my day in serving the sick. Oh, how happy should
1 be!" Then speaking of a priest, well known to his visitor,
"He wished," said he "to enter religion; he would have
joined the Marist fathers. Theirs is a work according to
God's own heart, for it combines humility, simplicity, and
contradictions. They go on bravely. If I could, I would
become a Marist. But the friends of this priest having
made sacrifices for him, he thought it best, in order to relieve them, to accept a cure, as he said, *for a time*. He
thinks no more now of his purpose of entering religion. Oh,
when we have taken this first step, it is hard to get loose?"

"M. le Curé, if you could get Mgr. Devie's consent, you
would soon *get loose*."

The holy curé began to laugh: "Most assuredly! Well,
my friend, we must not lose confidence. But the breviary
is not overburdened with canonized parish-priests. This
saint was a monk, that a missionary; there are many others
of different callings. St. John Francis Regis and St. Vincent of Paul did not remain parish-priests to the end of

their days. There are even more Bishops canonized, though their number is so small compared with that of priests. My friend, the ruin of priests is the habit of continually going to visit each other. By all means let them go occasionally to visit a brother for mutual edification, or for confession. But to be always running about! Alas!—You are a sub-deacon, my friend; you are happy. When once we are priests, we have nothing to do but to weep over our *poor misery*. That which prevents us priests from becoming saints, is the want of reflection. We do not enter into ourselves; we do not know what we are doing. What we want is reflection, prayer, and union with God. Oh, how unhappy is a priest who is not interior! But to be interior, we need silence and retirement, my friend,—retirement. It is in solitude that God speaks to us. I say sometimes to Mgr. Devie, 'If you want to convert your diocese, you must make saints of all your parish-priests.' Oh, my friend, what a fearful thing it is to be a priest! Confession! the Sacraments! What a charge! Oh, if men knew what it is to be a priest, they would fly, like the saints of old, into the desert, to escape the burden. The way to be a good priest would be to live always like a seminarist; but this is not always possible. One of our great misfortunes is, that our souls become callous. At first we are deeply moved at the state of those who do not love God; at last we come to say: 'These people do their duty well, so much the better; these others keep away from the Sacraments, so much the worse.' And we do neither more nor less in consequence."

He added, that the isolation of priests was another dangerous snare, and source of manifold temptation. "Unfortunately," says M. Monnin, "his words upon that subject were not recorded; which is the more to be regretted, as they touch upon a vital question, and would have completed this remarkable enumeration of the duties and dangers of the life of a parish-priest."

M. Vianney once said in the anguish of his heart, to a beloved brother in the priesthood, " I am withering away with sadness upon this poor earth ; *my soul is sorrowful, even unto death.* My ears hear nothing but horrors, which pierce my heart. I have no time to pray. I can hold out no longer. Tell me, would it be a great sin to disobey my Bishop by running away secretly ?"

" M. le Curé," was the reply, " if you wish to lose all the fruit of your labor, you have nothing to do but to give way to this temptation."

Another day, as he came from his confessional more broken down than usual, he stopped to look at some fowls which had scratched a hole in the sand of his court-yard, and were resting there asleep in the cool shade, with their heads under their wings. " I think these hens are very happy," said he. " If they had but a soul, I should like to be in their place."

But the bitterest drop in his chalice was the perpetual vision of sin; the daily insults offered to the Master he adored. " My God," cried he one day, " how long shall I dwell among sinners? when shall I be with the Saints? Our God is so continually offended, that one is tempted to pray for the end of the world. If there were not here and there some few holy souls, to console our hearts, and rest our eyes, from all the evil which we see and hear, we could not bear up against all we have to endure in this life. When we think of the ingratitude of men towards the good God, we are tempted to go to the other side of the earth, to see no more of it. It is horrible. If only the good God were less good; but He is so good! O my God! my God! what will be our shame when the day of judgment shall discover to us all our ingratitude! We shall then understand it; but it will be too late."

"No," said he, in one of his catechetical instructions, with an accent of the bitterest anguish, " there is no one in this world so unhappy as a priest. In what does he pass his life! In beholding the good God offended; His holy name continually blasphemed; His commandments continually violated; His love continually outraged. The priest sees nothing but this; hears nothing but this. He is always like St. Peter in the pretorium of Pilate. He has always before his eyes his Lord insulted, despised, mocked, covered with ignominy. Some spit in His face, others strike Him, others set a crown of thorns upon His head, others load Him with stripes. They push Him, they trample Him under their feet, they crucify Him, they pierce His heart. Ah, if I had known what it is to be a priest, instead of entering a seminary, I would have escaped to La Trappe."

It was observed that on Fridays the countenance of the holy priest indicated, by its paleness and the deep sadness of its expression, the intensity of his sympathy with the sufferings of our Lord.

Generally speaking, however, there was no outward indication of the conflict within, such was the strength of the *patience in which he possessed his soul.* "Only," as M. Monnin tells us, " the countenance whose prevailing expression, when he looked at others, was benevolence, unconsciously assumed a look of sadness when he gazed inwards upon himself, and found himself face to face with all the faults, weaknesses, and *miseries of his poor life.*" Yet he flinched not, for all this : " he bowed his head; suffered the storm to pass over him; made no change, absolutely none, in his resolutions or his conduct. He prayed more than usual; redoubled his fasts, his disciplines, and macerations; he kept himself more closely united to God, and labored no less. Whatever might be the aspect of the heavens or the state of his heart, he went on his way with the same energetic step, and the same calm and tranquil bearing. No suffering of mind or body ever had power to make him swerve one hair's breadth from the way of duty, or to relax in the slightest degree the steady onward speed of his course."

CHAPTER XI.

The pilgrimage of Ars—The daily labors of the holy Curé.

The pilgrimage of Ars, which, for a period of thirty years, seemed to bring back a scene from the times of St. Bernard into the broad daylight of the nineteenth century, began shortly after the foundation of the *Providence*. It owed its origin, partly to the rumors afloat of the wonders attending that work; partly to the desire of certain holy souls to avail themselves of the spiritual direction of the saintly curé; partly to the throng of poor who crowded to him for relief of their temporal wants; but chiefly, in the opinion of Catherine Lassagne, to "the prayers of M. le Curé for the conversion of sinners. The grace which he obtained for them was so powerful that it went to seek them out, and would leave them no rest till it had brought them to his feet." The numerous miracles wrought, one after another, in succeeding years, added to the concourse; but

the origin of the pilgrimage cannot be better explained than in Catherine's words : *" Grace was so powerful, that it went in search of sinners."*

" Divine Providence," says M. Leon Aubineau, " has so ordered it, that during the course of thirty years, the men of the nineteenth century, so enamored of all manner of vanities, should come in crowds to do homage to humility and simplicity. While the philosophers of our day have been inveighing against confession and its consequences, the people have replied by flocking to Ars to venerate a *confessor."*

The first object of the pilgrimage was unquestionably the confessional. Such instances as the following were very frequent at its commencement. M. Vianney was in his room about nine o'clock at night when he was startled by a vigorous knocking at the door. Upon opening it, he saw a great, robust, and very determined-looking man standing there, who thus addressed him :

" Come to the church. I want to make my confession. I have made up my mind to do it, and that at once."

The good curé, not without some lurking apprehension of robbery, took the sturdy penitent to the church. He was a wagoner, and had left his wagon and horses at the church-gate. He made his confession, and before he departed, he thrust a pair of worsted stockings into M. Vianney's hand, saying :

- " Sir, you have got a bad cold; put these on your feet as quick as you can."

Curiosity doubtless had its place among the motives which brought pilgrims to Ars. Many came simply to look at the magnificent ornaments which enrich the little church, and to wonder at the ascetic form of the curé, who was spoken of far and wide, as a wonder of mortification and sanctity. A letter written in 1827 thus describes the church during the Octave of Corpus Christi. "At 8 o'clock we went to Benediction. The church was filled with worshippers, of whom a considerable number were strangers. The walls were covered with rich hangings and banners, the Tabernacle splendidly gilt, the Remonstrance sparkling with jewels; the light of a multitude of tapers played upon the gold and diamonds; and kneeling amid all these splendors was the priest worn out with vigils and fasts, breathing forth in a scarcely audible voice the fervor of his love."

The difficulty of procuring food and lodging in so poor a place as Ars would soon, however, have put an end to the concourse of pilgrims, had curiosity or novelty been their only attraction. Persons of the highest rank and most refined and luxurious habits were content, in the words of one of the pilgrims, to be ill lodged, ill fed, to rise early, to be squeezed, elbowed, repulsed; they braved cold, hunger, thirst, fatigue, want of sleep, all to catch a few words from the holy curé; they would not have done so much for a king.

The inhabitants of Ars at last saw the necessity of providing accommodation for the increasing influx of pilgrims; the greater number of houses immediately round the church were, in fact, built for this purpose. New roads were made, and a regular system of public conveyances organized in 1835 between Lyons and Ars. At the same time packet-boats were established on the Saône, which greatly facilitated the arrival of the pilgrims. It was calculated that more than 20,000 persons then visited Ars in the course of each year. M. Vianney soon arrived at that state to which St. Philip Neri bound himself by vow,—never to have an hour or a moment to himself. From the year 1835 he was dispensed by Mgr. Devie from the usual pastoral retreat.

" You have no need of a retreat," said the Bishop; "and there are souls at Ars which have need of you."

M. Monnin's personal reminiscences of the pilgrimage, date from the year 1848. "At that time," says he, "the number of pilgrims who arrived at Ars by the omnibuses alone, which connected the village with the Saône, amounted to the incredible number of 80,000 in the course of the year. They came from all parts of France, from Savoy, Belgium, Germany, and England. They were of all ranks and conditions; some bringing offerings, some begging alms, all imploring to be healed of some malady either of soul or body. The lame, the blind, the deaf, the epileptic, the insane, the sick of every kind of malady, walking a hundred or two hundred miles in the strength of their invincible confidence. We shall not attempt to bring that long procession of human miseries before our reader's eyes, lest he should imagine from the numerous cures that the design of God in the pilgrimage was the healing of the body, whereas the conversion of sinners was the special work of M. Vianney, to which all the rest was merely accessory.

"Even the presence of the patient was not in all cases necessary. St. Philomena and the Curé of Ars could exert their power at a distance; and many a sufferer, too poor, too weak, or too sick to make the pilgrimage in person, has come from far distant lands to render thanks in the humble village sanctuary for his perfect recovery, after a novena to St. Philomena, or an application by letter, or through some charitable friend, to the holy curé. The oil from the lamp before St. Philomena's altar has proved the means of healing to many a distant sufferer."

It was not only sickness, but sorrow of every kind which found relief at Ars.

"Great and small flocked thither, when wounded by the

hand of God or man. The widow and the orphan; the prosperous and the sorrowful; the young, full of the illusions of hope; the old, weary of the conflict of life; men disgusted with the world, and women tired of frivolity; sinners, above all, flocked thither in crowds, attracted by a wisdom and a sanctity alike supernatural in their eyes. Among this living mosaic, many came also from curiosity, and some to scoff and contradict. There were to be seen the most whimsical complications, the most startling contrasts: virtues in the midst of vices; heartrending misery under an exterior of enviable prosperity; perplexities to be solved only on Calvary; sorrows without hope on this side heaven."

No wonder that the heart of the holy priest was sad within him at the sight of this long array of human misery, continually passing in sad procession before his eyes. "We must come to Ars," he would say in the anguish of his heart, "to know what sin is, and to see what evil Adam has done to his poor family. We know not what to do; we can but weep and pray."

The pilgrims were admitted to the confessional, each in his turn; but M. Vianney would sometimes call out of the crowd such as, by the supernatural light vouchsafed to him, he perceived to be in most urgent need of spiritual succor. No other claim of precedence was allowed. Some amusing incidents are recorded by M. Monnin of the disconcerted self-importance of some of his aristocratic penitents.

"A lady of high rank arrived one day at Ars in a grand carriage, which drew up at the church. The lady entered in great haste, and addressing the persons who blocked up the entrance of the little chapel in which the curé was hearing confessions, in a tone of authority she bade them make way. Having in vain tried commands and persuasions in turn, she betook herself to the assistant priest. 'M. l'Abbé,' said she, 'it is incredible. I have been trying for a full quarter of an hour to make my way to the confessional of M. le Curé; it is impossible to get through the crowd. I am not fond of waiting; I wait neither at the court of the King of Bavaria nor of the Pope.' 'I am very sorry, madam,' replied the inexorable abbé, with the utmost composure; 'but I really can do nothing to help you; and you will be obliged to wait at Ars.'"

Mdme. la Comtesse submitted to her fate, and was reduced, like common mortals, to the necessity of watching for the moment when M. Vianney should leave his confessional. She then advanced to him, and said in a tone and manner which unconsciously betrayed her:

"M. le Curé, I am come to make my confession to you."

"It is well, madam," replied he, with a smile which was significant and slightly malicious; "we have heard confessions before."

A young man, whose wife wanted to make her confession, was forcing a way for her through the crowd, and, by elbowing right and left, succeeded in reaching the chapel of St. John.

"What is the matter, my friend?" said the curé, with his wonted placidity, to the husband.

"It is my wife, who wishes to make her confession."

"Very well; she will come in her turn."

"But, M. le Curé," said the lady in a slight tone of pique, "I cannot wait."

"Madam, I am exceedingly sorry, but were you the Empress, you must wait your turn."

The following picture of the pilgrimage in the year 1857, only two years before the death of the holy curé, is from the pen of M. Louis Lacroix. "Two years ago I had

determined to devote a part of my holidays to a visit to
Rome; and a few days before my departure I met a friend
at Paris, who is both a thoughtful writer and an enlightened and sincere Christian. He warmly approved my plan;
'but,' added he, 'since you are setting off this time as a
pilgrim, make a pilgrimage at the beginning of your journey as well as at the end; and as you pass by Lyons, go to
see the Curé of Ars. It will not take you out of your
way; it will not delay you long; and you will see there
what you would vainly seek elsewhere—what can be seen
nowhere else.' My friend had seen the Curé of Ars, of
whom I had only heard some vague reports from distant
hearsay evidence, nothing from the mouth of an eye-witness. He spoke to me of what he had seen at Ars in a
way which excited my curiosity, and finished his vivid
and animated picture by the following reflections:

" 'You study history, and teach it; you ought to understand it and catch its secret lesson. Go to Ars, and
you will learn how Christianity was established, how nations were converted, and Christian civilization founded.
There is a man there in whom dwells the creative action
of the saints of old, who makes men Christians as the
Apostles did, whom the people venerate as they did St.
Bernard, and in whose person all the marvels are reproduced
which we know only in books. Go and see him; speak to
him, if you can get near him, for he is besieged by penitents; look at him if you can do no more, and you will
see that you have not lost your time. When we enjoy the
blsssing of being contemporary with such a prodigy, we
must not pass by it with closed eyes. Philosophers put
themselves to great inconvenience to see phenomena, which
are often not worth the trouble. This is the greatest and
rarest of phenomena, for it is sanctity in full action. You

cannot, in your quality of historian, be dispensed from observing it. Do not fail, then, to go to Ars, and that without delay, for the Curé of Ars will not last much longer.'

"My friend was right; I felt it, and resolved to follow his advice. Instead, therefore, of proceeding direct to Lyons, I stopped at Villefranche. I had hardly got into the town, when, just as I was on the point of ascending the steep street leading to the church, which seemed well worth visiting, the clouds which had been collecting in the sky (I notice this circumstance purposely) poured down such a deluge of water as compelled me to take shelter in the office of the carriages which the growing celebrity of the abbé had caused to run between Villefranche and Ars. At the appointed hour we set off; the heavy rain continued; not a person was to be seen on the road; it had rained frequently during the whole day and the preceding day also. Well, said I to myself, there will be no crowd around the Curé of Ars. I shall lose the sight of the people eagerly flocking to see him; but I shall be able to approach him easily, speak to him, and set off without much delay.

"As I was making these reflections we arrived at Ars. The carriage set us down at a good village inn, where you are well treated, and not, as yet, imposed upon; the curé, I was told, forbade it. Knowing how difficult it is to moderate the charges of inn-keepers, especially at a place of pilgrimage, this was to my mind a strong indication of the mastery exercised by this holy man over the hearts of his people. Without further delay we now hastened to the church, where we were told that we should find M. le Curé. On the way I arranged matters in my own mind. I thought that the omnibus had brought all the pilgrims who would be there to-day; that there was no other mode of reaching Ars; and that we were the only visitors. In my simplicity I expected to find the good curé in the church waiting. In short, though well disposed to be touched and edified by all I expected to see, I was in no way prepared for the scene which awaited me.

" I entered the church, then, with an eager and perhaps somewhat impetuous curiosity. What was my astonishment, instead of the solitude which I had anticipated, to find the church thronged by a crowd of persons, all reverential and recollected in their demeanor; the women dispersed in groups about the nave, the men pressed together, in silent and serried masses, around the entrance to the choir, all calm and silent, in the attitude of meditation and prayer.

"Never did antechamber of sovereign or minister of state so impress me. I felt at once all the dignity of this humble minister of the sovereign Lord of heaven and earth, whose sanctity invested him with so much power, and attached to him so many suitors. Still my eyes sought him in vain. The door of the sacristy was pointed out to me, and I was told that he was hearing the confessions of the men in rotation. He was now receiving those who had come the evening before, and it was already 5 o'clock P. M. Evidently I had no chance of seeing the Curé of Ars that day, forming, as I did, the last link of the long chain which began at the door of the sacristy. But I did not complain; I was fascinated by the beauty of the scene before me; and I thought myself happy to be able to observe how the Curé of Ars ended his day, being fully resolved to come on the morrow to see how he began it.

" Still, however, the Abbé Vianney remained invisible. The door of the sacristy opened and shut alternately on

the penitents, who followed each other to the tribunal of
the holy priest. I saw them go in with recollected, absorbed, or anxious countenances, and come out again with
a calm, joyous, open expression on their faces. One, a
young artisan, stopped suddenly as he passed me, and
struck his forehead, exclaiming to himself, 'I must speak
to him again;' and he took up his position at the end of
the file, to get a second turn, in the course of another day
or two.

"More than two hours had thus passed rapidly away.
I had forgotten to count the minutes; so completely had
the scene before me filled my mind with divine and eternal
things, that it forgot time, which is but the succession of
those which pass away. It was now night, nearly eight
o'clock, but the church, far from becoming empty, was
fuller than ever. I was told that it was time for evening
prayers, at which, as well as the morning Mass, the villagers
failed not to be present; for the sanctity of their curé had
brought them all back to the practice of their religious duties. At that moment M. Vianney appeared, and proceeded to the pulpit. The sight of him made me forget
everything else. I had no eyes but for him. He wore
his surplice, which he never lays aside. His whole exterior bore witness to his extraordinary sanctity. His face
and his whole person were fearfully thin, betokening the
sublime and awful work of mortification and asceticism,
whence results what Bossuet calls that *dreadful* annihilation of the whole man,—dreadful to nature, but beautiful
in the order of grace; for if it kills in the one, it gives
life in the other. That bent and fragile form had an inexpressible majesty of its own. He walked with his head
bowed down, and his eyes on the ground; his long and
flowing hair fell around his neck, and encircled his face

with a white aureola. I felt a thrill of emotion as he passed close by me, and I touched the border of his garment. As soon as he was in the pulpit, he knelt down and said the evening prayers, but in so feeble a voice that only a confused murmur reached my ear. It was the voice of a man utterly spent and exhausted; which renders his unwearied assiduity in the church and the confessional the more remarkable. He spends whole days and nights there. After he had said the prayers, he came down from the pulpit, crossed the church, went out by a side-door, and, still bareheaded and in his surplice, passed into his house, between two walls of the faithful, who knelt to receive his blessing as he went along. I had witnessed the power of the Curé of Ars over my fellows; I had felt it interiorly myself; the essential end of my visit to Ars had been attained. Evidently the Abbé Vianney was no ordinary man, since he could thus draw around him, in this obscure village of La Bresse, as great a concourse as could be found in the most celebrated places of pilgrimage. I had seen this; I might now have departed, and have had wherewithal to bear witness to the wonder of Ars. But I could not endure to go away without having spoken to the holy priest, and received his blessing. I had ascertained what I must do to gain access to him. A man who marshalled the people in the church, and whom I took to be a sacristan, assured me that if I were at the church at four o'clock, I might see him in the course of the morning, and be able to leave Ars on the same day. I resolved to be very exact to the time appointed.

" In the meanwhile everybody went home; the peasants from the neighborhood returned to their villages. All the houses in Ars received guests, who wished to prolong their stay. I returned to my inn, where I found my omnibus companions, a lady from Besançon and her daughter, a priest from Grenoble, two seminarists from Lyons, a chaplain from Marseilles, a Marseillaise lady with her two daughters (one dumb, the other lame), and another family from Marseilles composed of three persons. This great concourse from Marseilles was explained by the fact of a miracle having been obtained by the Curé of Ars, about six weeks previously, for a person of that town. The conversation at supper turned entirely on the extraordinary man whom we had come to contemplate. Each expressed his admiration, and gave his impressions in his own way. 'Ah, I am glad I came,' said the father of the family from Marseilles; 'it was no wish of mine. I came only to please my wife and daughter, who had set their hearts on it. But I am glad I came; I know now what religion is.' And it was easy to see that the good man felt more than he said, and was ready to carry what he had seen to its legitimate conclusion.

"The next day, which was the 11th of September, 1857, I was up before four o'clock, and at the church before daybreak. I expected to be there in good time, and even before anybody else; but I experienced the same, and even a greater surprise, than on the preceding evening. A great crowd was already assembled, and, to my extreme disappointment, I was obliged to take up my position at a great distance from the blessed door, which was to admit me to the curé.

"'How long have you been here?' said I to the neighbors whom fate had given me.

"'Since two o'clock in the morning.'

"'And when did M. le Curé come?'

"'He came at midnight.'

"'Where is he? what is he doing now?'

"' He is down there in the confessional, behind the choir, hearing the women's confessions. This is what he generally does on Friday mornings; he will not hear the men until after Mass.'

"' What, then, are all these whom I see doing?'

"' They are keeping their places, that each may get in in his turn.'

"' When did they come?'

"' When the curé himself came in, they were waiting at the door, the first comer holding the handle. At midnight the church was opened, and they took their places.'

"This surpassed all I had seen the evening before. I knew well that men are capable of prodigious endurance when their pleasure or their interest is at stake; but what I did not know, and what I had never yet seen, was that they can make the same sacrifice of their time and their ease for purely spiritual benefits; and this spectacle, so wholly new to 'me, which seemed like a page out of the Gospels, penetrated to the bottom of my heart, and affected me even to tears. I gave myself up then, as on the previous evening, to the sweet influence of the scene before me, and, regardless of the lapse of time, remained in prayer and meditation, in the atmosphere of spiritual religious life which surrounded this great servant of God.

"I felt, however, a little out of charity with the sacristan for not having warned me of the necessity of passing the night at the church-door, and for having thus condemned me to so bad a position. I looked askance at him, for he was early at his post, as he came and went, marshalling the new-comers, answering everybody's questions, soothing the impatient, without ever becoming impatient himself. Struck by the calmness and perfect propriety of his manner, I made some inquiries about him, and learned that my supposed sacristan was a gentleman, who, having been cured and converted by the Curé of Ars, had devoted himself, out of gratitude and piety, to the painful and thankless office which he was so diligently fulfilling. He had volunteered to be the holy curé's assistant, by keeping order in the church while he is hearing confessions. With a curé who is thus employed for twenty hours out of the twenty-four, this is no trifling labor. This discovery was another new light to me. It showed me how the Saints, who do impossibilities themselves, lead others also to attempt them; and how, as well by what they do themselves, as by what they cause others to do, in a spirit of abnegation, absolute self-sacrifice, and boundless love of God and their neighbor, they are in truth the most active, the most influential, and the most beneficent of mankind.

"At six o'clock the vicaire came to say his Mass, while the curé continued hearing the women's confessions. At last, about seven o'clock, having been in his confessional since midnight, he came out with that air of tranquillity which was habitual with him, and went into the sacristy to vest for Mass. Still full of the desire to speak to him for a moment, to ask his blessing, and then to proceed on my way, I had made an effort, and had succeeded in slipping into the sacristy just as the vicaire reëntered it. 'Stay here,' said he, 'and perhaps when M. le Curé comes, he will hear you before he goes up to the altar.' I followed this advice, but without success. The Curé of Ars, who judges by a single glance of the state and needs of a soul, did not think it necessary to alter his course in order to satisfy my impatience; he put me off till after Mass, and began to vest. All that I gained by my attempt was to see him near, to feel his sweet and piercing glance fixed upon me, and to be allowed to assist him in vesting for Mass. While he was thus engaged, I had an opportunity of observing the extreme thinness of that mortified body, which resembled a shadow rather than the body of a living man. I noticed at the same time a singular vivacity and energetic decision in all his movements. I followed him to the altar of St. Philomena, to whom he had a special devotion, and by whose intercession he has obtained so many miracles. There he said his Mass. The votive offerings of every kind which hang all round the walls of the chapel speak of the number of sicknesses and sorrows which have there found relief. Here it was that a paralytic, having suddenly arisen and walked, as at the word of our Lord Himself, the holy priest, embarrassed and distressed by the enthusiastic admiration and gratitude of the spectators, complained to the Saint with a humility which betrayed the whole secret of his power. 'Ah St. Philomena, when you grant me such graces, let it be in secret. Heal them at home, and spare my unworthiness such confusion as this.'

"After the Mass was over, I hoped that the Curé of Ars would be at last accessible. It was the time he had appointed me. But I was again mistaken. The church was thronged, and the crowd had separated me from him as he returned to the sacristy. I was obliged again to play the part of a spectator, and I saw the rest of his morning work. He had reappeared in his surplice on the steps of the choir. A quantity of medals and rosaries were brought to him to be blessed; several children were led up to him, on whom he laid his hands. When he had satisfied everybody, he went into a little sacristy at the right side of the church, where he received, one after another, several ladies who had come to consult him.

"In an hour's time he reappeared, and returned to the

choir, when the confessions of the men immediately recommenced. Whenever I caught sight of him, I was too far off to get at him; he seemed always to escape me. I was on the point of losing my temper; but a little reflection made me ashamed of this movement of impatience, for the sight of this saintly man, thus spending himself and giving his whole time to the needs of others, made me feel how unworthy it would be in me to grudge a little of my own for the blessing of an interview with him.

"It was now nearly nine o'clock, and the same movement which had shut the door of the sacristy against me the evening before rendered it inaccessible to me now. Each took his place, and entered in his turn. There were indeed some exceptions to the rule. A few bustling and obstinate ladies contrived to make their way, in spite of all obstacles, to the great indignation of the rest of the assembly. Sometimes the curé himself pointed out some one whom he wished to admit; a preference which excited no displeasure. The sick and infirm always found immediate admittance. When the Marseillaise lady appeared, with her two afflicted children, she had only to wait M. Vianney's next disengaged moment. From time to time a group was seen kneeling before the altar, of those who had just been reconciled with God. The vicaire appeared, opened the tabernacle, and gave them holy Communion. All these various movements sometimes produced a certain degree of confusion, which required a little surveillance; but then the gentleman whom I no longer took for a sacristan, and for whom I felt great respect, went from bench to bench, calming everybody, and restoring order and peace.

"This sublime scene of charity had now gone on for ten hours; he who was its hero had never for a single moment relaxed or suspended his labors. I had come into the

church four hours after him, and though I had been all
the time a simple spectator, I was overpowered with fatigue,
and began to think of retiring. But before giving up hope,
I determined to make one more attempt upon the inaccessible sacristy. Aided by the saint's obliging auxiliary, I
continued to place myself just at the opening of the door,
and when the curé opened it to admit a new penitent, he
saw me straight before him, seemed to recognize me, and
allowed me to enter. We remained standing opposite to
each other. Being unwilling to take up much of his precious time, I put to him briefly and rapidly the two questions which I had prepared. He replied at once decidedly,
without apparent reflection, without the slightest hesitation,
but at the same time without precipitation; his replies were
in the highest degree wise and judicious, and his advice
susceptible of the easiest and most beneficial application.
Generally speaking men are compelled to deliberate, and
maturely weigh a plan, before they can decide what will
be the wisest course to take. The Curé of Ars seemed to
improvise wisdom. I was amazed to see this calmness, attention, and presence of mind under the circumstances.
Ever since midnight he had been besieged as he was even
now; he had not given himself a moment's rest; he had
returned answers to hundreds of persons. There was a
man kneeling beside us at the priedieu of the confessional,
waiting his turn. Masses of others were pressing to the
door, like the waves of the rising tide. Yet the holy priest
was present to all, giving himself to all, without impatience
or apparent fatigue. Assuredly this was not natural, or
simply human; and no one can reflect for a moment upon
such facts without being compelled to recognize the intervention of Divine grace, raising a man, ever faithful to its
inspirations, to a miraculous power of action. He had an-

swered my questions in as short a time as it had taken me to ask them. When he had finished I said, 'I have one more favor, father, to ask : I am going to Rome, to pray at the tomb of the Apostles; give me your blessing, that it may go with me throughout all my journey.' At the name of *Rome*, the Abbé Vianney smiled; the eyes, which had been cast down, were raised; the recollected and interior expression changed in a moment to a glance of bright and vivid interest. His eyes sparkled as he said, 'And you are going to Rome; you will see our Holy Father. Well,' added he after a slight pause, 'I beg of you to pray for me at the tomb of the Apostles.'

" After this last reply, and an exchange of words, which certainly did not occupy more than five minutes, I knelt; he blessed me; I kissed his hand, and withdrew, full of joy, strength, and veneration. I was glad to be once more at liberty. I made the best of my way into the open air, and took a turn through the village of Ars, which I had not yet seen. Almost all the houses have been turned either into inns for the reception of the pilgrims, or shops for the sale of rosaries and other objects of piety. Many likenesses of the Curé of Ars were to be seen among them. I bought one which seemed to me the best. I then took a walk in the direction of the castle ; and returned at the end of half an hour, to be present at the catechetical instruction which M. Vianney, after all the labors of the confessional, gives daily for half an hour before the midday Angelus.

" The church was again filled, and I had difficulty in regaining a place in the choir. Assuredly the eloquence of the Curé of Ars was not in his speech. Though at a very short distance, I could hardly hear him ; for besides the feebleness of his exhausted voice, the total loss of his teeth had deprived him of all clearness of articulation. But he was eloquent in his gestures, in his countenance, and, above all, in the authority of his life, and the ascendency of his works. What a mighty influence did he exercise over his hearers! This was the last, and the most impressive scene of all. The multitude was crowded around him; at his feet, on the steps of the altar, on the pavement of the choir, were pressed together persons of every age, sex, and condition, especially women with their children in their arms, all absorbed in breathless attention, with their heads bent forward, and their eyes fixed upon him. If they could not hear, it was enough to see him; for his exterior conveyed all his meaning, so much expression was there in his gesture, his eyes, and his whole countenance. He shuddered with horror when he spoke of sin; he wept at the thought of the offences offered to God; he seemed rapt in ecstasy when enlarging on the Divine love; he alternately reddened and grew pale. His language was easy and abundant. His subject was, the end of man, which is happiness in God. Sin sets us afar off from God; repentance brings us back to Him. This was his daily theme, and he enlarged on it with all his heart. As I said before, we heard very little, but we felt it all. Now and then we caught something; such thoughts as these: 'It is a strange thing—I have met with many people who repented of not having loved God; never with one who repented or sorrowed for having loved Him.' It was not an eloquence which strikes and subdues, but an unction which enkindles and penetrates. Like St. John, he continually repeated, 'My children.' And the multitude listened to him as to a venerated father. A painter might have found subjects here for a picture of the Sermon on the Mount.

"The clock struck twelve as the Curé of Ars finished his discourse; and he then returned to his presbytery, to seek in prayer and mortification the strength to resume, at the end of two or three hours, his life of immolation and sacrifice. In the course of another hour I left the village of Ars, carrying away with me, as a treasure dearly prized, the blessing of the Abbé Vianney, and the indelible remembrance of the marvels of sanctity and charity which I had witnessed there. I had seen no particular miracle; but I had beheld the miracle of his ordinary life, every successive day of which was a counterpart of that which it had been my privilege to contemplate."

It is this daily unremitting labor for souls which constitutes the miracle of the life of M. Vianney. "It was passed," as M. Monnin tells us, "in the confessional." Of the eighteen or twenty hours which he gave to labor, he reserved only the time to say his Mass and Office, and to snatch the semblance of a meal at midday. It is difficult to conceive how he endured such continued toil and unremitted stretch of attention, without injuring his head, and without impairing in any degree the full and free use of his faculties. A priest can go through a day of sixteen hours in the confessional, as an occasional and exceptional case; but who would not shrink from encountering such a labor the next day and the next, without rest or pause, and that not for a week or a month, but for thirty years—for life?

" When the servant of God had finished his day's work, at nine o'clock in summer and seven in winter, the crowd of women who had not been able to approach him during the day would gather together in the little porch of the church which faces the presbytery. Each kept her place with jealous care until the church-door opened at midnight, or at latest two hours after. Others would rise after a short sleep, and station themselves near the entrance of the presbytery, to seize upon the curé on his way, and exchange if it were but a passing word with him. He replied to them without stopping. M. Vianney had often great difficulty in making his way into the church, and from the church-door to his confessional in the chapel of St. John the Baptist.

"At six or seven o'clock, according to the season, M. Vianney left the confessional to prepare to say Mass. So closely did the crowd press upon him on his way, that it was necessary to clear a passage for him, and to defend him from the rash attempts of certain persons, who would catch hold of his arm, his surplice, or his cassock. How often has he been almost thrown down or pushed violently! how often have his clothes been torn! Yet he never complained. Having with difficulty gained the sanctuary, he knelt before the high altar, and remained for a moment motionless, as if absorbed in the presence of our Lord. One would have said that he saw Him. A man was always near him to keep back the crowd. He then vested; and there was generally a little struggle for the honor of serving his Mass, which was a privilege usually granted to some eminent person among the pilgrims, or to a priest.

"After Mass M. Vianney blessed the various objects of piety which were presented to him; then he returned to the presbytery, and drank a little milk, which was his breakfast in the latter years of his life, when he had been at last persuaded to take breakfast. He then heard the confessions of from thirty to fifty men, who had been waiting their turn from the time the church-doors had been opened.

"At ten o'clock he suspended his labors, shut himself up in the sacristy, and recited his Office kneeling on the floor, without any support. Having finished his Office, he went into a little room to the right, under the belfry, where he confessed the sick or other persons who were unable to remain longer at Ars. What a crowd was wont to choke the entrance! We were sometimes obliged to use considerable determination to rescue M. le Curé, and prevent the old sacristy from being carried by storm.

"At 11 o'clock he catechized; as he descended from the little pulpit the throng was thicker than ever around him. Letters, money-offerings of various kinds, were thrust upon him. One begged his blessing, another a medal, a rosary, a picture, a token of remembrance of any kind. Mothers brought their children; the sick threw themselves on their knees before him, and barred his way. Those who could not get near him appealed to him by supplicating gestures. It was a difficult undertaking to pierce this human rampart, and to conduct M. Vianney to one of the chapels at the lower end of the church, where he was accustomed to give audience to a few more persons. The people pressed after him with such impetuosity that two men were almost always employed in restraining or regulating the movement.

"When the Curé of Ars re-entered his house for dinner, he had to make his way through a crowd which grew thicker and thicker as he advanced. Sometimes he frustrated the expectations of the pilgrims, either by going to visit the sick (whither, however, his regiment continued to follow him), or by returning to the presbytery by another way. He would often find within his gate some privileged persons, who had been secretly admitted, that he might see them unknown to the others.

"While he was at dinner an impatient multitude stationed itself without, keeping watch upon every outlet of the house; and when, at a quarter to one o'clock, he passed across the market-place to converse with his missionaries at

the *Providence** on matters affecting the parish or the pilgrimage, there was an instantaneous rush upon him, so vehement that two men were generally needed to restrain it.
He merely passed through the refectory of the missionaries,
without ever sitting down. The few minutes which he devoted to this visit were divided between his fellow-laborers
and such pilgrims as by special favor had gained an entrance
into the house, and now filled all the rooms, corridors, and
passages.

"When he returned to the church, he had to pass through
the same unavoidable lines of living fortifications, which
had re-formed during his absence. Here, above all, it became necessary to use force, in order to repress disturbance,
and to install M. Vianney again in his chapel, spite of the
murmurs of some and the violence of others. He first said
his Vespers on his knees, and then heard confessions until
five o'clock. Then he proceeded to the sacristy, where he
heard the men as in the morning, having first confessed
some of the women, who were unable to wait, behind the
high altar. There was always a press of people before him,
whenever he moved from one part of the church to another.
The greater number of those who came to Ars made general confessions. M. Vianney willingly devoted himself to
this laborious ministry, as the means of snatching souls
from hell by the reparation of sacrileges.

"This was, perhaps, the most consoling result of the
pilgrimage. Ars was a great spiritual hospital, where every
variety of moral evil was laid open for healing. Notwithstanding" (might we not rather say because of?) "the

---

* The house formerly used for the orphanage was latterly appro-
priated to the missionaries sent by the Bishop to assist M. Vianney,
to whose zealous efforts this congregation of missionary priests owed
its foundation.

sublime sanctity of the servant of God, sinners felt themselves drawn to him, spite of themselves.

"It might have been supposed that labors so absorbing
and incessant would have prevented the Curé of Ars from
giving his full attention to each soul in particular. Nothing could be farther from the truth. There was not one
of his penitents who might not have believed himself the object of his special solicitude. Our saint had that great art
and great wisdom which enables a man to shut himself up
in the present moment. He did his work, like a good work-
man, in its own hour, leaving the past to the mercy, and
the future to the providence, of God. He thus avoided
fruitless anxiety, precipitation, and confusion. In the midst
of the overwhelming pressure of the multitudes around
him, he listened to the penitent at his feet as if he had
nothing else to do or to think of."

Such, for thirty years, without change or relaxation, was
the life of the Curé of Ars. "People tell me," said a man
of the world, "of marvellous things which go on at Ars.
I doubt not the power of God; it is as great in this nineteenth century as in the first days of Christianity. I am
convinced that the prayers of the holy priest, whom men
go there to see, can obtain surprising and even miraculous
cures; but to recognize the presence of the supernatural
there, I have no need of all this. The great miracle of
Ars is the laborious and penitential life of its curé. That
a man can do what he does, and do it every day, without
growing weary or sinking under it, is what surpasses my
comprehension; this is to me the miracle of miracles."

CHAPTER XII.

Illness of M. Vianney—His miraculous recovery.

UNTIL the year 1843, the Curé of Ars had no assistant in his prodigious labors. A severe illness, which had nearly proved fatal to him at that time, induced the Bishop to appoint him a coadjutor.

Soon after his arrival at Ars, M. Vianney had been attacked by the fever so frequently prevalent in the unhealthy atmosphere of the Dombes, nor did he ever afterwards fully regain his former health. He was subject to headaches so acute that, as Catherine used to relate, he would often, when she wanted to speak to him, point to his forehead, with an indescribable expression of pain. Other sufferings were soon added to this habitual malady; but under them all he was ever calm and cheerful, testifying neither by look nor word what he was enduring. His constitution was so strong and elastic, that his recovery was usually as prompt and sudden as his attacks of illness.

In the beginning of May, 1843, he was assailed by a sickness which seemed destined to be his last. The concourse of pilgrims for the month of May was greater than in any former year, and he sank beneath the weight of his unassisted labors. He was accustomed during the month of May to address an exhortation to his people every evening. On the third evening he was obliged to break off suddenly, and with difficulty reached his house and his bed, where the most alarming symptoms soon discovered themselves.

The following extracts, giving the details of the holy
curé's illness, are from the correspondence of the family
which succeeded Mdlle. d'Ars at the castle, and succeeded
her, also, as M. Monnin tells us, in her devotion to God
and the Church, and in her love and veneration for M.
Vianney :

"Ars, May 6th, 1843.

" Our holy curé," writes Mdme. des Garets, " is ill, so
ill as to make us think that his crown is ready, and heaven
open to receive him. The joys of heaven are often the
sorrows of earth ; and I cannot describe to you the grief and
consternation of the whole parish. He has been in bed for
the last three days, and has permitted me to approach that
pallet of suffering and of· glory. There I beheld a Saint
upon the cross, with all the peace of heaven depicted on
his suffering countenance. He told me that he was going
to begin his preparation for death. Prosper" (the Comte des
Garets) " hardly ever leaves him. The saint likes to have
him with him ; and he has had sufficient influence to induce him to allow the straw, or rather the board on which
he sleeps, to be exchanged for a mattress. The doctor
thinks very seriously of the illness. We are afraid—very
much afraid. How can we venture to ask our Lord to leave
him to us still ?

" I cannot tell you what this loss will be to us. He was
our Saint, our angel, our glory, our consolation, our shield,
our hope, our stay. The whole parish is in tears and in
prayer. Will these prayers be heard ? He has spoken to
many of his departure. Every one calls to mind expressions, to which we now attach a sadly prophetic meaning."

"You cannot form an idea of the touching and religious spectacle continually before us since the illness of this holy man. The church seems deserted without him, and yet it is constantly filled with a sorrowful multitude, praying for him with their hearts, their thoughts, their tears, and their sighs. Tapers burn at every altar, rosaries are in every hand. In the first days of his illness they were obliged to set guards at the door of the presbytery to restrain the indiscreet affection of those who were clamoring to see him once more and to receive a last blessing. They could only be pacified by receiving notice of the moment when the Saint would raise himself on his bed of pain, and give a general benediction.

"It is not without a heartache that I see another priest at the altar, and hear other words than those breathings of love which continually fanned the flame that was consuming our Saint. It is at least a consolation to witness the touching manifestation of the love and veneration felt for his exceeding sanctity. It is a great lesson for my sons, if God will vouchsafe, in His mercy, to engrave it deeply on their hearts, so that in the last years of their lives they may call to mind that solemn moment when, kneeling round the sick-bed of their holy pastor, they saw what God does even here below for His elect. They heard him reply to the questions addressed to priests when they are administered, by exclamations of love and faith, which bespoke the whole tenor of his life. They saw him, as it were, spring upwards to meet His God, when He came to visit him. They have seen all this, my beloved mother, and it seems to me that I ought to bless God for it, and take good hope for their future life. It is a ray from Thabor, which will enlighten their course; a pang from Calvary, which will give them strength, confidence, and hope.*

" Prosper is almost always in or about the presbytery. The Saint always receives him with pleasure and affection. One night he wanted to send him to bed. ' M. le Curé,' said Prosper, ' if I were ill, you would come and watch by me.' ' Oh, I think so, indeed,' replied he ; and he let him remain with him for the rest of the night. The holy man has read the chapter of Ecclesiastes, upon obedience to physicians, to such good purpose, that he always shows the most perfect docility to the prescriptions of his medical attendants."

" In the retirement of my little parish," writes the Abbé Renard, "I soon learned the sorrowful news of the holy curé's illness. An express came to me at midnight with the information that M. Vianney was dangerously ill, and wished to see me. I rose and set off immediately. On my arrival at Ars, I had the happiness of embracing the holy priest, whom I found in such a state of exhaustion, that his death seemed close at hand. ' You wish to leave us, then, M. le Curé?' said I, with emotion. ' I shall leave you my body, and my soul will go up there,' said he, pointing upwards with his trembling hand. There was a sub-

---

* Of the two sons of this pious mother, Eugene, the eldest, died, consoled and strengthened by M. Vianney, after a long illness, sanctified by angelic patience, childlike submission to the will of God, and the generous sacrifice of his young life of twenty years. The second, Joanny, the favorite child of the Curé of Ars, fell five months afterwards at the first siege of Sebastopol. He had written home a few days before : "If anything happens to me, you may be assured, and may tell all who know me, that my last thoughts will have been for God and my family." One of his companions in arms thus wrote of him : "Ever in the path of honor, he took all he could of duty, and only what he could not avoid of pleasure." M Vianney wept when he heard of his death, and said : "This blow is indeed severe."

limity in the expression of his countenance, in his gesture,
and in that upward glance towards heaven, which I cannot
describe, but which deeply moved me. I could not add
another word. I felt my throat swell, and left the room
with my heart and my eyes full of tears. A mournful silence reigned throughout the village; there was sadness in
every face, as if death were in each man's house. The pilgrims were wandering around the church, like sheep without a shepherd, with their eyes turned towards the presbytery, to catch the slightest incident, or gather the most
trifling detail. Whenever any of the attendants in the sick-
room appeared, a hundred questions were asked. ' How
is the holy curé ?' ' How is the good father ?' And when
the sad reply told that he was no better, they flocked into
the church, redoubled their prayers and tears, endeavoring
to do violence to heaven, and to obtain of God, by the intercession of our Lady and St. Philomena, the restoration
of health so precious to them all."

Meanwhile the malady gained ground rapidly, and the
Abbé Valentin, M. Vianney's confessor, judged that it was
time to administer the Last Sacraments. Seven ecclesiastics,
who were at the time in the presbytery, were alone to be
present; and it was agreed, in order to avoid increasing the
sorrow and desolation of the people, that the bell should
not be rung. The holy curé overheard these arrangements
from his bed, and turning to the person who was watching
him, said quickly: "Go, and tell them to ring. Ought
not the parishioners to pray for their pastor?" No sooner
was the mournful sound heard than the whole village was
astir. "Tidings of this kind," says M. Monnin, "have
rapid wings; they fly with the air, they glide with the
light, they travel everywhere, though no one can trace their
electric path."

All his children would fain have knelt around the bed of their dying father; but a very small number only could enjoy this privilege; the rest knelt on the staircase, in the court, and even the market-place, praying and weeping.

When M. Vianney was asked, in the formula of the ritual, whether he believed in all the truths of our holy religion, he replied, "I have never doubted;" whether he pardoned his enemies, "I have never, thank God, wished ill to any one."

The next day the Curé of Fareins said Mass at the altar of St. Philomena. At that very time the patient fell, for the first time, into a peaceful slumber, which was the precursor of his perfect recovery. It was a general report at Ars, that St. Philomena had then appeared to him, and revealed to him things which, to the end of his long life, were a subject of joy and consolation to him.

The following is the testimony of M. Pertinant, the schoolmaster of Ars, who had been his affectionate and assiduous nurse throughout his illness:

"Our holy curé, finding himself at the last extremity, begged that a Mass might be said in honor of St. Philomena, to whom he had consecrated himself by a special vow. The Mass was said by a neighboring priest, and all in Ars, whether residents or strangers, assisted at it. Before the holy sacrifice began, M. le Curé seemed to me to be laboring under a kind of terror. I observed something extraordinary about him—a great anxiety, an unwonted disturbance. I watched his movements with redoubled attention, believing that the fatal hour was come, and that he was about to breathe his last. But as soon as the priest was at the altar, he became suddenly more tranquil; he looked like a man who was gazing at something pleasing and consoling. The Mass was hardly over, when he said: 'My friend, a great change has taken place in me; I am cured.' Great was my joy at these words. I was convinced that M. Vianney had seen a vision, for I had several times heard him murmur the name of his sweet patroness, which led me to believe that St. Philomena had appeared to him; but I dared not question him."

The following letter from the castle tells of his continued convalescence:

"Ars, May 14th.

"It is now two days since the physicians pronounced our holy curé to be much better, and the third morning now confirms this blessed news. The happiness is the greater as we were far from any hope of it. If you had but seen the desolation of the whole parish; if you had only heard the sobs which have echoed through our little church for the last ten days, you would understand the excess of our joy. When the death of M. le Curé was anticipated, baskets full of medals, rosaries, crosses, and images, were brought to him to bless. I doubt whether all the Bishops in France put together bless so many. The docility of the venerable patient is exemplary. He takes everything which is prescribed to him. Yesterday, indeed, he wanted to send away his chicken-broth; but his confessor came and scolded him, and he took it without another word.

"The other day, seeing all the faculty round his bed, he laughed, and said, ' I am at this moment engaged in a great conflict.' 'With whom, M. le Curé?' said they. 'With four physicians. If a fifth comes, I shall die.'"

"Ars, May 17th.

"The strength of our holy curé increases with a speed which his physicians call marvellous. 'Say *miraculous*,'

replied he. He attributes his cure to the intercession of
St. Philomena. He said very graciously to his doctors:
'You are the means which God has used to cure me.' And
he often speaks of the care they have taken of him. He
is continually expressing a lively gratitude for the affection
of which he has received so many touching proofs. I saw
him yesterday on his sofa, or rather on *our* sofa, wrapped
up in Prosper's cloak. He is not more emaciated than before his illness. Perhaps, if anything, his features bear
less tokens of suffering. His whole conversation expresses
a desire to recover his strength as soon as possible. But
what will he do with this life which he has prayed to be
prolonged, and with this strength which he now asks to be
restored? These are questions which we ask each other
with a sort of vague, undefined uneasiness. We now fear
to lose, in another way, him whose life has been so merci-
fully spared to us; and the joy of his restoration to health
is shadowed by most painful apprehensions. This poor
Saint has an extreme desire to go and breathe his native
air; foreseeing also that the reverence and affection of which
he is the object here, will not leave him the repose of which
he stands so much in need. In truth, the holy man wrings
the hearts of his people in every possible way; but tender-
hearted as I have ever known him to be, I cannot bring
myself to believe that he really intends thus to leave us
orphans. He speaks of his children with all the affection
of a father. 'There is a great deal of faith yet left on the
earth,' said he to Prosper; 'I was much moved when I
saw the gray heads of my parish bowed down at my bedside to receive my blessing.' These tokens of affection are
still lavished on him. Sentinels are needed to repress the
pious eagerness both of parishioners and strangers. They
are not ungrateful to God; they pray, they praise, they

give thanks; but most of all, they beseech Him to keep their beloved pastor in the parish."

On the 19th of May, M. Vianney was so far recovered, that at his earnest desire, he was led, or rather almost carried, to the church, where, after adoring with intense love and thankfulness the Divine Master who had permitted him still to live and labor for Him, he went to pay his tribute of gratitude to his "dear little Saint."

For the next week, M. Pertinant daily led the holy curé to the church at a little past midnight to say his Mass, his weakness being still so great as to make it impossible for him to go without nourishment till the morning. As soon as he entered the church, the bell gave notice of his Mass, at which his people all hastened to assist.

"It was more like Christmas than Ascension-tide," says the good schoolmaster, "to see our venerable curé among us once more, as if come down from heaven, which he had so nearly entered, to be born again amongst us on earth."

A profound terror of the judgments of God, and an intense fear of death, characterized this first illness of M. Vianney. "No, no, my God!" cried he, "not yet, not yet! I do not wish to die; I am not ready to appear before Thy dreadful judgment-seat!" And his terror was increased by the presence of a troop of demons, who kept repeating around him in a horrible voice, "We have him, we have him!"

When the hour of his departure was really at hand, we find no trace of these fears, which had then given place to the simple trustfulness of a child sinking to rest in its mother's arms. They were at this time a portion of that bitter chalice of desolation and seeming dereliction on the part of his Heavenly Father, of which he drank so deeply during the greater portion of his life. And now, too, the fear that he was out of his place, that he was marring instead of fulfilling the will of God, became intolerable, and the desire of solitude a temptation irresistible, because it seemed to him to come from God. He prayed for prolonged life and restored strength; not that he might labor for others, but that he might do penance for himself. The one cry of his wounded spirit was for some lonely cell, where he might weep over his *poor sins.*

"No one knows," said he, to his faithful friend, the Compte des Garets, "how many tears I have shed upon my poor pallet. Ever since I was eleven years old, I have asked of God that I might live in solitude; but my prayer has never been heard."

CHAPTER XIII.

First flight of M. Vianney—IIis return.

PERHAPS the most severe of all the spiritual conflicts of the holy curé was the continual wrestling with what seemed to him to be his vocation. Of the intensity of this trial, those only can judge who have a hunger and thirst like his to do the will of God, and have found that will to be their stay and their shelter in all temporal sorrow and in all spiritual desolation. To be where God has placed him, to do or to suffer what God has given him to do and to endure, is the meat and drink of the servant of God, and he is content to hold on his way, even in such obscurity as shrouds all the beauty of earth, and darkens all the face of heaven, if only he has light enough to show him that he is in the right path.

Even this was withheld from the Curé of Ars; he had to
toil in rowing with the wind and tide of his attraction to
solitude full against him; to do the work of a pastor and
evangelist with, as it seemed, the vocation of a Carthusian;
to struggle onward for life with the heavy burden of that
doubt which beset St. Francis on the first foundation of his
order. It was not the will of his Master to give him the
assurance which sent the holy patriarch on his way rejoicing: "Tell My servant Francis," said our Lord, by the
mouth of St. Clare, "that it is not my will that he should
labor for his own soul only, but for the souls of his brethren
also."

Three years before the period of his illness, about the
year 1840, M. Vianney had left his home in the midst of a
very dark night, under the overmastering pressure of the
desire to hide himself in some solitude, that he might
"weep over his *poor sins*, so that God might perchance
have mercy on him." He went some considerable distance
on the road to Villefranche. There he suddenly stopped,
and said to himself, "Am I really doing the will of God
now? Is not the conversion of one single soul worth more
than all the prayers I çan offer up in solitude?" An interior voice seemed to give him an answer, which brought him
back to his work.

On his recovery in 1843 a larger number of pilgrims than
had yet been seen at Ars threatened once more to break
down his restored strength. The bishop saw the necessity
of giving him assistance, and appointed M. Raymond, the
Curé of Savigneux, who had often asked to share his labors,
to be his coadjutor. In thus giving him a fellow-laborer,
for whom he had a special esteem and affection, Mgr. Devie
hoped to set at rest the desire for retirement, which he attributed to over-work and over-anxiety Unfortunately the

change had a directly contrary effect. M. Vianney no sooner saw a young and zealous priest at work among his people than he thought he might now safely leave them in better hands than his own, and that Divine Providence had thus set him free to follow the long-cherished desire of his heart. He thought also that he should be relieving others as well as delivering himself. "If he could have been persuaded," says M. Monnin, "that he was of any use in the world, he would have remained firm at his post; but he was fully convinced that he was good for nothing but to ruin everything he took in hand; that he knew not how either to speak or to act to any good purpose; that he was, in fact, simply a useless burden to the Church. He resolved to put an end to it." Some particulars of his flight are given in the following extract from a letter written at the time by the Comtesse des Garets:

"M. le Curé, our holy curé, is gone. He left us last night at one o'clock, to go we know not whither. What we do know, alas! is, that he is probably gone forever. It was reported in the parish the evening before that he was going the next day. We could not believe it; but this morning have been obliged to yield to the evidence which tells us he is gone. He wished to have escaped alone; but fortunately the rumors afloat in the village kept many watchers around the presbytery, and Pertinant and another have gone with him. He left a letter for M. des Garets, containing these words: 'My respected benefactor,—I have determined to spend a few days with my brother until this great concourse of people has in some measure subsided. I wish you a thousand spiritual and temporal blessings, in return for all the charity which you have shown towards me. You and all your family will always have a place in my grateful remembrance. Receive the best wishes of my heart,

and beg your venerable father to accept all that my heart
has to offer him.   VIANNEY, Curé of Ars.' "

Catherine's narrative is as follows :

" It was in the night between the 11th and 12th of September that M. Vianney tried to carry into execution the
thought which had so long tormented him, of retiring from
his charge to prepare himself for death by penitential exercises.   He had spoken to no one of his design until the
evening before, when he imparted it to us in his house of
La Providence, under the strictest injunctions of secrecy.
By the permission of God, he was overheard by a person
without, who lost no time in spreading the report all over
the village.   Great was the consternation; persons came
from all parts to inquire of us as to the truth of the report.
They determined, at all events, to be on their guard, and
watch all night.   Suddenly, between one and two o'clock,
a light was seen, and M. le Curé issued from the presbytery by a side-door; he was not walking slowly.   A troop
of people, who were waiting round the church till the door
should be opened, began to run.   M. le Curé ran too; they
ran after him.   Some wanted to speak to him, others to get
him to bless objects of devotion ; he continued his course
without noticing them.   He carried a bundle under his
arm, containing some linen wrapped up in a pockethand-
kerchief, and his little purse.   He gave this packet to the
young man who insisted on accompanying him, but who,
being in his working-dress, wished to return home first for
his Sunday clothes, so that he did not join M. le Curé till
he had reached the place of his destination.   He was replaced by the faithful Pertinant.   They went all the way
on foot to the house of François Vianney at Dardilly.   M.
Vianney had taken the precaution of avoiding the beaten
track for fear of pursuit, and had therefore gone consider-

ably out of his way.   When he arrived his feet were torn
and bleeding, and he was so unwell as to be obliged to go
to bed."

A letter from the castle, dated the 16th of September,
continues the narrative :

"I wrote to you of the flight of our holy curé on the day
when it took place.   Since then we have almost lost the
hope we at first cherished of keeping him with us, and have
strong reasons for believing that the gift of God, which we
have enjoyed for so many years past, will not be restored
to us.   The Bishop desires, at any cost, to keep him in the
diocese, and will not refuse the petition made to him to
give him anything but a parish to govern.   The poor
Saint hopes to escape the concourse and the kind of celebrity which pursues him here.   His humility does not allow
him to see that it would be the same everywhere.   ·There
would be no solitude nor repose for him, except at La
Trappe or the Grande Chartreuse.   It is believed, however,
that he will resist the interior voice which seems to call
him thither, from the fear of displeasing his Bishop.   I
could write you pages on the subject of the sudden and
nocturnal departure of our Saint, flying from the people
who pursued him, clinging to his cassock, and imploring a
last benediction.   His heart was torn ; yet he pursued his
flight with a rapidity which exhausted his strength.   He
was several times so much out of breath as to be obliged to
sit down by the roadside.   At last, assisted by Pertinant,
and leaning upon his stick, he arrived, without strength or
voice, after seven hours' walking, at his brother's house.
His first care was to send back a good young man, who had
overtaken him in his flight, to *that good M. des Garets,
who must be very uneasy.*   But not a word as to his plans,
nor any kind of explanation.   The *good M. des Garets,* re-

versing the parable of the lost sheep, had set off without delay in search of his pastor. After a journey of ten leagues, he learned on his arrival at Dardilly that M. Vianney had left it an hour before, without saying whither he was going, nor how long he should be away. You may conceive poor Prosper's disappointment. He wrote a letter at Dardilly, a copy of which I have read, for him to find on his return; which, if it fails to shake the resolution of the man of God, will no doubt increase his affection for the writer."

The letter is as follows:

"DARDILLY, September 15th, 1843.

"I need not tell you, my dear Curé, all the sorrow I feel at not finding you here. I came with a great desire to see you, and to receive your blessing once more. I wished to speak with you, and to impart to you my plans, and the means which it is in my power to employ,* and which, if we have the happiness of keeping you with us, I certainly shall employ, to prevent the abuses of which you complain. God refuses me this favor; I must submit. All that I ask of you, my dear Curé,—and you will not, I hope, refuse it, for the sake of the friendship which you have been so good as to show towards me,—is, that you will take no step till you have seen me, and we have conversed together. I will come to see you again in a few days, as soon as possible. Do not decide upon anything yet. You need rest, as no one knows better than I do. Stay with your brother as long as is necessary for you; but do not forget your poor parish of Ars. If any of your flock have caused you uneasiness, remember that they are the *few*, and that the greater number are strongly attached to you.

* M. des Garets was Maire of Ars, as well as Seigneur of the Castle.

Think of all those holy souls whom you are guiding on the way to heaven, and of those who were far off, and whom you are leading back again. Think of your *Providence*, of which you are the stay and support, and which cannot subsist without you. Think, lastly, of the good of religion, which God Himself has called you to maintain and glorify.

"Tell me, my dear Curé, are not the trials which God sends you, the sufferings of body and mind with which He afflicts you, all for His glory and your future happiness? It is not for me, my dear Curé, to say these things to you; but you will forgive me, in consideration of the sincere love which you know I bear you. Many will be coming to see you from Ars. Send me word how you are; and, once more, let me beseech you to take no step until I have seen you.

"The whole parish is in consternation; this is only the bare truth. Be assured that the sorrow felt here, and the fear of giving you pain, will prevent many abuses, and bring back many souls to virtue and religion. Be assured that, for my part, I will use every means in my power for the establishment of good order, and that I will do better than I have done hitherto. Whatever may be the will of God, do not forget me, my dear Curé, in your good prayers. Do not forget my family; do not forget my little Joanny, whom you had promised to prepare for his first Communion, which would have been a great source of hope and consolation to Madame des Garets and myself, and a great blessing to our child. Do not forget your desolate flock, which, widowed of its pastor, utters most fervent prayers that he may be restored to it, and that the good God will be pleased soon to bring you back among us.

"P. DES GARETS."

This letter made a great impression upon M. Vianney, who read it many times over. He had not left his brother's house, but was actually concealed in the room above that in which M. des Garets wrote his letter, having disappeared in the morning, after telling his nephew to say to any one who might inquire for him, that he did not know where he was.

Among the appeals made to him by his forsaken parishioners, are a few lines from the village innkeeper, who feared that something in his house might have displeased him.

"Monsieur," he writes, "I hasten to implore you not to desert us. You know what I have always said, and I repeat it now from the bottom of my heart: If there is anything which you disapprove in my house, I submit myself entirely to your wishes."

Catherine alone had been in his secret; he knew her perfect obedience too well to have any fear of intrusting it to her. A note which she sent to him at this time is a touching proof of the perfect resignation to the will of God to which the holy curé had trained her soul.

"We thank you with all our heart," she·writes, "for your goodness in thinking of us; and we should be most ungrateful were we ever to forget so great a proof of your charity. The object of almost all our prayers at this moment is, that the holy will of God may be accomplished in you."

The unsuccessful journey of M. des Garets to Ars had taken place on the 14th of September. On the 16th M. Raymond arrived there, after an interview with the Bishop at Belley, fully resolved to bring back, if possible, its lost treasure to the diocese.

Tidings of the place of M. Vianney's concealment hav-

ing got abroad, the pilgrims poured from Ars to Dardilly;
and the consequent disturbance and inconvenience caused
to his brother's family induced him to think of again changing his retreat. Meanwhile the inhabitants of Dardilly had
set their hearts upon detaining him there, in the hope of
one day obtaining him for their curé. M. Raymond accordingly met with an exceedingly cool reception; nor was it
till the end of the second day that, after employing all the
resources of his diplomacy, be could get speech of the holy
curé and deliver the message of Mgr. Devie. The Bishop
positively forbade him to leave the diocese of Belley; but
gave him the choice of two other positions, which he might
occupy should he persevere in his desire to leave his present parish.

M. Vianney promised to accompany M. Raymond to the
chapel of Beaumont, one of the places pointed out by the
Bishop. On their way the two priests went into a church
to say their Office. When they rose from their knees to
go out, they saw, to their great amazement, that the church
was as full as if the faithful had been summoned together
by the sound of the bell. M. Raymond said to his companion that he could not do less than address a few words
to these good people. He began to speak, and the voice
which since his illness had been so feeble and broken as to
be scarcely audible in conversation, was heard distinctly
and easily by the whole assembly.

The travellers slept at a village not far from Beaumont;
and the next day they both said Mass in that ancient sanctuary of the Mother of God. They were devoutly making
their thanksgiving together, when M. Vianney, leaning towards M. Raymond, whispered in his ear, in a tone of great
decision: "Let us return to Ars." "It was doubtless,"
says M. Monnin, "an inspiration from our Lady of Beau-

mont;" and a favor which the grateful people of Ars have never forgotten.

M. Raymond despatched a messenger to announce to the people of Ars the speedy return of their beloved pastor. "Never," says Catherine, "were better tidings heard."

The news spread like lightning; the village street was lined with people. The laborer left his work, the thresher threw down his flail, the women ran out of their houses. Videttes were posted along the road to give notice of his approach. At last a great cry arose, "There is the Saint!" and his children crowded round him, struggling which should be first to get his blessing, to touch his cassock, or to kiss his feet. He walked round the market-place, leaning on the arm of M. Raymond, and shedding blessings around him like a Bishop. As soon as he could extricate himself from the eager crowd, he went straight to the church, and said the evening prayers, amid the joyful and grateful tears of his people.

We cannot refrain from giving one more letter from the Comtesse des Garets. The tender and reverential affection of the pious family at the castle for their holy pastor brings to mind the household at Bethany whom "Jesus loved." It would seem that our Lord was pleased to vouchsafe to His faithful servant that refreshment in his toils which he disdained not to accept Himself,—the consolation of a holy and faithful friendship.

"Let us bless and praise the Lord! Yesterday, at five o'clock in the evening, the whole parish was still under the burden of sorrow. We were seeking our Saint, whom we feared to have lost forever. A quarter of an hour afterwards the bells rang out a joyous peal; all hurried to the market-place to see the holy curé arrive, dragging himself along with difficulty, leaning on his pilgrim's staff, and ac-

companied only by M. Raymond. The people all crowded
round him, laughing, crying, nearly stifling him with their
joy and gratitude. As for himself, he stopped and smiled
at their madness. 'It was all lost then,' said he. 'Well,
now it is all found again.' Prosper had hurried to the
spot; the Saint embraced him with the delight of a father
who has found a lost child. He does not conceal his satisfaction. He is pleased with everything and everybody;
pleased with the Blessed Virgin, who gave him the inspiration to return to his flock; pleased with the Bishop, who
has shown wonderful kindness to him, and great goodness
to his poor desolate people; and, lastly, he is pleased with
his poor children themselves, who have received him with
such overflowing delight. We are setting out in haste for
Trévoux, after having heard the Mass of our recovered
Saint. I saw him for a moment afterwards. There was
peace and joy in his eyes and in his voice, and, as he told
me, in his heart. . . . You said in your last letter that,
like his Divine Master, the Curé of Ars, after having fled
from the applause of men, would return to consummate his
sacrifice. I had always cherished the same hope myself.
The desolation of the village shook my faith, but could not
wholly destroy it. I did not think that this devoted man
was intended to end in tranquil retirement the life which he
had consecrated to apostolic labors. Notwithstanding my
reverence for his sanctity, I could not help thinking that
he had mistaken the will of God concerning him. That
will has now been manifested to him; and here he is again
in the midst of us, restored to our earnest prayers.

"The mourning of our little church has given place to
intense joy. It is about again to resume its wonderful
celebrity. And to what is that celebrity due? Neither to

talent, nor learning, nor eloquence, nor to the attraction of any external gifts ; but to the surpassing sanctity of a poor priest, like his Divine Master, meek and humble of heart."

CHAPTER XIV.

The Curé of Ars and La Salette.

"THE Curé of Ars," says M. Monnin, "had been one of the first to believe in the appearance of the Blessed Virgin to the little shepherds of the Alps, and to rejoice in the pledge of hope thus given to the world." As a proof of this, we have a letter addressed by him to the Bishop of Grenoble, in which he expresses his great confidence in our Lady of Salette, and states the fact of his having blessed and distributed a great number of medals and pictures representing the apparition.

In the autumn of 1850 Maximin came to Ars. The Abbé Raymond was then acting as the coadjutor of the holy curé. In order to put the boy's veracity to the test, he received him coldly, and told him that, though he might have deceived others, he would not deceive the Curé of Ars. He reminded him of a case of some young girls who had invented a story of an apparition some thirty years before, and who had lately come to acknowledge their imposture. Maximin at last said, in a temper (as we are told he had done before on similar occasions), "Well, have it then that I am a liar, and have seen nothing." The next day he had two interviews with M. le Curé, one in the sacristy, and the other behind the altar.

Maximin did not make a very favorable impression at

Ars. Those who saw him there were struck in the same manner as the Bishop of Orleans, who thus describes him in his account of a visit to La Salette in 1849 : " I have seen many children in my life," says Mgr. Dupanloup; " but seldom or never one who gave me so painful an impression. His manners, gestures, countenance, in fact his whole exterior, struck me as extremely repulsive."

After his interview with Maximin, the Curé of Ars refused to distribute the pictures and medals of Salette; by which it was discovered that he no longer believed in the miracle. When questioned on the subject, he invariably replied : " If what the child said to me is true, we cannot believe in the apparition."

" This report," says M. Monnin, " soon spread far and wide; to the joy of some, and the sorrowful amazement of others. But, after all, what did Maximin say ? Much has been written on the subject. Perhaps, however, the missionaries of the diocese of Belley may have had better means than others of ascertaining the truth. We have twice had a serious conversation with M. le Curé on this delicate subject, in the presence of a few witnesses, who must be able to remember, as well as ourselves, the particulars of this confidential conversation. We give them in their simplicity, as exactly as we can call them to mind after an interval of six years."

" M. le Curé, what are we to think of La Salette ?"

" My friend, you are at liberty to think what you will of it; it is not an article of faith. For my part, I think we ought to love the Blessed Virgin very much."

" Would it be indiscreet to ask you to be so kind as to tell us what took place between yourself and Maximin in that interview which has been so much talked of ? What was the exact impression which it left upon your mind ?"

"If Maximin spoke the truth to me, he did not see the Blessed Virgin."

"But, M. le Curé, it is said that M. Raymond had tormented the child with questions, and that it was to get rid of his importunity that he said he had seen nothing."

"I don't know what M. Raymond had done; but I know very well that I did not torment him. I merely said to him, when he was brought in to me, 'It is you, then, my friend, who have seen the Blessed Virgin?'"

"Maximin did not say that he had seen the Blessed Virgin, he only said that he had seen a great lady; perhaps there was some misunderstanding on this point."

"No, my friend; the child told me that it was all untrue; that he had seen nothing."

"Why did you not require of him to make a public retraction?"

"I said to him: 'My child, if you have told a lie, you must retract it.' 'It is not necessary,' he replied; 'it does good to the people; many of them are converted.' Then he added: 'I should like to make a general confession, and to enter some religious house. When I am there, I will say that I have told everything, and that I have nothing more to tell.' Then I replied: 'My friend, things cannot go on like this; I must consult my Bishop.' 'Well, M. le Curé, consult him. But it is not worth the trouble.' Thereupon Maximin made his confession."

M. Vianney added: "We must not torment ourselves about it. If it is not true, it will fall to the ground of itself. If it is the work of God, men may do what they will, but they will not be able to destroy it."

"M. le Curé, are you quite sure that you rightly heard what Maximin said to you?"

"Oh, quite sure. Many have said that I am deaf.*
What, indeed, have they not said? This does not seem to
me the way in which truth is defended."

We have gathered all these words from the mouth of
the veritable M. Vianney, who never varied in his statement. He assuredly believed that Maximin had told him
that *he had not seen the Blessed Virgin ; that he had seen
nothing.* And this clear and positive assertion occasioned
him great perplexity. He was inclined to believe, both by
the natural disposition of his character, and, after the pub-
lication of the decree of the Bishop of Grenoble, by his
reverence of episcopal authority; but in the truth and simplicity of his nature it was impossible for him to persuade
himself that he had not heard what had been so distinctly
articulated; and he struggled hopelessly against the painful doubts excited by the words of Maximin. Hence the
seemingly inconsistent answers which he gave to various
inquirers. On the strength of the approbation of the
Bishop of Grenoble, he would reply that the apparition
might be believed; he permitted, and even, in certain
cases, encouraged, the pilgrimage. If pressed to give his
personal opinion, he evaded an answer; or, if the character and position of the person who questioned him did not
allow of his doing this, he would reply, as we have seen,
*that if the child had spoken the truth to him, he had seen
nothing.* When eagerly pressed by persons, unconscious
of the indiscretion they were committing, to impart to them

---

* This unfortunate assertion, first made by Maximin, is the exact
contrary to the truth. M. Vianney's hearing was so acute that he
was obliged to wrap up his watch at night, lest the ticking should
keep him awake. The hypothesis that, in consequence of his imperfect articulation from the loss of his teeth, Maximin misunderstood
his questions, and answered at random, would be more admissible.

the particulars of his interview with Maximin, and to repeat the words which he had heard, we have sometimes seen him, with a kind of nervous movement, pass his hand over his forehead, as if to efface some painful memory, saying, in a supplicating tone, 'This pains me; this hurts my head.'"

"If you did but know," said he one day to a pilgrim, who vouches for the accuracy of the words,—"if you did but know how this chills and tortures my heart! Oh, I can bear it no longer! My God, deliver me! When I can shake off the doubt, I am light as a bird! I fly, I fly! But the devil casts me into my doubt again, and then it is as if I were being dragged over flints and thorns."

This trial lasted for eight years. At last a day came when it was given out that the uncertainty and fluctuations of the holy priest had come to an end. This statement was not at first believed; but the testimony was too strong to be long considered doubtful. In the month of October, 1858, M. Toccanier, the missionary then assisting M. Vianney at Ars, wrote thus to a member of the bar at Marseilles, well known as the author of several works upon La Salette:

"Since my last letter I have received from M. le Curé a fuller explanation of his return to his primitive faith in La Salette, of which he had been deprived by the unhappy retractation of Maximin. These are the details; which will, I know, give you pleasure:

"M. le Curé told me that he had prayed to be delivered from the doubt which, out of reverence for episcopal authority, he smothered within his breast. 'For a fortnight past,' he added, 'I had been suffering under great distress of mind, which ceased not till I said *Credo*. I wished for an opportunity of manifesting my faith to some person from the diocese of Grenoble; and the next day, behold! a priest whom I did not know came to the sacristy, and said to me, "May we, and ought we, to believe in La Salette?" I answered, "Yes; I have asked a temporal blessing from God by the mediation of the Blessed Virgin, invoked under the title of *Our Lady of La Salette*. I have obtained it."' In spite, then, of the retractation of Maximin, M. le Curé of Ars believes in La Salette."

"In the end of June, 1858," writes the Abbé des Garets, Chanoine of Lyons, "I met at Grenoble, on his way, like myself, to La Salette, M. l'Abbé B—, chaplain of the hospice of D—. This priest is wholly devoted to good works, especially for the spiritual benefit of the military. A particular intention now brought him to the holy mountain. Some pious women under his direction had been long begging him to unite them in a congregation under the invocation of Our Lady of La Salette.

"M. l'Abbé B—, having long considered this plan, wished, before taking any further step, to consult Our Lady on the very spot of her appearance. He left the mountain, telling me that he was going to consult the Curé of Ars. I made no remark, nor did I warn him of the doubts of M. Vianney on the subject; of which, indeed, he could scarcely have been ignorant. I said not a word to put him on his guard, but awaited the event. On the Abbé B—'s return home, he wrote to me as follows:

"'I have had the happiness of a long conversation with the holy curé. There is no doubt that he is wholly for Our Lady of Salette. Would that I could repeat to you word for word all that he said to me on the proposed work! His first salutation was an inquiry when I was going to begin; though I had not said a single word on the subject, and he had no means of knowing anything whatever about it. This is certainly most extraordinary. I was so much struck by it, that I have not yet recovered from my amazement. There must now be no further hesitation. The holy interpreter of the will of Heaven desires that the work should proceed without further delay. · "But is it quite certain, father?" said I, as I took leave of him; "does God really will this work?" "Come, come, my child," said he, "why do you make me repeat it? You want faith. Make a novena to the Holy Ghost and to St. Philomena, and then set to work." '

"It was evident to me," continues the Chanoine des Garets, "that a great change had taken place in the mind of the good curé; but how had it come to pass? This was an important point to ascertain, and yet not so easily accomplished as might be imagined. The Curé of Ars was not very accessible, amid the crowd of pilgrims which continually besieged him. One felt a scruple of conscience, too, in occupying any portion of his precious time, unless upon some matter of great moment, so that I had long ceased to attempt it.

"Now, however, I determined to try; and in October, 1858, having succeeded in approaching him for a moment, I said: 'M. le Curé, do you remember the visit you received early in July from the Abbé B—?'

" 'Yes.'

" 'And do you remember also the plan which he communicated to you?'

" 'Yes; it will succeed.'

"I was silenced by these brief, clear, precise replies, and pursued my interrogations no further. But M. le Curé proceeded: 'As to me, my friend, I have suffered unspeakably. I was most unhappy for many days; I suffered like a soul in hell. I knew not whether I ought to believe or not to believe.   I wanted to know the truth.   At last I determined to say quite simply, *I believe.*   It was as if a stone had fallen from around my neck.   I was delivered.   I am at peace.   I had asked a sign of God, and the next day I received a visit from a professor of the seminary (of Grenoble), who asked me what ought to be believed about La Salette.'   Here followed some words so indistinctly pronounced that it was impossible for me to catch them; but the sentence ended with these, most distinctly articulated, ' *So I believe firmly.*' "

CHAPTER XV.

Establishment of a Congregation of Missionary Priests—M. Vianney , attempts a second time to retire into solitude.

In the course of his forty years' ministry at Ars, M. Vianney was enabled to establish religious communities for the education of young persons of both sexes in his parish, and to found a still more important and extensive work for the benefit of the diocese at large.   The sight of the numerous pilgrims who flocked to Ars suggested to him the idea of extending to other parts of the diocese the benefits which he saw to arise from the instructions there addressed to them.   He was thus led to the foundation of a society of missionaries, which was established at Pont d'Ain, under the auspices of Mgr. Devie, towards the end of that holy prelate's episcopate.   Before his death M. Vianney had found the necessary funds for founding in perpetuity nearly ninety decennial missions in an equal number of parishes of the diocese of Belley.   It had been one of the latest thoughts of Mgr. Devie to connect the missionaries of Pont d'Ain with the parish of Ars, that, having the example of the holy curé continually before their eyes, they might be formed after the same pattern of humility, poverty, and mortification.

This design of the holy Bishop was carried into execution by his chosen successor, Mgr. Chalandon, the late Bishop of Belley, who in 1853 appointed the Abbé Toccañier, one of the missionaries at Pont d'Ain, to be the co-adjutor of M. Vianney. M. Toccanier thus relates the circumstances of his appointment:

"I was following the exercise of the annual retreat at the great seminary of Brou, and preparing to return to my beloved solitude at Pont d'Ain, when my superior, M. Camelet, came to tell me that Mgr. Chalandon, in pursuance of the wishes of his venerable predecessor, had appointed us to assist the Curé of Ars, in order to meet the increasing exigencies of the pilgrimage, and that he had made choice of me to represent the society.

"The Curé of Ars received me with his accustomed kindness; but I noticed somewhat of reserve and anxiety in his manner. That craving after solitude, which has always haunted him, was again aroused by the change just made, which seemed to him to offer a favorable opportunity of escaping from a position of which he was not so much weary as afraid."

Accordingly, the day after the installation of M. Toccanier, on Sunday, the 3d of September, M. Vianney imparted his plan, under an injunction of secrecy, to Catherine Lassagne and Jeanne Filliat. About midday he said to Brother Jerome (one of the brothers of the Holy Family, who had the charge of his school):

"Catherine has a thousand francs under her care; this sum will just complete the capital devoted to the establishment of the brothers of the Holy Family. Ask her for them at once, in case I should not see you again."

These words struck Brother Jerome. He at once reported them to his superiors, whose suspicions had been already roused by hearing that Mdlle. Lassagne had received orders, some days before, to prepare a trunk and some linen.

The preparations were all made, and M. Vianney seemed full of joy; he laughed at all the arguments and entreaties employed by the two poor women to detain him. Catherine was met by Brother Jerome with a sad countenance, and eyes red with weeping. She said as she passed him:

"You seem very merry, Brother Jerome?"

"Why should I be sad?" said the good brother.

"I am very sad."

"What is the matter, then?"

"I cannot tell you."

Her mouth was sealed by the injunction of her pastor, but she had recourse to a little innocent artifice, and, turning her back to the brother, that she might not seem to address him, she fixed her eyes on the windows of the presbytery, and said, as if to herself:

"Oh, my God! M. le Curé is then going to-night!"

"What do you say?" exclaimed Brother Jerome.

"Nothing; I say nothing. I am not speaking to you."

Brother Jerome had heard enough. He went at once to his superior, and they both together carried the heavy tidings to M. Toccanier, who charged them to watch carefully, and to bring him word of any movement on the part of M. Vianney. Catherine now acknowledged that the signal, of which he had given her notice, was to be the striking of three blows on the door of the room where the church-vestments were kept. She lay awake all night, weeping and praying that M. le Curé might not awake.

The brothers stood sentry in the garden ; having previously sent word to M. des Garets, who, though rather incredulous, desired to be sent for, should their fears be confirmed.

At midnight a light was seen, and the three knocks were heard. The missionary, who had thrown himself ready dressed upon his bed, was awakened, as he tells us himself, by repeated·knocks at his door.

"I stood in the market-place with the two brothers, watching the movements of M. le Curé by the light of his lamp, which enabled us to observe him unseen. We saw him take his hat and Breviary, descend the stairs, and go in the direction of Catherine's little house. We shrank back, not to be discovered ; but as soon as, having knocked, he pronounced the words, 'Are you ready? let us set off quickly,' we all three showed ourselves on the door-step.

"Seeing himself thus surrounded, M. Vianney said in a severe tone to Catherine, who was in tears :

"'Catherine, what have you done? You have betrayed me.'

"Brother Athanasius, who was the first to speak, said :

"'Where are you going, M. le Curé? We know that you want to leave us ; but if you go, we shall ring the tocsin.'

"'Do so,' said M. Vianney, in a brief and resolute tone ; 'do so, and let me pass.'

"I did not wish to act as gaoler ; so I contented myself with keeping close to the fugitive, and haranguing him to the best of my power. Finding all my reasoning useless, a new idea struck me. The night was pitch dark. I contrived to get rid of the lantern which had been provided ; foreseeing, what came to pass accordingly, that M. le Curé would lose his way. In fact, instead of taking the high-road to Lyons, he advanced at great speed towards Juy, escorted by the crowd of pilgrims, who had passed the night under the belfry, and some of his parishioners. When we reached the plank, which had been now replaced by a bridge across the stream, I tried to stop his passage. As he persisted in his resolution with desperate energy, it occurred to me to take his Breviary from him, in order to compel him to a retreat; but he contented himself with telling me that he should recite his Office when he got to Lyons.

"'What, M. le Curé!' said I, with an air of great astonishment, 'you will pass a whole day without saying your Office?'

"At this unexpected apostrophe, he said with a little embarrassment:

"'I have another Breviary at home, which belonged to Mgr. Devie.'

"'Well, M. le Curé, we will go and fetch it.'

"And he consented to return; which was more than I had hoped for. As we turned back, the first strokes of the tocsin sounded.

"'They are ringing the Angelus,' said Brother Jerome.

"M. Vianney knelt down, and began to say the Angelus aloud.

"'Suppose,' said I, leaving him in his illusion, and desiring above all things to gain time,—'suppose we say a decade of the rosary for a good journey to you?'

"'No, no; I can say my rosary on the way.'

"As we approached the church, the crowd grew thicker and thicker. M. le Curé seemed neither surprised nor disconcerted. He arrived at the presbytery, mounted the stairs in great haste, and went into his room. I followed, and remained there with him, making a show of looking among his books for the one he wanted, but in reality turning everything over, and making such a confusion that it was impossible to find anything. I contrived to retard the discovery of the desired volume as long as possible, and then to put it out of his way again, just as his hand was about to lay hold of it. In the midst of these subtle manœuvres, my eyes suddenly lighted upon a portrait of Mgr. Devie. Calling to mind the history of his first flight, which I happened to have heard related the evening before by M. Raymond, I suddenly addressed him :

"'M. le Curé, look at Mgr. Devie! I am sure that he is at this moment looking at you with astonishment !* We ought to respect the will of a Bishop during his life, and much more after his death. Remember what he said to you ten years ago.'

" Disturbed at the remembrance of one whom he had always loved and venerated with all his heart, M. Vianney faltered out, with the simplicity of a child threatened with its father's displeasure :

"'Monseigneur will not scold me ; he knows very well that I have need to go and weep over my poor life.'

" As we left the room, we met M. le Comte des Garets, who came in his turn to use the authority of his character and long friendship with M. Vianney to induce him to change his purpose.

" M. le Curé seemed not to listen to him, replied coldly to his remonstrances, and left him under the impression that he was acting under a presentiment of his approaching end."

There was something ironical and bitter in the tone and manner of M. Vianney throughout this scene, which struck all who were present as different from his usual sweet serenity.

* " Il vous fait de gros yeux."

"It no doubt betrayed," says M. Monnin, "the presence of temptation."

Meanwhile the old village had been roused by the first strokes of the bell, the continued clang of which was now mingled with confused cries of "M. le Curé!" Nobody knew in what direction the danger lay. The women crowded the market-place, and prayed aloud in the church; the men armed themselves with whatever weapons came first to hand,—guns, forks, sticks, axes; some apprehending fire, brought buckets of water.

M. Vianney had great difficulty in making his way through the·crowd. It was much worse when he tried to go out. They refused to let him open the street-door. A person well known at Ars for his devotion, placed himself in the doorway, clenched his fists, and vociferated in the most determined manner:

"No, M. le Curé, no! I tell you, you shall not pass!"

"Leave me alone, then," replied M. Vianney, with his accustomed gentleness.

He tried another door, which he found also·blocked up.

"He went thus," says Catherine, "from one door to another, without getting angry; but I think he was weeping."

At last he made his way into the street, and stood still for a moment, to consider by which way he could make his escape.

"The moment," says M. Toccanier, "seemed to me favorable for a last effort. I addressed to him, with all possible energy, the words which God put into my lips, of which I only remember the following: 'M. le Curé, do you, who are so well acquainted with the lives of the Saints, forget the generous and persevering zeal of St. Martin, who with the crown already within his grasp, said, *"I refuse not to labor ?"* And will you leave the furrow before the day's work is done? Do you forget those words of St. Philip Neri, *" If I were at the very gate of Paradise, and a sinner were to ask the aid of my ministry, I would leave the whole court of heaven to hear him ?"* And will you have the courage to leave unfinished the confessions of these poor pilgrims who have come so far? Will you not have to answer for their souls before God?' Every word was echoed by the crowd of strangers and parishioners, who fell at the feet of the holy priest, crying with heartrending sobs, 'Yes, father; let us finish our confession; do not go without hearing us.' And thus saying, they rather carried than led him to the church."

The holy curé knelt, according to his custom, before the sanctuary, and wept for a long time; then he went into the sacristy, remained there for some minutes with M. des Garets; and then went quietly into his confessional, as if nothing had happened.

Meanwhile the Vicar-General of the diocese, the Abbé Baux (M. Vianney's confessor), and M. Raymond, his former coadjutor and beloved friend, had been summoned, and used every argument in their power to induce him to remain. He would make no promise.

In the three following days, as if in recompense of the sacrifice he had made of his own will, the holy curé was visited by extraordinary graces and consolations. When questioned afterwards by M. Toccanier as to the motive of his intended flight, he answered, that he wished to throw the responsibility upon the good God, and to be able to say to Him, " If I have died a parish-priest, it has been Thine own doing, and no fault of mine."

Our Lord seems to have been willing to show that He

accepted the burden thus laid upon Him, by interposing on
more than one occasion to prevent his removal.

"On the 26th of January, 1855," writes M. Toccanier,
"M. Vianney's nephew came from Dardilly to beg him to
come and visit his father on his death-bed. The good curé
said to me :

" 'I am going to see my brother, who is very ill.'

" 'M. le Curé, we will go together.'

" ' My nephew is with me ; it is very cold ; there is no
occasion to trouble you.'

" After rapidly exchanging these words, I went with him
to his room, begged him to breakfast like a man about to
take a journey ; and a few minutes afterwards one of his
parishioners arrived with a carriage. M. le Curé got in ;
his nephew, Brother Jerome, and I followed him, under the
anxious eyes of the crowd, who begged his blessing, and
wished him a good journey and a safe return. The parish,
notwithstanding its uneasiness, felt a certain confidence in
seeing him set off under so good an escort."

They had scarcely started when M. Vianney began to
feel exceedingly tired ; soon afterwards, so ill that he was
obliged to ask to have the carriage opened, and to get out ;
he was no sooner in the fresh air than he was seized with a
fit of trembling, and became quite unable to walk. He was
at last obliged to confess that he could proceed no farther.
M. Toccanier was too happy to seize the opportunity of
saying :

"In that case I will go on with your nephew to Dardilly."

"Yes, my friend ; you will be doing me a kindness.
Ask my brother if he has anything particular to say to me,
and commend me to my sister."

M. Vianney again got into the carriage, which returned

at full speed to Ars, without his feeling the smallest return of illness. All his bad symptoms disappeared as soon as the horse's head was turned homewards. He went into the confessional the moment he returned, and said the evening prayers as usual, without the slightest fatigue. On his way, M. Vianney was met by the omnibus from Lyons full of pilgrims, who, as soon as they recognized him, left their carriage empty, to escort him on foot to the village.

"Among these pilgrims," said M. Toccanier to him, "there were no doubt some old sinners."

"Oh, yes, my friend; there were some who had not been to confession for forty years."

"You see, M. le Curé, that our good God stopped you Himself, to bring you back to the work which is so dear to Him."

M. Vianney looked at him with a smile.

M. Toccanier had explained at Dardilly the cause of the holy curé's non-appearance, and consoled his sick brother as well as he could. A few hours only after his return to Ars a deputation arrived, consisting of the vicaire and some of the religious of Dardilly.

"Happily," says M. Toccanier, "I was with them in the sacristy when they were trying to demonstrate to M. Vianney that, by taking the railroad, and stopping at the different stations, he would be able to accomplish his visit.

"'It is impossible,' said the good curé; 'I have done what I could.'

"Then M. le Vicaire, unmasking his last battery, suffered these words to escape him : 'It is very sad that your brother should be obliged to carry to his grave the secrets which he may have to confide to you.'

"Remembering what I had said on my arrival, M. le Curé immediately replied: 'My brother has no secret.

M. Toccanier, who went to see him, questioned him on the subject.'

"Disconcerted by this unexpected reply, the assailants gave up the undertaking, or rather deferred it to another day; for soon after this unfortunate attempt they returned at night, at the hour when M. le Curé was accustomed to go from the presbytery to the church, bringing a carriage with them, which they tried to persuade M. Vianney to enter. But he stood firm, and said: 'No, no! I have not given notice to Monseigneur, and I am not ready.'"

Four times had the holy man been compelled to resign his cherished hope by the unmistakable manifestation of the will of Divine Providence. He now understood that what he had believed to be an inspiration was in fact a temptation. It was a temptation which continued to harass him at times to the end of his life; but it never, after the instance just related, had power to perplex him as to the path appointed for him.

He would often repeat, that it was "a fearful thing to pass from the cure of souls to the tribunal of God;" but he never again sought to find relief in solitude. It would have been in vain; the sins and sorrows of his fellow-creatures would have pursued him whithersoever he fled.

CHAPTER XVI.

Homage paid to the sanctity of M. Vianney.

THE celebrity which became so keen a suffering to this holy and humble man of God was something the more extraordinary in our age, and in his country, from the fact that it rested on his sanctity alone.

That sanctity impressed the imagination, and commanded

the reverence, even of those whose hearts remained unchanged. "We once heard," M. Monnin tells us, "a distinguished but somewhat skeptical philosopher exclaim in his enthusiasm, 'I do not believe anything like this has been seen since the stable at Bethlehem!' Our philosopher was mistaken; he had not read the history of the Church; but he spoke truth in this sense, that the life of the Curé of Ars, as the lives of all the Saints, was but the continuation of the life of our Lord. Bethlehem was their cradle; there it was that sanctity had its birth; and from thence has it advanced, from age to age, and from land to land, under the impulse of the power of God."

A celebrated poet, who wished to see and hear the Curé of Ars, was so much overcome by the emotion produced by his presence, that the words escaped him unawares, " I have never seen God so near." He was called to himself by the quiet reply of M. Vianney, who said, pointing to the Blessed Sacrament exposed on the Altar, "True, my friend, God is not far from us; we have Him there, in the sanctuary of His love."

Another distinguished pilgrim observed of him: "The Curé of Ars is the very model of the childhood which Jesus loved, the very impersonation of Christian infancy; and therefore it is that God is with him."

The pilgrimage of Ars numbered, as we have said, names from almost every country in Europe, and even from the far banks of the Mississippi and La Plata. It was not only laymen, priests, and religious who came to visit and consult the holy curé, but bishops and princes of the Church. M. Monnin enumerates no less than twelve of the hierarchy of France alone; among them Mgr. Dupanloup, who came to impart to him the fears which filled his soul on receiving the burden of the episcopal office. "There are many bishops in the Martyrology," said M. Vianney to him; "there are hardly any curés. Judge, Monseigneur, whether you have so much cause to tremble as I."

In May, 1854, Ars was visited by an English Bishop. In his *Pilgrimage to La Salette* the Bishop of Birmingham thus describes his interview with the holy curé:

" We reached Ars a little before eleven; and a good priest, the curé's assistant, led us by a side-door into the church. The first object on which my eyes fell was the head, face, and shrunken figure of the curé straight before me; a figure not easily to be forgotten. He was saying his Office, and the nave of the church was crowded and heated with the number of people it contained. His face was small, wasted, and sallow; many expressive lines were marked around the mouth. His hair was white as snow; his expansive forehead pale, smooth, and clear; whilst his eyes were remarkably deep in shadow, and covered with their lids. He soon moved to a little side tribune in the nave, and holding his Breviary in his left hand, and leaning, or rather supporting himself erect, against a pillar in the nave, as if to sustain his feeble frame, he began to preach. As he opened his eyes, they sent forth a light, pale indeed, as if from his incessant fasting, but so preternaturally bright and tranquil, as to awaken at once the deepest interest. As he went on, the vigor and vivacity of his spirit, mantling through his thin and suffering frame, increased in energy. His voice, soft, yet shrill, rose into cries of anguish as he spoke of sin; his contracted hand was placed between his eyes, his brows shrank together, and tears began to fall, as they always do when the thought of sin comes to his mind. He again opened his eyes, and those shaded recesses became full of light; and he threw his feeble hand appealingly towards the people, who, fixed in the positions they had first taken, listened with profound attention, and even awe.   Then his eyes were cast up, and his whole figure seemed to follow.   He spoke of God, so good, so amiable, so loving, and his hands, his shoulders, his very person, seemed to gather on his heart.   It was impossible not to feel that God alone was there, and was drawing the whole man to the seat of His repose. Then there was a word about being in the Heart of Jesus, and in that word one felt that he was *there*.   He spoke for twenty minutes, and with a simplicity, a self-abandonment, an energy, and variety of tone and action, as his subject varied, all spontaneous, all from the heart. One thing I cannot describe,—such a force of spirits, with such an absence of animal warmth ; it was as if an angel spoke through a body wasted even to death.   Owing to the loss of his teeth, and to my distance from him, I could not well make out the words of his discourse ; but if I had not understood a syllable, I should have known, I should have felt, that one was speaking who lived in God.   His instruction was on a Confession, and was interspersed with one or two brief anecdotes and many ejaculations.   He then went out ; and in his surplice, bareheaded,—for he never covers his head,—proceeded, through the hot sun, to visit a sick person.   A crowd followed, and pressed upon him.

" Before he reached his house I had looked it over with his reverend assistant.   The walls were naked and ruinous ; there was scarcely anything there besides the poor furniture in his own room, and his little bed.   In one room, however, as ruinous as the rest, there was a good piece of furniture, containing sets of rich vestments, which the Vicomte d'Ars, at a cost of 40,000 francs, had presented to the church.   Before he came in, I was told he would escape from me as soon as he could for a little solitude.

But no. His manner of receiving me was as free and simple as it was full of humility and charity. There was nothing of a tone and gesture straining itself to maintain a character, but the disengaged self-abandonment and simple politeness of a saint. The chair which he presented was recommended as the chair of his predecessor in the parish. And he often repeated that he was very grateful for my visit. I was speaking of prayer for England, and of the sufferings of our poor Catholics on account of their faith; and he was listening, his eyes nearly closed, when suddenly he opened their singular light in all its brightness full upon me, and breaking in on the narrative in a way I shall never forget, with the manner of one giving a confidence, he said: 'But I believe that the Church of England will return again to its ancient splendor.' It is remarkable how often one meets with this conviction in France, and to how much prayer it gives rise. To understand him, one should see his face, always glowing when he speaks of God, always bathed in tears when he thinks of evil.

" His poor eyes, though so sweet and tranquil, are worn with his tears, and habitually inflamed.

" His spirit of direction has that largeness in it, which, unless it be infused, can only be attained by prayer and a long experience of souls. So long as the soul has God for her object, and acts with God, the mode of her interior employment is but an accident. The love of God, and the protection of Mary,—these are his two great themes. Amongst the rest of the saints his favorite is St. Philomena. He has built a beautiful little chapel in her honor, the first raised under her invocation in France. Like his church, it breathes of order, cleanliness, and piety. I felt it would be wrong to detain him from his short time for rest and food, so I asked him for a medal, by which to re-

member him. He took a few in his hand, and said : 'Take
one.' 'No,' I said; 'give me one.' 'There,' he said, 'is
the Immaculate Conception, and there is St. Philomena.'

"At my request he saw my companion for a short time;
and saying he would go and meet him, he had no sooner
shown himself at the door than the crowd of people rushed
upon him.   He can never stir out without being thus surrounded and pressed upon by the people.   He took my
friend affectionately by the hand, and walked with him
round his little garden; and when an offering was made to
him for his church, he said : 'Oh, let it be for my poor.'
He was then left to himself; but his meal was quickly over,
and he returned to the confessional.   He is now required
by his Bishop, under obedience, to add to the single poor
meal that used to be all he had in the day, a second, and
to eat a little meat at one of them.   At this he shed tears—
that a sinner like him should eat meat!—and he thinks
himself a glutton.

"He never begins his labors in the confessional later
than two o'clock in the morning, often at one; and when
the numbers waiting are very great, at midnight.   Penitents will lie all night on the grass, fifty at once, either in
order to gain the earliest admission to the church and the
confessional, or because of the houses being already quite
filled with those who come from a distance.   Except while
he says Mass, or preaches his little discourse, or for the
very short time he takes for his scanty food, the holy curé
lives almost entirely in the confessional.   From midnight
or early morn he is there till nine at night; then he retires
for his Office; a little reading, and some two hours at the
very most, for rest.   Such has been the unbroken course
of his life for many years.   In his soul, he lives for God;
in his poor earthly frame, he suffers from a complication of

most acute maladies, which give him no repose. As he said to one who is intimate with him, he suffers all day for the conversion of souls, and all night for the souls in purgatory. Of his penetration into the interior state of souls many instances are recounted."

The celebrated P. Lacordaire paid a visit to Ars in May, 1843, and carried away with him a profound reverence for the sanctity of the holy curé, and some treasured words of prophetic encouragement as to the revival of his illustrious order. The son of St. Thomas of Aquin disdained not to ask and receive the oracles of spiritual science from the lips of the lowly village pastor, and the most eloquent preacher in France listened in silent reverence to the words of life which flowed in his rustic patois from the mouth of the peasant's son.

M. Vianney said on this occasion, "Do you know what struck me during the visit of the Père Lacordaire? That which is greatest in science is come to humble itself to what is least in ignorance; the two extremes have met."

The pilgrims were not satisfied with seeing and hearing M. Vianney; their devotion showed itself in a way exceedingly annoying and inconvenient to the holy man. In their ambition to possess themselves of something that had belonged to him, they would cut off pieces of any part of his dress which they could get hold of. It has been stated already that he always wore his surplice, and never his hat; a circumstance which arose from the fact that if he laid down either the one or the other for a moment when he had taken it off, it was cut to pieces by these pious spoilers; so that in despair of correcting the evil, he left off his hat altogether, and wore his surplice continually. Even this did not wholly protect him; pieces were continually cut off his cassock: and women have been known to slip behind him during the Catechism, and cut off bits of his hair. When he perceived it, he would turn round and say quietly, "Leave me alone."

There was a general desire to get hold of his portrait; and the sight of those multiplied representations, sometimes grotesque in the extreme, which garnished all the houses in the village, was a perpetual mortification to the holy curé, who never would consent to sit for his portrait. M. Cabuchet,—"an artist," says M. Monnin, "of the Christian school, who prays before he paints,"—having furnished himself with a recommendation from the Bishop, came to beg for a sitting. "Willingly," said M. Vianney, "provided that Monseigneur will permit me to leave the place immediately afterwards." The young artist was compelled to catch the likeness by stealth. He concealed himself among the crowd, and made a wax model in his hat.

He had not been two days at Ars before he felt a desire to make his confession to the good father. "Take care," said the missionary, "that you do not betray yourself, or you will receive as your penance an order to break your model." M. Cabuchet could not refrain from making another attempt to gain the desired permission; but M. Vianney again repulsed him, saying this time, with somewhat of severity in his tone, "No, my friend, no; it is useless to ask me; neither for you nor for Monseigneur, will I ever consent."

After this conversation M. Vianney again caught sight of his penitent watching him attentively during his catechetical instruction; and guessing what he was about, he leant towards him, and said in a low voice: "Come, come, my friend, you have gone on too long giving distractions to me and to everybody else." Happily the work was already far advanced. The patient artist, however, interrupted it

for a day or so, and reappeared when he thought the good
curé had had time to forget him. "My friend," said M.
Vianney, catching sight of him again, "have you then nothing to do at home?"

"M. le Curé, one would think you wished to turn me
out of doors."

"No, my friend; but I have a great desire to excom-
municate you."

"What crime have I committed?"

"That's good! that's good! you know quite well; you
have been giving me distractions all the morning."

"It has been one of the great blessings of my life," said
M. Cabuchet afterwards, "to have known the Curé of Ars.
We must have *seen* saints, to be able to paint them."

Among the marks of honor bestowed upon M. Vianney
are to be ranked the dignity of Canon, conferred upon him
by Mgr. Chalandon; and the Cross of the Legion of Honor,
sent to him by the Emperor. He never wore his *camail*,
except at the ceremony of his reception, which was a grievous mortification to him. As to the badge of knighthood,
he said, "I don't know why the Emperor has sent me this,
except for having been a deserter." He opened the case
containing it, supposing it inclosed a relic; and his look of
blank disappointment is well remembered as he said, "Nothing but this, after all."

M. Monnin gives us the particulars of a singular debate
which arose between the parishes of Dardilly and Ars, as
to which should possess the mortal remains of him who had
rendered the one illustrious by his birth, and the other by
his labors. While he was yet alive, the parishioners of
Dardilly sent a deputation, begging the holy curé to leave
his body to his native village. Considering the request a
very unimportant one, and being at all times unwilling to

refuse any boon asked of him, M. Vianney made no difficulty in doing as they desired. But no sooner did the fact become known than an outcry arose, not only in Ars but throughout the whole diocese of Belley. The Bishop was obliged to interfere, and asked M. Vianney the motive of his bequest. "Alas!" said he, "if but my soul be with God, it matters little where my poor body rests."

The Bishop claimed this *poor body ;* and the curé, deeply mortified at the strife about what he accounted so contemptible a matter, promised to make another will, which he accordingly did the day before his death, in favor of the parish of Ars. But Dardilly was not to be so easily foiled ; the parish authorities set on foot a subscription for the maintenance of what they called their rights, and the people of Ars had no little trouble in establishing their just claim. Such a struggle as this in the nineteenth century is certainly no slight indication of the estimation in which the holy curé's sanctity was held by those who had the nearest and longest experience of its deep reality.

CHAPTER XVII.

Portrait of M. Vianney—His natural qualities and supernatural graces.

"THE venerable Curé of Ars," says M. Monnin, "exhibited in his person all the characteristics which constitute, if we may be allowed to use the expression, the *physiology of the Saint.* Sanctity is ordinarily accompanied by certain exterior signs, which indicate the sensible presence of the Divine element in the human personality,— the life of God in us. To have life, in the language of the

Gospel, is to have Jesus Christ, the Life Eternal, dwelling in us. Sanctity is, then, nothing else but the life of Jesus Christ in man, whom it transforms and deifies, so to speak, by anticipation, making him to appear, even here below, what he shall be when the Lord shall come in His glory, and 'we shall see Him as He is, without cloud or shadow, and be transformed into His likeness from glory to glory, as by the Spirit of God.' This transformation is already begun in the Christian, who, retracing, line by line, upon his soul the image of the Son of God, is at last able to say, 'Christ is my life;'* 'I live, yet not I, but Christ liveth in me.'† The Saint bears Christ within him, not only in his soul, but in his body. Jesus Christ breathes in his thoughts, his sentiments, his actions,—in the very throbbings of his heart, and the features of his countenance, which reflect, as far as it is possible for the human face to do, the dignity, grace, and loveliness of the Redeemer of men.

"The whole person of the Saint thus becomes a most pure and clear crystal, through which shines forth the glorious and divine form of Christ, our beloved Lord, *that the life of Jesus may be manifested in our mortal flesh.*‡

"This fact alone renders the Divine action evident, and in some sort palpable, to experience, and even to scientific observation. It is the intimate fusion of the natural and supernatural order, the shining forth of the Divinity through the transparent veil of the body. And such is the energetic power of this manifestation, that men most destitute of religious feeling are subdued by the ascendency exercised over all around them by the Saints. They recognize them, they know not why, as superior beings; they admire without understanding them; as those who have been born blind feel the sun's rays, though they see them not.

"To M. Vianney might be applied the words in which the Père Condren was described by M. Olier: 'What appeared outwardly was but the shell of what was really there. He was like one of the Hosts on our altars. Outwardly we behold the accidents and appearances of bread, but inwardly it is Jesus Christ.' So was it with this great servant of God. And this is the secret of the wonderful power which he exercised over the human heart. Without thinking of it, without knowing it, without willing it, this man, *so weak in bodily presence*, drew all who approached him within the sphere of his attraction. Once to meet his eye or hear his voice was to be fascinated by his look and word. Men of the world, accustomed to the power of far different spells, have acknowledged that, after they had seen the Curé of Ars, his image seemed to haunt them, and his remembrance to follow them, whithersoever they went. . It would have been difficult indeed to image to oneself a form more clearly marked by the impress of sanctity."

M. Monnin thus describes the outward appearance which, in his later years, so lightly veiled the indwelling of Jesus:

"M. Vianney was small of stature; his form, though not devoid of a certain degree of vigor, indicated a highly nervous temperament. Age and toil had not robbed his limbs of their elasticity and suppleness. His movements were quick and decided, and their agility bore tokens of a childhood developed in the healthy exercise of rustic labor. By a rare privilege, he preserved to the last the full use of the organs and faculties necessary for the fulfilment of his mission. Thus his hearing retained its acuteness, his sight its keenness, his mind its clearness, and his memory its fresh-

ness, even to the day of his death. Yet his body had reached
such a degree of extenuation as to seem almost immaterial.
There seemed to be nothing under the large folds of his
cassock. His step, though heavy, was rapid, as of a man
who, weary and exhausted, yet hastens on in the service of
God. His head fell slightly forward on his breast, from
the habit of recollection and adoration. His hair fell thick
and long, like a white aureola round that calm expressive
head; beneath the sweet majestic expression of which
might perhaps be discerned some traces of the early rusticity of his life,—a rusticity now tempered and subdued
by benevolence. On that emaciated face there was no token of aught earthly or human; it bore the impress of
Divine grace alone. It was but the frail and transparent
covering of a soul which no longer belonged to earth. The
eyes alone betokened life; they shone with an exceeding
lustre. There was a kind of supernatural fire in M. Vianney's glance, which continually varied in intensity and
expression. That glance dilated and sparkled when he
spoke of the love of God; the thought of sin veiled it with
a mist of tears; it was by turns sweet and piercing, terrible
and loving, childlike and profound. It was a very furnace
of tenderness and compassion when fixed upon any one. It
had then that mysterious power of attraction bestowed by
our Lord upon the eyes which are continually raised to
Him; and, wonderful to say, that glance, which searched
all hearts, and before which all spirits bowed, never affrighted any one.

"The most remarkable thing, next to the eyes, in the
countenance of the Curé of Ars was the profile, the lines of
which were bold, harmonious, and well defined. Although
the sweetness and serenity of his face betokened the Divine
peace which dwelt within, its characteristic and familiar

expression, when at rest, was that supernatural melancholy which belongs to the habitual sentiment of the invisible while yet in this visible sphere. It was deepened by the continual contact with sin and sorrow, impressing many a bitter thought upon his soul, and casting their mournful reflection upon his countenance. But when he came forth from that habitual state of recollection to converse with men, it was with a bright and gracious smile, which was ever ready to respond to every look which was turned upon him. There was not one of his features which did not seem to smile."

Such was the outward man of this holy priest of God, as described by one admitted to his intimate familiarity, and afterwards privileged to close those eyes, when their marvellous light had been withdrawn from earth, and to compose for its *last* (we might also say its *first*) repose that frame which had labored and suffered night and day for so many weary years in the service of Christ.

A remarkable circumstance is noticed by M. Monnin, which is indeed evident to any one who has seen a portrait of the Curé of Ars and of the infidel philosopher of Ferney,—the striking resemblance in the shape and outline of the face between the two. The expressions are as strongly contrasted as the forms are alike; but that there should be even this material resemblance between Voltaire and J. B. Vianney,—two men who seem to stand at the very extremities of human nature; the one as intense in his love as the other in his hatred of Jesus Christ,—is a thought which thrills through the heart with a pang akin to what we feel on contemplating the infancy of Judas.

There was an hour when the baptismal water fell upon his infant brow, and the soul of that most miserable and wicked old man was as lovely and as beloved in the sight of God as his who in feature was so closely to resemble him. And now who can help shuddering at the thought of the great gulf fixed? Oh, holy and humble lover of Jesus, pray for us now, while there is yet time for us to learn to love Him like thee, lest we also fall after the same example of pride and unbelief!

If the power of sanctity thus ennobles and transfigures the most earthly and material portion of our being, still greater is its empire over that which is in its nature spiritual. The influence of grace in raising, quickening, and deepening the mental faculties is seen with especial clearness in the history of M. Vianney.

"We have seen," says M. Monnin, "what he was as a young man; we have followed him in his maturity; we have not concealed the fact that he did not possess various or extensive human learning. What means had he of acquiring it? But he had what supplies the place of knowledge, and, if need be, of experience,—the faith which foresees all things and knows all things. He had great practical wisdom, a profound sense of the ways of God and the miseries of man, a wonderful sagacity, a quick and sure practical discernment, an acute, judicious, and penetrating mind. He was, besides, endowed with a supernatural memory, an exquisite tact, and a power of observation which would have been alarming to those who approached him but for the sweet charity which set its indulgent seal upon all his judgments.

"It was once observed in the presence of a learned professor of philosophy, 'There is great sanctity in the Curé of Ars, and nothing but sanctity.'

"'There is,' was the reply, 'great illumination. In his conversation it is cast upon every kind of subject,—upon God and upon the world, upon men and things, upon the present and the future. Oh, how well do we see, how far and wide do we see, when we see by the light of the Holy Spirit! To what a lofty pitch of sense and reason is a man elevated by faith!'

"Absorbed as he was in the functions of his ministry, M. Vianney was indifferent to none of those exterior questions which affect, either directly or indirectly, religious and social order. He had clear and ready perceptions upon many subjects hard of solution to the most skilful and practised intellects, and yet plain to him, from the one point whence he viewed all things, human and divine,—the glory of God, and the salvation of souls."

Nor was it only in the graver and severer exercises of the intellect and judgment that the faculties of this holy man had acquired so wonderful a development.

"Hard as he was to himself," says his friend, "and bearing on his whole person the traces of most austere penance, he was gentle, cheerful, and even playful in conversation. With those whom he knew and loved he was perfectly frank and open. Unhappily, it would be impossible to convey in writing the charm of that happy intercourse. A smile cannot be written down, and the conversation of the Curé of Ars was like the smile of his soul. He never laughed but with this smile of his soul, which rarely quitted his lips, encouraging gayety, and inspiring confidence. The Spirit of God, which dwelt in him, gave to his lightest word an incomparable exactness, fitness, and simplicity. The exquisite sensibility with which his heart was endowed shone through his expressions, animating, warming, and coloring them.

"Thus he long mourned for his pious friend Mdlle. d'Ars with a mingled feeling of tenderness and veneration. At his first visit to the new inhabitants of the castle, he gave way before them to the keenness of his regrets, saying, 'Poor lady, how sad it is not to see her in her old place at church!' Then, fearing that he had been wanting in delicacy to the heirs of his benefactress, he added, drying his tears, 'Yet, we are very wrong to complain. The good God treats us as He did His people of old: He took away Moses, and gave them Caleb and Josue.' Soon afterwards, in replying to their congratulations on the new year, he said to the same family, which was soon to share his heart with Mdlle. d'Ars, 'I wish I were St. Peter; I would give you the keys of Paradise as my new year's gift.'"

To Mgr. de Langalerie, who, on one of his frequent visits, said to him, "My good Curé, you will kindly permit me to say Mass in your church," he replied, "Monseigneur, I am sorry that it is not Christmas, that you might say three."

On the first visitation of Mgr. Chalandon, M. le Curé was told that he ought to say something in compliment to the new prelate. He accordingly addressed him thus:

"Monseigneur, the days on which your holy predecessor visited our parish were days of benediction. And no wonder; for *when the Saints pass, God passes with them.* We have lost nothing, Monseigneur; on the contrary, we have gained; for Mgr. Devie still blesses us from Heaven, and you, Monseigneur, whom He chose to carry on his work, you bless us upon earth. Bless us, Monseigneur; bless the pastor, bless the flock, that we may always and altogether dearly love the good God."

At the time of the cholera, the Abbé Toccanier having returned after a long absence, the holy curé embraced him, saying, "Oh, my friend, what happiness is this! I have often thought what must be the misery of the lost souls in being separated from the good God, when we suffer so much in separation from those we love!"

At the end of the long procession on the feast of Corpus Christi, some of his friends wished him to take some refreshment. He declined, saying, "It needs not. I want nothing. How should I be tired? *I have been bearing Him who bears me.*"

A religious once said to him, with great simplicity: "Father, people believe generally that you are very ignorant."

"They are quite right, my child. But it matters not, I can teach you more than you will practice."

Notwithstanding his decided taste for solitude, he loved to open his heart to those whom he loved and trusted. He seldom, indeed, spoke of himself; but when he did, it was with simplicity and openness, and always of such matters as were most humiliating to him. Of the gifts and graces with which he was favored he spoke to no one. Thus M. Monnin tells us that "he never revealed himself entirely; he led you to the threshold of his soul, and stopped you there." "How often," adds he, "have we said to ourselves, when we left him after those evening conversations, which it was the privilege of the missionaries to enjoy, 'How blessed must it be in Paradise, if the company of the Saints is thus sweet upon earth!'"

"At the close of his day of heavy, wearisome labor, standing before his little table, or at the chimney-corner, that his chilled and cramped limbs might feel the warmth of the fire, the innocence and joy of his heart found utterance in a thousand bright plays of fancy, and in thoughts and images full of grace and sweetness. According to the counsel of St. Paul, he avoided vain and profane discourses, and idle questions, which minister strife rather than edification. If any trifling debate arose in his presence, he kept a modest silence, as if he feared, by giving an opinion, to disoblige one of the parties. If appealed to, he intervened by some gracious and conciliating word, or by the enunciation of some of those great principles which cannot be disputed, and which restore peace between adversaries by bringing them off the ground of division to that on which strife is no longer possible. His soul hovered, like an angelic spirit, above the medley of vulgar passions and interests. He looked at everything from that point of view, familiar to the Saints, where light dwells without a shadow. Conscience was his only horizon.

"Never did labor or suffering diminish the interest of his conversation, or lead him to cut it short. The sweetness and brightness of his mind seemed, on the contrary, to grow amid the infirmities of old age. That dark time seemed to have been suppressed for him, and replaced by a freshness of feeling and imagination, which endured beneath the frost of age, like the eternal youth of the blessed. The conversations which we had with him within the last two months of his life often recalled to our mind the words of one whose memory is justly venerated: 'That the last thoughts of a heart filled with the love of God are like the last rays of the sun, brighter and more intense before it disappears.'*

"The courtesy of M. Vianney was not the cold and artificial politeness of the world, but that courtesy steeped in charity, cordiality, and sincerity, which sets every one at his ease. After the example of Him in whom grace and goodness first appeared in bodily.form, the servant of God, thought of all, cared for all, forgot none but himself, and forgot himself entirely. He wanted nothing for himself, not even consolation and sympathy; for he accounted him-

* Madame Swetchine.

self unworthy of them. Never did he utter a contradiction
or a refusal, except when he saw there would be error or
sin in compliance. During his long life he never opened
his mouth but to console; his heart, but to receive and
treasure up the sorrows of others; his hand, but to dispense
alms and benedictions.

"It is a difficult task, and one under which the best of
us sometimes fail, to preserve tranquillity in activity; recollection amid the most absorbing exterior labors; entire and
free self-possession, and constant union with God, in the
midst of hurry, noise, and press of work. The Curé of
Ars rose superior to this trial. As a pure current passes
through the salt waters of the ocean without contracting
aught of their bitterness, his soul passed daily through the
strife and tumult of human passion without losing a parti-
cle of its purity and peace. He was subject to none of
those vacillations which so often affect the strongest spirits.
At whatever moment he might be seen, surrounded, pressed,
assailed by the indiscreet multitude; harassed by absurd
and idle questions; tormented by impossible requests; called
hither and thither; intercepted whichever way he turned;
knowing not how or whom to answer,—he was always himself, always gracious, always amiable, always compassionate,
always ready to yield and to grant everything to all with a
tranquil and smiling countenance. Never could we discern
in him the slightest token of abruptness or impatience;
never the most imperceptible shade of discontent, or the
shadow of a cloud upon his brow; never a reproach or a
complaint, or one word louder than another on his lips.
When surrounded by the most clamorous and unrestrained
tokens of respect, confidence, and admiration; applauded,
followed, borne in triumph by the multitude; when he saw
them haunting his steps, hanging on his words, kneeling

for his blessing,—still was he the same: simple, modest, and ingenuous as a child; never seeming for a moment to suspect that his sanctity had anything whatever to do with this extraordinary concourse,—with the miracles celebrated by so many voices,—with that standing miracle which Ars, for a period of thirty years, presented to the world.

"Nor need we marvel at the equanimity of the servant of God. The life of severe restraint and austerity to which he had devoted himself is, at the same time, the purest and the calmest which it is possible to conceive. One thing alone enthrals the liberty of man, and disturbs his peace, and that is fear,—the fear of suffering. There is nothing, therefore, which can fetter or trouble him who has taken suffering for his glory and his delight. All the troubles and perturbations of the soul arise from the desires which are cherished, or at least suffered, there. We suffer only because we have still some will of our own; had we no will but God's, we should be always content. No more desires, no more pains. The holy priest had early attained to that true treasure of the heart, universal detachment. Having detached himself from all things and from himself, he had found himself and all things in God. He had established himself in the imperturbable possession of that peace, which is nothing else but perfect charity,—the pure love of our Lord, which is indifferent to all things but its object; which fears *neither death, nor life, nor angels, nor principalities, nor powers, nor things present, nor things to come, nor height, nor depth, nor any creature.**

"One remarkable feature in the character of the Curé of Ars, and one to which all who had the privilege of living in familiar intercourse with him will agree in bearing tes-

* Romans viii, 38, 39.

timony, was its singular consistency. There was never a single moment in which his brow did not bear, with unruffled majesty, the pure and delicate aureola of sanctity. In whatever position he might be found, wherever he was seen or heard, the *Saint* was always visible. Almost all men have their bad days, their hours of weakness and obscurity; when the stoutest hearts betray themselves, and the most masculine courage quails. It was not so with our venerable father. He might be observed closely and leisurely; his soul might be sounded to its most secret depths, and his life scrutinized in its minutest details, and nothing was lost in the analysis. He was never seen to act but in the most perfect manner; never to take any but the wisest and most heroic part; never to choose any but the most excellent objects. In all his actions he combined the utmost purity of intention with the greatest intensity of fervor; so that we know not, in truth, where to find an instance in which he could have been reproached with doing less well that which he might have done better. His least actions taught as eloquently as his greatest; and this is important to state, that the twofold instruction of his word and his works may survive him in that marvellous harmony of excellence by which even prejudice is disarmed. That which was visible to the world of this miraculous existence is nothing to what was hidden. Many have known the active life of this holy priest of Jesus Christ; it is above admiration; from whatever point we consider it, it is a miracle. Some few have witnessed his life of mortification; it would have been fearful even in days when penance was not so rare a thing as it is now. Very few indeed have been admitted to the knowledge of his interior life; and it is by that chiefly that we must estimate him."

The tender and considerate kindness, which was one of

this holy man's loveliest qualities, sprang from his total self-forgetfulness. He who never sought for sympathy under the severest sufferings of mind or body had all his own to give to those of other men, for he wasted none upon his own. He was kind to all; kind, most especially, to the poor, the weak, the ignorant, and the sinful. He was prodigal of consideration and attention for the meanest beggars who approached him, seeking not only to relieve, but to please them. He was sedulous in warding off from those around him the slightest pain, the most trifling contradiction.

"He had the same heart on earth," says M. Monnin, "that he has now in heaven." Perhaps the refinement of its tenderness was never so fully known as by his missionaries. "He was as sensitively careful and anxious for their health and comfort as he was sternly regardless of his own." "On one of the first Sundays that I had the happiness to spend with him," says M. Toccanier, "he had observed that I coughed a good deal during Vespers. What was my astonishment, after night prayers, to see my venerable curé come to me, through a stormy night, with his lantern in his hand, to say, 'My friend, I see that you have a bad cough; I am not at all tired; I will say the first Mass in your place, and catechize the children.'" He did the same thing several times when M. Monnin was with him. "Remonstrance was useless; for he would suddenly leave the confessional, and take possession of the pulpit before I had time to anticipate him."

He observed one day, when the cold began to set in, that the superior of the missionaries had not brought his cloak with him. He had one made for him immediately, of very good warm cloth. Another day, when M. Monnin had been seen crossing the market-place on a rainy day without an umbrella, he found one placed in his room on his return, which the good curé had sent for on purpose from Villefranche. ·

It has been said that, as in all high genius, so in all exalted sanctity, there is a feminine element, which is seen stamped upon the very features of the medieval Saints; and in this minute and considerate tenderness for all the creation of God, and all the redeemed of Christ, we recognize a love, passing, indeed, the mere natural love of woman, yet akin to it; a restoration to man of a gift and grace lost in Paradise, and surviving (in the natural order) only in woman's devoted affection for her nearest and dearest.

The considerateness was carried into the most insignificant details of the courtesies, as well as the charities, of his daily life. He never sat down in the presence of others; he never allowed others to stand in his own. When the missionaries took leave of him at night, wearied and worn as he was, no persuasion could induce him to omit paying them the respect of accompanying them to the door of the house.

"It has been truly observed," says his biographer, "that to acquire a great influence over the hearts of men, and to change the indifferent and the hostile into friends, sanctity alone is not sufficient,—that the Son of God became *man* when He willed that religion should become a law of love. In the holiness of the Curé of Ars there was this ineffable union of the Divine and human. How could men help loving him, who was so full of love, and whose only aim was to do them good, without a thought of requital? It was not by his alms and his material liberality that he mastered all hearts; it was by his graciousness, his benevolence; by the active and heartfelt interest which he took in others. With the growth of the interior life, his solicitude for his neighbor seemed to develop day by day. He became more and more tender towards others, as he redoubled his severity towards himself."

CHAPTER XVIII.

Virtues of the Curé of Ars—His faith, hope, charity—His humility, poverty, and mortification.

"THE Curé of Ars," says M. Monnin, "had received the gift of faith in a supereminent degree. His intimate union with God had rendered Divine truths sensible and palpable to him.

" Faith was the moving principle of his life. It was his only science ; it explained all things to him, and by it he explained all things to others. 'The faith of M. le Curé,' says Catherine, ' is so vivid, that he seems to *see* the things of which he speaks. He is so penetrated with the thought of the Real Presence of our Lord in the Blessed Sacrament, that he speaks of it in all his instructions. He would often repeat : *Oh how blessed are our eyes, which behold our good God !* and this with such an accent of intense joy, and an expression of such radiant delight, that it seemed as if he were beholding the vision of God.' "

Flashes of joy would sometimes flit across his eyes, which spoke of a bliss derived from no created source. He used to say, "We have but a distant faith, as if our good God were on the other side of the sea, some three hundred miles off. If, like the Saints, we had a living, penetrating faith, like them we should see our Lord. *There are priests who see Him every day in the Mass.*" We are told: " The idea that the holy curé actually saw our Lord at the altar, and knew Him in the breaking of the bread, occurred to all these who had the happiness to be present at his Mass. He seemed touched by a ray of the Divine glory. His heart, mind, soul, and senses were absorbed in God. In the midst of the crowd, and under the influence of the multitude of eyes which were fixed upon him, he enjoyed as undisturbed communion with our Lord as if he had been in the solitude of his poor chamber. He bathed His sacred feet with an abundant effusion of holy tears, which usually flowed during the whole time of the celebration of the Divine Mysteries. M. Vianney's Mass was neither too quick nor too slow. He made his own devotion give way to the service of his neighbor. The only time, as we are told by one of the pilgrims who used to serve Mass, at which he was longer than other priests, was that just before Communion. ' He then seemed to hold a mysterious colloquy with our Lord. He looked lovingly at the Sacred Host. His lips moved; then he stopped, as if listening; and again his lips moved, as if in reply; at last, by a visible effort, as if cutting short a conversation with a beloved friend, he consumed the Sacred Species.' "

When the Blessed Sacrament was exposed he gazed upon it with such an ecstatic smile, that a brother priest, who once caught the expression of his countenance when thus in adoration, instinctively turned towards the tabernacle, as if expecting to see something. He saw nothing; but the expression of M. Vianney's face had struck him so forcibly, that he said : " I believe the time will come when the Curé of Ars will live upon the Holy Eucharist alone."

" The Curé of Ars," says M. Monnin, " had received the gift of prayer in a supereminent degree. His soul was more closely united to God than to his body. In the midst of his most overwhelming labors, he never relaxed from his state of holy contemplation, dwelling continually in the presence of God, and beholding Him with a tender love in all His creatures.

"His mind, being free from the earthly vapors which darken the intellect and cloud its clearness, received, instead of the limited and imperfect notions of human science, those transcendent lights which enabled him to comprehend the relations of all things with their Creator, and their destination in the wonderful order of His purposes. Dwelling thus, by continual contemplation, in a region far above this world, he used his purified senses only for the practice of virtue. His will tended solely to the Supreme Good; but all this was inclosed in the invisible sanctuary of the soul; the sensible part had no portion in it. No outward sign was wont to reveal the operations of grace, except a pious and recollected bearing, indicating great interior concentration, but without a shadow of affectation or singularity. He was not one of those who, in the words of the *dear St. Elizabeth*, seemed to wish to 'frighten the good God by a sad or severe demeanor; he gave Him what he could cheerfully, and with a glad heart.' He was far from all exterior exaggeration, and averse to it in others."

He once advised a good priest who came to him for confession, and whose devotion struck him as being somewhat demonstrative, not to assume any posture in church which might attract attention. "My friend," added he, "do not let us make ourselves remarkable."

"M. Vianney," says his biographer, "had but one only thought,—but that ardent, generous, active, indefatigable,—to love God, and to make Him to be loved. God, and nothing but God! God always! God everywhere! God in all things! *Deus meus et omnia!* The whole life of the

Curé of Ars is summed up in this sublime monotony. Thirty years of an existence, of which every day was like all the rest. Always God's work; never the slightest admixture of his own; never did he allow himself the most trifling relaxation; never an instant's respite; never a passing indulgence of fancy, a momentary glance of curiosity."

The light and fire of this intense love of God fell upon all, whether persons or things, which were related in whatever degree to the object of his supreme affection. From the Sacred Humanity in its Ineffable Presence on the Altar, from the Immaculate Mother of God, from the spouse of Christ purchased by His blood, and her august head His Vicar on earth, to the least object bearing her blessing upon it; he loved and reverenced each in its degree, as stamped with the Divine image and superscription of the King of Heaven and earth. He loved pictures, crosses, scapulars, confraternities, holy water, relics above all; of which he used to say that he had more than five hundred in his possession. He belonged to the Third Order of St. Francis, and to many pious confraternities and sodalities. His devotion from early childhood to his Immaculate Mother has been already noticed. It was, indeed, next to the love of Jesus, the very passion of his heart. One of his great practices was to recommend a novena to the Immaculate Heart of Mary. "I have so often drawn from that fountain," he used to say, "that I should have exhausted it long ago, were it not inexhaustible."

He dwelt and conversed with the saints as his familiar friends. After St. Joseph, St. John Baptist, and St. Philomena, there were none whom he invoked more frequently than St. Teresa and St. Francis. His special devotion to the Seraphic Patriarch no doubt rested on a certain very perceptible resemblance of spirit between himself and the great pattern of poverty and simplicity.

He had a great devotion to the souls in Purgatory, for whom he offered up all his .sleepless and suffering nights, and a third part of his daily labors, crosses, and tears; the other two being devoted to the expiation of his own sins, and of the sins of his brethren still on earth.

"The fear of the judgments of God was," says M. Monnin, "his predominant thought; despair his besetting temptation." And yet the overmastering power of the love of Jesus with him, as with Blessed Paul of the Cross, cast out fear, and made him long for death, that he might look upon His face, who was, even here, "his life, his heaven, his present, his future." Once, after listening to one of his thrilling discourses upon the bliss of Heaven, some one asked him what was to be done to obtain so glorious a recompense. "My friend," replied he, "this only is needed,—grace and the cross."

"O Jesus," would he often exclaim, with his eyes full of tears, "to know Thee is to love Thee! Did we but know our Lord loves us, we should die of joy. Our only happiness on earth is to love God, and to know that God loves us. To be loved by God, to be united to God, to live in the presence of God, to live for God—oh, blessed life, and blessed death!" Hearing the birds singing before his window, he exclaimed with a sigh: "Poor little birds! you were created to sing, and you sing. Man was created to love God, and he loves Him not."

As we read these words we seem to catch a passing fragrance from the *Fioretti* of St. Francis; and again, "There was something which can never be forgotten in the tone in which he used to pronounce the adorable name of Jesus, and in which he would say, *our Lord*—as if his whole heart was overflowing on his lips." Who does not think of the long night's reiteration of *Deus meus et omnia*, or *The little Babe of Bethlehem*, which was as honey in the mouth of the Seraph of Assisi?

"It is impossible," says Catherine Lassagne, "to conceive how much M. le Curé had at heart the salvation of souls." He labored and wept for them by day; he suffered for them by night. He had prayed that he might suffer much during the day for the conversion of sinners, and during the night for the souls in Purgatory; and his prayer had been amply granted. A burning fever and unceasing cough tormented him on his poor pallet. He would rise at intervals of a quarter of an hour to try to get some relief out of his bed. And when worn out with pain and unrest, he was just beginning to find some repose, the time came for him to rise for his day of unremitting labor. So worn and weary was he that he had to drag himself along from one chair to another; and yet, without even a thought of giving himself another moment's rest, he went eagerly whither he was called by his burning love for souls, and, by the aid of the good Master who proportions His aid to the need of those who look to Him alone, was enabled to labor on, day after day, and year after year, in the same unceasing round of daily toil and nightly martyrdom.

"You have prayed," said he one day to a parish priest, who had been complaining that he could not touch the hearts of the people,—"you have prayed, you have sighed, you have wept. But have you fasted? have you watched? have you slept on the ground? have you taken the discipline? Unless you have come to this, you have not done all."

M. le Curé," said one of the missionaries, "if our Lord were to give you your choice, whether to ascend at once to Heaven, or to remain on earth to labor for the conversion of sinners, which would you do?"

"I think, my friend, that I should remain here."

"Oh, M. le Curé, is it possible? The saints are so happy in Heaven; no more temptation—no more miseries."

With an angelic smile he replied, "True, my friend; but the saints cannot labor for God. They *have* labored well; for God punishes idleness, and rewards only labor. But they can no longer, like us, glorify God by sacrifices for the salvation of souls."

"Would you remain on earth till the end of the world?"

"I think I would."

"In that case you would have plenty of time before you; you would not then get up so early in the morning?"

"Oh, yes, my friend, at midnight. I am not afraid of trouble. I am only afraid of appearing before God with my *poor curé's life*. But for this thought, I should be the happiest priest in the world."

Next to sinners, those nearest to the heart of M. Vianney were the poor. He loved them as the favorite and chosen representatives of our Lord. Not content with relieving the multitudes who came to seek him, he sought for those who shrank from making their wants known; and it was generally believed that he supported a number of families, who had fallen from better circumstances into indigence, in Lyons, and the neighborhood. Once, on being refused payment by a person to whom he had lent a sum of money, he said quietly: "He thinks that I have no need of money; yet St. Martin's day is near at hand, and I have the rent of thirty families to pay."

"We should never repulse the poor," he used to say. "If we cannot give them anything, let us pray the good God to inspire some one else to do so. Some say, 'They will make a bad use of what I give them.' Let them make what use of it they will; they will have to answer for the use they make of your alms, and you will have to answer for giving or not giving it."

To satisfy the demands of his insatiable liberality, the holy man would sell everything he possessed, even to his clothes. The old ones fetched a high price, as having belonged to him; and when he had nothing new to dispose of, he would sell old shoes, cassocks, surplices. If anything new were given to him, especially if of a better material than ordinary, it always went first. According to Catherine, if some one else had not taken charge of his wardrobe, he would soon have left himself without a change of linen.

M. Monnin observes, that "wealth has received this singular property from God, that division multiplies instead of diminishing it; and when it is cast from the right hand it falls into the left. Thus the ocean receives all the waters of the earth, because it returns them all to heaven. The heart and the hands of the Curé of Ars were like the ocean. This poor priest, so poor that he used to say he had nothing of his own but his *poor sins*, enriched all the world around him by his bounty. Gold and silver flowed into his hands from France, Belgium, England, and Germany, by a thousand imperceptible channels. He had but to will it to obtain immediately the sum necessary for a foundation or a work of charity. He often received considerable sums without ever being able to discover the source whence they were derived.

"Sometimes, though very rarely, it seemed as if the fountain were dried up. Then M. Vianney set to work to *torment his good Saints*,* till the mysterious stream began

* Cassait la tête à ses bons Saints.

once more to flow. He found money which he had never reckoned upon in his pockets, on his table, in his drawers, and even among the ashes of his hearth."

"When he wanted," says Catherine, "to establish a foundation in his church in honor of the Heart of Mary, he addressed this prayer to her: 'Oh, my Mother, if this work is pleasing to thee, send me the means to establish it.' On the same day, after Catechism, he said to us, 'I have found two hundred francs in my drawer. Oh, how good God is!'

"'Well,' said Jeanne Marie Chaney, 'since this is miraculous money, we must keep some of it. Who knows? Perhaps it may bring more.'

"'Yes,' replied M. le Curé, 'this is *celestial money.*'

"Jeanne Marie, in fact, took four of these five-franc pieces in exchange for others. She was sorry afterwards that she had not taken the whole sum."

Again:

"On the 19th October, 1839, M. le Curé said to us, ' A strange thing happened to me yesterday. I laughed at it all by myself. I perceived that my purse had been growing, growing. I looked into it, and found a handful of crowns, and a double Louis d'or.'

"'Some one has given them to you, M. le Curé.'

"'I don't know, but I think not. My bureau is locked, and the key was there in my table-drawer. Besides, this is not the first time such things have happened. I found a cask of wine in my cellar. It was not brought there by me, nor by my order. The poorer we make ourselves for the love of God, the richer we are in reality.'"

M. Vianney had set the children of the *Providence* to make a novena for an important object. In the course of the novena he met M. Tailhades, a priest who was staying with him at the time, and said to him, "I am in great perplexity. I owe three thousand francs. Ah, we ought to take great care not to get into debt."

"Be at peace, M. le Curé," said his friend. "The good God will settle it all for you."

In the evening they met again after the Catechism, and exchanged a few words. M. Vianney said, "I am going to count my money." A few moments afterwards he returned, saying joyfully, "Well, we have found money— plenty of money; I have been really loaded with it this morning. My pockets were quite weighed down, so that I was obliged to hold them up with both my hands. I was ashamed and afraid to be seen."

"You see plainly, M. le Curé, that our Lord wills you to remain here, since He works miracles in your aid."

"Oh, what our Lord does here, He can do quite as well elsewhere. When St. Vincent of Paul went right and left making his foundations, Divine Providence followed him everywhere."

"But, after all, M. le Curé, where *did* you find this money?"

"I found it somewhere. See here, again; a lady gave me this handful of crowns."

"M. le Curé, please to teach me how to work these miracles."

Instead of making a direct reply, M. Vianney said very seriously, "My friend, there is nothing which more disconcerts the devil, and more powerfully attracts graces and favors from God, than fasting and vigils. When I was alone, and could do as I would on this point, I obtained everything which I desired. Now," added he, with tears, "I cannot do the like. If I remain so long without food, I lose all my strength, and am unable to speak."

The next day he came again to M. Tailhades with a very bright countenance.

"I have found some more money. I said yesterday to the Blessed Virgin, ' My most holy Mother, if devotion to your Immaculate Conception is pleasing to you, get me some money to enrich the foundation which I propose to make in honor of your Immaculate Heart.' This morning I repeated my prayer; but I added, ' You must find me two hundred francs this evening. If the money comes later, it will not be for you.' And here is a person who has just brought me three hundred francs. I said to him, ' Oh, no, this would be too much; but I will thankfully accept two hundred.' "

"One day," says M. Monnin, "in the visit which he paid us after dinner, the Abbé Toccannier and I observed that he looked much brighter than usual.

" ' M. le Curé,' said I, ' you look quite radiant to-day.'

" ' I believe so, my friend. I have, at any rate, reason to be content. I have discovered this morning that I have wealth to the amount of two hundred thousand francs. And what is better still, this capital is placed out at enormous interest on the most secure bank in the universe. I have lent it to the three richest Persons I could meet with.'

" We did not at once understand this enigma, and asked Brother Jerome to explain it, who replied by producing the register of foundations. The sums collected for the single work of the missions amounted to 200,000 francs.

" The Curé of Ars founded also more than 1000 annual Masses, at the expense of 40,000 francs."

The intentions of some of these are singularly touching and characteristic.

Some were to be in honor of the Sacred Humanity of our Lord, to make preparation for the insults which He receives in the Divine Sacrament of His love; in honor of His Five Wounds, for the conversion of sinners; in honor of His agony in the garden, to obtain the conversion of the dying.

In honor of the Holy Ghost, to obtain the establishment of the Catholic faith amongst infidel nations.

In honor of the Immaculate Heart of Mary, for missionaries working among idolaters.

In honor of the same Immaculate Heart, for the priests of the diocese of Belley.

In honor of the twelve privileges of the Blessed Virgin, to ask her protection for those who receive the Sacrament of Penance.

In honor of our Lady of the Seven Dolours, to ask her protection for the dying.

To thank God for having preserved the Blessed Virgin from original sin; to praise the Holy Ghost for the honor conferred upon His Spouse by the proclamation of this blessed dogma; and to ask the protection of Immaculate Mary for children before their birth, that they may attain the grace of holy baptism.

Money never rested in M. Vianney's pockets. He took care to empty them twice a day. He was obliged to take certain precautions against his own lavish prodigality when he wanted to reserve a sum for any special purpose.

"Here," he would say to the widow Renard, who often acted as his treasurer on these occasions, "Claudine, I intrust this money to you; take good care of it. But, above all, be on your guard against the Curé of Ars; and if he asks for any of it, refuse him point-blank."

A priest who was building a church, and who was in consequence exceedingly short of money, said to him one day, " M. le Curé, I wish you would teach me your secret, that I may not have to stop half-way in the building of my poor church."

" My friend," replied the holy curé, " my secret is very simple—*to give everything, and keep nothing.*"

Humility, poverty, mortification—these links have formed the threefold chain of the marvellous life we have been following. A few more instances in illustration of these virtues must be noticed before we pass on.

" Our good God has chosen me," said the Curé of Ars, almost in the words which St. Francis had used before him, " to be the instrument of His grace to sinners, because I am the most ignorant and the most miserable priest in the diocese. If He could have found one more ignorant and worthless than myself, He would have given him the preference."

Such was his estimate of himself; and the proof of its sincerity was the reality of his desire to be so esteemed by others. Praise was a sensible suffering to him. When Mgr. Devie once called him unawares " my holy curé," his distress was painful to witness.

" Miserable wretch that I am !" cried he; " even my Bishop is deceived in me. What a hypocrite must I be !"

His mortification, as we have seen, extended to his whole being; heart, mind, and senses were all alike brought under its dominion.

" In this path," he used to say, " the first step is everything. Mortification has a sweetness which, when we have once tasted it, we can never bear to be without. We feel that we must drain the cup to the dregs. There is but one way of giving ourselves to God in the way of self-renunciation and sacrifice, and that is, to give ourselves wholly, without keeping anything back. The little we try to keep is good for nothing but to embarrass us, and afford food for suffering."

Of the austerity of his fasting, and the severity of his bodily sufferings, both from ill-health and by the direct infliction of the spirits of darkness, we have already had ample evidence. To these he added other severe corporal penances,—iron chains, heavy and sharp disciplines, and, perhaps more affliction still, the perpetual self-restraint by which he closed every avenue to the most innocent enjoyment of the senses, and refused to avail himself of the most ordinary alleviations of pain and discomfort. He had imposed, as a rule, upon himself never to smell a flower, never to drink when parched with thirst, never to brush off a fly, never to appear to be conscious of an unpleasant smell, never to express disgust at any repulsive sight, never to complain of anything whatever which affected him personally, never to sit down, never to lean against anything when kneeling. He had a great shrinking from cold, but would never take any means to preserve himself from it. He told the Abbé Tailhades that once, during a severe winter, both his feet froze.

"When I leave the confessional," said he, "I am obliged to look for my legs, and touch them, to find out whether I have got any. I cannot stand; and, to leave the church, have to drag myself along by the chairs and benches. Well, well! in Heaven we shall be well repaid; we shall think no more of all this."

Another day, when, from acute pain, he could hardly get up stairs, M. Tailhades offered him his arm.

"Oh, no," said he; "I have often mounted these stairs before. What shall I do when I am alone?"

"Perhaps," said his companion, "you have only got what you have asked for?"

He replied, "It may be so. Some years ago I said to our Lord: 'Only grant me the conversion of my parish, and I consent to suffer whatever Thou wilt for the remainder of my life.'"

Neither look nor tone ever betrayed what he was enduring. He would go on conversing with his usual cheerfulness, till, overcome by intense pain, he suddenly sank down upon a chair, and, when anxiously questioned by his friends, would reply, with a sweet smile, "Yes, I am suffering a little."

At the time when he was undergoing the severe persecution which we have described in the earlier period of his ministry at Ars, he was on the point of addressing a letter to his Bishop, which would have freed him from much of his trouble, and prevented its recurrence; when, however, the letter was brought to him to sign, he tore it, saying, "To-day is Friday, the day on which our Lord bore His Cross. It is fitting that I should bear mine. To-day the chalice of humiliation is less bitter."

M. Monnin tells us that the holy curé often said that his character was naturally exceedingly impetuous, and that to overcome it he had been obliged to use great violence with himself. "And yet," adds he, "we have seen him pressed, stifled, overborne by the crowd without evincing on his countenance the slightest shade of annoyance. We have seen him at the moment when the throng around his confessional was greatest, leave it three times successively to give Holy Communion to three different persons, who could just as easily have come all together; and this without showing the slightest sign of impatience, or even making an observation. We have seen him more than annoyed, *harassed* every hour of the day by the same person, who wanted to get out of him something which he did not think fit to grant. She showed an obstinacy totally wanting in tact or delicacy, and therefore extremely irritating. M. le Curé did not give way to her in the least degree, but, with a gentleness equal to his firmness, received her each time that she approached him as if it had been the first." These traits of great self-mastery in little things bring vividly before us that great pattern for daily imitation, the meekest yet most majestic of spirits, St. Francis of Sales.

The following instructions on the mortification of the will have a sound too of Annecy.

"We have nothing of our own but our will. It is the only thing which God has so placed in our own power that we can make an offering of it to Him. Thus we may be assured that a single act of renunciation of the will is more pleasing to God than a fast of thirty days.

"As often as we can renounce our own will, to do the will of another, so that it be not against the law of God, we acquire great merits, which are known to God alone. What is it which renders the religious life so meritorious? the unremitting renunciation of the will; the continual death of that which is most alive within us. I have often thought that the life of a poor servant-maid, who has no will but that of her mistress, if she knows how to turn this renunciation to good account, may be as pleasing to God as that of a religious who punctually observes her rules.

"Even in the world we may at all times find some opportunity of renouncing our will. We can deprive ourselves of a visit which would give us pleasure; we can perform some distasteful work of charity.. We can go to rest a few minutes later, or rise a few minutes earlier. Of two things which occur to us to be done, we can choose that which is least pleasing to us.

" I have known some holy souls in the world who had no will, who were wholly dead to themselves. *It is this which makes Saints.* Look at that *good little St. Maur*, who was so powerful with God, and so dear to his Superior, for his obedience. The other religious were jealous of him. The Superior said to them, 'I am going to show you why I have so high an estimation of this dear little brother.' He made the round of the cells; every one had something to finish before he opened his door. St. Maur alone, who was busy copying the Holy Scriptures, left his work instantly to obey St. Benedict's call. It is only the first step which is hard in the way of abnegation. When we have once fairly entered upon it, all goes smoothly; and when we have this virtue, we have every other."

———

CHAPTER XIX.

The Curé of Ars as a catechist, preacher, and director—His supernatural insight into the souls of his penitents.

" WHO was your master in theology ?" was a question once somewhat ironically addressed to the Curé of Ars. " I had the same master as St. Peter," replied he, with the most perfect simplicity. We are told that, both in his sermons and in his catechetical instructions, M. Vianney was not only precise and exact in his theological statements, but that he frequently expressed them in terms known only to scholastic divinity. *Whence had this man this wisdom,* but from Him who reveals it to little ones ? He spoke French— as we have been told St. John wrote Greek—incorrectly;

but, like him, *he declared that which he had seen, which he had heard with his ears, which he diligently looked upon, and his hands had handled, of the Word of Life.*[*]

His faith was his only science, his only book our Lord Jesus Christ. Those who heard him carried away the impression that he *saw* what he spoke of. " He spoke without any other preparation than his habitual recollection in God," passing at once from the confessional to the pulpit, and with that perfect self-possession which arises from entire forgetfulness of self.

"Timid and modest," says M. Monnin, "as was his ordinary bearing, he was not the same man when his audience, no matter how distinguished, was before him. He carried his head erect; his eyes flashed fire. ' You were not alarmed at your audience ?' was said to him one day. ' No; on the contrary, the more there are, the better am I content;' and then added, with a smile, ' conceited people always think they do things well.'

" If kings, cardinals, or the Pope himself had been listening to him, he would have said neither more nor less: for he thought only of souls, and made them think only of God. This true oratorical mastery stood him instead of talent or rhetoric, and gave to the simplest words from those venerable lips a singular majesty and irresistible authority."

In M. Monnin's pages we find many striking and beautiful passages taken down from the holy curé's sermons and instructions; but he tells us that it is impossible thus to give any idea of the power and energy of his words. "It was his whole being that preached;" and even when his voice was inaudible, as we have seen by the testimony of Bishop Ullathorne and M. Lacroix, the very sight of him moved

---

[*] 1 St. John i, 1.

and stirred the heart.   As to his style, he always used the very simplest expression in which it was possible to clothe the idea he wished to convey.   He availed himself freely of images drawn from nature, and from the associations of his early life of rustic labor.   His instructions, as well as his ordinary conversation, were full of incidents from the lives of the saints, told with the life-like freshness of one who lived habitually in their company.   The Curé of Ars," says M. Monnin, " without ever suspecting it, was a poet in the highest sense of the word; his heart was endowed in the highest degree with the gift of sensibility, and it opened only to give out the true note and the just accent."

"One spring morning," said he, " I was going to see a sick person : the thickets were full of little birds, who were singing their hearts out.* I took pleasure in hearing them, and I said to myself, ' Poor little birds, you know not what you are singing; but you are singing the praises of the good God.' "   Again we are reminded of St. Francis of Assisi. The following passages are from his catechetical instructions:

" Prayer disengages our soul from matter; it raises it on high, as the fire inflates a balloon.   The more we pray, the more we wish to pray.   It is as with a fish, which at first skims over the surface of the water, then sinks lower, and plunges still deeper.   The soul plunges, engulfs itself, loses itself in the sweetness of its communing with God.

" Time passes quickly in prayer.   I know not whether we then even desire Heaven.   Oh, yes.   The fish which is swimming in a small stream is happy, because it is in its · element; but it is still happier in the sea.   When we pray, we must open our heart to God, like a fish when it sees the

* Se tourmentaient la tête à chanter.

wave coming. God has no need of us; if He commands us to pray, it is because He wills our happiness, and because we can find happiness in nothing else. When He sees us coming, He leans His heart down very low to His little creature, like a father who bends down to listen to his child when it speaks to him. In the morning we should do like the infant in its cradle. As soon as it opens its eyes, it looks quickly through the room to see its mother. When it sees her, it begins to smile. When it cannot see her, it cries.

"We must do like the shepherds who are in the field in winter-time. (Life is, indeed, a long winter!) They make a fire; but, from time to time, they run in all directions to collect wood to keep it up. If, like them, we knew how to keep the fire of the love of God alive in our hearts by prayers and good works, it would never go out. When you have not the love of God in your heart, you are very poor; you are like a tree without flowers or fruit.

"In the soul which is united to God it is always spring.

"Like a beautiful white dove, which rises from the midst of the waters and shakes its wings over the earth, the Holy Ghost comes forth from the infinite ocean of the divine perfections, and hovers over pure souls, to infuse into them the balm of love.

"The Holy Ghost reposes in a pure soul as on a bed of roses.

"The soul wherein the Holy Spirit dwells exhales a sweet perfume, like the vine when in flower.

"He who has preserved his baptismal innocence is like a child who has never disobeyed his father. When we have preserved our innocence, we feel borne upwards by love as a bird by its wings.

" They whose souls are pure are like the eagles and the swallows which fly in the air. A Christian whose heart is pure is upon earth like a bird which is held by a thread. Poor little bird! He waits but the moment when the thread shall be cut to fly away.

" Good Christians are like those birds which have large wings and little feet, and which never rest on the ground, lest, being unable to rise again, they should be taken; so they make their nests on some high place, as on the point of a rock or the eave of a house. And thus should the Christian dwell ever on the height. As soon as we lower our thoughts to earth, we are taken.

" A pure soul is like a beautiful pearl: as long as it remains hidden in its shell at the bottom of the sea, no one thinks of admiring it; but if you place it in the light of the sun, it attracts all eyes. Thus the pure soul, which is now hidden from the eyes of the world, shall one day shine before the angels in the sunlight of eternity.

" The pure soul is as a beautiful rose, and the Three Divine Persons descend from Heaven to breathe its perfume.

" The good God makes greater speed to pardon a penitent sinner than the mother to snatch her child out of the fire.

" The elect are like the ears of corn which escape the reaper's hand, and like the bunches of grapes left after the vintage.

" Imagine to yourself a poor mother compelled to bring down the knife of the guillotine on the neck of her child: such is the good God when He dooms a sinner to hell.

" What will be the bliss of the just, when, at the end of the world, the soul, embalmed with the fragrance of Heaven, shall come to seek its body, to enjoy God for all eternity! The bodies of the just shall shine in Heaven like brilliant diamonds, like globes of love!

"What a cry of joy when the soul shall unite itself to its glorified body, which shall no longer be to it an instrument of sin or a cause of suffering! It will bathe itself in the balm of love as the bee in the flower, and so shall it be embalmed for all eternity.

"The priest is to you like a mother, like a nurse to an infant of a few months old: she gives him his food; he has but to open his mouth. The mother says to her babe, 'Here, my little one, eat.' The priest says to you: 'Take, and eat: this is the Body of Jesus Christ. May it keep you, and lead you to life eternal!' O blessed words! A child, when it sees its mother, springs towards her; it struggles with those who would hold it back; it opens its little mouth, and stretches out its little hands to embrace her. Your soul, in like manner, in the presence of a priest, naturally springs towards him; it runs to meet him; but it is withheld by the bonds of the flesh in men who give everything to the senses, and live but for the body.

"Our soul is swathed in our body like a child in its swaddling bands; nothing can be seen but the face.

"To love God: oh, how beautiful this is! We shall never understand what love is till we get to Heaven. Prayer helps us in some degree; for prayer is the raising of the soul to Heaven.

"The more we know of men, the less we love them. It is the contrary with God: the more we know of Him, the more we love Him. That knowledge enkindles so intense a love of God in the soul, that it can no longer love anything or desire anything but God. Man was created by love; therefore is he so prone to love. On the other hand, he is so great that nothing on this earth can satisfy him.

It is only when he turns to God that he is content. Take a fish out of the water, it will die. Well! such is man without God.

"There are people who do not love the good God, who never pray to Him, and yet who prosper. It is a bad sign. They have done some little good amid a great deal of evil, and God is repaying them for it in their life.

"Earth is like a bridge for crossing the water; it serves but to support our feet. We are in this world, but we are not of this world, for we say daily, *Our Father, Who art in heaven*. We must wait for our reward, then, till we shall be *at home* in our Father's house. Therefore it is that good Christians are always on the cross,—in the midst of contradictions, adversities, contempt, and calumny. So much the better. But we are surprised at this. We think that, because we love the good God a little, we are to have nothing to cross us, nothing to suffer. We say, Such a one is not good, yet everything prospers with him; do what I will, nothing succeeds with me. This is because we do not understand the value and the blessedness of crosses. We say sometimes, God chastises those whom He loves. It is not so. *To those whom God loves, trials are not chastisements, but graces.* We must not look at the labor, but at the recompense. A merchant looks not at the toil which his commerce costs him, but at the profit he makes by it. What are twenty or thirty years compared with eternity? After all, what have we to suffer? A few humiliations, a few rebuffs, a sharp word or two: these things do not kill.

"Oh, how blessed a thing it is that we can please God, little and low as we are!

"Our tongues ought to be used only to pray, our hearts to love, our eyes to weep.

"We are great, and we are nothing. There is nothing greater than man, and nothing less. Nothing greater, as regards his soul; nothing less, as regards his body. We take such care of our body, as if we had nothing else to care for; whereas, on the contrary, it is the only thing we ought to despise.

"We are God's work. A man always loves his own work. It is easy to understand that we are God's work; but that the crucifixion of God should be our work, is incomprehensible.

"Some people suppose that God the Father has a hard heart. Oh, how do they deceive themselves! The Eternal Father, to disarm His own justice, has given a heart of exceeding tenderness to His Son. No one can give to another that which he possesses not himself. Our Lord has said to His Father, 'Father, punish them not.'

"Our Lord has suffered more than was necessary to redeem us. But what would have satisfied the justice of His Father would not have satisfied His own love. Without the death of our Lord, all the race of men put together could not have made satisfaction for the smallest untruth.

"In the world Heaven and hell are kept out of sight: Heaven, because if men could but see its beauty they would hasten thither at whatever cost, and leave the world to itself; and hell, because if they knew the torments to be endured there, they would neglect no means to escape them.

"The sign of the cross is formidable to the devil, because by it we escape his power. We should make the sign of the cross with great reverence. We begin by the head, signifying the Chief, the Creator,—the Father; then the heart, love, life, redemption,—the Son; the shoulders, strength,—the Holy Spirit. All things remind us of the cross. We ourselves are made in the form of the cross.

" In Heaven we shall be nourished by the breath of God. The good God will place us as an architect places the stones in a building,—each in the place fitted for it.

" Heaven melts into the souls of the Saints. They bathe and drown themselves in its overflowing waters. As the disciples on Tabor saw Jesus only, so interior souls see our Lord alone in the Tabor of their heart. They are two friends who never grow tired of each other.

" There are some who have lost faith, and never see hell till they enter it.

" The damned shall be enveloped in the wrath of God, as the fish in the water.

" It is not God who damns us, but we damn ourselves by our sins. The damned do not accuse God, they accuse themselves; they say, I have lost God, my soul, and Heaven by my fault.

" No one has ever been damned for having committed too much evil to be forgiven; but many are in hell for one mortal sin of which they would not repent.

" If a lost soul could but once say, 'My God, I love Thee,' it would be no longer in hell. But alas for that poor soul! it has lost the power to love, which it had received, and which it refused to use. Its heart is dried up, like a bunch of grapes which has passed through the wine-press. There is no more happiness in that soul, no more peace, because no more love.

" ' Unhappy souls!' said St. Teresa; ' they do not love.'

" The goodness of God kindles the fire of hell. The lost will say, 'Oh, if God had loved us less, we should suffer less! Hell would be endurable. But to have been so much loved ! What anguish !'

"The friends of a dying man asked him what inscription they should place upon his tomb. 'Write this: Here lies a madman, who went out of this world without knowing how he came into it.' There are many who leave this world without knowing or caring why they came into it. Let not us do like them.

"If the poor lost souls had the time which we waste, what good use would they make of it! If they had but one half-hour given them, that half-hour would unpeople hell.

"When we die, we make restitution; we give back to the earth what we received from it. A little morsel of dust about the size of a nut: this is what we shall become. We have much indeed to be proud of!

"We must labor in this world, we must suffer and struggle. We shall have all eternity to rest in.

"If we rightly understood our happiness, we should almost say that we are happier than the Saints in Heaven. They live on their earnings, they can gain no more; while we can add something each moment to our treasure.

"The grace of God helps us to walk, and sustains us. It is as necessary to us as crutches to the lame.

"When we go to confession, we must fully understand what we are going to do. We are going to take our Lord down from the cross. When you have made a good confession, you have chained up the devil.

"The sins which we hide will all appear again. If we want to hide them well, we must confess them well.

"Our faults are like a grain of sand by the side of the great mountain of God's mercy.

"I know no one so much to be pitied as these poor people of the world; they have a mantle lined with thorns upon their shoulders, they cannot move without pricking themselves; while good Christians wear a cloak lined with rabbit-skins.

"The good Christian cares nothing for the goods of this world. He escapes from them as a rat from the water.

" Unhappily, we do not keep our hearts sufficiently pure and free from all earthly affections. Take a sponge which is very dry and very clean; plunge it into water, and it will be filled to overflowing; but if it is not dry and clean, it will absorb nothing. And so, when the heart is not free and disengaged from the things of earth, try as we may to plunge it in prayer, it will absorb nothing.

"When we give ourselves up to our passions, we twine thorns around our heart.

" We are like moles of a week old : no sooner do we see the light, than we bury ourselves in the ground.

"The devil keeps us amused till our last moment, as a poor man is kept amused while the soldiers are coming to take him. When they come, he cries and struggles in vain; they seize him for all his resistance.

"When men die, they are often like a bar of iron all covered with rust, which must be put into the fire.

" Poor sinners are frozen like snakes in winter.

"The slanderer is like the caterpillar, which leaves its slime upon the flowers.

" What would you say of a man who should cultivate his neighbor's field, and leave his own untilled? This is just what you do. You are continually turning up your neighbor's conscience, and leaving your own fallow. Oh, when death comes, how much shall we repent of having thought so much of others and so little of ourselves; for it is of ourselves, and not of others, that we shall have to render an account! Let us think of ourselves, of our conscience, which we should look at continually, as we look at our hands to see if they are clean.

"We have always two secretaries: the devil, who writes down our bad actions to accuse us; and our good angel, who writes down our good actions to justify us at the day of judgment. When all our actions shall be presented to us, how few will there be, even among the best of them, really pleasing to God! So many imperfections, so many thoughts of self-love, of human satisfaction, of sensual pleasure, of selfishness, will be found mixed with them! They have a fair appearance; but it is only an appearance: like those fruits which look ripe and mellow because the worm has touched them." *

He would often, though with great reserve and discretion, make use of recent events or personal allusions to illustrate some truth, or enforce the practice of some duty. Thus:

"Because our Lord does not show Himself in all His Majesty in the Blessed Sacrament, you remain in his presence without reverence. Yet it is *He Himself*. He is in the midst of you. Like that good Bishop who was here the other day; everybody was pushing against him. Oh, if they had but known it was a Bishop!

"We give our youth to the devil, and the dregs of our life to the good God, who is so good that He contents Himself even with this. Happily, all do not act in this way. There is a young lady, of one of the first families in France, who left this place to-day. She is hardly three-and-twenty: she is rich, very rich. She has offered herself as a victim to the good God for the expiation of sins and the conversion of sinners. She wears a girdle garnished with points of iron; she mortifies herself in a thousand ways, of which her parents know nothing. She is as pale as a sheet of paper. Hers is a beautiful soul, as pleasing to God as any now on earth ; it is such souls as this which keep the world from perishing.

" Two Protestant ministers came here the other day, who disbelieved our Lord's real presence in the Blessed Sacrament. I said to them, ' Do you believe it could detach itself, and, of its own accord, place itself upon the tongue of a person who was approaching to receive it ?' ' No.' ' Then it is not bread. A man had doubts about the real presence. He said to himself, What do we know about it ? It is not certain. What is the Consecration ? What passes upon the altar at that time ? But he desired to believe, and he prayed to the Blesed Virgin to obtain the gift of faith for him. Now listen well to what I am going to tell you. I do not say that it happened *somewhere*, but I say that it happened to me: when that man presented himself to receive Holy Communion, the Sacred Host detached itself from my fingers while I was yet a good distance from him, and went and placed itself upon the tongue of that man.' "

The Soul.

" How beautiful a thing is a soul! When our Lord showed one to St. Catherine, it seemed to her so beautiful that she said, ' Lord, if I did not know that there is but one God, I should take this to be a god !' The image of God is reflected in a pure soul like the sun on the water. A pure soul is the admiration of the Three Persons of the Blessed Trinity. The Father contemplates His work : This is my creature ! The Son, the price of His blood. We estimate the worth of a possession by the price it has cost us. The Holy Spirit dwells in it, as in His temple.

"Again we may know the value of our soul by the efforts which the devil makes to destroy it. Hell arrays itself against it—Heaven on its side. Oh, how great it must be! To form an idea of our own dignity we must often think of Heaven, Calvary, and hell. If we did but understand what it is to be children of God, we should be incapable of committing sin, we should be like angels upon earth. To be children of God—oh, what an exalted dignity! It is something grand to have a heart, little as it is, with which we can love God. What a shame is it to man to descend so low when God has placed him so high! When the angels had revolted against God, that God of infinite goodness, seeing that they could no longer enjoy the bliss for which they had been created, made man, and this little world which we see, for the nourishment of his body. But his soul also requires nourishment; and as nothing created can nourish the soul, which is a spirit, God was pleased to give Himself to be its food.

"But our misery is that we neglect to have recourse to this Divine nourishment as we pass through the desert of this life. Like one who dies of hunger at a well-spread table, there are those who go on for fifty or sixty years without nourishment for their souls!

"Oh, if Christians could but understand the language in which our Lord speaks to them: 'Notwithstanding all thy misery, I desire to see near Me that beautiful soul which I created for Myself. I have made it so great that nothing but Myself can fill it; I have made it so pure, that My Body alone is meet to be its food.'

"Our Lord has always singled out pure souls. St. John, the beloved disciple, rested upon His bosom. St. Catherine was remarkable for her purity; and so was she favored with frequent visions of Paradise. When she died, the angels took her body and bore it to Mount Sinai, where Moses received the Commandments of the Law. God showed by this miracle that so pleasing in His sight is a pure soul, that it merits that the body which has been a partaker of its purity should be buried by the hands of angels.

" God looks lovingly upon a pure soul; He grants all its petitions. How should He refuse anything to a soul which lives but for Him, by Him, and in Him? It seeks Him, and God shows Himself to it; it calls Him, and God comes; it is one with Him; it enchains His will to its own. A pure soul has an irresistible power over the loving heart of our Lord.

" A pure soul is with God, as a child with its mother. It caresses and embraces her, and its mother returns all its endearments."

Prayer.

"See, my children; the treasure of a Christian is not upon earth, but in Heaven. Well; our thoughts should be where our treasure is.

" Man has a high calling,—to pray and to love. You pray, you love: this is the bliss of man upon earth.

" Prayer is nothing else but union with God. When our heart is pure and united to God, we feel within us a balm which inebriates, a light which dazzles. In this intimate union, God and the soul are like two pieces of wax melted together: they can be separated no more. This union between God and His little creature is a beautiful thing. It is a bliss which surpasses our comprehension.

"We have deserved to be forbidden to pray; but God, in His goodness, has permitted us to speak to Him. Our prayer is an incense which he receives with exceeding pleasure. My children, you have a narrow heart; but prayer enlarges it, and enables it to love God. Prayer is a foretaste of Heaven, a drop from Paradise. It never leaves us without sweetness. It is a honey which flows into the soul and sweetens everything. Troubles melt away before a fervent prayer like snow before the sun.

"Prayer makes time pass with great rapidity, and so happily that we are unconscious of its duration. When I was travelling over La Bresse, at the time when almost all the poor curés were ill, I prayed to the good God all the way as I went. I assure you, the time did not seem long to me.

"We see some who lose themselves in prayer as the fish in the water, because they belong wholly to God. There is nothing between them and Him. Oh, how I love these generous souls! St. Francis of Assisi and St. Colette saw and spoke with our Lord as we speak to each other. While we—how often do we come to church without knowing what we come to do, or what we wish to ask! There are some who seem to say to the good God, 'I am going to say two words to You, to get rid of You.' I often think that when we come to adore our Lord, we should obtain everything we want, if we would ask for it with a very lively faith and a very pure heart. But, alas! we are without faith, without hope, without desire, and without love.

"There are two cries in man : the cry of the angel, and the cry of the brute. The cry of the angel is prayer ; the cry of the brute is sin. Those who do not pray crouch

upon the ground, like a mole which is searching for a hole
to hide itself in. They are all earthly, all brutish, and
think of nothing but the things of time; like the miser
to whom, when receiving the last Sacraments, a silver crucifix was presented to kiss: 'That cross,' said he, 'must
weigh full ten ounces.'

"If one day were to pass in Heaven without adoration,
it would be Heaven no longer; if the poor lost souls, in
the midst of their sufferings, were able to adore, there
would be no more hell. Alas! they once had a heart to
love God with, and a tongue to bless Him; it was the end
of their creation. And now they are condemned to curse
Him throughout all eternity. If they could hope that a
time would ever come in which, but for one minute's
space, they might pray, they would expect that minute
with an impatience which would make them forget all their
torments."

M. Vianney would sometimes thus paraphrase the Lord's
Prayer: " *Our Father, Who art in heaven.* Oh, my children, what a blessed thing it is to have a Father in Heaven!
Thy kingdom come. If I make the good God to reign in
my heart, He will make me to reign with Him in His glory.
Thy will be done. There is nothing so sweet as to do the
will of God, and nothing so perfect. To do things well,
we must do them as God wills them to be done, and in
conformity with His designs. *Give us this day our daily
bread.* We have two parts, our body and our soul. We
ask the good God to feed our poor body, and he replies by
causing the earth to bring forth all things needful for our
sustenance. But we ask Him to nourish our soul, which
is the most precious part of ourselves; and the earth is too
little to furnish our soul with that which will satisfy its

craving; it hungers for God, and nothing but God can fill it. And so our good God thought it not too much to come and dwell upon this earth, and to take upon Him a body, that this body might become the food of our souls.

"'My flesh,' said our Lord, 'is meat indeed. The Bread which I will give is My Flesh for the life of the world.' The Bread of souls is in the Tabernacle. The Tabernacle is the garner of Christians. Oh, my children, how beautiful this is! When the priest holds up the Host before you, and shows it to you, your soul may say, 'This is my food.' Oh, my children, we are too happy. We shall never understand it till we get to Heaven: how sad this is!"

The Priesthood.

"My children, we are come to the Sacrament of Order. It is a Sacrament which seems to have no relation to any of you, and which yet in fact bears a relation to every one. This Sacrament raises man to God. What is a priest? A man who holds the place of God, a man vested with all the powers of God. 'Go,' says our Lord to the priest; 'as My Father has sent Me, so send I you. All power is given to Me in Heaven and on earth. Go, therefore; teach all nations.'

"When the priest remits sins, he does not say, 'God absolve thee;' he says 'I absolve thee.' At the Consecration he does not say, 'This is the Lord's Body.' He says, 'This is My Body.'

"St. Bernard tells us that all comes to us by Mary. We may say also that all comes to us by the priest; yes, all happiness, all grace, every heavenly gift.

"If we had not the Sacrament of Order, we should not

have our Lord. Who placed Him here in this Tabernacle? The priest. Who first received your soul on its entrance into life? The priest. Who nourishes it, to give it strength for its pilgrimage? The priest. Who will prepare it to appear before God, by washing it for the last time in the Blood of Jesus Christ? The priest; still the priest. And if that soul should die, who will raise it again, who will restore it to tranquillity and peace? Once more,—the priest. You cannot recall to mind a single blessing from God without beholding by the side of that remembrance the image of the priest.

"Make your confession to the Blessed Virgin or to an angel,—will they absolve you? No. Will they give you the Body and Blood of our Lord? No. The Blessed Virgin cannot cause her Divine Son to descend into the Host. You might have two hundred angels round you, but they could not absolve you. A priest, simple and humble as he may be, can; he can say to you, 'Go in peace; I pardon you.'

"Oh, how great, then, is the priest! The priesthood can only be understood in Heaven. If we could understand it upon earth, we should die, not of fear, but of love.

"The other gifts of God would avail us nothing without the priest. What would be the use of a house full of gold, if there were nobody to open the door for you? The priest has the key of all the treasures of Heaven: it is he who opens the door; he is the steward of the good God, the administrator of His goods. Without the priest, the Death and Passion of our Lord would profit us nothing. Look at the poor heathen: of what benefit is our Lord's death to them? Alas, they can obtain no share in redemption so long as they have no priests to apply His Blood to their souls. The priest is not a priest for himself; he does not absolve himself, he does not administer the Sacrament to himself. He is not for himself, but for you.

"Next to God, the priest is everything. Leave a parish for twenty years without a priest, and it will worship the brutes.

"If M. le Missionaire and I were to go away, you would say, 'What should we do in this church? There is no Mass now. Our Lord is no longer there; we may as well pray at home.' When people want to destroy religion, they begin by attacking the priest; for when there is no priest, there is no sacrifice; and when there is no sacrifice, there is no religion.

"When the bell calls you to church, if you are asked, 'Whither are you going?' you may answer, 'I am going to feed my soul.' If they point to the Tabernacle, and ask you 'What is that golden door?' answer, 'It is the store-house of my soul.' And, 'Who has the key? who provides the food? who spreads the table?' 'The priest.' 'And the food?' 'It is my Lord's precious Body and Blood.' Oh, my God, my God, how hast Thou loved us!

"Now see the power of the priest. His word changes a morsel of bread into God! this is more than creating a world. Some one said, 'Does St. Philomena, then, obey the Curé of Ars?' She may well obey him, indeed, since God obeys him.

"If I were to meet a priest and an angel, I would salute the priest before the angel; for the angel is the friend of God, but the priest holds His place. St. Teresa kissed the ground on which a priest had trod. When you see a priest you ought to say: This is he who made me a child of God and opened Heaven to me in holy Baptism, he who has purified me when I have fallen into sin, who gives my soul its nourishment.' At the sight of a church you may say: 'What is there? The Body of our Lord. How comes it there? A priest has been there, and has said the holy Mass.' ✗

"What was the joy of the Apostles, after the resurrection of our Lord, once more to behold the Master whom they so dearly loved! The priest ought to feel the same joy at the sight of our Divine Lord whom he holds in his hands. We attach a great value to objects which have touched the shrine of the Blessed Virgin and the Infant Jesus at Loretto. But the fingers of the priest, which have been plunged into the chalice where His Blood has been, and into the ciborium where His Body has been laid, are surely far more precious.

"The priesthood is the love of the Heart of Jesus. When you see a priest, think of our Lord Jesus Christ."

The Holy Spirit.

"Oh, how blessed is this, my children! The Father is our Creator, the Son is our Redeemer, and the Holy Ghost our Guide.

"Man is nothing by himself, but he is much with the Holy Spirit; the Holy Spirit alone can elevate his soul and lift it on high. Why were the Saints so detached from earth? Because they suffered themselves to be led by the Holy Spirit. Those who are led by the Holy Spirit have a right judgment in all things. Therefore it is that there are so many ignorant souls who are far more keen-sighted than the learned. When we are led by a God of light and power, we cannot go wrong.

"The Holy Spirit is a light and a power. It is He who

makes us to discern between truth and falsehood, good and evil. Like those glasses which magnify the objects on which we look, the Holy Spirit shows us evil and good in all their magnitude. With the aid of the Holy Spirit we see all things on a large scale : we see the greatness of the smallest action done for God, and the greatness of the slightest fault. As a watchmaker discerns by the help of his magnifying-glass the most minute wheels of his watch, so by the light of the Holy Ghost we discern the most secret details of our poor lives. Then do the slightest imperfections appear great, the lightest sins horrible.

"The reason why the Blessed Virgin never sinned is, that the Holy Spirit revealed to her the hideousness of evil. She shuddered with horror at the slightest fault. Those in whom the Holy Spirit dwells cannot endure themselves, so conscious are they of their own misery. The proud are those who have not the Holy Spirit.

"Worldly men have not the Holy Spirit; or if they have Him, it is only at intervals. He does not dwell with them; the noise of the world drives Him away. A Christian who is led by the Holy Spirit feels no difficulty in leaving the good things of earth to pursue those of Heaven. He can discern the difference between them. The eye of the world cannot see beyond this life, as mine cannot see beyond that wall when the church-door is shut. The Christian's eye sees into the depth of eternity. The man who suffers himself to be led by the Holy Spirit feels as if there were no world; the world feels as if there were no God. It behooves us, then, to know by whom we are led. If we are not led by the Holy Spirit, do what we may, there is neither substance nor savor in anything we do. If we are led by the Holy Spirit, there is a sweet fragrance—an exceeding joy!

"Those who suffer themselves to be led by the Holy Spirit experience every kind of happiness within themselves, while bad Christians roll amid flints and briers.

"A soul in which the Holy Spirit dwells is never weary in the presence of God. Without the Holy Spirit we are like a stone by the wayside. Take in one hand a sponge filled with water, and in the other a flint; press them both equally : nothing will come out of the flint, while the sponge will give forth water in abundance. The sponge is the soul inhabited by the Holy Spirit, the flint is the cold hard heart in which the Holy Spirit dwells not.

"A soul which possesses the Holy Ghost enjoys a sweetness in prayer which makes the time spent in it seem always too short : it never loses the holy presence of God. Such a heart before our loving Saviour, in the holy Sacrament of the Altar, is like a bunch of grapes in the winepress.

"It is the Holy Spirit who forms the thoughts in the heart of the just, and inspires his words. Those who have the Holy Spirit bring forth nothing evil: all the fruits of the Holy Ghost are good.

"Without the Holy Spirit all is cold; thus, when we feel that we are losing fervor, we must hasten to make a novena to the Holy Ghost, to ask for faith and love.

"When we have made a retreat or a jubilee we are full of good desires; these good desires are the breath of the Holy Ghost, which has passed over our soul and renewed all within it, like the warm wind which melts the ice and brings back the spring. You even, who are not great Saints, have moments in which you taste the sweetness of prayer and of the presence of God. When we have the Holy Ghost, the heart dilates and bathes in Divine love. The fish never complains of having too much water; and so

the good Christian never complains of being too long with
God. There are some who find religion irksome; but it is
because they have not the Holy Spirit.

"If we were to ask the lost souls why they are in hell,
they would answer, 'Because we resisted the Holy Spirit.'
And if we were to ask the blessed why they are in Heaven,
they would answer, 'Because we followed the leading of the
Holy Spirit.' When good thoughts come into our minds,
it is the Holy Ghost who is visiting us.

"The Holy Spirit is a power. It was the Holy Spirit
who supported St. Simeon on his pillar; it is He who sup-
ports the martyrs. But for the Holy Spirit the martyrs
would have fallen like the leaves from the trees. When
the fires were kindled for them, the Holy Ghost extinguished the fierceness of the flames by the fire of Divine
love.

"When the good God sent us the Holy Spirit, He dealt
with us as a great king who sends his messenger to bring
one of his subjects to him, saying, 'You will accompany
this man whithersoever he goes, and bring him back to me
safe and sound.' What a blessed thing, my children, to
have the Holy Spirit for our companion! He is a good
Guide, and yet there are those who will not follow Him.

"The Holy Spirit is like a man with a good horse and
carriage, who offers to take you to Paris. You have nothing to do but to say 'yes,' and to get in. It is no hard
matter to say yes. Well, the Holy Spirit wishes to take us
to Heaven. We have nothing to do but to say yes, and to
let Him take us there. The Holy Ghost is like a gardener,
who cultivates our souls. The Holy Spirit is our servant.

"Here is a gun. Well, you load it, but there must be
some one to fire it off. So there is material in us wherewith to do good; the Holy Spirit fires the train, and good

works are the consequence. The Holy Ghost rests in the soul of the just, like the dove in her nest. He hatches good desires in a pure soul, as the dove hatches her little ones.

"The Holy Spirit leads us as a mother leads a child of two years old in her hand—as one who can see leads a blind man. The Sacraments which our Lord instituted would not have saved us without the Holy Spirit. The death even of our Lord would have been useless to us without Him. And therefore, our Lord said to His Apostles, ' It is expedient for you that I go away; for if I go not away, the Paraclete will not come to you.' The descent of the Holy Ghost was needed to render that harvest of graces fruitful. As with a grain of wheat: you cast it into the earth, but it needs the sun and rain to make it spring up and bring forth the ear.

"We should say every morning: 'My God, send me Thy Holy Spirit, to teach me what I am and what Thou art.'"

Suffering.

"Look at St. Catherine, who has two crowns,—the crown of suffering and the crown of purity. How glad is she now, that dear little Saint, that she chose rather to suffer than to consent to sin!

"There was a poor boy in a parish quite close to us who was lying sick upon his miserable bed, all covered with sores. I said to him, ' My poor little boy, you suffer very much!' He answered, 'No, M. le Curé. I do not feel my yesterday's pain to-day, and to-morrow I shall not feel the pain of to-day.' 'But you would like to get well?' 'No; I was naughty before I was ill; perhaps I should be naughty again. I am better as I am.' There was vinegar indeed, but the oil had the better of it. We do not understand this because we are too earthly. Children in whom the Holy Spirit dwells put us to shame.

"If the good God sends us crosses, we resist, complain, and murmur. We are so averse to everything which crosses us, that we want to be in a box full of cotton-wool, when we should be in a box full of thorns. The Cross is the way to Heaven. Sickness, temptations, and sorrows are so many crosses, which are to bring us to Heaven. All this will soon be over. Look at the Saints who have arrived there before us. The good God does not ask of us the martyrdom of the body, He asks of us only the martyrdom of the heart and the will. Our Lord is our pattern; let us take up our cross and follow Him. Let us do like the soldiers of Napoleon. They had to cross a bridge on which the enemy was firing; no one dared pass over it. Napoleon seized the standard, went forward, and all followed him. Let us do the same; let us follow our Lord, who has gone before us.

"A soldier told me one day, that in a battle he had walked for half an hour upon corpses; he could hardly find a spot to set his foot upon; the ground was red with blood. It is thus that in the journey of life we must tread upon crosses and sufferings, in order to reach our home.

"The Cross is the ladder of Heaven. How consoling is it to suffer under the eye of God, and to be able to say to ourselves in the evening, in our examination of conscience, ' Come, my soul, thou hast had two or three hours to-day of resemblance to Jesus Christ. Thou hast been scourged, crowned with thorns, and crucified with Him. Oh, what a treasure for the hour of death ! How sweet to die when we have lived on the Cross !'

"We must suffer, whether we will or no. Some suffer like the good thief, and some like the bad. Both alike suffer. But one knows how to render his sufferings meritorious; he accepts them in a spirit of reparation, and, as he turns to Jesus crucified, he catches those blessed words, 'To-day shalt thou be with Me in Paradise.' The other, on the contrary, howled, cursed, and blasphemed, and died in the most frightful despair.

"There are two ways of suffering: to suffer with love, and to suffer without love. The Saints suffered all things with patience, joy, and perseverance, because they loved. We suffer with vexation, impatience, and anger, because we love not. If we loved God, we should love crosses; we should desire them, and delight in them. We should be able to suffer for Him who vouchsafed to suffer for us. What have we to complain of? Alas! the poor heathen, who have not the blessing of knowing God and His infinite loveliness, have the same cross as we, but they have not the same consolations.

"You say it is hard: no, it is sweet, consoling, delightful; it is happiness. Only we must love while we suffer; we must suffer and love.

"Mark this, my children: in the way of the Cross it is only the first step that is hard. Our greatest cross is the fear of crosses. We have not courage to bear our cross—we are very wrong; for, do what we will, the cross holds us in its arms, we cannot escape it. What, then, have we to lose? Why not love our cross, and make use of it to take us to Heaven? But, on the contrary, most men turn their back on the cross and fly from it. The more they run, the more the cross pursues them, the harder it strikes, and the more heavily it weighs upon them. If you would be wise, go like St. Andrew to meet it, saying: 'Hail, good cross! admirable cross! O cross greatly to be desired! Receive me to thine arms, take me from among men, and restore me to the Master who redeemed me by thee.'

"Take good heed to this, my children : he who goes to meet crosses finds them indeed, but is glad to find them; he loves them; he bears them courageously. They unite him to our Lord; they purify him; they detach him from this world; they remove all obstacles from his heart; they help him to pass through this world, as a bridge helps us to cross water. Look at the saints; when no one else persecuted them, they persecuted themselves. When God did not send them sufferings, they invented sufferings for themselves. A good religious was complaining once to our Lord that he was persecuted. He said, ' Lord, what have I done to be treated in this way?' Our Lord replied, ' And what had I done to be led to Calvary?' Then the religious understood; he wept, asked pardon, and never again dared to complain. People of the world are in despair when they meet with crosses; good Christians weep when they have none. The Christian lives in the midst of crosses, as the fish in the water.

"We ought to run after crosses, as the miser after money. Nothing else will give us confidence in the day of judgment.

"The good God wishes that we should never lose sight of the Cross; therefore He places it everywhere,—along the road, on the heights, in the market-place,—that at the sight of it we may say to ourselves, 'See how God has loved us!'

"The Cross embraces the world; it is planted at the four corners of the universe; there is a piece for every one.

"If any one said to you, 'I wish very much to grow

rich; what must I do?' you would answer, 'You must work.' Well: to go to Heaven we must suffer. Our Lord shows us the way in the person of Simon the Chanaanite: He calls His friends to bear His Cross after him.

" Crosses are, on the road to Heaven, like a fine stone bridge over a river. Christians who do not suffer pass that river by a frail bridge, a line of wire, which is always ready to break under their feet.

" He who loves not the Cross may perhaps be saved, but it will be with great difficulty: he will be but a little star in the firmament of Heaven. He who has fought and suffered for his God will shine like a glorious sun.

" Crosses transformed into the flames of love are like a bundle of briers which are thrown into the fire and consumed to ashes. The briers are hard, but the ashes are soft.

" Oh, what sweetness do those souls experience in suffering who belong wholly to God! It is like the mixture of a little vinegar with a great quantity of oil. The vinegar is still vinegar indeed, but the oil corrects its sharpness so that we scarcely perceive it.

" If you put a fine bunch of grapes under the press, a delicious juice exudes from it: our soul under the pressure of the Cross gives forth a juice which nourishes and strengthens it. When we have no cross, we are dry; if we bear our cross with resignation, we feel a consolation, a sweetness, a happiness, which is the foretaste and commencement of Heaven. The good God, the angels, and saints surround us; they are at our side, and see us. The passage of the good Christian tried by suffering to the other world is like that of a person carried upon a bed of roses.

" Thorns give forth balm and the Cross sweetness. But

we must squeeze the thorns in our hands, and press the
Cross to our heart, to make them distil the fragrance which
is within them."

"Those who have only heard the Curé of Ars in his catechetical instruction," says M. Monnin, "only half know
him. They know the infused light, the supernatural grace,
the solidity, the transparency, and at times the elevation,
depth, and originality of his teaching; but they cannot estimate its unction, energy, and power. It was in his Sunday discourses that the missionary, the apostle, the inspired
prophet, the saint consumed with thirst for the salvation of
souls, came forth in his full power and mastery. These
discourses began with our Lord Jesus Christ, and ended
with Him. He was always before the eyes of the holy
curé, and always on his lips, because always in his heart."

The following extract is from a sermon on the Feast of
the Presentation:

" Have you meditated on the love which consumed the
heart of the holy old man Simeon during his ecstasy? For,
assuredly, he was in ecstasy when he held the Infant Jesus
in his arms. He had asked of God that he might behold
the Redeemer of Israel, and God had promised to grant his
prayer. Fifty years did he spend in this expectation, burning with desire for its fulfilment. When Mary and Joseph
came into the Temple, God said to him : ' He is here.'
Then taking the Infant Jesus in his arms, and pressing
Him to his heart, which overflowed with love, and kindled
at the touch of the Holy Child, the good old man exclaimed:
' Now, O Lord, let me die !' Then he gave back Jesus to
His Mother; he was only suffered to keep Him for one
moment. But we, my brethren, did we know it, are far

happier than Simeon. We may keep Him always if we will. He comes, not only into our arms, but into our heart.

"O man, how happy art thou, didst thou but understand thy happiness! Didst thou understand it, thou wouldst die for joy; ay, thou wouldst surely die for joy! Thou wouldst die of love! That God gives Himself to thee; thou mayest carry Him away with thee, if thou wilt; whither thou wilt,—He is one with thee!"

Sometimes he would allude to passing events which affected the welfare of religion or the Church. In 1849 he thus spoke of the sorrows of the Holy Father:

"It would seem that, in the absence of His Vicar, our Lord Himself is returning to earth to manifest Himself once more among men in His suffering humanity. You have heard of the new miracle which has taken place at Rome; the veil with which St. Veronica wiped the sacred face of our Lord was exposed the other day. While the Cardinals were kneeling before this sacred portrait, which had been nearly effaced by time, the sad and tearful countenance of our Divine Lord reappeared in perfect distinctness. Some, indeed, refuse to believe the miracle. You may as well try to make a blind man distinguish colors. By this apparition and these tears our Lord seemed to say to the Cardinals: 'Where is your father and My son? They have driven him away; where is he?' just as Mary said to St. Peter, after the death of Jesus: 'Where is thy Father and my Son? I see him no longer.' Our Lord wept for His Vicar, as a father who has lost his son, as a husband who has lost his wife. He has worked a miracle in behalf of the Pope. How holy, then, must he be! What alms can be so acceptable to God as to give to the Holy Father? You will have a share in his holy prayers. Our Lord has always shown a deference towards His Vicar: he is the depositary of all His treasures. We can do nothing, therefore, more acceptable to God than to pray for His Vicar until he is restored to his dominions. Jesus Christ asks us to do so by His tears."

In 1830, when crosses had been broken down in some parts of France,—

"They may do what they will," cried he, in the midst of his catechizing, with an indignant energy which electrified his hearers; "they may do what they will! The Cross is stronger than they; they will not always overthrow it. When our Lord shall appear in the clouds of Heaven, they will not be able to pluck it out of his hands!"

M. Monnin gives the following fragments from some of the holy curé's Sunday homilies on the gospel for the day; "very incomplete," he tells us, "yet having at least the merit of fidelity. They give the thoughts, and sometimes the expressions and images in which they were clothed. They may suffice to give an idea of his manner of preaching."

"We see in to-day's gospel, my brethren, that the master of the field having sown his seed in good ground, the enemy came while he was asleep, and sowed cockle in the midst of it. The meaning of this is, that God created man good and perfect, but that the enemy came and sowed sin in his heart. This is the fall of Adam,—a dreadful fall, which let in sin into the heart of man. This is the mixture of the good and the evil; we find sin among virtues. Do you say, We must root up the cockle? 'No,' replies our Lord, 'lest with it you root up the wheat also. Wait till the harvest.' The heart of man must endure thus unto the end,—a mixture of good and evil, of vice and virtue, of light and darkness, of good seed and cockle. The good God has not been pleased to destroy this mixture, and make for us a new nature in which there should be nothing but good seed. We must struggle and labor to hinder the cockle from overgrowing the whole field.

"The devil will come indeed to sow temptations around our steps, but by the help of Divine grace we shall be able to overcome them and stifle the cockle. The cockle is impurity and pride. 'Without impurity and pride,' says St. Augustine, 'there would be no merit in resisting temptation.'

"Three things are absolutely necessary as defences against temptation,—prayer to enlighten us, Sacraments to strengthen us, and vigilance to preserve us. Happy are the souls which are tempted! It is when the devil foresees that a soul is tending to union with God that he redoubles his rage. O blessed union!

"In to-day's gospel we read, my brethren, that a householder went out early in the morning to find laborers to work in his vineyard. Was there no one, then, already in this vineyard? Yes, my brethren, there was the most holy Virgin, who was born in the vineyard. What is this vineyard? It is the state of grace; and our Blessed Lady was born in it, for she was conceived without sin.

"We have been called into it. The householder came to seek us; but the holy Virgin was born there, for she was conceived without sin. Oh, what a blessed and beautiful laborer! The good God might have created a more beautiful world than this, but he could not have given existence to a creature more perfect than Mary. She is the tower built in the midst of the vineyard of the Lord.

"See, my children, this is an imperfect comparison. You know those eggs in the sea out of which we see the little fishes come forth, which cleave the waves with such exceeding swiftness: thus the holy Virgin, at the first moment of her creation, had the plenitude of life, and walked upon the wide waters of the ocean of grace.

" After the Blessed Virgin there was one who was for a few moments out of the vineyard, but lost no time in entering it: this was St. John the Baptist. All the rest came later, and needed the householder to come forth to seek them.

" Who are the laborers of the first hour? St. Louis Gonzaga, St. Stanislas Kostka, St. Colette,—all these entered the vineyard at holy Baptism, and never left it again, for they always preserved their innocence. Happy souls who could say to the good God, ' O Lord, I have always belonged to Thee !' Oh, how blessed it is, how great a thing it is, to give one's youth to God ! What a source of happiness and joy !

" Next come those who give themselves to God in the strength of their manhood. These also may be sincerely converted, and become good and faithful laborers in the vineyard of the Lord. But those poor hardened sinners who have spent their life far from God, who come and labor in His vineyard when they can no longer do anything else,— who wait to forsake sin till sin has forsaken them,—oh, they are much to be pitied. When they have wallowed for years on years in the mire of sin, it needs a miracle to rouse them from it. My brethren, let us ask this miracle for them."

On the Gospel of the first Sunday in Lent.

" Our Divine Saviour, having been our pattern in all things, was pleased to be our pattern also in temptation.

" For this end he suffered Himself to be led into the wilderness.

" As a good soldier fears not the battle, so a good Christian ought not to fear temptation. All soldiers are good in garrison; it is on the field of. battle that the brave man is distinguished from the coward.

" The worst of temptations is to be without temptation. We may almost say that we are happy to have temptations; it is the season of the spiritual harvest, in which we are garnering up stores for Heaven. It is like the harvest-time, when men rise early, and labor hard, but make no complaint, because they gather much.

" The devil tempts those souls only which are in a state of grace, or are trying to emerge from sin. The others are his own; he has no need to tempt them. A Saint, passing one day before a convent, saw a multitude of devils, who were tormenting the religious, but without succeeding in seducing them. He came afterwards to a city, at the gate of which one devil was seated, with his arms across, making all the inhabitants go wherever he chose. Then the Saint asked him how it was that he alone was sufficient for a whole city, while so great a number was employed to torment a handful of religious. The devil replied that he was quite enough for the city, because, when men are inclined to hatred, impurity, and intemperance, he took hold of them thereby, and the thing was done; while with the religious it was more difficult. The army of demons employed to tempt them lost their time and their labor; they could make nothing of them. So they were waiting till others should come who would weary of the austerity of their rule.

" In a monastery, one of the brothers saw a devil, during the time of the Holy Sacrifice, hammering on the head of one, and another, who alternately advanced and retreated.

After Mass, the brother asked the two religious what they had been thinking of. The one said that he had been thinking of some carpenter's work which he wanted to do in the couvent; and the other, that the devil had often come to attack him, but that he had each time driven him away. That is what all good Christians do, and so temptation becomes a source of merit to them.

"The most ordinary temptations are to pride and impurity. One of the best means of resisting them is an active life to the glory of God. Many people give themselves up to sloth and ease. No wonder, then, that the devil gets the upper hand of them.

"A religious complained to his Superior that he was subject to violent temptations. The Superior ordered the cook and the gardener to call him continually to help them. Some time afterwards he asked him how he was going on. 'Ah, father,' said he, 'I have no time now to be tempted.'

"If we were deeply impressed with a sense of the holy presence of God, it would be very easy to us to resist the enemy. With this thought before us, *God sees me!* we should never sin.

"There was a Saint once who complained to our Lord after a temptation was past, saying, 'Where wast Thou, O my loving Jesus, during this horrible tempest?' Our Lord replied, 'I was in the midst of thine heart, and was pleased to see thee combat so bravely.'

"At the moment of temptation we must firmly renew our baptismal promises. Listen, and mark this well. When you are tempted, offer to God the merit of that temptation to obtain the opposite virtue. If you are tempted to pride, offer the temptation to obtain humility; if by impure thoughts, to obtain holy purity; if to thoughts against your neighbor, to obtain the virtue of charity. Offer the temptation also for the conversion of sinners. This enrages the devil, and causes him to fly, because the temptation is turned against himself. After that, he will leave you very quiet.

"A Christian ought always to be ready for battle. As, in time of war, sentinels are always placed here and there to see if the enemy is advancing, so we ought always to be on our guard, to see whether the enemy is laying snares for us, or is about to surprise us.

"We are, in this world, like a ship at sea. What produces the waves? The storm. In this world the wind is always blowing. Our passions raise the tempest in our soul. These are the conflicts which win Heaven.

"We must not imagine that there is any spot upon earth where we can escape this conflict. We shall find the devil everywhere, and everywhere will he strive to rob us of Heaven. But everywhere and always we may come off victorious. It is not as in other contests, where, of two parties, one must be the vanquished: here, if we will, by the grace of God, which will never be wanting to us, we may always triumph.

"When we think all is lost, we have but to cry, '*Lord, save us; we perish!*' For our Lord is there, close to us; and He says to us, 'Of a truth thou lovest Me; I see that thou lovest Me.' And, indeed, it is in our combats against hell, and our resistance to temptation, that we prove our love to God.

"How many unknown souls there are in the world whom we shall one day see rich with the spoils of the victories they have gained moment by moment here! It is to these souls that the good God will say, '*Come, you blessed of My Father; enter into the joy of your Lord.*'

"Our guardian angel is always at our side, with his pen

in his hand, to write down our victories. We should say every morning, 'Come, my soul; let us labor to win Heaven. This evening our labors will be over.' In the evening: 'To-morrow, my soul, all the troubles of life will perhaps be ended for thee.' We have not yet suffered like the martyrs. Ask them if they are sorry now. God does not require so much from us. There are some whom a single word overcomes. One little humiliation is enough to wreck them. Courage, my brethren, courage! When the last day shall come, you will say, 'O blessed conflicts, which have won Heaven for me!' Let us, then, fight generously. When the devil sees that he has no power over us, he will leave us in peace. This is how he generally deals with sinners who return to God: he lets them enjoy the sweetness of the first moments of their conversion, because he well knows that he shall gain nothing by attacking them then,—they are too fervent. He waits a few months, till that ardor shall be passed; then he begins to make them neglect prayer and the Sacraments—he attacks them by various temptations; then comes the conflict; then is the time to pray hard for strength, and not to suffer ourselves to be discouraged. Some people are so weak, that when the slightest temptation comes upon them they give way like a piece of soft paper. If we would always march right onward, like good soldiers, when conflict or temptation comes upon us, we should raise our hearts to God and take courage. But we lay behind, and say, 'So that I be saved, it is all that I want. I don't mean to be a Saint.' If you are not a Saint, you will be a reprobate; there is no half-way; we must be one or the other; look well to it. All those who shall possess the kingdom of Heaven shall one day be Saints. The souls in Purgatory are holy, for they have no mortal sins; they have but to be purified, and they are the friends of God. Let us labor on, my children; a day is coming, in which we shall find that we have not done a whit too much to gain Heaven."

In a sermon on the second Sunday in Lent M. Vianney was enlarging upon the rapture of the Apostles on the Mount of the Transfiguration, which brought to his mind the bliss of the soul when admitted in Heaven to the clear vision of the sacred humanity of our Lord. Suddenly he exclaimed, as if in ecstasy,

"*We shall see Him! We shall see Him!* O my brethren, have you ever thought of it? We shall see God! We shall see Him as He is—face to face!" And for a quarter of an hour he ceased not to weep and to repeat, "*We shall see Him! We shall see Him!*"

On the twenty-first Sunday after Pentecost.

"My God, forgive us as we forgive.

"The good God will forgive none but those who forgive. This is His law. There are some who carry their folly so far as to omit this clause of the *Pater noster*. As if God did not see the bottom of our hearts, and took notice only of the movement of the tongue!

"The Saints have no hatred, no malice in their hearts. They forgive all who injure them, and always think that they deserve to suffer far more for their offences against the good God. But bad Christians are vindictive.

"As soon as we begin to hate our neighbor, God hates us. Hatred is like a dart, which returns into the bosom of him who hurls it. I said to a man one day, 'But you don't want to go to Heaven, then, since you will not see that person?' 'Oh, yes; but we will try and keep as far

as possible from each other, that we may never meet.'
They will not have this trouble, for the gate of Heaven is
closed against hatred.   In Heaven there is no rancor.   And
so good and humble hearts, who receive insults and calumnies with joy or indifference, begin their paradise in this
world, while those who harbor rancor are miserable; they
have a careworn brow, and eyes which seem ready to *de-
vour all who come near them.*

"There are some people who, under an exterior of piety,
take offence at the slightest insult or the least calumny.
Though we were so holy as to work miracles, yet if we have
not charity, we shall never enter Heaven.   A certain religious, who had never performed great austerities, enjoyed
great tranquillity at the point of death.   His Superior expressed surprise at his composure.   The religious replied,
'I have always pardoned all the injuries which have been
inflicted on me with all my heart.   I hope, therefore, that
the good God will pardon me.'

"The way to overcome the devil, when he excites feel-
ings of hatred against those who injure us, is immediately
to pray for their conversion.

"The devil leaves bad Christians very quiet; he troubles not himself about them; but he stirs up calumnies
and persecutions without end against those who are doing
good, and thus furnishes them matter for great merit.
This is the way to overcome evil with good; and this is
the way to be Saints.   But these mere outside Christians
will endure nothing; everything chafes them; they answer
sharp words by sharp words.   When fairly unloosed, they
give full vent to their hatred.   Their heart is like a reser-
voir full of gall, which they are always ready to disgorge
upon those who happen to be nearest to them.

"Our self-love makes us believe that we deserve nothing but praise; whereas we ought to acknowledge that we deserve nothing but insult. 'But I am innocent,' you will say; 'I do not deserve to be treated in this way.' You do not deserve it perhaps for what you have done to-day, but you deserve it for what you did yesterday. You deserve it for your other sins, and you ought to thank God for giving you this means of expiating them.

"In the parish where I was vicaire there was a person who devoted herself to placing out young girls. People often came to find fault with her. She always humbled herself, taking all in good part, and asking their pardon. And it came to be said of her, 'Oh! as to her, she is a Saint.' And indeed the Saints act in this way. This is true devotion. It is like St. John of God, who passed himself off for a madman. When the Superior of the house in which he was had received a letter inquiring if he had a Saint with him who passed for a madman, he went and asked his pardon; but St. John felt only one regret,—that he had been discovered, and should no longer have to endure the humiliations, blows, and painful remedies brought upon him by his supposed malady, which he had endured with imperturbable patience and obedience. A woman, whose son had been taken prisoner by the barbarians, came to impart her trouble to a priest. The good missionary, having no means of ransoming the prisoner, was much embarrassed. After a moment's reflection, he said to the poor mother, 'I will take the place of your son. Sell me, and redeem him!' She refused at first, but overcome by the urgency of the missionary she yielded. The son was restored to his mother, and the missionary remained a slave to the Turks, who loaded him with every kind of ill-treat-ment. This was perfect charity. He preferred his neighbor to himself. But we, on the contrary, are grieved at the prosperity of others.

"If one of your friends is praised, and nothing is said of you, you are discontented. If you see some one, after his conversion, making rapid progress in virtue, and arriving, in a short time, at a high degree of perfection, you feel pained at being left behind. If you hear him praised, you are grieved, and say, 'Oh! but he was not always like this. He was much like other people; he committed this fault, and that fault.' This is all pride; and there is nothing so contrary to charity as pride. They are like fire and water.

"The good Christian, my children, is not like this; he is compared to a dove, because he has no gall. He loves everybody: the good, because they are good; the bad, out of compassion, because he hopes that by loving them he will make them better, and because he beholds in them souls redeemed by the Blood of Jesus Christ. He prays for sinners, and says to our Lord, 'My God, suffer not these poor souls to perish!' This is the way to Heaven. While those who think themselves to be something, because they adopt certain practices of piety, but who are a continual prey to jealousy and hatred, will find themselves miserably deceived at the last day.

"*We ought to hate nothing but the devil, sin, and ourselves.*

"We ought to have a charity like that of St. Augustine, who rejoiced to see any one very good. 'At least,' he used to say, 'here is some one who will make amends to the good God for my want of love.' A man of quality, when passing through a wood, met the murderer of one of his kinsmen, whose death he had often promised to avenge. As soon as he saw him, he drew his sword. The other threw himself at his feet, and said, 'For the love of God, forgive me.' At the name of God the intended assassin, fearing to strike, sheathed his sword, and said, 'I forgive thee.' The next day he went into a church, and said to the good God, 'Thou wilt forgive me, for I have forgiven.' There was a large crucifix there, which bowed its head in token of assent. A man who had been imprisoned on an unjust charge of sheep-stealing was about to fall into despair. An angel appeared to him, and said, 'It is true thou art not guilty of that of which thou art now accused; but dost thou not remember how thou didst neglect to draw that drowning man out of the water whom thou mightst have saved, and didst not save? It is for this that thou art suffering to-day.' "

On the last Day of the Year.

" The world passes away; we pass away with it. Kings, emperors,—all pass away; they are swallowed up in eternity, whence they return no more. We have but one thing to do,—to save our poor souls. Look at the Saints; they were not attached to the things of earth; they cared only for the things of Heaven. Men of the world, on the contrary, think of nothing but the present.

"A good Christian does as those who go into a foreign country to amass wealth; they never think of remaining there; they have nothing so much at heart as to return to their own country as soon as their fortune shall be made. We must do like kings on the point of being dethroned; they send their treasures before them, to wait for them in the land whither they are going. So a good Christian sends all his good works before him to Heaven. The good God has placed us upon earth to see how we behave ourselves, and whether we will love Him. But nobody remains here. A man from Bourg, who had been condemned to a hundred years on the galleys, is said to have lived to return. All his contemporaries had disappeared; he recognized nothing but the houses.

"If we considered this well, we should keep our eyes continually raised to Heaven, our true country. But we suffer ourselves to be carried hither and thither by the world, riches, and material enjoyment; and think not of the only subject which ought to occupy our attention.

"Look at the Saints, how detached they were from the world and all material things! With what contempt did they regard all this! A religious, on the death of his parents, found himself in possession of great wealth. 'How long have my parents been dead?' said he to the person who brought him the news. 'Three weeks,' replied he. 'Tell me, can a dead man inherit property?' 'Certainly not.' 'Well, I cannot inherit from those who have been dead three weeks, for I have been dead twenty years.' Ah, the Saints understood the nothingness and the vanity of this world, and the happiness of quitting it for that bright hope of Heaven!

"There are two kinds of avarice,—the avarice of Heaven, and the avarice of earth. He who is avaricious of earth never carries his thoughts beyond time; he is never rich enough; he still grasps and grasps for more. But when the hour of death comes, he will have nothing. I have often told you. It is as with those who have laid in too large a store of provision for the winter; when the next harvest comes, they know not what to do with it, and find it much in their way. And so, when death comes, our possessions are only in our way. We carry away nothing; we leave everything behind.

What should you say of one who should heap up provisions in his house which will spoil, and be obliged to be thrown away, while he neglects to gather up precious stones, gold, and diamonds, which he could take with him wherever he goes, and which would make his fortune? Well, but, my children, we do just the same; we fix our affections on material things, which must all come to an end, and think not of gaining Heaven, the only true treasure.

"A good Christian, who is avaricious of Heaven, makes small account of the goods of earth; he thinks only of adorning his soul, and of gathering together that which will always satisfy, and which will last forever. Look at the kings, the emperors, the great men of this world: they are very rich; are they very happy? If they love God, yes; but if not, no; they are not happy. For my part, I think there are no people so much to be pitied as rich men who do not love God.

"The Saints were not attached, like us, to earthly goods, they were attached to that alone which shall abide with them to all eternity. Go from world to world, from kingdom to kingdom, from wealth to wealth, from pleasure to pleasure,—in none of these things will you find happiness. The whole world will as little suffice to satisfy an immortal soul as a spoonful of flour will revive the strength of a starving man. When the Apostles had beheld our Lord ascend into Heaven, they found earth so sad, so vile, so contemptible without Him, that they rushed upon the tortures which would deliver them from it, and unite them the sooner to their good Master. The mother of the Macchabees, who saw her seven sons die, and herself died seven deaths in the sight, encouraged them by these words: 'Look up to Heaven.'

"Our Lord has rewarded the faith of the Saints by

vouchsafing to them a sight of Heaven. Some of them have walked with Him in Paradise. St. Stephen, while he was being stoned, saw Heaven open over his head. St. Paul was ravished thither, and declared that he could give no idea of what he had seen there. St. Teresa had a sight of Heaven, and ever after, as she tells us herself, everything on earth seemed but as mire and dirt to her.

"But we,—alas, we are all earthly! We creep along on the earth, and know not how to rise above it. We are too dull, too heavy.

"Earth is a bridge for crossing the water.

"A bad Christian cannot understand that bright hope of Heaven which consoles and animates the good Christian. All that constitutes the happiness of the Saints seems hard and irksome to him.

"Consider, my children, these consoling thoughts: With whom shall we live in Heaven? With God, who is our Father; with Jesus Christ, who is our Brother; with the Blessed Virgin, who is our Mother; with the angels and saints, who are our friends.

"A king said sorrowfully in his last moments: 'Must I, then, leave my kingdom, to go to a country where I know no one?' This was because he had never thought of the happiness of Heaven. We must make friends there now, that we may find them after death; and we shall not be afraid, like this king, that we shall know no one there."

The extraordinary gift of illumination with which M. Vianney was endowed shone forth pre-eminently in his direction of souls.

"It seemed," says M. Monnin, "that in the mind of this humble priest there was a type of truth; a latent but infallible criterion; a key which opened to him the door of the most securely and carefully closed hearts; a clue which guided him through the labyrinth of the most intricate consciences; a chord which vibrated in unison with all that is right and just, and with which everything wrong or false jarred discordantly.

"In the words of Mgr. Devie, *the Curé of Ars was not learned, but he was enlightened.* The most lucid intellect does no more than receive the rays of light. With many men the light which they receive from Heaven is obscured by the shadow which the image of self casts upon their soul. Liberty and purity of heart are indispensable conditions of illumination.

"'Every passion,' says St. Thomas Aquinas, 'injures (in so far as it affects the soul) the rectitude of the judgment, and its faculty of giving good counsel. A man under the influence of any passion whatever always sees objects as either greater or less than they are in reality.'"

There was neither pride, ambition, nor avarice in the heart of M. Vianney; and consequently there was neither tenacity nor feebleness in his mind. He was not beguiled by the flickering light of the imagination, nor subject to the tyranny of the senses. He had that clearness and exactness of vision which comes from purity of intention, and which the Holy Ghost Himself infuses before time has bestowed the teaching of experience. In all his judgments reason was his law, and the will of God his guiding light. To him accordingly were brought for solution questions of every kind and degree, from the most intricate case of casuistry to the simplest detail of daily life; from the foundation of a monastery, or the inauguration of some new work of expansive charity, to the marriage of a daughter or the hiring of a servant.

The following questions have been heard by M. Monnin himself:

"Father, my mother is very ill. Some think she may recover; others that the case is hopeless. What am I to believe?—Father, I have a relation who is threatened with loss of sight; should he try an operation?—Father, will my daughter recover?—Father, my health will not allow me to do anything alone; will the good God procure me an assistant? A person has been recommended to me who would suit me in many respects; should I receive him?—Father, should I increase the number of my workmen?—Father, should I change my servant?—Should I sell my property?—Should I give up my business?—Should I go and live in the country?—Father, tell me in what college my son will be best placed, both with regard to soul and body?—My son has just taken his bachelor's degree; what career should he pursue?—Father an offer of marriage has been made for my daughter; should I give my consent?—Father, what ought we to think of La Salette?—Father, what ought we to think of the miracle of Rimini?—What ought we to think of Louis XVII?—Father, what ought we to think of such and such a mode of dress?"

"This question," says M. Monnin, "was often addressed to him."

The gravity of our subject will not allow us to introduce a letter, in which the question of a fashion then becoming prevalent was treated at great length, and with a seriousness which greatly amused M. Vianney.

"Poor ladies!" said he, speaking of the tyranny of this fashion; "they drag mountains after them. They incommode themselves and incommode others. They have done well to enlarge the streets; but they will soon have to widen the doors. Poor ladies! with all their fashions, they suffer in this life, to suffer in the other."

When the questions were idle, indiscreet, or painful to

his humility, he marked his perception of it by something slightly ironical in his reply :

"Father," said a lady, "I have been here three days, and have not been able to speak to you yet."

"In Paradise, my child; we will speak in Paradise."

"Father," said another, "I have come two hundred miles to see you."

"It was not worth while to come so far for that."

"Father, I have not yet been able to see you."

"You have not lost much."

"Father, only one word."

"My child, you have already spoken twenty !"

"Father, is my husband in Purgatory ?"

"I have never been there."

"Father, I wish you would tell me what is my vocation."

"Your vocation, my child, is to go to Heaven."

"Father, I have such a great fear of hell."

"Those who have a great fear of hell are in less danger of going there than others."

"Father, I am very bad and very slothful."

"When people address such severe reproaches to themselves, it is a sign that they do all in their power not to deserve them."

When he perceived that some lurking vanity or egotism mingled with the inquirer's desire to know his opinion, he would cut the matter very short :

"Father," said a very good young person, in whom he, however, perceived something of this kind, "tell me where I should go to make my novitiate,—to the Dames de la Nativité, or to the Dames du Sacré-Cœur? I should prefer the Dames de la Nativité, because they know me."

"Alas!" was M. Vianney's only reply, "they know no great thing, then."

The poor young lady was sorely disconcerted; but the mists of self-love were scattered, and she learned to look to God alone in the choice of her vocation.

"My child," said he with his sweet smile, to another, who had been long pursuing him with the same story, which he knew by heart,—"my child, in which month of the year do you speak least?" As she bit her lips in silence, "It must be the month of February," continued he, "because it has three days less in it than any other."

In all cases but such as these, the good father, as he was universally called, listened and replied with unfailing patience and attention to every question addressed to him.

His singular gift of discernment enabled him to give that counsel to every person who came to him which proved to be the most conducive to the perfection of each. He would advise one to enter religion at once, another to wait till some present call of duty had been fully discharged; he would advise a third to marry, and a fourth to lead a single life in the world.

A young lady, on recovery from a severe illness, had made a vow of chastity. Being afterwards sought in marriage with much perseverance, and finding in herself no marks of vocation, she was on the point of yielding; when M. Vianney showed her that nothing could compensate for the gift which she had made of herself to Jesus Christ, who had vouchsafed to accept her. He told her plainly that were she to prove faithless to her vow she would be miserable, and advised her at least to make a trial of the religious life. After much hesitation, she followed his advice, and is now an excellent religious.

"Father," said another, "from the time of the retreat

preparatory to my first Communion, I have felt an urgent desire to enter some cloistered order; I wish to fulfil what seems to me to be the will of God; but my family throw obstacles in the way. I am very unhappy. I get impatient with those who oppose my wishes. And at other times the thought comes into my mind that these desires are illusions and devices of Satan, who wants to disturb me and make me offend God."

"Poor child! It is indeed God who is calling you, and I believe that He means you one day to be a religious; but it must be with your parents' consent. If you leave home against their will, there will be no need of sending you out of the convent; you will come out of your own accord. Besides, your father and mother would die of grief, so strongly are they attached to you. In every house there is a privileged child, who is loved more tenderly than the rest. Well, you are the darling of your family. You must stay with your parents as long as they live. If you leave them, all will go wrong with you from that day forward."

This counsel was likewise followed; and after being the stay and comfort of her aged parents to their last hour, the dutiful and cherished child is now the happy spouse of Jesus Christ.

"M. le Curé," said a priest, "when I leave this place, I wish to make a retreat at the Novitiate of Flavigny?"

"You will do well, my friend; you will do very well.. Would that I could go with you!"

"M. le Curé, suppose our Lord were to bid me remain there, and take the habit of St. Dominic?"

"No, my friend, no; this desire does not come from Him. Stay where you are."

"Do not you think that our Lord may ask an account of

me of a good desire, which may have come from Him, and which I shall have stifled?"

"No!" very decidedly; "you are where He would have you to be. You will always have more good to do there than you will be able to accomplish."

"M. le Curé, give me your blessing, that I may always know and do the will of God."

"May that blessing, my friend, *urge you on and restrain you.*"

A parish-priest of the diocese of Autun came to him with a very complicated case, upon which no one whom he had hitherto consulted had been able to throw any light.

M. Vianney replied in one word; but that word threw so vivid and instantaneous a light upon the most obscure point of the question, that the priest could not help saying to himself, "Well! you have certainly some one who counsels you!" adding aloud, "M. le Curé where did you study theology?"

M. Vianney pointed to his prie-dieu.

So great was the estimation in which the holy curé's judgment was held, that there was scarcely a work of charity or a religious congregation, among the many which have sprung up with such wonderful rapidity within the last half century in France, which was not brought in its infancy to Ars, to be submitted to the ordeal of his spiritual sagacity and marvellous common sense.

M. Monnin gives the following instance of a congregation especially dear to the holy man's heart:

"On the 1st of November, 1853, a noble-hearted Christian* felt an inspiration in the presence of the Blessed Sa-

* Eugénie Smet, a native of Lyons.

crament to establish an association of prayers for the relief of the souls in Purgatory.' She asked our Lord to give her a token of His will on the subject. This token was granted to her prayer. The next day, being the festival of All Souls, it occurred to her, whilst making her thanksgiving, that there were religious orders for every want of the Church militant, and that there were none for those of the Church suffering. It seemed to her that God was calling upon her to fill up this void. She was at first terrified at the thought of the mission which seemed to be laid upon her, and she besought our Lord, by His five Wounds, to grant her yet further evidence of His will upon the subject.

From the month of November, 1853, till the June of 1855, this thought never left her. She obtained the manifestations she had asked. She felt irresistibly impelled to the task which she dared not look in the face, when she suddenly remembered the Curé of Ars, whom she had heard mentioned for the first time a little while before. The idea that this holy man had been chosen by Divine Providence to aid her in her undertaking became more and more deeply fixed on her mind, and she only waited an opportunity, which was soon afforded her, of entering into communication with him. In the month of August she received an encouraging reply. On the 30th of October she begged M. Vianney to think over her project on All Souls' Day. The holy curé remained for a long time with his head between his hands. Then he said with tears, " This is the work which God has been so long asking for." He then dictated the following reply, which was written by M. Toccanier on the 11th of November:

" The idea of founding an order for the relief of the souls in Purgatory comes directly from the Heart of our Lord, who will bless and prosper it.

"You may," added the Abbé Toccanier, "rest assured of these two things: that M. le Curé approves your vocation to the religious life, and also the new order, which he believes will extend rapidly in the Church."

The foundress, foreseeing difficulties on the part of her family, had recourse once more to the Curé of Ars, and received, on the 25th of November, the following reply: "To my great surprise, M. Vianney, who generally advises young persons not to oppose the wishes of their parents, but to wait for their consent, has no hesitation in your case. He says that the tears of natural affection will be sooner dried than those which are shed in Purgatory. He will pray that this terrible conflict between grace and nature may end in the triumph of grace."

By the advice of M. le Curé, the foundress went to Paris on the 29th January, 1856. Crosses of all kinds assailed the little band of fellow-workers whom she had succeeded in drawing together. No money, no work, much suffering. The holy curé only smiled at the recital of these trials.

"She had reflected well before she made her decision," said he to his missionary. "She prayed, she took counsel, she weighed beforehand all the sacrifices that were to be made; she has all possible guarantees of success; what is wanting to her? She wanted but one thing; she wanted only crosses. She has them. Tell her that these crosses are flowers, which will soon bring forth their fruits."

"Strengthened by these invigorating words," says M. Monnin, "the little community redoubled their prayers. Soon afterwards, in July, 1856, they obtained the house which they now occupy. From that time they have lived on the bounty of their Heavenly Father, receiving from Him their daily bread, and devoting to the care of the sick poor the time which is left free from their religious exercises. As the number of sisters increases, Providence increases their store; and fresh proofs of sanctity, as we can attest on our own knowledge, give token of the presence of God with them. Fully do they act up to their motto: *To pray, to suffer, and to work for the souls in Purgatory.* On the death of Mgr. Sibour, their first and zealous protector, M. le Curé thus consoled them: ' A house founded upon the Cross shall fear neither wind, nor storm, nor rain. Trials show clearly how pleasing a work is to God. You cannot doubt that your sufferings and sacrifices have already greatly served the cause of the suffering souls.'

"On the question whether they should continue to abandon themselves to Divine Providence, by devoting themselves exclusively to the care of the sick poor, he gave a speedy and very positive decision. ' Oh, yes, yes, unquestionably. These ideas of poverty and abnegation are excellent. In laboring for the deliverance of souls, and taking the works of mercy for the means, they realize in all its fulness the spirit of Jesus Christ; they relieve at the same time all His suffering members, both those on earth and those in Purgatory.' "

M. Vianney always showed a special kindness and cordiality to religious. He seemed more at home with them than with others, and greeted them as fellow-countrymen and countrywomen of the region in which he dwelt. His direction was suited, with the most exquisite tact and discrimination, to the state of the souls with which he had to deal. With some he confined himself within the circuit of the precepts, while he led others forth into the large and green pastures of the counsels. There was the keen eye, and the sure foot, and the tender guiding hand of the Good Shepherd.

"In direction," says M. Monnin, "the principal, as well as the most delicate, point is to follow the call of God, and to lead others to follow it; not to go before the Holy Spirit, but to proportion ourselves to the souls of others, that we may bring them into conformity with Jesus Christ. The diversity between the faces of men has its parallel in the diversity of their consciences. Each man is intended to walk in the way by which God calls him to come to Him. Each is to sow and reap in his own furrow, that there may be degrees in merit and shades in virtue,—stars of greater or less brilliancy in the firmament of the same glory."

" To render this discernment of spirits so sure and so intuitive as it was with the Curé of Ars, we have unquestionable evidence that he was endowed with a gift of reading the hearts of his penitents, not only supernatural, as are all gifts of the Spirit, but, strictly speaking, miraculous.

"To our certain knowledge," says M. Monnin, "he made known to many that they were making false confessions. It was a matter of daily occurrence for him to tell those who came to him, at first sight, what was their attraction, or their vocation, and by what ways God purposed to lead them."

An old sinner was sent to him from a distance. No one in the parish knew how long it was since he had been to the Sacraments. M. le Curé besought him, with tears, to return to his duty; and as he still resisted, laid his hand on his heart, saying, "There is something wrong there. How long is it since you made your last confession?"

"Forty years."

"It is more than that, my friend; it is forty-four."

A miserable man, who had signalized himself by highway robberies and every kind of evil deed, having ruined his health by his excesses, came to Ars in hope of obtaining a bodily cure. He presented himself to the curé, who at first refused to receive him. He was going away in a very bad humor, when he bethought him to go into the church. M. Vianney saw and beckoned to him. He went into the sacristy, saying to himself: "M. le Curé wants me to make my confession; but I shall confess what I like." When he had finished his pretended confession, M. Vianney, who had listened in silence, said, "Is this all?"

"Yes," replied the penitent.

"But you have told me that on such a day, in such a place, you committed such a crime." And he told the man the history of his own life better than he could have done himself.

The sinner's heart was changed; he made a good confession, obtained the cure both of body and soul, and, on his return to his home, became a model of penitence and piety.

A young man, who wished to put M. Vianney's discernment to the test, came to him with an air of great apparent contrition.

"I am a great sinner," said he, "and desire most earnestly to open my heart to you."

M. Vianney, instead of receiving him with open arms, replied very dryly, "My friend, I have not time; you will find priests to hear you elsewhere." And he turned away from him.

The young man expressed astonishment, and was told that M. le Curé had no doubt read his heart, and seen that there was no purpose of amendment there. He was advised to return to the church; and there he was struck by one of those sudden inspirations which sometimes bring a sinner back, spite of himself, to God. He was no sooner on his knees than he felt pierced with a sincere desire for conversion. He once more sought out the holy curé, who did not this time turn from him, but received him with all that overflowing tenderness with which he ever welcomed the returning sinner.

CHAPTER XX.

Miraculous cures and conversions at Ars—M. Vianney's knowledge of future and distant events—His visions and revelations.

THE life of its saintly curé was, as has been often said, the great miracle of Ars; yet our sketch of it would be incomplete were we to omit all mention of the supernatural cures, both of body and soul, of which we find so many interesting and fully attested relations in the narrative of M. Monnin. We have only space for a very few of these cases.

The earliest mentioned is related in Catherine's journal of the year 1838.

" One of the directresses of the *Providence* was dying of malignant fever, accompanied by delirium. The physicians had given her up. She had lost both sight and hearing. It was thought that she could not live out the day. This was on a Saturday. When she seemed to be actually in her agony, the prayers were read for the recommendation of the soul; she was quite unconscious of it. But suddenly she opened her eyes, and said, ' I am cured !' The blessed candle was still burning beside her. She asked, ' What is that candle for?' She was told that M. le Curé had just been saying the last prayers for her soul. She wished to

rise, which she did with the help of her companion, and
continued sitting up for a moment, feeling no remains of illness. The doctor was sent for, who found no vestige of
fever left, and could hardly believe his eyes. He declared
it to be a miracle. M. le Curé had said the evening before,
' I have almost scolded St. Philomena; I have been tempted
to reproach her with the chapel built in her honor;' by which
we saw that he had prayed for this cure. One of us," continues she, " gave a poor woman an old cap of M. le Curé's.
She put it upon her child, who had a wound in his head,
thinking to herself as she did so, ' The Curé of Ars is a
saint; if I had faith, my child would be cured.' In the
evening, when she was going to dress the abscess as usual,
she found that it had disappeared, and the wound was perfectly dry."

A poor man came to M. Vianney to implore the cure of
his child, who was a cripple. The curé exhorted him to
make his confession, which he was unwilling to do, as he
knew that he would be enjoined to give up his calling,
which was that of a violin-player to all the dances in the
neighborhood. However, he made his confession, and on
his return home took his violin, broke it to pieces in the
presence of his wife, and threw the fragments into the fire.
At the same moment his child jumped with joy, and ran
through the house crying, " I am cured !"

A poor soldier had a child about six years old, who was
a perfect cripple. Having lost his wife, he was on the
point of being obliged to leave the service, in order to look
after the poor little orphan. Happily it occurred to him to
make a pilgrimage to Ars. He obtained three days' leave
of absence, and went to Lyons. While he was waiting for
the omnibus which was to take him to Ars, some people,
who saw him carrying his poor little cripple in his arms,

cried out, "Where are you going with that poor child? You are very simple. The Curé of Ars is not a doctor.˙ You should take him to the incurable hospital."

No way disconcerted, the honest soldier made his way to M. Vianney, and told his story.

"My dear friend," was his reply, "your child will be cured."

The sentence was hardly finished, when a slight crack was heard; the crippled limbs were stretched out, and the child began to walk.

"In the February of 1857," says M. Monnin, "while we were preaching the Lent, a poor woman came to Ars, carrying in her arms a child of eight years old, who could not walk. For twenty-four hours did this poor creature hang upon the steps of M. le Curé, standing sentinel at the door of his confessional, rushing towards him the moment he appeared, and showing him her child with a gesture so expressive, and a countenance so moving in its suppliant energy, that we had not the heart to drive her away, as the Apostles would have done the woman of Canaan.

"M. Vianney had often blessed this child, and spoken words of hope and consolation to the mother. When they returned to the place where they were to lodge for the night, 'Mother,' said the child, 'will you buy me some shoes (sabots)? for M. le Curé has told me that I shall walk to-morrow.' Whether M. Vianney had really made this promise to the poor child, or he had so interpreted the kind looks and words which he had received from him, the sabots were bought, by the advice of the people of the house where the two poor creatures lodged.

"The next day, to the amazement of every one, the child who had been seen carried in so painful a manner by its mother, ran through the church like a hare, crying out to

any one who would listen to him, 'I am cured! I am cured!'
The poor mother was hiding her joy, her amazement, and
her tears in one of the chapels.   We saw her, questioned
her, and wished to present her at once to the holy curé,
who was at the moment preparing to say Mass.   She wanted
to see him, to speak to him, to throw herself at his feet.
The gratitude was choking her.   M. Vianney listened to
our petition in a cold and almost severe silence, which forbade our insisting upon it further.   After Mass, we made
another more successful attempt.   ' M. le Curé, this woman
begs that you will help her to thank St. Philomena.'   He
returned, and silently blessed the mother and child.   Then,
in a tone of the deepest annoyance and mortification, he
said, ' *St. Philomena really ought to have cured the little
thing at home.*'   A month afterwards we received the following letter :

" St. Romain, March 12th, 1857.

" Monsieur le Missionnaire,—In accordance with the
desire which you expressed to me at my departure, I write
to give you an account of my little boy, and to assure you
that he is perfectly cured.   He has had no return of pain.
He walks and runs as if nothing had ever ailed him ; and
yet the doctors had all given him up.   I am very happy.
Accept for all your goodness the sincere thanks of your
very humble and respectful servant,

F. Devoluet.

" In the summer of 1858, a sudden cure took place,
which was witnessed by all the pilgrims and inhabitants of
Ars.   A young man of Puy-de-Dome, who could only walk
with difficulty by the help of crutches, came to M. Vianney,
saying, ' Father, do you think I may leave my crutches

here?' 'Alas, my friend,' was the reply, 'you seem to have great need of them.' The poor cripple was not to be repulsed. Whenever he had an opportunity, he repeated his question. At last, on the Feast of the Assumption, just before evening prayers, he caught hold of M. le Curé on his way from the sacristy to the choir, and once more asked his never-ending question, 'Father, shall I leave off my crutches?' 'Well, my friend, *yes*,' said M. Vianney, 'if you have faith.' At the same moment, to the astonishment of all present, the young man walked with a steady step to the altar of St. Philomena, and laid his crutches on the step. He has never needed them again, and has since, in gratitude for his recovery, embraced the religious life in the Institute of the Brothers of the Holy Family."

At the close of a long series of cases, no less remarkable than the preceding, and of the full and numerous attestations which he annexes of their veracity, M. Monnin proceeds as follows:

" Besides, and above all these testimonies, the series of which is far from being exhausted, the mighty voice of public opinion proclaimed aloud the existence of a superhuman power at Ars, manifesting itself in these prodigies. For the last thirty years thousands of sufferers have come yearly to Ars, with a confidence which has never failed, and which has often been richly rewarded. All, indeed, did not find the health they sought; but all, according to the measure of their faith, received the graces of fortitude and resignation, a more Christian view of suffering, and a clearer insight into the privileges attached to it. No one that we have known went away without a blessing. The Curé of Ars received all with kindness; he consoled and encouraged them, and gave them the best part of his time, his counsels, and his prayers. But he was far from promising a cure to all. We have often spoken to him of one tried by long and intense suffering, borne with angelic sweetness and piety, for whom we could never obtain any answer but this, ' It is a cross well placed.' ' But she suffers so intensely; is there no hope of relief?' ' Yes, my friend, in Heaven.' This was his usual answer, when questioned about a sick person whom he knew he was not to cure. ' Patience; there will be no more suffering in Paradise.' There is now at Ars a poor man who waits, like the paralytic in the Gospel, for his cure. He spends his life in quarrelling with St. Philomena, and making it up again, according as his soul ascends or descends in the scale of resignation. On the whole, however, he is a model of conformity to the will of God, and a rare example of the power of faith to sweeten and render endurable the bitterest trials. This good man has always been, and still is, convinced that M. Vianney wanted but the will to cure him ; ' *his humility,*' he used to say, ' *spoils his charity.*' M. Vianney often went to see him on his poor bed. He exhorted him, cheered him, made him laugh ; for poor Michel was always ready to laugh ; but he never gave him the faintest hope of recovery. On the contrary, when spoken to of the hopes and desires of his obstinate client, he always said, ' He does not want his legs to go to Heaven. He will go there without them, and perhaps he would not have got there with them.'

" A religious was sent to Ars by his superior, who exceedingly desired his cure. The holy curé said to him, ' My friend, we must will what God wills. He wills to sanctify you by patience. You will see, at the hour of death, that you will have saved more souls by this illness than by all the works of zeal which you could have accomplished in health.'

"The superior was not to be discouraged, and two years afterwards the invalid returned by his orders to Ars. 'No, no,' said M. Vianney, once more; 'you will remain in this state; you are doing more good in it; you are more useful to your congregation; you are saving a greater number of souls.' The companion of the religious observed that the superior had great need of him; when M. le Curé made a gesture, indicating that God had no need of any one; and added, 'We must see things in God; we must enter into the ways of God.'

"One word more," continues M. Monnin, "before we close this chapter. In the world these things will not be believed: Christians, who know the value of humility before God will find no difficulty in believing them. They know what it costs to make a Saint; and they account the cure of a hopeless malady a far less miracle than that of the existence of a man wholly dead to self; seeking himself in nothing; humble and unmurmuring in humiliation; rejoicing to suffer amid continual sufferings. This miracle Ars has witnessed for half a century: the life of a man so austere and so loving, so gentle and so strong, so simple and so enlightened; so full of candor, sweet cheerfulness, and invincible courage; who suffered every contradiction, and endured every pain, without ever uttering a complaint, or being for one single day unlike himself; who was humble in the plenitude of the gifts of God, and amid the radiance of a popularity with which no contemporary renown can bear a comparison; who lived for forty years almost without food, sleep, or rest, under a daily toil of from sixteen to eighteen hours a day; and who finished his career of labor, suffering, and glory, without ever giving way to a sign of impatience or a moment of pride. In truth, if the holy man worked miracles, it was no fault of his, and above all it was no benefit to him. Of all the crosses which he had to bear, this was assuredly the heaviest. On account of this gift of miracles his patience was cruelly tried, his humility alarmed, and his time consumed by the exactions of the multitude. Well might he complain to St. Philomena, and beseech her to work these wonders in secret at a distance, to signalize her power over the soul rather than the body, and sum up his complaints in the naïve reproach, '*St. Philomena really ought to have cured this little one at home.*'"

"The justification of the sinner," says St. Thomas, "is the greatest of the works of God." And how often did He vouchsafe to work this greatest of His wonders by the means of the Curé of Ars? It was emphatically his work, his daily work, to which all the bodily cures and other miracles wrought at Ars were but secondary and subsidiary. In the sixteen hours which he spent daily in the confessional, he must, at a moderate computation, have heard no less than a hundred penitents, and that for more than thirty years.

"It will never," he once said himself, "be known in this world how many sinners have found their salvation at Ars. The good God, who has need of no man, has been pleased to make use of. me for this great work, though I am a very ignorant priest. If He could have laid His hand upon another, who had greater cause to humble himself than I, He would have made choice of him, and have done a hundredfold more good by his means."

It was not by his words only that M. Vianney made his way to the hearts of sinners; he moved by his tears those whose own eyes were dry. "Father," said a hardened sinner, who had long knelt unmoved at his feet, "why do you weep so bitterly?"

"Alas, my friend," replied he, "I weep because you do not weep."

The following narrative of a conversion effected by a look of the holy curé is given by the subject of it, M. Maissiat, who, after trying every phase of unbelief and misbelief, from Mahometanism to Mesmerism, died two years after his conversion a sincere and fervent Catholic.

"A week ago," said M. Maissiat to a priest who met him at Ars, "I left Lyons to make a month's botanical excursion across the mountains of the Beaujolais and Mâconnais. In the carriage which brought me from Villefranche, I met by accident an old gentleman of my acquaintance, who was on his way to Ars. He begged me to accompany him. 'Come with me,' he said; 'you shall see a curé who works miracles.' 'Miracles!' replied I, laughing; 'I have never believed in miracles.' 'Come, I say; you will see, and you will believe.' 'Oh, if you make a believer of me, you may indeed cry out a miracle.' 'Well, come for a walk to Ars.' 'I don't mind if I do; I have plenty of time before me. Ars is not far from the country I want to explore. I will come with you.'

"On our arrival, my friend took me to the house of the widow Gaillard, where we shared the same room. He woke me very early, and said, 'Maissiat, will you do me a favor? Come with me to Mass.' 'To Mass? I have not been at Mass since the day of my first Communion; could not you ask something else?' 'You will come to please me. There you will be able to see and judge of the Curé of Ars. I only ask one thing of you—to look at him well. I will find you a place whence you can observe him at leisure.' 'Oh, as to that, I care very little about it; but I care very much about obliging you. You wish to take me to Mass? Be it so; I am at your disposal.'

"We entered the church. My old friend placed me on the seat opposite the sacristy. Presently the door opened, and the Curé of Ars came out, vested for Mass. His eyes met mine; it was but one glance, but it pierced to the bottom of my heart. I felt as if crushed beneath that look. I bowed down low, and hid my face between my hands. I remained motionless during the whole of the Mass; then I tried to raise my head, and would have gone out; but as I passed the sacristy, I heard these words: 'Go out, all of you!' At the same moment a hand was laid upon mine, and I felt attracted as by some invisible force. The door was closed upon me, and I found myself face to face with that glance which had struck me to the earth. 'M. le Curé,' stammered I, 'I have a crushing burden on my shoulders.' A voice of angelic sweetness, which seemed not like any human utterance, replied: 'My friend, you must get rid of it immediately. Kneel down and tell me all your poor life; and our Lord will take up your burden; for He has said: *Come to Me, all you who are heavy laden, and I will refresh you.*' My trouble began to disappear; and without thinking that I was making my confession, I began to tell the holy man all the history of my life, since the day of my first Communion. During the whole time he wept over me, exclaiming from time to time, 'Oh, how good God is! how He has loved you!' I did not weep; but my heavy burden seemed gradually to be lifted off me, and at last I felt as if it were altogether gone. 'My friend,' said the curé, 'you will return to-morrow. Go to the altar of St. Philomena, and beg her to ask your conversion of our Lord.' I had not wept in the sacristy, but I wept plentifully at the feet of St. Philomena. To-morrow I am to receive absolution, and after it the Body of our Lord: have the charity to say

Mass for me, that I may not be wholly unworthy of so great a grace."

The Mass was said for M. Maissiat's intention; "And," says the priest who offered it, "I saw him afterwards receive Holy Communion from the hand of the venerable M. Vianney, peace and joy being depicted on the countenances of both."

In the course of the year 1842, a man advanced in years came to Ars with his niece, who wished to consult the curé upon the choice of a state of life.

"My friend," said the holy curé, "you are come for confession ?"

"No, Monsieur," replied he, somewhat disconcerted at the directness of the attack; "I have no such intention. I came simply to accompany my niece; and as soon as she has received your advice, I purpose returning home again."

"No, no, my friend; you must seize the opportunity; it may not return. I am old, and you are not young. In our long life we have witnessed the death of many of our fellows. There are men who reject mercy, and whom mercy in return rejects. Come, my friend, let us not lose time; for time will not wait for us."

"M. le Curé, this is all very true; but my confession will not be the work of a day. I should have to stay here some time, which would cost money."

The holy curé saw the kind of man he had to deal with, and said with a faint smile:

"My friend, do not let this disturb you; when your money is spent, you can apply to me."

"M. le Curé," said the old miser, in a tone of no slight annoyance, and at the same time taking some gold pieces out of his pocket, "I can pay my own way, thank God, and have no need of alms."

"My friend," was the grave reply, "fear not to spend this money for the salvation of your soul; it is the best use you can possibly make of it. Our Lord has said: *What shall a man give in exchange for his soul?* Remain here as long as is necessary for settling the affairs of your conscience, and prepare for confession at once."

This exhortation had an immediate effect.

"In the month of May, 1856," says M. Monnin, "we witnessed the conversion of an old blasphemer of eighty. The mention of the name of God, or of M. Vianney, never failed to put him in a fury. He used to call the holy curé an old sorcerer or an old hypocrite. The good father, who had been told of it, had the charity to go to the hotel to see this miserable hardened old man; for it was impossible to get him to the church. He went up to his room, and threw himself on his knees before him, weeping bitterly, and crying: 'Save your poor soul! save your poor soul!' The old man was converted; he began to weep, and to recite the *Ave Maria*, which he continued to repeat, almost night and day, all the time he remained at Ars. M. le Curé came morning and evening to hear his confession.

"A good and fervent Communion sealed the reconciliation with God of this poor laborer of the eleventh hour.

"On another occasion, the Curé of Ars saw a person come into the sacristy, whom it was easy to recognize by his appearance and manner as a man of the world. The stranger approached him respectfully; and the good curé, concluding he came for confession, pointed to the little prie-dieu, on which his penitents were accustomed to kneel.

"The fine gentleman, who perfectly understood the gesture, hastened to explain:

"'M. le Curé, I am not come for confession; I want to reason with you.'

"'Oh, my friend, you have made a great mistake; I am no reasoner: but if you are in need of consolation' (his finger again pointed inflexibly to the prie-dieu), 'place yourself there, and be assured that many have done so before you, and have not repented of it.'

"'But, M. le Curé, I have already done myself the honor of telling you that I did not come for confession, and that for a reason which appears to me simple and decisive,—I have no faith; I believe as little in confession as in anything else.'

"'You have no faith, my friend! Oh, how I pity you! You are living in a mist. A little child of eight years old, who has learnt his catechism, knows more than you. I thought myself very ignorant; but you are far more so, for you are ignorant of the very first things which we ought to know. You have no faith! Well, that is a reason for me to torment you, which I should not otherwise have ventured to do. It is for your good. Place yourself there, and I will hear your confession. When you have made it, you will have travelled a long way on the road to faith.'

"'But, M. le Curé, it is neither more nor less than a comedy that you are advising me to act with you. I beg of you to believe that I have no taste for it; I am no comedian.'

"'Place yourself there, I tell you!'

"The man, overmastered by the tone of mingled sweetness and authority in which the words were spoken, fell upon his knees in spite of himself. He made the long-unused sign of the cross, and began the humble acknowledgment of his faults. He arose, not only comforted, but fully believing, having experienced the truth which rests on the eternal word of our Divine Master: *He that doth the truth cometh to the light.*

"As he left the little sacristy, where he had found the peace so long and vainly sought elsewhere, the infidel of but an hour ago could not restrain the expression of his joy: 'What a man,' said he,—'what a man this is! Nobody ever spoke to me in this way before. If he had not taken hold of me in this manner, it would have been long enough before I should have made my confession!'"

"The confessions effected by the Curé of Ars," says M. Monnin, "however sudden, were solid and durable. Men abandoned to a reprobate mind, addicted to passions which are commonly judged to be incurable, yielded to the grace which wrought and spoke in him. We know a drunkard of sixty years who has never fallen into his habitual vice since he visited Ars. The vicaire of his parish describes him as one of his most fervent penitents and most constant communicants."

Numerous instances are given by M. Monnin in proof of the infused knowledge possessed by the holy curé of future or distant events. A pilgrim came to ask his prayers for the recovery of a servant.

"Yes, my friend," said M. Vianney, who had never seen her; "it is for Marie; I see her in the choir."

"Strange," said the pilgrim to himself, "that he should know her name; he is mistaken at least on one point, for she is at the end of the church." On leaving the sacristy he found her in the choir.

A religious of the convent of St. Clotilde at Paris wrote to ask his prayers for a relation then in the Crimean war, and also for a nun in the convent who was very ill.

"The arms of the soldier," said he, "will be prosperous.

The religious will be more useful to her community in Heaven than on earth."

The soldier returned unwounded, after passing through manifold dangers; and the invalid died within a month after the words were spoken.

A young lady was in great anxiety as to the fate of her husband.

"What shall we say to this poor child?" said one of the missionaries.

"Say that there is nothing to fear, and that peace will soon be concluded." The interview of Villafranca took place a few days afterwards.

Of revelations, visions, and sensible and extraordinary graces, the following instances are related:

"On the 25th September, 1858," says M. Toccanier, "in the presence of M. Martin, our Saint confessed to me, that on two different occasions our Lord had made known to him, by a strong inspiration, that the best use to which he could put the money intrusted to his disposal was the foundation of missions. He added, 'Such is my love for the missions, that when I die, I would sell my body, if I could, to found one.'"

A person very intimate with the holy curé related the following fact to M. Monnin the day after his death:

"On the 3d of May 1859, in a visit which I paid to M. le Curé, I spoke to him of my attraction for those works which relate to the salvation of the soul in preference to any other. He signified his approval, and added:

"'I was in a little difficulty how to ascertain the will of God on this subject. St. Philomena appeared to me. She descended from Heaven, all luminous and beautiful, enveloped in a white cloud, and said to me: Thy works are good, for there is nothing more precious than the salvation of souls.' While he was speaking to me of this vision, M. Vianney was standing by his hearth, his eyes raised to Heaven, his face radiant with the remembrance, which seemed still to fill him with ecstasy." He had told the same thing, though with fewer details, to Catherine.

"By dint of cross-questioning," says M. Toccanier, "I drew from him the confession that our Lord had given him wonderful signs to prove that his ministry was acceptable to Him. He told me that one night a person had stood by his bedside, and spoken sweetly to him. 'It was not the *grappin*,' added he; 'the grappin has a shrill voice.' 'It was, then, a holy apparition?' said I. He suddenly changed the conversation, as if repenting of having said so much.

"Another day he said with much simplicity: 'About two months ago, when I could not sleep, I was sitting on my bed weeping over my poor sins. I heard a very sweet voice whisper in my ear, *In te, Domine, speravi; non confundar in æternum*. This encouraged me a little; but as the trouble of mind still continued, the same voice repeated still more distinctly: *In te, Domine, speravi;* 'This time it was certainly not the grappin.' 'It would seem not.' 'Did you see anything?' 'No, my friend.' 'Perhaps it was your guardian angel.' 'I know not.'"

On another occasion, when speaking of the foundations he had just made, he acknowledged to M. Toccanier, in the presence of the Brothers of the Holy Family, that in the night-time he wearied the Saints with prayers.* "You pray in the night, too, M. le Curé?" "It is when I wake. I am old now, and have not long to live. I must make the

---

* Qu'il cassait la tête à ses bons Saints à force de les prier.

most of every moment." "You lie on the hard boards, and do not sleep much." He replied, with an expression of singular solemnity on his countenance, "One is not *always* sleeping on the hard boards," and immediately changed the conversation, as if he feared those few words might suggest to his friend an idea of the heavenly visitants sent to make joyful and glorious the place of his unrest.

CHAPTER XXI.

Death and burial of M. Vianney—Funeral sermon by the Bishop of Belley.

A LETTER written from Ars during the Lent of 1840, nearly twenty years before the death of M. Vianney, gives the following picture of his sufferings at that time:

"The sight of what our holy curé endures is really heart-rending. It is impossible to see and hear him without unbounded pity and admiration for this sublime and continual sacrifice; for the zeal, the resignation, and the sweetness, with which he suffers himself, day after day, to be oppressed and stifled by the ever-increasing multitudes who come to him for a last counsel or a last benediction. Will he be able to continue the prayers and instruction, which he gives us every evening, till the end of Lent? or will that feeble voice soon pass away from earth, to swell the eternal *alleluia?* We know not, in fact, what to hope or expect, such is now the weakness and exhaustion of the holy penitent. The doctor has discovered the seeds of many maladies, all accompanied by acute suffering. You would have wept yesterday to see him sink into his seat during the singing of the *Vexilla*. I thought it would be the last time that he would ever salute that cross, his *only hope*. The contractions of his limbs bore evidence of the agony he was enduring. Suddenly he rose, and, in a voice trembling with pain, described to us, in words of fire, the might of prayer. Nothing but a miracle can account for this marvellous existence."

Again: "The holiness of our curé goes on increasing, and his nourishment decreasing."

In 1859, M. Monnin writes: "For a long time past M. Vianney had seemed to retain but a breath of life. The little thread of voice which remained to him was so feeble that it could be heard only by a very attentive ear. All the energy of his life and mind seemed concentrated in his eyes, which burned like two brilliant stars in their deep recesses, betokening strength in weakness, and life in death.

"The intense heat of the month of July, 1859, had tried him cruelly: he had fainted several times. The heat of the church, filled night and day by an immense crowd, was suffocating. Those who were waiting their turn for confession were obliged to go out continually, to breathe a little fresh air, from the heat of this intolerable furnace. But *he* never went out; he never left his post of glorious suffering; he never thought of shortening those long hours of endurance, which lasted in the morning from one o'clock to eleven, and in the evening from one to eight; he breathed nothing but that burning, vitiated, deadly air, which is fatal to human life. It killed him at last; he sank under this slow and painful martyrdom.

"Yet we were far from anticipating his end; so accus-

tomed were we to enjoy his presence, to believe in the miracle of his preservation; such care did he take to conceal to
the very last moment the prostration of nature. We only
know that, when he rose in the night to return to his dear
sinners, he had several times fallen down in his room or on
the stairs. And when we remarked that the sharp cough,
from which he had suffered for five-and-twenty years, was
more tearing and incessant than usual, he only answered
with a smile: 'It is troublesome; it takes up all my time.'
The Curé of Ars had exhausted all his remaining strength
in this last struggle of his closing years, this desperate conflict with the infirmities of age. He was at the haven where
he had desired to be. And when death càme, he had nothing to yield up to its power but members broken by labors,
vigils, and fasting; a body reduced by a slow and cruel
immolation to the transparency of what the ancients were
wont to call a *shade*.

"His end was remarkable only for its astonishing simplicity. His death was as hidden as his life had been.

"Many expected to see, at the last moment, a manifestation of those transports of love, those raptures, those burning words and holy tears, the source of which had become
daily more abundant. But nothing of the kind appeared.
It seemed as if he still desired to shroud himself as much
as possible in silence and obscurity. He had the very
manner of death he would have preferred, had the choice
been left to him."

"What should we expect" (has been said of the death
of St. Vincent of Paul),*—"what should we expect of one

* *The Glory of St. Vincent of Paul.* By the Right Rev. II. E.
Manning, D.D.

whose life was so like the life of our Lord, and whose mind was so much the life of a little child, but that when he came to die his death should be childlike too? And certainly, among all the deaths of the Saints of God, we hardly see one marked with greater tranquillity and calmness, peace and sweetness; like the sleep of a little child. All his long eighty-five years, from the time that he kept his father's sheep, and among the herds of the field lived in the spirit of prayer, was the life of a child of God. He had a right to die as a child, for he had lived as a child; and they who live as children of God have a right from their heavenly Father to die in His bosom, to die as the patriarch died of old, *by the mouth of the Lord;* that is, as it were, by the kiss of the lips of their heavenly Father."

Such, as we have seen, had been the life, and such was the death of the holy Curé of Ars. The words just quoted might have been written of him.

" We begged him in vain," says M. Monnin, " to take a little rest. He always answered, 'I shall rest in Paradise.' On Wednesday, the 29th of July, he went through his usual routine of labor, catechized, passed sixteen or seventeen hours in the confessional, and ended this laborious day with prayer. When he returned home, more broken and exhausted than usual, he sank upon a chair, saying, '*I can do no more.*' He had repeated several times before: 'Ah, sinners will kill the sinner;' and again : 'I know some one who would be finely taken in if there were no Paradise ! And yet,' added he, 'I often think that if there were no other life, it would be happiness enough to love God in this, to serve Him, and to do some little thing for His honor.'"

What passed after the missionaries had retired from the room, which the Saint was never more to leave alive, during

that night which preceded his terrible agony of four days,
is known to none.   No one ever dared to intrude upon the
secrecy of those sleepless nights, during which Heaven and
hell seemed to vie with each other in soothing or torturing
his bed of pain.   All we know is, that at one o'clock in
the morning, when he attempted to rise to go to the church,
he was seized with a faintness which obliged him to call
for aid.

"You are tired, M. le Curé!"

"Yes; I think it is my *poor end.*"

"I will call some one."

"No; do not trouble anybody; it is not worth while."

M. le Curé had certainly foreseen and foretold his approaching death. In the month of August, 1858, he declared
positively that he had but a year to live, and that by that
time in the year 1859 he should be no longer in this world.
When the morning came, he did not speak of saying Mass,
and resigned himself to the cares and attentions which he
had hitherto rejected.   These were alarming symptoms.
He would not, however, submit to the use of a fan, which
he considered a luxury.

"Leave me," said he, "with my poor flies."

"You are suffering very much," said one who watched
beside him.   A resigned movement of the head was the
only reply.   "M. le Curé, let us hope that St. Philomena,
whom we are going to invoke with all our might, will cure
you now, as she did eight years ago."

"Oh, St. Philomena can do nothing here."

The consternation was deep and general when M. Vianney's absence from the confessional was perceived.   Strong
and tender were the ties which bound every heart around
him to his, whose sacrifice of all human affections for Christ

had been repaid by the hundredfold even in this life, which is its never-failing reward. The missionaries and the Brothers of the Holy Family watched continually around the dying bed of him whom they reverenced as their father, while night and day his pillow was tended by his old and beloved friend of thirty years, the Comte des Garets. Another of his parishioners took up his station on the roof of the presbytery; and, under the burning sun of August, during the whole time of his illness, continued watering the roof and the walls, to keep up a refreshing coolness around him.

"For three days," says M. Monnin, "every means was resorted to which the most ingenious piety could devise; invocations of every Saint in Heaven, applications for prayers to every religious community, pilgrimages to every sanctuary. But the purpose of God now to crown His faithful servant became daily more manifest.

"On Tuesday evening, M. Vianney asked for the last Sacraments. Providence had brought together, as witnesses of that touching spectacle, priests from the most distant dioceses. The whole parish was present. A person who had a right to approach the sick man came with joined hands to implore him, at that last moment, to ask our Lord to restore him.

"He fixed his deep and brilliant gaze upon her, and shook his head. Silent tears flowed from his eyes when the bell announced the last visit of the Master whom he so fervently adored. A few hours afterwards he wept once more. These tears of joy were his last. They fell upon the cross of his Bishop, Monseigneur Langalerie, who, warned by urgent messages of the progress of the malady, came in breathless agitation, praying aloud as he forced his way

through the kneeling crowd which intercepted his passage.
He was but just in time. At two o'clock in the morning
which followed that holy and touching interview, without
struggle or agony, Jean Baptiste Marie Vianney fell asleep
in the Lord, while the priest who writes these lines, as he
recited the prayers for the commendation of the soul, pronounced these words : *Veniant illi obviam sancti angeli
Dei, et perducant eum in civitatem cœlestem Jerusalem.*
Two o'clock in the morning ; it was the hour when, in every
convent where the night office is said, those words of the
hymn of confessors were being chanted in honor of St.
Dominic :

> Dies refulsit lumine
> Quo Sanctus hic de corpore
> Migravit inter sidera.''

The Curé of Ars gave up his holy soul to God in the
arms of the faithful companions of his labors, the Abbé
Toccanier and the Abbé Monnin, and in the presence of the
Brothers of the Holy Family, the Comte des Garets, and
some others of his tried and dearest friends. The news
spread rapidly through the village and neighborhood, but
at first was hardly credited. It seemed impossible to that
faithful and loving people that such a misfortune could have
befallen them. He had been so near death before, and restored to them by a miracle, and by a continued miracle
had he been restored to them ever since. His life for thirty
or forty years would have been death to any other man.
And he was so much wanted ! What was to become of
that innumerable concourse of pilgrims, sick in body or in
soul, who hung upon his lips ? Had his hand been indeed
lifted up for the last time in benediction ? "We had
cradled ourselves," says M. Monnin, "in these hopes ; we

had rested on the thought that he was still to be left for a long time to us. We could not imagine Ars without its curé; its church always open and full; its midnight Angelus; its closely besieged confessional; its Saint, who was the sun of that privileged corner of the earth, who gave it its life, and filled its atmosphere with the odor of his virtues. And he was no more! He had blessed us for the last time; he had bidden us his last farewell; and that sacred bond between our souls and God, that golden link between us and all the mysterious glories of the communion of Saints, was broken.

"The Curé of Ars was dead! That life of devotion and prayer, of charity and patience, of humility and sacrifice, was over: *he had fought the good fight; he had finished his course; he had received his crown.* At last the toil-worn laborer of the Lord was at rest. As the words, *Depart, Christian soul,* were uttered, he entered into the joy of his Lord."

The emaciated body, seamed and scarred with the glorious stigmata of mortification, lay on his poor pallet, arrayed by the hands of his beloved missionaries in the poor cotta and soutane which in life he never laid aside. The Comte des Garets drew near the bed, took the hand of his revered pastor, and bade him this touching farewell: "You have been our friend on earth, be our friend still in Heaven!"

One of the lower rooms of the poor presbytery was hastily adorned with white hangings, decorated with crowns and flowers; and thither, for two long days and nights, came pilgrims from every part of France, to weep and pray around him, who, for the first time, had no answering tears to give, but whose prayers, now tenfold mightier than before, were rising for them before the throne of God.

The mournful sound of the death-bell from his own beloved church was echoed back from every neighboring steeple.

Two Brothers of the Holy Family knelt by the bed of death, protected by a strong barrier from the pressure of the crowd, their arms weary with the toil of passing backwards and forwards the crosses, rosaries, and medals which were brought to touch the sacred corpse, and to gain a last blessing from those hands which for the first time moved not to bestow a benediction.

Notwithstanding the intense heat, not a trace of decomposition appeared upon the body up to the night before the funeral. The venerable countenance lay uncovered, sweet, calm, and benign as in life. He seemed as if in a blissful sleep. Those who watched that beloved face even thought they could trace a gradual brightening, as if he were drinking in deeper and deeper of the vision of peace.

On Saturday, the funeral procession was formed. From early dawn thick masses of people had been collecting on every side of the village, amounting on the most moderate calculation to six thousand. More than three hundred priests, and representatives of almost all the religious houses in the neighborhood, came to pay their last tribute of reverence to their saintly brother.

"Until the removal of the body," says M. Monnin, "there was the greatest tranquillity throughout the whole assemblage: the women and children of the parish, the religious confraternities, the clergy, regular and secular, ranged themselves in two lines, in the most perfect order. But no sooner was the coffin carried out of the house, than the same electrical movement which was wont to accompany the servant of God, wherever he appeared in his lifetime, broke forth irresistibly; and, as the triumphal procession passed through the village, it was impossible to control it. No one who had come unexpectedly upon that spectacle would have taken it for a funeral. Never did the royal progress of a living prince excite so lively and heartfelt an expression of enthusiasm, as that which surrounded the mortal remains of this lowly priest."

The long procession halted at the square before the church; and there, in accents which have echoed through the length and breadth of France, the Bishop of Belley, as he stood before the coffin, told what had been the life and death of *the good and faithful servant who had just entered into the joy of his Lord.*

At the High Mass which followed the sermon, a brigade of *gendarmerie* kept back the multitude from pressing into the church, which could not have held a twentieth part of their number, and which none but the authorities and the family of the deceased were permitted to enter. The deepest silence prevailed during the celebration of the sacred mysteries, and every knee was bent when the bell gave notice of the elevation.

The body of the holy priest was then carried into the chapel of St. John the Baptist, and laid by the side of the confessional, where he had worn away his life in reconciling sinners with their God.

"The apostolate of the Saints," says M. Monnin, "ends not with their earthly life; their relics have a mission too. We hope that from his venerated tomb M. Vianney will carry on his work. Several instances of extraordinary graces, and of bodily cures wrought by his intercession, have already occurred. We hope, and look in humble confidence, for greater wonders still, in our Lord's own time.

We may not forestall it.   When it shall please Him to call this new star to shine in the firmament of His Church, it shall answer, ' I am here.'*   It will be the hour of His divine power, and miracles will reveal it."

We read in the following simple and thrilling words, spoken by Mgr. de Langalerie in the presence of the dead, the earnestness of his hope and desire to see the star of his diocese shine forth in visible radiance over the darkness of this world :

"Euge, serve bone et fidelis; intra in gaudium Domini tui" (Matt. xxv, 21).

"Keep silence, my brethren ; listen attentively, ye faithful and pious souls ; whom love, reverence, and grief, have brought in such a multitude to this touching and solemn ceremony.   I am about to repeat to you the words of our Lord in the holy Gospel; say, is there one among you who did not feel as if he heard these words from the mouth of God Himself, at the moment when the blessed soul of our saintly curé was at last released from the body so long worn down in the service of his Divine Master?   *Euge, serve bone et fidelis; intra in gaudium Domini tui,*—'Courage, good and faithful servant; enter into the joy of thy Lord and thy God.'

"Meditate for a few moments, my brethren, on these sweet and cheering words.   They must be our hope and consolation at this moment.   I may add, that they contain a salutary warning, in the name of him who shall speak to you no more, save by the example of his life, and proba-

* "The stars were called, and they said, We are here: and they shone forth with gladness to Him who made them" (Baruch iii, 35).

bly also by the marvels of his tomb. *Euge*, courage,—already does this first word, this single word, reanimate us. Courage, good and faithful servant! Jean Baptiste Marie Vianney, our holy Curé of Ars, was a servant of God, who numbered seventy-four years of good and loyal service. He took service in the house of the Lord from his very infancy. As a child, as a very little child, he served God ; as a young man, as an ecclesiastical student, he served God; no repulse or discouragement could turn him aside from his steadfast purpose to serve God in the highest and most perfect way possible, by devoting himself to the sacerdotal life. He desired to be a priest most assuredly only to serve God. His life has given full proof of this. As priest, as vicaire, and as curé, always and in all things, he served God.

"And this service at last, as you all know, so entirely filled his life, that the indifferent actions which we consecrate to the service of God, by offering them to Him, and thus referring them indirectly to His honor,—all these indifferent actions had, as it were, vanished from the life of the holy curé. He lived almost without food or sleep. Two or three ounces of nourishment a day, one or two hours of sleep, sufficed him. And how did he employ the rest of his time? Wholly in the service of God, in the service of souls,—fourteen, sixteen, eighteen hours in the confessional, interrupted only by his catechetical instruction which was so eloquent a sermon. The mere sight of the saintly curé, when his words were inaudible, preached, touched, converted. And how was the remainder of his time employed? In frequent communication with his beloved parishioners, in visiting the sick, in long and fervent prayers, in pious reading; in one word, his whole day was spent in acts directly to the glory and service of God.

And this day, thus devoted to God, was continually recommenced, Sunday and week-day, night and day, without respite or relaxation.

" *Euge, serve bone et fidelis, quia in pauca fuisti fidelis!* ' Courage, good and faithful servant, thou hast been faithful in little things !' O my God, permit me this word ; it was not only in *little* things that the Curé of Ars was Thy faithful and devoted servant. Let it be said to Thy glory, O my God ; for his life was a new miracle of Thy power and of Thy love ; to Thee, indeed, all this is doubtless little, very little, infinitely little, but to us, weak mortals, this life was a miracle, a glorious, a continual miracle. Through how many years, through how many centuries may we look back ere we find the life of another priest thus fruitfully, thus holily, thus continually occupied, employed, lavished in the service of God ?   And that service of God was accomplished with all the perfection and fidelity due to the sanctity of the Master whom we serve. *Euge, serve bone et fidelis!* 'Courage, good and faithful servant !'   *Good,* for a Christian, for a priest, is sacrifice, mortification, the Cross; *good* is the moan of natural sorrow turned into the sigh of expiation and love.   Sacrifice is an act of love, and at the same time the true proof of true love.   In this consists *good* service, service tried and proved; such was the solid and enduring goodness of the Curé of Ars.

" To the austerity of a life such as we have sketched, and you have witnessed, he added many other mortifications ; he had almost continual sufferings to endure, and God laid upon him, from time to time, the burden of secret and mysterious trials. So *faithful,* moreover, was this good and painful service, that no movement of self-love ever tarnished its perfect and entire fidelity.   What this holy priest

did for God, he left wholly to God. That poor country
curé was as simple as a child, amid the throng of pilgrims
which surrounded him. You have seen him, all you who
are here present; you have heard him. Is not this the
truth, the exact truth? Testimonies of admiration and reverence, the most numerous and most varied, had no power
to move him. He gave his blessing to the multitude, as
one who had himself received the benediction of a greater
than he.

"*Euge, serve bone et fidelis!* These sacred words, 'Courage, good and faithful servant,' have a marvellous fitness
when addressed to him! But no; I speak them not for
him, but for ourselves. Courage! *Let us not weep as
those who have no hope.** Hope here is almost faith. Suffer me now, my brethren, to open my inmost heart more
fully to you. Having been providentially warned of the
rapid progress of the malady of our dear and venerated
Curé of Ars, I hastened hither. 1 recited my Office on
the way. It was the Office of St. Dominic, another *true
and faithful servant.* In union with Jesus Christ, the
Head of the Church, I love, when I say the Breviary,
to unite myself with the Saint whose festival we cele-
brate. But now, unconsciously, the words of the prayers
brought continually before me the thought of the holy priest
to whom I was hastening. St. Dominic was with me, indeed, assisting my prayers; but by his side appeared
continually the good and holy Curé of Ars. *Who shall
dwell in Thy tabernacle, or who shall rest upon Thy holy
mountain? He whose life is without stain, and who practices justice;* and again, *Thou hast set him a little lower
than the angels, and hast crowned him with glory and*

<hr>

* 1 Thess. iv, 12.

honor. These and a thousand other passages seemed to bear so marked a relation to the servant of God. And some hours after his death, as I was saying Mass for him at the altar where he had so often stood, the same thoughts recurred to my mind, when I read these words which follow the Epistle : *Emitte lucem tuam, &c. Thy light and Thy truth have led me to Thy holy mountain, and to Thy tabernacle. Why, then, art thou sorrowful, O my soul? and why dost thou disquiet me ?* And then in the Gospel : *Levate oculos vestros, &c. Lift up your eyes, and behold the fields white for the harvest.* These fields seemed to me to be those covered by our holy curé with a rich and abounding harvest; and my heart overflowed, it overflows still, with confidence and with sweet and holy hope.

" *Euge, serve bone.* ' Courage, good and faithful servant; enter into the joy of thy Lord.' The hope which these words inspire, as applied to the holy Curé of Ars, is in itself a consolation amid the mournful and solemn circumstances which surround us; yet, by an attentive study of the sense of these sacred words, we shall discover a more direct and abundant source of encouragement under the severe sacrifice required of us by God. Great indeed is this sacrifice ! We have lost, we have *all* lost, what can never be replaced. God will not lavish such miracles of grace and sanctity upon us. France has lost a priest who was an honor to her, and to whom her children came from her remotest provinces for counsel. And poor sinners, what have they lost in the irresistible words, and still more resistless tears, wont to lure them back to God ! Our diocese has experienced a most heavy loss. The Curé of Ars was its glory and its providence, and the founder of the missionary work which has brought it so many blessings.

More than ninety parishes will owe to him the perpetual boon of a mission once in every ten years. And how many other works of charity did he encourage, bless, and foster!

"Your Bishop, too, has endured a heavy loss. He has lost a father, a friend, a model. Poor holy curé! At our first meeting he came to me trembling. Mgr. Devie and Mgr. Chalandon had been so good, so especially good, to him! There is always something of anxiety in the reception of a new Bishop, and he had so deep a reverence for the episcopal character. How often have I seen him, on the first tidings of my arrival, hasten to this very spot, and kneel for my blessing, amid the involuntary murmur of astonishment which would sometimes escape from the crowd, to see such exalted sanctity bow before the simple episcopal character! But the fear which was a restraint upon our first intercourse soon disappeared; and he came to love me, I believe—I am sure—as tenderly as I loved him.

"Yes, I repeat, we have all lost much; but these words, *Euge, intra in gaudium!*—'Courage, enter into joy,'— ought to stay the course, if not of our tears, at least of our complaints, our murmurs, even of our overkeen regrets. Good and faithful servant, your day's work is done; you have done enough, you have labored enough; come, and receive the reward of your toil. And such was the thought which filled my mind when, having blessed the dying Saint, and prayed with him and for him, I was borne, as it were, on the stream of his weeping people, to the foot of the altar. There I took part in the public prayers; there I heard one of his beloved sons, one of our missionaries who lived with him, ask for the miracle of that revered father's restoration to life and health; and as, in spite of myself, I felt that I could not join in that petition, I contented myself with an act of resignation and union with the will of God. What! said I to myself, after he has labored so much, shall we ask to keep him with us still? He doubtless would say, with St. Martin, to his weeping disciples, *Non recuso laborem*, 'I refuse not to labor still.' In his goodness, and moved by our tears, he would have consented to live on; but can we have the heart to ask it? He is wearied out, exhausted utterly; for a long time past he has seemed to live only by a miracle. Has not God left him to us long enough? We indeed have need of him; but he has need of repose; he has a right to his reward. Let him enter, then, let him enter at last, into the joy of his Lord. *Intra in gaudium Domini tui*. And will he be so lost in the joys of Heaven as to be unable still to think of us, to pray for and assist us? No; Heaven is very near to earth, for God unites them both. Courage! courage! In the bosom of God, where he reposes, the Curé of Ars is not lost to us. And the first lesson we may learn from this tomb, and from the words which are to be engraven upon it, is the knowledge of the great benefits which he can still confer upon our souls.

"What would have been his answer during his lifetime to the words which we have now applied to him? 'Courage, good and faithful servant; enter thou into the joy of thy Lord.' Would you believe it, beloved brethren; and ought I to make it known to you? Yes, most assuredly; and I ask of God, in the name of him whom we have lost, that my words may be wholly episcopal and apostolic.

"The holy curé would not only have replied in the words of the Gospel, '*I am an unprofitable servant;* why call you me good and faithful?' but he would have felt a desire (shall I say a temptation?) to deal still more hardly with himself. This was one of the secret trials, by which, as I have said, God was pleased to exercise His servant.

"'M. le Curé,' said one of the missionaries to him, 'how, in the midst of this concourse, which continually surrounds you, can you resist the temptation of vain-glory?'

"'Ah, my child,' replied the holy priest, 'say rather, how can I resist temptation to fear, discouragement, and despair?'

"Strange excess of the grace of God, which explains the pertinacity with which this good and venerated pastor clung to his desire to leave his flock, in order to end his days in penance and retirement!

"'Ah, Monseigneur,' he said to me, hardly a fortnight ago, 'I shall soon ask you to let me go and weep over the sins of my life.'

"'But, my good curé,' said I, 'the tears of the sinners whom God sends to you are worth far more than yours.'

"'Do not speak to me in this way, or I shall not come to see you any more.' And all my words of affection and encouragement seemed powerless to convince him.

"He was in his own eyes a miserable sinner. He dreaded the responsibility of the pastoral office, and feared that he had discharged it ill. The judgments of God at times filled him with terror. The last days of his life were, however, passed in the deepest tranquillity; the Divine voice had doubtless whispered *Euge* in his ear, and filled his heart with courage. But in his first illness, in that dark valley of the shadow of death, through which it pleased the Lord that he should pass some fifteen years ago, to give so sweet and glorious a consecration to your prayers, the trouble and perplexity of his soul was manifest. What lesson are we to draw from this revelation of the interior of so saintly a spirit?

"Timorous and over-fearful souls, of which perhaps there is many a one among the pilgrims here, learn from the holy curé to resist the excessive fears which obedience bids you lay aside. This temptation was to him the *ne magnitudo revelationum* of St. Paul. By these fears God saved and shielded the humility of that gifted soul; they gave a higher merit to that unswerving confidence in God, which was, after all, the master-key of his life; and they taught him, by trial and experience, the words of compassionate sympathy by which he reached and healed your hearts. Do you know what was the secret balm which flowed with them? It was the perfume of his tears, his prayers, of all the graces which God had poured forth upon that wound in his heart, which was also, which perhaps is still also, your own.

"But above all, do you, indifferent and presumptuous souls, whom, though rarely to be met with in this pious assembly, the rumor of these solemn obsequies may have attracted from the world,—do you, I say, learn that there were moments when the Curé of Ars, the saintly Curé of Ars, trembled at the judgments of God. A striking example this, in an age in which there is so little fear; an age in which fear has given place, not to love, but to torpor, indifference, and forgetfulness. Oh, when will you awake? When will you tremble, who have so much cause to fear? When will you do seriously the most serious work you have to do?

"For you, beloved and venerated priest, there is no more temptation, no more fear. We have full confidence that, even now, you have entered into joy, peace, and rest eternal : *Intra in gaudium Domini tui.*

"You have been ushered into that joy by the Mother of Mercy, whose name you bore, and whom through life you have loved so well; by St. John Baptist, your patron, so great in his humility; by St. Philomena, your chosen patroness, who seemed to live again in you, and to hide her name under yours, as yours was shrouded under hers.

"Oh, from your abode of glory and of bliss, watch still, watch ever over us. Chariot and guide of Israel, leave us your twofold spirit of devotion to God's service, and of holy fear, tempered and mastered by confidence and love.

"Leave it to this community of missionaries, which glories to call you father.

"Leave it to your dear, your well-beloved people of Ars, whose only consolation for your loss will be to think of you, and love you daily more and more.

"Leave it to the clergy of this diocese, which, with a holy pride, numbers you among its members.

"Leave it to your Bishop, so sorrowful, and yet so joyful, as he speaks of you. And be well assured that the brightest and the most earnestly desired day of his episcopate will be that on which the infallible voice of the Church shall permit him to chant solemnly in your honor: *Euge, serve bone et fidelis; intra in gaudium Domini tui. Amen.*"

And now, O holy priest, humble follower of Jesus, while you shed your benediction upon those devoted hearts which knew and loved you when on earth, forget not us, who look wistfully to you from afar.

Have you but one blessing, O tender and loving father ?

Have you none for this poor land, once the Island of Saints and the dowry of Mary; which has sold her birthright, and cast away her blessing ?

Our hearts have thrilled at your words of consolation, which bade us hope for the conversion of England.

Pray for us then, holy confessor of Christ.

By the slow martyrdom of your life-long toil for souls, pray for our priests; that their labors may be multiplied, and their numbers and their strength be made equal to their labors.

Pray for our unbaptized children, O father of the orphan and the outcast. Pray still more for those whose baptismal robes have been stained and blackened in the streets of this sinful city, for lack of a Christian mother's care, or a Christian pastor's eye.

Pray for us all, poor sinners that we are, O pitiful and loving Saint, that our cold hearts and listless lives may catch some distant gleam, and reflect some faint and feeble ray, of your intense and burning love for Jesus and Mary.

We have only to add, in the words of M. Monnin, that wherever, in the course of this work, the title of Saint or Blessed has been applied to M. Vianney, it has been simply in token of our veneration, and with no thought of anticipating the decision of our holy Mother the Church.

www.ingramcontent.com/pod-product-compliance
Lightning Source LLC
Chambersburg PA
CBHW051129120726
47905CB00005B/1480